W9-AKE-822

RED JACKET

ALSO BY JOSEPH HEYWOOD

Fiction

Taxi Dancer
The Berkut
The Domino Conspiracy
The Snowfly
Ice Hunter
Blue Wolf in Green Fire
Chasing a Blond Moon
Running Dark
Strike Dog
Death Roe
Shadow of the Wolf Tree
Force of Blood

Non-Fiction

Covered Waters: Tempests of a Nomadic Trouter

RED JACKET

A LUTE BAPCAT MYSTERY

JOSEPH HEYWOOD

LYONS PRESS
Guilford, Connecticut
An imprint of Globe Pequot Press

Lyons Press is an imprint of Globe Pequot Press.

Text design: Sheryl Kober
Layout artist: Melissa Evarts
Project manager: Ellen Urban
Maps © Morris Book Publishing, LLC

Library of Congress Cataloging-in-Publication Data is available on file.

ISBN 978-0-7627-8253-6

Printed in the United States of America

10 9 8 7 6 5 4 3 2 1

To educator, administrator, coach, and friend, Ed Jarvie, who helped to spark my interest in history more than a half-century ago. And to Mike Vairo, whose relatives lived through the Italian Hall tragedy of 1913.

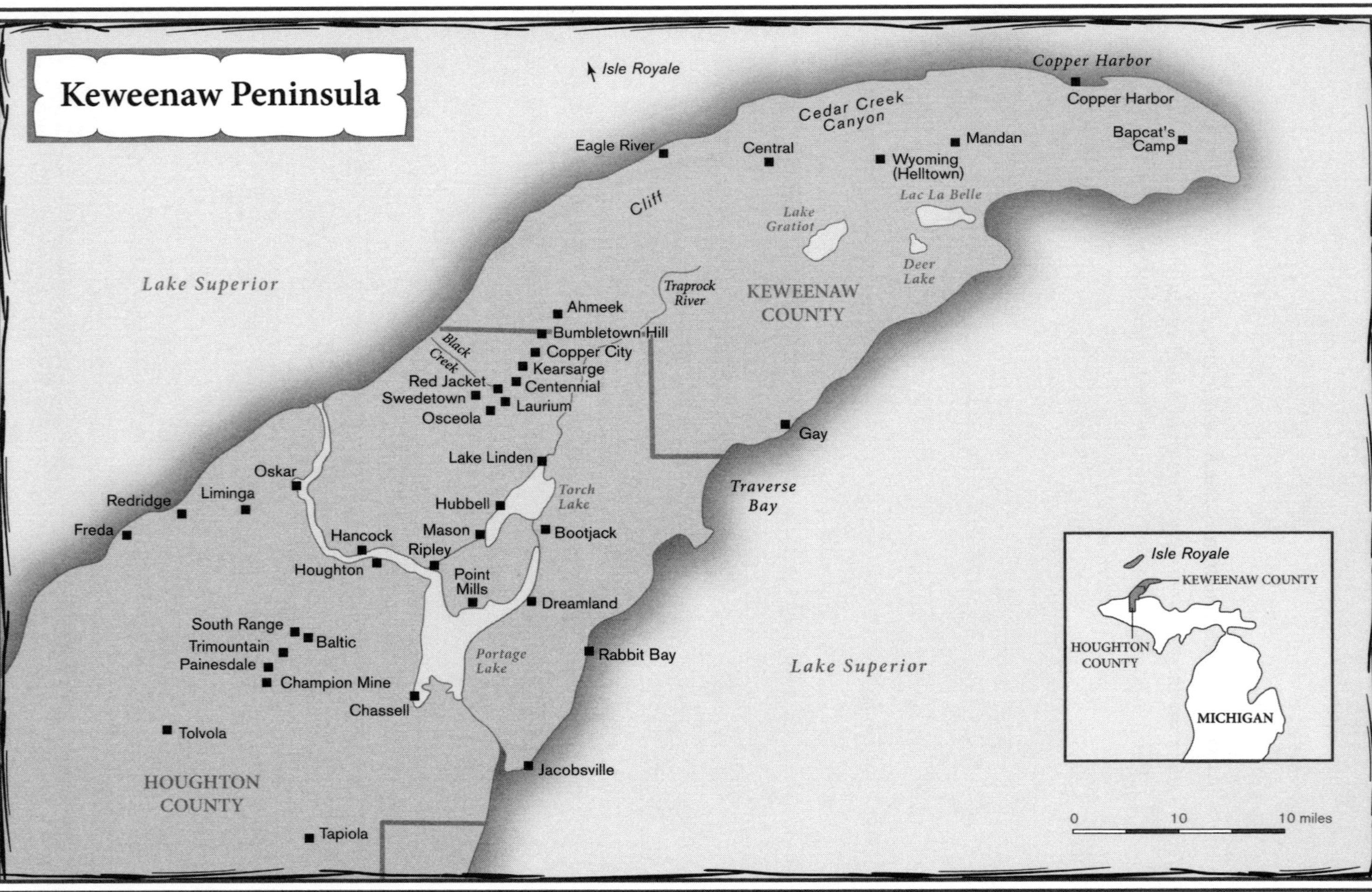

Keweenaw Peninsula
Isle Royale
Copper Harbor
Copper Harbor
Cedar Creek Canyon
Eagle River
Central
Mandan
Bapcat's Camp
Wyoming (Helltown)
Lac La Belle
Cliff
Lake Gratiot
Deer Lake
Lake Superior
Traprock River
KEWEENAW COUNTY
Ahmeek
Bumbletown Hill
Black Creek
Copper City
Kearsarge
Red Jacket
Centennial
Swedetown
Laurium
Osceola
Gay
Lake Linden
Oskar
Torch Lake
Traverse Bay
Redridge
Liminga
Hubbell
Freda
Hancock
Mason
Bootjack
Ripley
Houghton
Point Mills
Dreamland
South Range
Baltic
Trimountain
Painesdale
Champion Mine
Portage Lake
Rabbit Bay
Lake Superior
Chassell
Tolvola
Jacobsville
HOUGHTON COUNTY
Tapiola
Isle Royale
KEWEENAW COUNTY
HOUGHTON COUNTY
MICHIGAN
0
10
10 miles

. . . beyond the most distant wilderness and remote as the moon.

—Patrick Henry,
describing the Keweenaw Peninsula to Congress

1

San Juan Heights, Cuba

FRIDAY, JULY 1, 1898

"Sharpshooter to me!" Colonel Theodore Roosevelt shouted in his oddly pitched voice, sweat streaming down the sides of his face, forming a thin red paste and leaving him looking more flushed than he actually was, his skin color matching the blood trickling down his left arm.

The dismounted First Volunteer Cavalry had begun their assault from the bed of the San Juan River, where enemy snipers had picked away at them and artillery rounds had rained from above, Roosevelt alone on horseback. The climb was steep, causing them to go single file and watch their footing through the high grass.

"Sir," Corporal Bapcat said calmly, standing beside his colonel.

"What are you hearing, Corporal?"

"Not much, sir."

"Nothing?"

"Some birds, sir."

"Tell me about them."

"Not quite crows, but something that sounds like crows, sort of."

"I see. What about them?"

"To our left and right, Colonel, never directly ahead or behind, always to the sides."

"Good man, Corporal Bapcat. Mangrove cuckoos, *Coccyzus minor*, solitary creatures. They only call during breeding season in the spring. Conclusions?"

"I'm thinking the enemy's got scouts and pickets out there marking our route and numbers."

Roosevelt beamed his huge smile. "Well read, Corporal. All senses to business—brain, eyes, nose, ears—all instincts. Pass the word to the men and carry on."

"Yessir."

Roosevelt loved his birds, and even here in the middle of battle it was like being on the hunt back in the Dakotas. Old Four Eyes was one of a kind.

• • •

Midafternoon. They were atop a hill they had dubbed the Kettle, looking along the northern flank of the American line, not a mile from Santiago. The Spaniards were bombarding them relentlessly from multiple positions below. Having taken Kettle in a chaotic but determined fight, Roosevelt had then led his men up San Juan Hill, the greater height, but General Sumner had intercepted them and sent them back to Kettle to repel an expected counterattack. Bapcat had no idea how many men the brigade had lost so far, but he had seen bodies all the way up. Sumner ordered the Rough Riders to defend and hold the advantage they had earned with their spilled blood. Gatling guns had opened their way to Kettle, where there had been brief but fierce hand-to-hand fighting, and now Bapcat guessed Gatlings would throw back the Spaniards attempting to regain lost ground. War was not so much about courage as firepower. The ten-barrel guns were lethal, and it struck him that army weapons were getting deadlier and deadlier, but soldiers' ways were not changing.

Roosevelt walked over to him, pointed along the ridge, asked almost matter-of-factly, "Your ears telling you anything, Corporal?"

"Those pesky cuckoos are at it again, sir, moving around us. I think maybe the Spanish boys are looking for a good place to climb back up."

"Suggestions?"

"Let me follow the sound, see if I can find where they settle on, and we can set up there."

"You think they'll mark a spot for their comrades?"

"That's what we'd do," Bapcat said.

"Just like Indians," the colonel said.

"Yessir."

"Do it, Corporal."

Twenty minutes later Bapcat had heard enough and waved for his colonel, pointing, "Just below right here is fairly flat, not as steep as where we came up, and the birdcalls are on both sides of the spot."

Roosevelt stood by the lip of the hill, the blue polka-dot bandanna tied around his slouch hat billowing like a guidon in the breeze, and rubbed his eye. “Sar’nt Green, put your Gatling here.”

Green and another man from the Gatling Gun Detachment began to haul the lethal weapon into place.

“With me, Corporal,” Roosevelt said, walking, his spyglass aimed downhill.

“This is the right place. Skirmishers in red trousers—see how the buttons sparkle even with all this dirt? They’re pressing up to clear a path for a maneuver in force, which is forming directly behind them. You can see the wide-brim hats farther back.”

Roosevelt took off his khaki slouch hat and rubbed his neck with the soiled blue neckerchief. The man held his spectacles and rubbed them with the tail of the cloth, chuckled at some unspoken thought, as he sometimes did when pressure was high, and put them back on his nose. “How many you reckon you see down there?” he asked Lute Bapcat, his former civilian hunting companion and guide, now his personal military sharpshooter.

“Seeing seven, sir,” Bapcat reported.

“I’ve counted ten. I’ll spot, eh? Just like a hunt in the Badlands, Lute.” Roosevelt took a small brass spyglass, extended it, and pointed it downhill.

“Sharpshooter ready?”

Bapcat took a knee and dropped five rounds into the carbine’s internal magazine. “Ready, Colonel.”

“Very well. Two trees in a marked vee, left one half the size of the right tree, some sort of yellow melon broken on the ground by the left one. Acknowledge?”

“Have it, sir.” Bapcat silently chambered a .30-40 round with the remarkably smooth bolt.

“First target, right ten feet from the marker trees. There is a stump, one man behind it with rifle flat against his chest.”

“Have him, sir.” Bapcat’s shot was swallowed by the din of hundreds of rounds being expended all around the mountaintop. There was no smoke or muzzle flashes from either side, both armies having adopted flashless powder, each thereby canceling the other’s theoretical tactical military advantage.

Bapcat retracted the bolt. The empty cartridge flew up and end over end to his left.

The Rough Riders had intermingled with Negro regulars of the Ninth and Tenth Cavalries. All wore the same dark shirts sweated black, bled red, and helped each other stay alive. They had doggedly fought their way up the hill more or less as a single integrated unit, led there by the unflappable colonel.

"Bully shot," Roosevelt said. "Two and three, right eight feet, prone men, hats off."

"Just head shots, Colonel?" Head shots were risky, a chest shot better, even if your aim was a bit off.

"Concern noted," the colonel said. "Let's take what they give us, son."

The M1896 Krag bullet was not particularly large, but its thin jacket shredded upon impact with flesh, leaving a monstrous, mushrooming bite. Bapcat racked another round into the chamber, held his breath, released slowly, squeezed the trigger once, ejected the empty, chambered a second and fired again, both shots taken within three seconds and each on target. He felt almost serene amid the cacophony of battle.

"Double hit," the colonel announced.

They worked together, colonel and corporal, until there were ten dead Spaniards on the ground less than seventy yards below, each of them dispatched by twenty-year-old Corporal Lute Bapcat, Rough Rider, sharpshooter, North Dakota cowboy, hunting guide.

When the Spanish forces turned back from the hill, the minor counterattack was broken and American soldiers all along the ridge stood like fools, cheering and waving their hats and rifles. Roosevelt sat on the ground beside Bapcat. "Bit different than sniping elk from a hillside, eh, Lute?"

"Yessir." Very different—if you stopped to think about it, which he hadn't. He had made up his mind to just do what had to be done and to hell with danger or anything else. *Don't think, just do.*

"Hard to kill a man?" Roosevelt asked.

"Not easy." He'd seen the colonel firing with his revolver, hitting a man as the rest of them went hand to hand to run the Spaniards off the hilltop.

"Good; better that way. It's the natural order, ordained by our creator. Always remember: Killing is not against God's will. It's only *murder* that offends the commandment. Thou shalt not murder, the original translations proclaimed. The Good Book prohibits murder, Corporal."

"Good to know, sir." But killing this way seemed so easy that it was hard to embrace the differences in definition the colonel was suggesting. *Can you murder someone—an enemy—in wartime?* Bapcat wondered, and quickly admonished himself. *No thinking.*

"Should be equally hard to kill, whether you're a colonel or a corporal," Roosevelt said. "Fine job you did here, Lute. How many did you take climbing the hill today?"

"Not sure, sir. I hit nine and saw them fall, but I guess I don't know any more than what I seen." It was not widely known that Corporal Lute Bapcat served as Roosevelt's personal guardian on the field of battle, watching for any visible threat to his colonel and erasing it. He was fairly certain he'd hit all nine men he'd shot at, and probably killed most of them, which now left his right, trigger hand trembling ever so slightly. He'd never killed a man before today, never even seriously entertained the possibility.

"Going back west after we muster out?" the colonel asked.

"Nossir. Thought I'd go home."

Bapcat saw that this information seemed to catch Roosevelt by surprise.

"You're not a Westerner?"

"No sir, from Michigan, a place in the Keweenaw Peninsula called Red Jacket."

Roosevelt grinned. "Ah, the Keweenaw . . . Copper Country. I know its reputation well. Bloody hard place requiring equally plucky men. Home, eh? Family?"

"Orphan, sir. I left when I was twelve and went west to become a cowhand and hunter."

"Why go back?"

"Trapping, sir."

Roosevelt flashed a huge, toothy smile. "Trapping's a fine, honest living of the old school. Furs floated our country for centuries. Good for you, Lute. I expect you'll be a fine trapper, or whatever you choose to pursue in life. You sure are one fine shot with that Krag." The colonel squeezed Bapcat's shoulder affectionately and started to march off toward a group of men clustered together, talking.

Bapcat knew it had been Sergeant Green and his Gatling gun that had shattered the counterattack. His work had been more mosquito than predator.

Ten feet away, Colonel Theodore Roosevelt stopped, wheeled around, came rigidly to attention, and solemnly saluted his young sharpshooter.

"History made here today, Corporal Bapcat. *You* identified where the enemy would come up. You, sir, were our boulder, our unmoving force on these heights."

All Rough Riders and many of the men from the regular army units within earshot stood and joined in the salute. Bapcat wished they would stop. He could tolerate just about anything but being singled out.

Roosevelt stopped beside a sitting black soldier and offered his canteen to the man, who took a sip, smiled, and handed it back. Roosevelt grinned, took a drink for himself, and stalked away stiff-legged like a predator who was not yet close to sated. The colonel might have been born with a silver spoon in his mouth, but by God, he had more pluck and grit than any man Lute Bapcat had ever met, and if his colonel asked, he'd follow him into Hell itself.

Bapcat began to clean his Krag and saw Sergeant Frankus Fish glaring at him. Fish had been his NCO until the colonel selected Bapcat for his personal retinue. Fish made it clear then that he resented the younger cavalryman, especially after Bapcat stopped him from beating another soldier by holding a skinning knife to the sergeant's throat and reminding him, "Every man here is a volunteer, Sar'nt Fish."

2

Chicago

FRIDAY, JANUARY 30, 1903

Lute Bapcat realized too late that coming to Chicago had been a mistake, but his trip was nearly finished and he decided to see it through. Three years underground in the copper mines had given him a stake for a new life, and he had come to Chicago to buy equipment from Kisor's Silver City Fur Supply House. Kisor had salesmen traveling through trapping country, and one of them had told Bapcat he could get items a lot cheaper by going directly to the main depot at the home office.

The salesman, a Spanish-American War veteran who claimed to have seen action in the Philippines, gave Bapcat a ticket for the comedy *Mr. Bluebeard,* the seat for a matinee performance, which suited him. He found all the lights and activity at night in the cluttered, stinking city both disturbing and disorienting. Living alone in the North Woods seemed natural; alone in Chicago, he felt out of place, even unsafe. Tomorrow he would catch a train back to Copper Country, haul his supplies to the extreme tip of the Keweenaw Peninsula, and begin his new life as an independent and unbeholden trapper.

Not wanting to be pressed in by other theatergoers, Bapcat found a tavern called Muley's on West Randolph Street, across from the Iroquois Theater, and toyed with a tepid beer, wondering if he should even bother to attend the play. Bluebeard, he thought he'd heard somewhere, had been a murderer. *How the hell do you make a musical show about a killer? Chicago is a damn strange place.* The ways of the city confounded him. One beer led to two, and a decision to forgo the show. Besides, it was well past the performance's starting time. *No point going over there.* He ordered another glass of beer, which was the only truly good thing to come from the day.

"What's going on over by the theater?" Someone at the bar asked. Bapcat looked out across the street, saw firefighters milling around the front of the building. Then he thought he saw smoke, and without thinking it through, pulled on his bearskin coat and fur cap and burst outside into a howling, icy wind. The firefighters were all screaming instructions at each other, several of them trying to pull open doors, which seemed blocked.

An alarm bell sounded in the distance, and police and more firemen began to converge on West Randolph Street. Bapcat grabbed a large cop by the arm. "You need help? I helped fight some fires out west," Bapcat said, adding, "Soldier."

"Stick with me, bub," the cop said. "Name's O'Doyle."

"Lute."

Three hours later Bapcat had helped carry out dozens of bodies, mostly women and children. One woman had a perfect boot print on her crushed forehead, her nose, lips, and teeth smashed. There had been mass panic inside and hundreds were dead. He'd never imagined such carnage out of nothing. The smell of charred human flesh and shit was so overpowering that cops and firemen gagged repeatedly as they carried out the dead. Bapcat reacted the same way. It was one thing to kill a man from afar, another to pick up the parts of a burned corpse, whose flesh sloughed at the slightest touch.

Finally he and O'Doyle took a break for a cigarette. He'd not seen the cop lose his stomach. Instead, the man had resolutely continued to retrieve bodies, Bapcat staying with him the whole time. "The actor, that Foy fella," the cop said as they carried out yet another body.

Bapcat had never heard the name before.

"Seems he tried to maintain order. Told people from the stage to sit where they were, ya know, not to panic—how everything would be all right. Then some jamoke opened the big doors behind the stage and that let the wind in from outside and made the bloody fire flare. It swept over them poor dumb bastards and suffocated and cooked 'em right there where they sat. Some's callin' da man a hero, but I dunno. Your number comes up, seems nuttin' you can do, God bein' an almighty prick about such things, don'chu know."

Bapcat had seen the blackened, still-smoking corpses in the seats, wondered what had happened. He had killed Spaniards, had been given medals, called a hero. Now some actor who had tried to save lives had failed because of another man's mistake. *Is it the outcome that makes for a hero, or the attempt?* He had no idea. *Too damn deep for the likes of me.*

His only certainty: Those responsible for this fire needed to be punished. Kill kids, you deserved not just jail, but death.

"Will somebody be held accountable?" Bapcat asked the cop.

O'Doyle laughed sardonically. "In this town?"

3

Montreal River, Keweenaw County

THURSDAY, MAY 15, 1913

It had been a flinty, moody, relentless sort of winter, with storm after storm keeping fur-bearers hunkered down for long periods, the fluxing conditions forcing the trapper to run his line only when weather conditions permitted, not when he wanted to. Bapcat had been cold so often for such extended periods that back in his hillside dugout, he could barely tolerate even marginal heat from his small wood-burning stove.

In March, just before a raging weeklong blizzard, he had seen a man's tracks and intuited that the snooper was Zakov, the Russian wolfer some other backcountry Keweenawians called Borzoi, the Wolf Hound.

Timber wolves dined mainly on venison, but the whitetail herd this far north up the seventy-mile-long peninsula was infinitesimal compared to larger Houghton County herds to the south, where there were some farms raising potatoes, rutabagas, and beets. If wolves were moving north it would be for beaver, which meant they would be his competitors, but only if they stayed into autumn. The presence of the wolves did not concern him; Zakov did.

The wolfer's tracks were brushed with great skill, but Bapcat had still seen them and read the sign. The Russian seemed to be probing and measuring Bapcat's skills, and Bapcat himself. Why? Eventually there would be a confrontation of some sort. The direction and tenor would rest on the Russian's attitude, and explanations.

Three inches of snow had fallen on nearly barren ground on May 1 and was mostly gone now, but Bapcat had kept several sets out near blue ice structures in cedar swamps along the smaller creeks and ponds, and soon would have to go fetch the traps to boil, clean, and store them away for summer. Once summer arrived in earnest, he would prospect for silver and float-copper chunks, and start making next winter's wood. *Life here may not be that varied, but it's busy and steady, and there's little place here for an idle, lazy man.*

He was not far from his dugout and looking at a fiddle fern trying to unfold when a brutish shadow stretched over his light path and startled him. He flinched, swallowed hard, and looked up to see the hulking, entirely naked form of Big Louie Moilanen, the town of Hancock's justice of the peace.

"Mr. Justice," Bapcat greeted the man.

"Holy wah, dere, Lute. You know I ain't one a dem formal fellas. Youse t'ink mebbe youse seen my duds around?"

"Can't say I have. What makes you think they're around here?"

The eight-foot-one justice of the peace, reputedly the tallest man in the world, nervously rubbed the corner of his mouth. "I don't know, Lute. Widow Frei asked me come fetch you."

Jaquelle Frei was thirty, beautiful, sensuous, sneaky, money-minded, and assertive. She owned and ran Frei Dry Goods and Outfitters in Copper Harbor.

"The widow mention why?"

Big Louie looked skyward, scratched at stubble on his chin, frowned, and answered, "I don't t'ink she did, Lute."

Because of his size, many people thought the giant stupid, or mentally slow, but he was just an ordinary man, a careful thinker who liked to mull things over before he talked. However, today's odd behavior was not at all characteristic of the man who had spent three seasons as a sideshow attraction with Ringling Brothers, and used his lucre to buy a Hancock tavern. Two years back he'd been elected justice of the peace, and had since done a fine job in that role. No, this was not the normal Big Louie Moilanen, and it concerned Bapcat, who liked the big man a lot.

"Did you have your clothes on when you left the widow's place?" He'd not be surprised if she'd seduced the man and had her way with him.

More lip tugging. "Pretty sure I had 'em, Lute. Not certain, though."

"Did you have your Bible?"

"Always carry da Blessed Word," Moilanen said.

No Bible in sight now. "How about you go take a seat in my shack and I'll backtrack you?"

"You can follow me?"

"It's like tracking a deer." *One the size of a Belgian draft horse.* "Your feet all right?"

The big man looked down, wiggled his toes. "Seem ta be."

"I'll be back, Louie. Help yourself to anything you need."

"Lute, you t'ink dere might be somet'ing wrong wit' me?" Moilanen asked.

Bapcat heard concern in the man's voice. "I'm not a doctor, Louie, and truth be known, I ain't even much of a trapper, but if it worries you, let's see if you can talk to a doctor down there to Hancock. What brought you here—besides the widow?"

"I don't quite remember," the man said. "Can you follow da tracks of t'oughts, too?"

"That's way outside my ken, Mr. Justice. You sit tight. I'll be back soon as I can."

"Good t'ing she ain't so cold out, eh," Big Louie said.

"Yessir," Bapcat said with a chuckle. "Lucky for all of us."

He found the man's neatly folded clothes along with his Bible near one of the abandoned copper mines dating from the Civil War era, fetched them back to the dugout, and handed them to the giant. Moilanen teared up when Bapcat gave him his Bible.

"Shall we head for town, find out what the Widow Frei wants?"

"Wants you ta come ta her store," the justice of the peace said as he dressed.

"You take the train up from Hancock?"

"I t'ink so," Moilanen said. "But I couldn't say for certain."

Bapcat wondered if he should go with the man to make sure he got to a doctor. This behavior was not at all like the Louis Moilanen he'd known since his time in the mines a decade ago.

4

Copper Harbor, Keweenaw County

THURSDAY, MAY 15, 1913

Bapcat didn't allow time for the widow to get her dander up, which was pretty much her normal demeanor. She seemed eternally addled or perturbed, if not by anything specific, then by the vagaries and inexactitudes of life itself, which she considered unpredictable, annoying, and largely unfair.

"Why'd you send Big Louie to find me?" he asked. "He's waiting outside."

"*Somebody* had to go, and you know perfectly well I have a thriving commercial enterprise to manage. You think I can just pick up and leave the likes of *him* in charge here and come traipsing after *you?*"

"Louie seems to run his saloon just fine down in Hancock."

"We are in the respectable dry goods business, and do *not* cater to the swilling public," she countered sharply. "Word's going 'round that Theodore Roosevelt himself is coming to Marquette for a libel trial. Seems some fool newspaperman over that way opined in print that the former president's a lush; the president, bless his plucky, righteous heart, has taken exception and filed suit. As well he should; a respectable person cannot let scoundrels have their way with their reputations. That particular allegation ring true to you? His drinking, I mean."

Bapcat shrugged. He was not precisely sure what the word *allegation* meant, but it was the widow's way to sling about expensive words most real people had no sense of. Fact was, he'd seen Roosevelt take a glass of wine on rare occasions, but never anything stronger, and always just one small glass with some of his suppers. "I wouldn't know," he told the volatile proprietor of Frei Dry Goods and Outfitters.

Widow Frei had the slithery moves of a Manx cat. Her response to him was to touch an eyebrow with her pinkie, as if she were tidying up. "Why then do you suppose you have gotten a summons to appear in Marquette for the trial?" She held out an envelope.

The trapper squinted at her. "That don't add up."

"Deputy Sheriff Valo come up from Eagle River and asked me to send a messenger, but Big Louie volunteered, and I never turn down a man willing to do honest work or to act like a *real* man. Lord knows the world has few enough of them, and some places have an even larger void. Valo insists you were a Rough Rider with Roosevelt down there in Cuba. Is it true you've seen the elephant, Lute?"

Valo is dumber than an ice wagon! Bapcat had tried to keep his past to himself, but some people, including Valo's boss, knew the facts. Bapcat tended to be a private man, happiest and most secure in his own counsel and company. He gave the widow a noncommittal shrug.

"*Good God, Lute!* Don't you dare dissemble! I cannot tolerate the lack of verisimilitude in a man. If you were an honest-to-God Rough Rider, I'll venture that makes you about the most special man in these parts." She leaned over the glass counter and whispered lasciviously, "On occasion, as I recall fondly, in certain of *my* parts, too."

He took the envelope, extracted the typewritten letter, and read it. *Office of W. S. Hill, Esq., Attorney at Law, Washington Street, Marquette.* He was ordered to present himself on the morning of Friday, May 23. "Not enough time to get myself all the way over there."

Jaquelle Frei expelled a noisy breath. "Good God and foo, Mr. Bapcat, these here times are the epitome of the *modern* era we are privileged to inhabit: electric lights, telephones, motorcars . . . Ye God, Lute, you can take the train and electric trolley down to Houghton, and a train from there to Marquette. How difficult can *that* be? I daresay you could be there as early as tomorrow if you so choose."

"Valo still around?"

"I'm not my brother's keeper, and in any event, he isn't my brother, is he? I don't know where the fool is. My guess, look in a doggery. All you men seem to have a weakness for forty rod, perhaps including the former president."

"Oh, I doubt *that*," Bapcat mumbled, letting it out and regretting he had. "I need someone to escort Big Louie back south."

Frei grabbed his arm and turned him. "See, I *knew* you knew Roosevelt! Why would the giant Moilanen need help?" She glanced at the justice of the peace standing serenely outside on the porch of her store.

"I don't think he's feeling quite himself."

"He looks normal to me."

"He showed up at my place naked," Bapcat said.

The widow's eyes glazed over and she absentmindedly nibbled her lower lip and grasped Bapcat's wrist. "Ye God! *Totally* disrobed, Mr. Bapcat, all secrets revealed and there for the whole world to gaze upon?" Her face was strained. "Ye God. Is he . . . you know, almighty? That is, *all* of him?"

Bapcat pushed her hand away. "I'm going to go find Valo," he said, turning to leave, but she caught his arm again with a viselike grip.

"Been hesitant to raise the issue, dear friend. You've got quite a tab with this establishment, and I know you won't be selling your furs 'til July, but this lady has got bills year-round, and if all my customers paid as erratically as you, I'd have to close, and where would that leave the community? I'll have you know this enterprise is at the center of village life, and that makes me the linchpin of the entrepreneurial community. But," she added in a low and conspiratorial whisper, "if you were to stay the night, we might could arrange to reduce some of your considerable and long-standing deficit."

"I don't have money for a room, Jaquelle."

She brayed. "*Ye God! Why* these games, sir. *Why*? You *know* very well the very room I allude to is directly *upstairs*, Trapper Bapcat!"

Once, in a moment of weakness, he'd made the mistake of bedding her, and now she expected and demanded intimacy every time he came to town, which was as often as two or even three times a year. She was insatiable in such matters, and the reality was that she wore him out in all ways, *especially* with her palaver, which just about never stopped, and at times even got considerably pronounced once her clothes were shed and vigorous coupling commenced (fornicating with Jaquelle Frei being an always vigorous and physical undertaking).

"You render a woman both wanton and carnal," she said. "I'll testify that the late Mr. Frei surely fell far short in these categories, though he was a fine provider and a polite and proper gentleman, as we all surely expect from pure German-born stock. I shall not speak unkindly of him, but tell me the truth straight-out, Lute: Were you one of Teddy Roosevelt's Rough Riders? I mean, were you in that mean bloody scrap down there with him and all those fine boys?"

Bapcat nodded, and Widow Frei picked up a piece of paper and began frantically fanning herself and exhaling loudly. "Sakes alive, my flesh is on fire, Mr. Bapcat, and I do believe you should commence to dowsing said flames before I swoon like a randy doe in a clutch of horned bucks. I say, I swear you'll turn me into a devotee of *cinq à sept*, Mr. Bapcat, have me shedding my gear and panting before high tea."

Sankaset? What the blazes is she on about? She made more turns than a snowshoe hare, and there was no sense fighting or trying to resist her. Once she got a notion into her mind, it would not be dislodged by logic or emotional appeal. She knew what she wanted, and what you wanted was a distant second, if it was a factor at all.

"All right, but I have to see to Big Louie first," he said.

"That's the difference betwixt us," she said. "When the wantons overcome yours truly, when that lovely twitching commences in her netherings, such urgencies override all else—but I suppose a soldier must learn to contain his emotions and not give in to bestial impetuosity." She did not sound at all happy about the syllogistic conclusion she had constructed.

• • •

As predicted, he found the rotund deputy Valo at Sigmund's Tavern. "Almo, when are you going back to Eagle River?"

"I guess mebbe I ain't yet decided," the surly deputy crowed defiantly.

"Could you escort Justice of the Peace Moilanen down that way, and make sure he gets on south on the electric toward Hancock?"

"Tallest man in the damn world ought to be able to look after himself," the deputy said with a snarl.

Sheriff John Hepting of Keweenaw County was one of the finest individuals Bapcat knew, but many of his deputies, especially this one, were lacking in many ways. "Justice Moilanen's feeling a little poorly."

"Well, boo-hoo for the damn giant. *How* poorly?"

"You recently get you a doctor's license, did you?" Bapcat asked sharply, leaning into the man.

Valo, a devout coward, caved under the sharp question. "No cause to pull your tongue-gun."

"Shorty like you got something against a man bein' tall?"

" 'Course not, and I ain't short. I'm average."

"Then act like an average lawman and see that he gets down the line. In fact, finish your beer and get over to the train station now. I'll send him over."

Valo looked pained, but obeyed, belching once he'd swallowed his remaining beer in two gulps.

When Bapcat got back to the widow's place, he asked her, "Has Zakov been around?"

"The Borzoi?" She shook her head. "I daresay that one's even less social than you. And why are you changing the subject? I got intimate notions fluxerpating my mind, and other anatomical reaches that shan't be mentioned by a proper lady in public."

"Just wondering."

"I suppose he might have been around, which is to say most emphatically, *not* with me—here, I'd say late February, early March, and he wouldn't say why, only grinned like a simpleton when people spoke to him. Ask me, Russians are odd as two-tine forks on their best days."

"He have pelts?"

"None I seen, but wouldn't wolves be took down to the sheriff in Eagle River? I thought that's where bounties get settled, or am I misinformed?" She made a sour face and cringed dramatically. "Who'd *want* a nasty old wolf pelt?"

"Fur's real warm," Bapcat said.

"Don't tell me *you* trap them?"

"I do not, madam, and I don't agree with the bounty neither. Wolves ain't no threat to people, Jaquelle."

The widow smiled. "I reckon our famous and legendary Little Miss Red Riding Hood might assert a diametrically opposed viewpoint." Jaquelle Frei suddenly loosed an amazingly accurate imitation of a howling wolf, smacked his behind, took his belt and pulled him up the stairs to her living quarters as she ascended backwards, tugging relentlessly at his trousers.

"Guess I'm gonna find out why you fellas were called Rough Riders," she said, a leer in her husky voice. "Treat me like I'm the enemy, Lute. Give me the real what-for, and don't you spare me any rough stuff. I can take it just fine. God's honest fact is, he seems to have made me especially *for* rough stuff, though I can't imagine why."

5

Montreal River

FRIDAY, MAY 16, 1913

It had been both a long and a short night in the widow's soft bed. The strange summons to the lawyer in Marquette was unsettling on too many levels to deal with. On principle, Bapcat took umbrage at being ordered anywhere by anyone. It was not like he was without pressing chores to get done, as the Keweenaw's short spring plowed unceremoniously into an equally short summer. And there was the mystery of the Russian's wolfer's snooping; this needed to be addressed when he had time to sit and think about it. On the other hand, Roosevelt was a truly great man, and if the colonel needed help, it was Bapcat's duty to render it.

But a trip all the way to Marquette? It was inconvenient at best.

Worse, he'd have to pass through Copper Harbor again, which would bring another rutting with the sweaty, screaming widow. After some thought he had concluded that it was more than merely possible her insatiable lust had contributed to her late husband's demise. A reputedly frail man, he had surely been subjected to her massive demands, which had surely depleted his life fluids. Intimacy too often—like baths, by some accounts—was a risky proposition in terms of a man's longevity.

Despite all of these considerations, Bapcat could not get his mind off Big Louie's unusual and disturbing behavior.

Reaching his hillside refuge, he saw that someone had been in the cabin since yesterday. Hair and porcupine quill telltales had been dislodged and reset differently than he had left them. Four boxes of Winchester .30 caliber cartridges were gone. His Model 94 was still there, but not his full ammo supply. The intruder had tried to be careful and appeared to have moved cautiously, but Bapcat could track a shadow, and having seen he'd been burgled, he easily interdicted the trail and overtook his interloper some three miles southwest, finding the man on his back at the bottom of a crude copper pit, hammered out by Indian miners hundreds or thousands of years ago. This part of the peninsula contained many such pits, which could be extreme walking hazards.

"Zakov," he said to the man, who looked to be in some pain, "I would have shared bullets if you'd asked."

"*Na lovtsa I zver'beshit*. Here I've broken my leg and arm, and your sole concern is such a bourgeois pittance as ammunition."

Pinkhus Sergeyevich Zakov was a small, lean man with black hair and a neatly trimmed black mustache that swept past the corners of his severe mouth. He always wore a black hat that sat on his head like a pot, and carried a sword. The shoulders of his coat bore red and gold epaulets.

"I want it all back—what's mine is mine. Comes down to it, I could shoot you where you lay and take back what's mine."

"You would murder a man for mere bullets?"

"Out here, ammunition is life. You stole and ran."

"Your future as a social philosopher, my friend, seems bleak. Bullets are solely and irretrievably about death. One needs to know war to truly grasp this truth."

"I ain't your friend, Zakov. You have been to war?"

"Ninth Royal Cavalry, the Czar's Own Golden Regiment, we were called, though we seemed *his* only when ceremonial duties called. When fighting erupted, our fearless emperor was of course nowhere to be found. His Majesty got the gold; the rest of us got the war. We were in the great debacle in Manchuria, the battle for Darien, in China."

"What war you talking about?"

"Russo-Japanese, 1905. Your own President Roosevelt with the legendary Big Stick played peacemaker."

"And brought you to America?"

"*Nyet*, though this certainly might be construed. I brought myself. In my country, one invariably must see to oneself. The government is the enemy and the beast, not the domesticated pet of citizens as it sometimes seems to be here, at least on the paper you Americans seem to worship so much. To the rest of the world you seem rich beyond words, which is a very misleading perception."

"Your accent doesn't seem Russian."

"I doubt you are a linguistic expert on accents and patois. My father was a diplomat. I was born and raised in England. My unit repaired from

Manchuria back to Piter, but I went east alone through Siberia, crossing eventually into Alaska, and made my way from there to America across Canada."

"You are a bounty hunter," Bapcat said.

"You are as obvious as Newton's apple."

What? "There are more wolves in Alaska than here."

Zakov grunted. "Russia, too, but I prefer these milder southern climes."

The man was clearly demented. "You're sure your leg is broken?"

"Yes, but there is little pain. My arm is at an angle I doubt the creator intended—if one clings to such baseless superstitions and fantasies such as deities."

"You do not believe in God?"

"The question is, does God believe in me? The only jury which might answer that query, I believe, remains sequestered until the very moment of our demise. Why should I invest in an imaginary creature which by all worldly evidence does not appear to reciprocate by investing in me, *or you*, for that matter?"

Bapcat had harbored similar thoughts since childhood. He turned away from the pit.

"Wait!" a clearly alarmed Zakov squawked.

Bapcat stopped. "I am going to cut aspen poles, make a travois, splint what can be splinted, and pull you out of there."

"Are you always so cold-bloodedly logical?" the Russian wanted to know.

"Are you always so damn dramatic?"

"*Lez hoc hevo ne b'yut*," Zakov said with a grunt.

"What?"

"Don't beat the one who falls. It is widely known in these parts that Citizen Bapcat is a difficult man, a near hermit. In my country, hermits are revered and tend toward holiness. I detect none of that in this instance."

"I don't much care what's widely known or what you detect."

"I rest the case. *Na chuzhoy karavay rot ne razevay.*"

"You spout nonsense. I speak no Russian."

"It is convenient, then, that you have Zakov to translate."

"As I said, nonsense."

"You see, you do understand some Russian after all, my friend."

Bapcat cut aspen saplings and used vines to fashion a hammocky mesh and climbed down to the Russian. A leg bone was bulging against the flesh, and one of the man's arms was useless. Bapcat asked, "How long have you been down here?"

"Hours."

"I can splint the leg, but a doctor needs to see it. A break of this kind can go bad fast."

"There are no doctors near here," Zakov said.

"Not here—Red Jacket."

"Forty miles on your crude contraption?"

"No, nine or ten to Mandan, and from there we'll go south by rail." By going direct they could avoid going back down the hill to Copper Harbor, and Bapcat could thereby avoid the Widow Frei.

"I am going to immobilize your leg, but the pain will increase until I'm done."

"Vodka would be most welcome."

That would be an even greater luxury than a physician. "What you get is a stick, Zakov. You want me to do this, or not? It's your choice. Either way I get my ammo back."

"Do what you must; my point is made," the Russian said.

Bapcat nodded, put a stick in the man's mouth, and began to immobilize his limbs, cleaning the open wound with water from a freezing seep in the rock.

The man winces, but doesn't squirm. Doesn't cry out. This Russian is tough. "Why did you want the cartridges?"

"My supply is low."

"You could buy more."

"That, alas, requires rubles."

"There is credit for men such as us. Or you could employ poison in your wolf killing, as more sensible wolfers do."

"Credit is an entrepreneurial trap, and poison is without honor. This train will cost, *da?*"

"I'll make arrangements for us when we get there, and you will pay me back."

"I have no money, and few prospects for earning any."

Bapcat said, "It will work out. We'll see how philosophical you feel when the pain settles in."

"Some trapped wolves will chew off a leg rather than submit. Pain is a state of mind, nothing more."

"We shall see," Bapcat said.

"Your skepticism shows you know nothing of a Russian's heart."

"The same heart that teaches thievery?"

The Russian sulked.

In Mandan, Bapcat made his patient comfortable in the train station, but decided the breaks were too serious to haul him another forty miles down the line. Better he get him back to Copper Harbor and take him to Frei Dry Goods until he could get a doctor over there to tend to the man's injuries.

Once Bapcat had gotten the Russian settled upstairs, the widow began eyeing him with lust.

"I want you to keep Zakov here until a doctor can come and take a look at him. Only after that can he be moved. I will pay."

She leered. "I mean this from the deepest and kindest reaches of my heart," she said, "but it is customary to make some payment on account before running up such impulse expenses—said payment expected today, before you run off to only the dear Lord knows where."

"But the Russian is upstairs in your bed, and there's no time. Make the call for me. Please."

Widow Frei went to her telephone and cranked it several times, made the call, and hung up.

She turned to Bapcat: "No answer. Doctors are such busy men. We'll have to keep trying. Why do you repeatedly insist on such lame logic, my dear Mr. Bapcat?"

She flipped the front window sign from OPEN to CLOSED and pulled him into a storeroom where she had assembled a cot. She peeled her dress over her head and lay down, smiling. "Let us be about our business anon, Trapper Bapcat. There are paying customers to look after."

6

Eagle River, Keweenaw County

SATURDAY, MAY 17, 1913

Sheriff John Hepting did not seem surprised to see Bapcat. "Valo was out of sorts when he got back," the sheriff said, hiding a smile. "You two have words?"

"I just said things plainly to your man. Did Big Louie Moilanen get on safely to the south?"

"He did," Hepting said, "though Valo seems unable or unwilling to explain your concern."

"Moilanen showed up at my shack naked as Eden and looking for his duds and his Bible."

Sheriff Hepting's left eyebrow arched slightly. "Any idea what the problem was? Tippling?"

"I don't think so, John. He seemed confused but mostly rational by the time I saw him, but I have to say what I saw disturbs me."

"I called down to Doc Kochendorfer to let him know you wanted him to have a look at the giant. Can't say he did or didn't. You here for the night?"

"Got to catch the next train to Red Jacket."

"Nothing to do back at camp?"

"Plenty, but some things take priority."

"The Roosevelt trial?"

"Hard to keep secrets up here," Bapcat complained.

"I won't argue the veracity of that statement. How long you think you'll be gone?"

"John, how'd Valo know I was a Rough Rider?"

"Saw it in a list in the Houghton paper. Only four of you fellas in the whole state. You come out of the woods once in a while, you'd know."

Bapcat grunted. "I don't even know why I've been summoned, but I have to get a doctor up to Copper Harbor to look at Zakov."

"What happened to the Russian?"

"Fell in a hole. Broke his leg real bad. An arm, too."

Hepting said, "Chaz Frinkois left for Houghton this morning for some sort of meeting. Your best bet is to find Doc Kochendorfer in Red Jacket and see if he can get up the line. Bad breaks?"

"One on the leg looks bad."

"Best hurry," the sheriff said. "Good seeing you, Lute. Don't be a stranger."

Bapcat laughed. "I'll always be a stranger in towns."

"The widow up your way still ruling the roost?"

Bapcat blinked and cringed.

7

Red Jacket, Houghton County

SATURDAY, MAY 17, 1913

It was well into dark when Bapcat walked from the station down a street lit with electric lights, and made his way to Dominick Vairo's saloon under the Italian Hall. Thick, choking smoke from mine operations hung over Seventh Street. Mine operations more or less surrounded Red Jacket and kept it clogged with smoke. Wagons clattered and echoed, dogs barked, and automobile motors crackled and popped. The electric lights brought a yellowish brightness the trapper found eerie.

Bapcat had known Vairo since his return to the Keweenaw, and enjoyed the man's company. Vairo sent a kid named Gipp to find Dr. Kochendorfer, who came over to the saloon immediately to have a beer with the men.

Vairo poured one for the messenger, too. The boy was tall and muscled, a handsome, seemingly good-natured lad, and obviously accustomed to tippling.

Bapcat extended his hand. "Lute Bapcat, trapper."

"George Gipp, ball player."

Bapcat liked the kid, a boy with a man's confidence.

"How's Louie?" the trapper asked the doctor.

"I wanted to do some tests, but the big man refused. In some ways he has the emotional stability of a child. Some sort of spell, I'd say, but that's a catchall bogus term we doctors use when we don't know what the hell's happening, and in this case, I don't, and won't unless he lets me try to figure it out. Why do I have the honor of being summoned to meet with you esteemed gentlemen?"

"Zakov the Russian wolfer has a bad leg break and a broken arm. Bone pressing against his skin," Bapcat reported.

"Did you clean it?"

"Best I could.

"Where is he now?"

"With the Widow Frei. I suspect she'll do further tidying."

The gray-headed Kochendorfer nodded. "Hope that's all she does." That said, he left to find a way to Copper Harbor.

"Didn't expect you until July for the fur sale," Vairo told his friend.

"Got other business."

Vairo grinned. "Word's out: Roosevelt. You hear about the troubles brewing hereabouts?"

"No."

"One-man drills."

"This is bad?"

"You were underground; you know. Fewer jobs, greater danger. A man from the Western Federation of Miners is here trying to stir the soup and make it boil over."

Bapcat had spent a horrendous three years as a trammer, hand-filling metal and wood cars with ore. He'd seen at least thirteen men die in his last two years, and was driven out by what became an uncontrollable fear of being in a tight place in the darkness. His heart would race, sweats would start, and he would nearly pass out. Kochendorfer had finally ordered him to stay aboveground and find another way to make a living. By then he had saved a stake, turned to trapping, and never looked back.

"Strike coming?"

"At first I thought not, but now I'm not so sure. The low-pay boys seem pretty troubled by everything. I hear the union will call for a member vote and ask mine operators to meet. If dey agree to meet the union, maybe stoppage can be avoided. If not, who knows? Seems to me likelihood of operators agreeing is nil."

"Mine owners always have the high ground," Bapcat said to Vairo.

"*Si,* is always the same. The country you are in does not matter," Vairo said. "Calumet and Hecla is Rome, *capisce*, a cold and ruthless city-state that enforces its will? C and H owns the town, and everybody lives here, me included. I doubt the WFM has faced the likes of C and H. How long you out of the woods, Lute?"

"Tonight, but I'll be back." He left coins on the bar, but Vairo pushed them back. "Dominick's friends don't pay. Good furs this winter?"

"Quality's the best ever, but numbers are way down."

"That mean anything, you think?"

"Just that there's fewer animals."

"What about nature's so-called bounty? Is such shortage in this country even possible?"

"I think it must be," Bapcat said.

"You'd think God would arrange it so man never runs out. Genesis tells us God made whales and fowl and so forth before He made man, and this was for man, his crowning creation."

"I guess it comes down to the fact that people keep making too many more people," Bapcat said.

"Like *coniglio,*" Vairo said, elbowing him. "Ah . . . but family is the only thing, my friend. We should find for you a fine Italian wife, and you should start making your *own* bambinos."

Bapcat held up his hands and laughed. Being with Jaquelle Frei three times a year was about as much distaff company as he could tolerate. To *live* with a woman? Not likely.

"*Ciao*, Dominick," Bapcat said on his way out, walking past two bloodied men who were whaling at each other in the street with sturdy barrel staves that looked like long black bones.

8

Houghton, Houghton County

SUNDAY, MAY 18, 1913

The electric trolley delivered Bapcat to Hancock, where he caught another trolley across the canal to Houghton and got a room at the Marjoanton Hotel. The desk clerk gave him the once-over. "Food down at Vertang's, whiskey's at the Miner's Hat, both on the Avenue," by which he meant Shelden, the town's main drag.

The clerk looked at the sign-in sheet. "Copper Harbor, eh? This is the big town, son; best be careful. Feelings sometimes run raw for strangers in these parts."

Bapcat got a venison steak and fried potatoes at Vertang's. It was tough, stringy meat, but he was hungry, and would have to put up with restaurant fare until he got back to his camp.

Not one to crave or need alcohol, the one-time Rough Rider wandered Shelden Avenue, listening to the din from various establishments, including a sporting house. Although there was no sign outside, the ladies preening and posturing on the porch made it clear what sport their employer catered to. A small red lantern illuminated the tableau.

Farther along the street a small wiry man crashed into him and viciously swatted him to the side, snarling, "Stay the hell out of my way, you bloody lummox!"

Immediately back on his feet, Bapcat drove his boot hard into the side of the man's leg, causing him to collapse in a heap on the walkway, his collision with the ground sounding like a sack of flour dropped from a high roof.

The man rolled over and tried to get up but Bapcat, his temper in full flare, kicked the man in the mouth with his heel and sent him careening backward.

The fracas ended with Bapcat being ganged and held by several men while others helped the downed man to his feet, all of them apologizing and fawning like drooling toads. "Sorry, Cap'n Hedyn. This man's clearly a public menace. Sheriff Cruse is just down the street. We sent a runner to fetch him."

The man called Hedyn rubbed his mouth, hocked up some blood, and spit. Bapcat sensed the man was getting ready to retaliate and the trapper wanted to be ready, but the men holding him were maneuvering him in a slow dance, keeping him just beyond the smaller man's reach.

"Men die for less," Hedyn said through loose teeth, his eyes bright red, his form glowing like a serpent crawling out of a fire.

"You knocked me down," Bapcat said, and he could immediately hear the man hiss in response.

"You know who I *am,* boy?"

"Not the world's bare-knuckle fighting champion, that's for damn sure."

Hedyn was glaring now, trying to move his jaw, wincing.

A large fat man with a square head arrived, huffing under the strain of moving too fast and demanding to know what was going on, like the others, kowtowing to the man called Hedyn.

Uniformed deputies arrived, handcuffed Bapcat, and led him away, slapping the side of his head as they went. It was impossible to retaliate.

He heard the fat man say behind him, "Sorry about this, Captain Hedyn. We'll take care of this troublemaker."

Hedyn said, "Cruse, you're supposed to keep order in this sad excuse for a town. If you can't do your job, I guess it won't be all that hard to find a replacement."

"You're right, Captain. You're absolutely right. It won't happen again."

• • •

Two hours later Cruse opened the door to the stinking cell, sat down across from his prisoner, and offered a cigarette. "Bapcat, is it?"

The trapper nodded, ignored the cigarette.

"One of Roosevelt's chosen few, we hear. Listen close, bub—it's one thing to snuff a bunch of Spaniards on some tropical isle, but you can't go roughing up leading white citizens. You know who that was you knocked on his ass like a discarded cur?"

"No."

"Captain Madog Hedyn of the Delaware, the hardest mine boss in Copper Country."

"He knocked me down."

"Nobody disputes that, Bapcat, but sometimes facts are irrelevant. See, we all got roles to play in life's grand drama, and yours and mine is to be politely subservient to the Hedyns of the world. I'm sure it happened just as you say, but I'm still gonna have to hold you a few days before I let you go. Appearances count in this life," the sheriff added.

"I have to be in Marquette on Friday."

"I can work with that," Sheriff Cruse said with a fat grin. "The justice of the peace will charge you with disturbing the peace and public drunkenness. You pay a fine and it's over."

"I haven't had a drop to drink," Bapcat said. "And, I want a trial."

Cruse looked pained. "These things are misdemeanors—infinitesimal matters in the greater scheme of the universe. We make it a point to not waste public treasure or time adjudicating petty matters."

"I have a right to a trial."

"Studied up on the law and the Constitution, have you?"

"No, but I know my rights—and President Roosevelt is expecting me Friday." He threw this into the stew, not knowing if it was precisely accurate.

Cruse reacted immediately with a sort of pained moan and sigh. "Well, I see how you want to play this," the sheriff said. "And to level with you, I'm not one to create a ruckus when it ain't needed, so you'll sleep it off here tonight, and we'll let you loose tomorrow."

"I already paid for a hotel room tonight."

"Good. You might want to consider that a cheap lesson in manners."

"The man called Hedyn came at me."

Cruse frowned and waved a hand. "You need to go to Marquette, then git, but don't let me catch you around here again—unless you're ready for the full bite of the court." Cruse slammed the steel door and left him alone to try to sleep in a room that stank of old vomit, sweat, blood, and shit.

One of the jailers looked in on him later. "Are you really going to see Roosevelt?"

Bapcat nodded.

"Makes this your lucky night," the man said. "Cruse protects them mining moguls like they was virgin saints, but you're going to get out without even a lesson-bearing beating."

"Am I supposed to be grateful?"

"Couldn't hurt."

"Pass a message to your sheriff and to Hedyn: I see them again, it won't end so quietly."

"Cruse won't like that, and as for Hedyn, I don't go near Beelzebub's spawn unless I have legal reason to be there, which I don't. I were you, I'd stay far away from the captain. Cruse, he's got deputies to fight his battles, but Hedyn likes to fight his own, and he doesn't stop until his opponents are totally done for. You know where the term *upstanding citizen* comes from?"

"No."

"Them's the ones still standing when the big fights are finished," the guard said. "You didn't win no fight tonight, son. You may have got one started, is all."

9

Marquette, Marquette County

FRIDAY, MAY 23, 1913

The office of W. S. Hill was on the third floor of a red stone building that housed Citizens Bank on the street level. Bapcat made his way up the wooden stairs to a door with the lawyer's name painted in gold on a smoky glass panel. The floors had no dust. He could smell wood polish. The door opened into a reception area with an older female receptionist, her mouth frozen in what looked like a rictus of permanent pride or confidence.

He held the envelope out to her. "Bapcat."

She hardly glanced at the document and nodded toward a door to her left. "Through there, second office on the right."

He followed her directions and found himself in a doorway looking at a grinning, gap-toothed Theodore Roosevelt, who popped to his feet and enveloped Bapcat in a powerful bear hug. "Corporal! Glad you came!"

"Colonel, uh, Mr. President . . ."

Roosevelt nickered enthusiastically. "I prefer 'Colonel' with my boys!" he said. "Sit, Corporal—take a load off."

Bapcat felt Roosevelt studying his face. "You have a scrap, did you, Corporal?"

Bapcat decided to be direct with his old CO. "Nothing important, Colonel. I don't mean to jump the gun, but I don't see how I can be much help in this trial of yours."

The former president's eyebrows danced. "Good gracious, son. To be honest, I don't see that you can help in the trial, either, but I'm sure you would if you could, and I truly appreciate such sentiment. The letter was my way of getting you out of the woods, Corporal. You're still trapping up in Copper Country?"

"Yessir."

"Making a go of it?"

"Ends meet . . . eventually," Bapcat admitted, more a statement of hope than reality.

Roosevelt smiled. "Never the complainer. Still ample animals up there?"

"Populations are shrinking, all species."

The former president frowned. "It's the same across the country, Lute. It's sad—a national shame."

Roosevelt was wearing the thick pince-nez eyeglasses the Rough Riders had referred to as his nose-pinchers. He adjusted them to a better perch on the bridge of his nose. "Want to do something about the problem, Corporal?" the colonel asked.

A man coughed from the doorway. Straight-backed, graying hair, high cheekbones, tall in stature, aristocratic in bearing. Behind him, another man, this one short and possum-like, with a protruding thin nose and a sweeping gray walrus mustache.

Roosevelt stood. "Corporal Bapcat, meet William R. Oates, your state's Game, Fish and Forestry warden."

The straight-backed man shook Bapcat's hand with a sharp, firm grip. Bapcat could feel huge calluses on the man's palms and fingers, a working man's honest hands.

"And this is Chief Deputy Warden David R. Jones," Oates said, stepping aside to allow his smaller companion to reach his hand out.

"David," the smaller man said.

Bapcat responded, "Lute."

"Please be seated, gentlemen," Roosevelt said.

Bapcat remained standing.

Oates began. "The president has given you his highest personal recommendation—very high indeed. He tells us you are a man cool of heart and head when circumstances are most dire."

He thought about Hedyn and Sheriff Cruse, and nearly laughed.

"You trap the Keweenaw?" Jones asked.

"Since 1903," Bapcat said.

"Productive?"

"Less and less."

"Market hunters?" Oates asked.

Bapcat tried to think before answering. "I hear they take deer and ducks and geese to the south of me, but I haven't seen them out where I am." Market hunters killed en masse, processed dead game, and shipped it to high bidders or contractors, almost always in the Midwest's big cities. "No market-hunting of beavers that I've seen," Bapcat added.

"It was endemic early in our country's history," Oates said. "But castor colonies are down, yes?"

Endemic? "Beaves is down some, I guess, but market-hunting them was long before my time," Bapcat said, trying to lighten what felt like a very tedious conversation in the making.

"Free enterprise," Oates said softly. "Which matches products to wants and sells to the highest bidder."

What do they want with me? Bapcat wondered.

"You know Sheriff John Hepting?" Jones asked.

"I do."

"Your opinion of the man?"

"Honest, a good man; has his own opinions on things."

"What about Sheriff Cruse of Houghton County?" Oates asked.

Until last night he'd never talked to the sheriff, but he'd heard about him. "It's said by some that he likes to curry favor with the mine owners." Last night pretty much supported this contention.

"Captain Madog Hedyn of the Delaware mine?"

"Met him just once," Bapcat said, reeling under the irony of being queried about the very man he'd thrashed just the night before.

"And?"

"They say he's a hard man."

"Ever hear Hedyn's name in connection with market-hunting?" Oates asked.

"No, sir. I live way out on the tip of the peninsula, and I don't get a lot of company." *Or welcome it.*

Oates exchanged a look with Jones. Bapcat was thin, almost six foot, with a short black beard, large hands, and dark hair. "I see your knuckles are abraded. You ever considered working as a lawman?" Oates asked.

Bapcat shook his head and looked at his hands. "I fell down. What kind of lawman?"

"Deputy State Game, Fish and Forestry Warden," Jones said.

"*Game warden?*" Bapcat said, seeking clarification. "Me?"

"Yes, deputy game warden. Chief Deputy Jones here would be your immediate supervisor," Oates said.

Roosevelt immediately weighed in. "These are fine men, Lute, and they need skilled and trustworthy men like you who know their way around the woods."

"Ordinarily," Jones said, "counties pay deputy wardens, and we jointly select the men, but past choices have often been entirely political. Warden Oates and I want to put the focus squarely on conservation and resources, not politics. We want our men hired for their knowledge and skills, not their connections. We want high-minded, dedicated, professional lawmen, not political hacks. The job is supposed to be about the resources, not who you know or who owns what. President Roosevelt did the same thing when he headed the Civil Service Commission in Washington."

"*Keweenaw* County?" Bapcat asked.

"Houghton *and* Keweenaw," Oates said, "but you will be paid from our offices in Lansing, not by either county. You can hire an assistant as our second deputy, but only on a trial basis. Let's take some time to measure people before we commit to permanent hires. You can, of course, hire other assistants on a temporary basis as you need them, when season or circumstances dictate. Your pay will be three dollars and fifty cents a day, every day."

Jones said, "You provide your own firearms and ammunition, and your own means of transportation. You own an automobile?"

Bapcat shook his head. "Doubt an automobile would help where I live. What roads we have outside the towns are bad when they're at their best. A horse might be more useful."

"Yes, about that—we want you to move to Ahmeek so you are close to both counties and can move north or south."

"Ahmeek?" That was nearly forty miles south of his place, and right at the top of the mining district.

"The house there is state-owned, free to you. You'll just need to keep the furnace supplied with coal and do your own repairs. The move to Ahmeek isn't optional, son," Oates added.

"We want you to hold off on identifying yourself at the outset," Jones chimed in. "Better to pick a time and use that moment for maximum surprise effect."

Bapcat looked at his colonel. "*This* is why you called me here, Colonel?"

"This, and because I always enjoy spending time with my boys. Take the job, Lute. Your colonel thinks it's the right thing to do for yourself, for your state, and for your country. You see, I'm still your spotter, even after all these years, my boy."

Lute Bapcat trusted Roosevelt, but he harbored doubts—especially when it came to living in Ahmeek. He loathed all towns. *Still, one can't turn down the former president when he asks you to serve.*

The former Rough Rider corporal nodded, and Teddy Roosevelt slapped his knee in delight. "Knew it!"

The colonel reached down to the floor and picked up a .30-40 Krag-Jørgensen carbine, which he held out to Bapcat. "Had this sent to me when you mustered out in New Jersey," Roosevelt said. "I want you to have it. Let it remind you of what the calm in a storm can accomplish."

Bapcat was speechless, and after collecting his wits, went to his pack and pulled a bayonet from its scabbard and popped the steel onto the Krag's barrel. The carbines wouldn't hold bayonets very effectively, but it looked lethal, and he had kept it since Cuba.

Roosevelt was smiling. "You saved that all this time?"

"Yessir."

Roosevelt smiled. "At the critical moment, show your enemy your steel, Corporal." Roosevelt was fond of bayonets—saw them as manly, lethal, and decisive in close fights.

Chief Deputy Jones said, "There's a green house up the hill on Rock Street. Ask for Deputy Warden Horri Harju. Good man. He'll see to getting you set up and properly and officially instructed."

Oates stood. "Raise your right hand and repeat after me."

Lute Bapcat was sworn in as the Michigan deputy warden for Houghton and Keweenaw counties.

Roosevelt grunted a happy, "Bully!"

The two state men departed, leaving the old Rough Riders alone. Roosevelt said, "Your state's new governor, Woody Ferris, is not the sort to meddle in local affairs. He's a genteel type, thinks of himself as a higher-education man, a man of cerebral and calm pursuits. Likes to remain far above the fray. I suspect you'll have free reign in your neck of the woods, Corporal, but choose your targets well. The Spaniards were pretty respectable as foes go, but these market hunters and the like are mankind's sorriest excuses for people. Watch your back at all times and cut them no slack.

"And remember this, Corporal: When times are hard—and they always get hard—just bear in mind there are other men (and even women) here and in other states doing the same thing you are doing, and through our mutual values and our collective efforts, we hope to protect and preserve the natural world we live in. I've been pushing for Rough Riders to be hired as forest rangers all around the country, in our parks and preserves. If we lose nature and the wilderness, we lose life itself. What you're about to undertake is more than a mere job. We need tough, no-nonsense men on our front lines, men like you. Always remember that, son."

"Yes, sir," Bapcat said, shaking hands with his former commanding officer.

10

Marquette, Marquette County

FRIDAY, MAY 23, 1913

The man who opened the door was stoop-shouldered, with a drooping blond mustache, head shaved smooth as a Lake Superior rock, and huge wing-like ears. "Bapcat?" the man greeted him.

The trapper nodded.

"Horri Harju. Any trouble finding the place?"

Bapcat shook his head. "Only green house on the street."

"So it is, so it is. Come in, come in."

The house looked from without like a residence, but the interior was more like a military warehouse with crates of ammunition, stacks of rifles and boxes of pistols, snowshoes, skis and bindings, iron skillets, rucksacks—all sorts of things.

"Coffee?" Harju asked. "I assume you accepted the job, or you wouldn't be here, would you?"

"No coffee," Bapcat said.

"I think half my blood's coffee," Harju said, and before the statement fully registered with Bapcat, it was punctuated with a looping roundhouse sucker punch that Bapcat barely deflected with his left forearm, while grabbing Harju by the shirt, pulling him over and forward, and driving his knee into the man's crotch. Harju staggered backward, laughing and rubbing his crotch, while Bapcat began massaging his knee, which hurt like the dickens.

Pain in the knee momentarily ignored, Bapcat stepped toward the man, who put up his hands and said, "I surrender. Ya, you'll do Bapcat. In this job you gotta be ready at all times. The beaver ban help make up your mind?"

Who is this lunatic? "What beaver ban?"

Harju groped in his trousers and pulled out a tin pot, which was dented, and tossed it to Bapcat. "Good idea to assume the worst going into any scrap. That pot's lined with heavy felt—my late wife's idea. She wanted me to invent armor to repel bullets, too, but I ain't had that sort of time. Truth is, I may need to redesign the pot. I felt your knee, and that's pretty rare. You're the first one to ever shed that first punch."

"You *wanted* me to fight?"

"Well, sure—we needed to know something more about you."

"Talk isn't good enough?"

"Sometimes action is far more compelling. Before we finish here, I'll show you how to put an opponent to sleep by pinching his neck." Harju motioned at his own neck. "The beaver ban will be announced in July. There will be no beaver trapping through 1920. Populations have crashed downstate, and they're in damn poor condition most places up here as well. You agree?"

"I don't know about down below, but there are a lot fewer over my way."

"Excellent distinction. A game warden needs to stick with what he knows and what he's seen. Avoid generalization when you can."

He'd noticed, but never thought about connecting his personal experience to a larger picture. "I've seen."

"So, if the ban wasn't the decider for you, what was?"

"Colonel Roosevelt."

"You hold the man in high regard?"

"The highest."

"He as brave as some make out, or just some reckless rich boy?"

"Bit of both," Bapcat said. "Not sure how to sort out which is which."

Harju smiled. "Yep, I think you'll do."

"What's *your* job here?"

"Deputy warden—like you, but for Marquette County. The chief likes for me to orient new Upper Peninsula deputies."

"Long at the job?"

"Ten years. Sometimes it feels longer, but with this civil service change, we're going to be hiring more qualified men, not a bunch of cowards, hacks, and sycophants. You hearing anything about a strike looming over your way?"

"There's been talk."

"It could get ugly fast," Harju said.

"For the miners."

"For everyone except us. For us it could be a windfall. See, in this job you need to keep your eyes and ears open all the time, pay attention to everything that happens around you. Comes a strike, businesses get in trouble, can't make payrolls, can't pay their employees—who can't eat—and that's when we can expect violations to happen. Whole world is cause and effect once you adjust to thinking that way."

"Am I to be the first warden over my way?"

"No. The first was a disaster named Case Bestemand. When they sent him to me, I wired the chief in Lansing and told him I had lots of doubts. Bestemand was once a deputy for Sheriff Cruse, who continued to use him as his personal dog. Bestemand didn't last a month. He went down to the Chassell area to look into rumors of wild fowl market-hunting in the marshes of the Sturgeon River. Trapper found him stumbling around the woods down by Pelkie a week later. He'd been severely beaten, his skull fractured. Hospital in Marquette sent him to the state mental hospital in Newberry, but he walked away from there and hasn't been seen since. That was two years ago."

Harju took a breath and looked into Bapcat's eyes. "This job we do is dangerous. People up here grudgingly accept law in towns, but they don't accept law in the woods, and I doubt they will in the time we're on this Earth."

"Are there a lot of laws?"

"Not yet," Harju said. "But there will be, by and by. Deer and small-game licenses start this year, no shooting waterfowl in spring, new deer-season dates, and down the road, maybe as early as next year, there will be shooting only deer with horns, no more does and fawns. The limit on possessed fish is reduced, and people from outside the state now need to buy a fishing license, just like we do. You and me will talk a lot about all this in more detail, but that's a pretty fair look at what we're in."

Bapcat was trying to process all the information.

Harju said, "Let's start with this principle: If a violator demands a jury trial, you'll probably lose. Few jurors will find a neighbor guilty of the same things they do themselves. This means your job is to be clever and get a confession from the man and then quickly get him to the justice of the peace for sentencing. If you can't get a confession, thrash the hell out of the man so that even if the case gets to the jury and he wins, he will already have lost because he'll remember what you did to him, which of course you will promise to mete out to him every single time you find him even stretching a law."

Bapcat was speechless.

"You didn't hear that as an official order from the department," Harju said. "I'm just telling you a way to handle some of our business. How'd you like being a miner?" Harju asked, changing subjects.

"Wasn't fond of being underground in the dark in closed spaces."

"Three years at the Mohawk Number One, I hear."

Do they know everything about me? "Yes, three."

Harju grinned. "Now that we're all civil servants, we're authorized to investigate personal backgrounds. Don't be alarmed. Were me in that mine job, I wouldn'ta lasted a month. You were a trammer, right?"

Bapcat nodded. "Yes, trammer."

"Hard work?"

"Hard and scary, everything done by hand. Most mine owners wouldn't invest in motorized equipment." Bapcat recalled the thirteen men he saw die in two years.

"The darkness drive you out?"

"A doctor told me he'd insist they fire me rather than let me go back underground again, so I took my leave. By then I had a stake saved."

"Why'd you take the job in the first place?"

"Money. I could live cheap and build my stake."

"Trap any while you were a miner?"

"No time. Mining takes all the tar out of you."

Harju nodded. "This job will do the same."

"This job's aboveground," Bapcat said.

"And it's outside," Harju added with a sly grin.

"How long will I be here?"

"Three, four days. That a problem?"

"No, sir, I'll wire people and let them know."

"Rule One," Harju said, holding up a forefinger. "Don't never let people know where you are going, or when, and don't never take the same route to or fro. The best game wardens are shadows of shadows. You bring enough duds with you?"

"Some."

"Don't worry; we'll get you fixed up. Just listen when I instruct, and for Pete's sake, ask questions. Ready?"

Bapcat held out his hands. "It's your show."

Harju grinned and shook his head. "*Our* show, Deputy. From this moment on, you and me, we're brothers, Bapcat."

11

Marquette, Marquette County

MONDAY, MAY 26, 1913

Horri Harju was a fair man, a demanding teacher, passionate about work, making a salient point each time he could find an opening about how Bapcat needed to achieve a big success early on to validate the change to civil service status for game wardens.

One morning Harju announced, "That house in Ahmeek won't be available. There's been a fire. You'll need to find another abode." Harju gave him a purchasing price range and told him, "Make it damn clear you're representing the state government."

"Won't that make them want to charge more?"

"It will, which is why you should be resolute on price haggling, and not settle for a cent more than what you think you would pay if it was your own money."

"I've never bought a house before," Bapcat confessed.

"There's a first time for everything," Harju pronounced. "Make them draw up a contract and send it to Chief Oates for his review and approval."

Bapcat immediately began to wonder if the house fire was somehow related to how unpopular game wardens were, and when he shared his concerns, Harju laughed and nodded. "Good, good. That's the right attitude for deputies. Accept no coincidence on its face value."

• • •

Bapcat settled into his role as student. The litany of duties wardens faced was awesome, far more extensive than Bapcat had ever thought, and it left him wondering if this job was the right thing for him. He didn't mind working hard, but he liked having time to think. How could he find time to supervise and train township fire wardens, enforce commercial fishing regulations, help plant fish sperm and fingerlings, patrol lands, lakes, ponds, and streams, all while looking for fish and game violations, apprehending and prosecuting violators, securing private land for use as state game refuges, lecturing the public on conservation and fire prevention, removing obnoxious fish from designated state waters, *and* keeping streams and rivers free of beaver obstacles?

Midday a white-haired man with a red face showed up at the green house and Harju said, "Omer Clarke, meet Lute Bapcat. Lute meet Omer, the department's school coordinator."

"Big title," Clarke said. "But I'm a deputy, paid the same as you and Horri. I was a schoolteacher down to Lansing, but Davey Jones came up with the idea of recruiting kids to do fire prevention and conservation. He offered me the job and I took it. Statewide we've now got more than five thousand boys in the Michigan Forest Scouts. The last warden over your way did nothing with this program, but we have a chapter in Red Jacket. Your contact there is a teacher at Laurium High School named Cornelius Nayback. Bestemand gave Nayback a hundred dollars for MFS uniforms and sundries, and we ain't heard from Nayback since."

"Has this program helped reduce fires in the state?" Bapcat asked.

"Has indeed, but more importantly, these scouting groups have allowed deputy wardens to move more freely in their communities and towns and to be accepted. Used to be it was damn near a local crime or cardinal sin to help the game warden. Now it's getting less so. More and more people are coming over to our way of thinking, which is why dealing with the public in a controlled and professional way is so important for our future *and* for our safety. Me, I work around Lansing, but you fellas are alone out in the deep bowels of Hell, and if you make enemies, your situation makes it real easy to get rid of you."

"Like the last warden?"

"Possibly," Harju said.

"We *know* Bestemand gave Nayback the money?" Bapcat asked.

Clarke said, "Draft drawn on Miners Bank in Laurium. We have the record."

"Has the man checked with anyone since Bestemand disappeared?"

"No," Harju said, "and we sent two letters asking that the money be returned to the State. No response either time."

"Who chose Nayback?"

"Cruse—same man who chose Bestemand," Clarke said. "Never mind Nayback for now. The big thing is to treat people fairly, don't let your temper loose unless it's warranted, and make sure you always pay attention to young people. They're the secret to our long-term success. If they grow up doing the right thing, it will make our job a lot easier someday."

That afternoon on the shooting field south of the federal prison, Bapcat had fired the .30-40 Krag-Jørgensen, 12-gauge shotgun, and .44 revolver. At the end of the shooting Harju looked impressed.

"Some might shoot better with a shotgun or pistol, but your rifle score is the best we've ever had, and your combined results are also the best," Harju said. "Word is that you used that rifle to lethal advantage during the Spanish War. Let's hope you never have to point a weapon at anyone in your career as a deputy."

Bapcat nodded. He'd killed enough in Cuba.

Harju asked, "Any thoughts on a warden's biggest advantage?"

"Surprise," Bapcat said.

Harju nodded. "Appear when and where they least expect it. Make folks think you are multiple people, and that you can work days on end without sleep and be everywhere and check on everyone." Harju leaned over. "You only have to do this a couple of times. Violators talk to each other. Word will get around, and you'll have them all looking over their shoulders all the time. You'll see. It's good that you can handle a firearm, but your main weapon will be your brain. Without that, you're sunk."

"Is this the end of things here?" Bapcat asked.

"Pretty much. Tonight we'll get you set up with report forms and law manuals, and you can head for home and get started finding a place to live."

"If Ahmeek's out, what about staying at my own place?"

"A trapper's shack way the hell back in the woods? That won't do, Lute. Take a deep breath here and now. Find a bloody place close to town right from the start. Get a hotel room first, and work from there. I'll be over in a couple of weeks to look in on you." Harju gave him a big grin and squeezed his shoulder. "All state wardens meet two or three times a year for training from the state biologist and senior deputies. It's always interesting. Your first group session will be later this year in Sault Ste. Marie. Now, don't you go running off like that last fella."

Lute Bapcat looked the man in the eye. "I don't run. Ever."

12

Laurium, Houghton County

MONDAY, JUNE 2, 1913

Mordella Rose DiSilvestro was Dominick Vairo's sister-in-law. Mrs. DiSilvestro was short with alabaster skin, and wore a floor-length heavy black frock with her black hair tied back so tightly in a bun it made her face look like a red skull. Set in the middle of a narrow lot, her house was two stories, long but not very wide. The room she had shown him was on the second floor and seemed secure for his gear. If he wanted meals with their family, that would cost extra. He had told her he'd think about meals, and they shook hands on the room.

That was yesterday afternoon. Bapcat was in Laurium now, east of Red Jacket, knocking on the front door of the house of Cornelius Nayback.

The man who answered the door was slight, with a nervous twitch that made his nose move continuously. His handshake was like a rag doll's, and his voice so soft and tentative that Bapcat had to strain to hear.

This man teaches rhetoric? "Nayback?" Bapcat began.

"Who is asking?"

"Deputy Warden Bapcat."

Nayback looked at him and showed no emotion. "What is it you want, Deputy?"

"Michigan Forest Scouts. Deputy Bestemand gave you one hundred dollars in state funds."

"You are misinformed, sir," the man said firmly. "He did no such thing."

"The State has the record of a draft drawn in your name."

"His word or the bank's?"

"Miners Bank here in Laurium. The State sent letters asking that the money be returned to a state account."

"How does one return what one does not possess?" the man countered.

Difficult to read his eyes or his tone. "Our records and the bank's say you got state money," Bapcat repeated.

"They show no such thing. By your own account the records show Bestemand got money from the bank, allegedly in my name. That is not the same as giving it to me. Please go away. Your business is with Deputy Bestemand."

The man tried to close the door, but Bapcat blocked it with his boot. "The State says my business is with you, and the State *will* have its money back."

"I can empathize, but I don't have said money."

"Because you spent it?"

"I'm no wastrel, sir! I don't have it because I never received said money. Please leave me alone. I find this insulting."

"The State *will* get its money back," Bapcat said forcefully.

"Spoken like a State puppet," Nayback responded angrily.

The man's sudden vitriol surprised Bapcat. "I beg your pardon?"

"Bapcat, you can't even give yourself a legitimate name! You cling to the State label of shame despite achieving majority."

"What're you talking about, Nayback?"

"Bapcat . . . Let me guess. Your first name is Luther, am I right?"

How does he know?

"The orphanage used the same naming convention for bastards abandoned on their doorstep. Lute Bapcat—ergo, Lutheran Baptist Catholic. Think back on names at the home, man. Use your brain, if you possess one."

Bapcat remembered. Billy Cathtist, Paul Orthometh, a few others. *Could this rodent be right? Why didn't someone tell me any of this*?

"Never mind the name," Bapcat said. "You owe the State money."

"You are speaking not to some hapless Bohunk, my good sir, but to a member in good standing of the faculty of Laurium High School, and I'll have you know that I have friends in high places. Prove your allegations if you can, sir." With this, Nayback closed the door and Bapcat heard the latch click.

Pretty feisty for a mouse. *Lutheran Baptist Catholic?* What do you care? A name's just a damn name.

13

Lake Linden, Houghton County

FRIDAY, JUNE 6, 1913

The county's St. Cazimer's Orphanage was much as Bapcat remembered it from the day he had walked away, only smaller than it seemed years ago. Back then it had seemed foreboding; now, just abandoned and empty. The sign was gone, no children were in sight, the yard was bosky and overrun, the old multistory stone building in a state of disrepair. An old man with one arm gone at the shoulder sat in an unpainted chair on the porch of a small house next door.

Bapcat approached the porch, saw the man's glazed eyes, and guessed he was blind. "Sorry to bother you," the deputy said.

"My specialty to be bothered, some might say. I'm Gurden Supanich; some call me Blackie. What you call me is up to you, it being a free country and all that."

"Lute Bapcat."

"The man chuckled. "Another runaway state bastard come home to the roost, eh?"

"What's that supposed to mean?"

Supanich then related the same explanation Nayback had provided. "This come as a revelation to you, does it?"

Bapcat sat on the edge of the porch. "I left when I was twelve," he explained.

"Stayed till sixteen, they would have explained everything, even helped you pick a new name. Run off, eh? See, patience sometimes pays, even in a shithole like St. Cazimer's."

"Couldn't tolerate the place anymore, and I had plans."

"Plans, eh? Soldier or sailor?"

"Cowboy."

The old-timer grinned. "Good for you, son. I went to work in the bloody mine at fourteen, was there till a magazine accident took my arm and my eyesight. Had a wood fragment skewered my brain, else we wouldn't be here making idle talk. You come back for nostalgia?"

"Explanations," Bapcat said. "I guess."

Supanich said, "I just gave you good as you're likely to get."

"Mrs. Hoogstratton was head matron."

"Cut her wrists and died, dispatching herself with a lot more efficiency than she ever showed when she was running this place. St. Cazimer's was abandoned for months. Vagrants used it, but now it's too run-down even for the likes of them. Listen, Bapcat—a name's just a damn label, and there ain't no shame in being a bastard. Back in the day of Queen Elizabeth, bastards were considered nature's little accidents, and kids weren't punished for something they had no say in."

"You were around back then?" He had no idea when Queen Elizabeth had lived.

Supanich laughed. "Seem old enough, don't I? Nossir, I read till I lost my eyes, and now and then a whore named Aurey Pentoga reads to me. Says reading out loud for money beats being on her back for stinky loggers and miners, and I guess I see her point."

14

Swedetown, Houghton County

FRIDAY, JUNE 6, 1913

Rose DiSilvestro met Bapcat on the front walk and seemed irritated or confused.

"What's wrong?" the new game warden asked.

Vairo's sister took a deep breath and said, "Your wife's here—up in your room."

"My *wife?* I don't have a wife."

"Not my concern, you being a grown man and all." His landlady stalked back into the house, shutting the screen door in his face.

He saw crude crutches next to his bedroom and on the bed sat Zakov.

"The doctor you sent is no better than a barber in the matter of medicine. The imbecile wanted to remove my leg, until I informed him that my first action as a one-legged cripple would be to kill him slowly. Your Widow Frei requested I inform you that payment on account will be expected at first opportunity. I joked to your new landlady of being your winter wife, and she became all worked up before I could explain. American women are too damn literal. Initially, I said I was your dogsbody, but she did not understand the word or the concept, and I mistakenly substituted the word *wife.*"

"I don't understand *dogsbody* either," Bapcat said sourly.

"The word refers to an officer's personal valet."

"I'm not no officer. You got something against using plain words?"

"You are far too touchy, my boy."

"I thought you would be in a hospital."

Zakov tapped a leg cast. "The latest thing. Plaster serves to immobilize bone until the bone can knit itself. I'm already a maestro on crutches."

"The hospital should have put that plaster on your head until your brain heals."

The Russian smiled thinly. "This is a poor way to address the dear wife you've not seen in so long."

"You ain't staying with me—is that more to the point?"

"I have nowhere else to go."

"That's not my problem. You tried to steal from me, remember?"

"Irrelevant, my friend, and moot. In Russia if you rescue a critically injured man, you are subsequently and eternally responsible for his welfare."

"This ain't your goddamn Russia, and what exactly does *critically* mean?"

Zakov waved a finger. "A hair of definition to be parsed, massaged verbally, and debated ad infinitum. It can mean what you wish, or not wish—your choice."

Bapcat slung a crutch at the man, who caught it. "Get out, thief."

Zakov didn't move. "The hospital has discharged me, but I cannot return to the taiga until I heal. You are responsible for my welfare. What about this elemental situation can you not grasp and understand?"

"I'm boarding here. *Alone*."

"The bed is solid," Zakov said. "There's room on the floor for you."

Bapcat took a step toward the Russian with the intent of administering severe bodily harm, but instantaneously decided against violence. "Why aren't you staying with the Widow Frei?"

"Her commercial interests extend far beyond Copper Harbor. She had no space or time for me."

"Let me guess: When the doctor moved you to a hospital, she told you to not come back."

"It was not nearly as bluntly stated as that, but certainly that's the unquestioned gist."

"Where's your place in this so-called *taiga*, and what's that mean?"

"East of Bootjack, and it translates in your vernacular as the backwoods. I was up McCallum Creek, toward Rice Lake."

"A lot of farm country over that way." The area was south of Red Jacket.

"Of course, which makes it a predictable deer magnet, which in turn, serves as a wolf magnet, my *raison d'être*."

"I'll get some help to move you back."

"That won't be possible."

"Why not?"

"I appropriated a space for myself. It was run-down with no signs of habitation. Some men appeared one morning and let me know that uninhabited does not mean un-owned. They chastised and forcefully banished me."

"You mean they beat the tar out of you?"

"No, I had a brace of pistols and the drop. It was a peaceable, albeit hasty departure, but I cannot go back there."

"They got your ammo, right?"

"Yes, all but that in the revolvers and in my rifle at the time."

"You could try to legally rent or purchase the building."

"No money, my young companion. I am a penniless state of one."

"I should drag you into the woods and shoot you like a broke horse," Bapcat said. "Put you out of your misery."

"I would be almost gratified for such a release from life's sour circumstances, but you seem neither the merciful, nor the killing, type."

"You're half right," Bapcat said, and went downstairs.

"The Russian up there is hurt and crazy. Do you have another room to let?" he asked the DiSilvestro woman.

"Dangerous crazy?" she asked.

"Just off kilter some due to life's hard circumstances."

The woman shrugged. "That defines all of us, Mr. Bapcat." DiSilvestro gave him a long, appraising look. "Talk to Dominick. He's the family's agent of commerce."

Bapcat nodded. "Okay if the Russian stays until we find another place?"

"Of course. Will you and your wife dine with the other guests tonight?"

"He's *not* my wife," the trapper said, using a tone he hoped would make it clear the joke was over.

15

Ahmeek Village, Keweenaw County

SUNDAY, JUNE 8, 1913

Dominick Vairo came with him. "It started as a basic miner's house, but my brother-in-law Giuseppe gave it a few additions, which he just finished. The miners 'round here got no money for such things. The water closet is the latest, eh?"

The house, unlike neighboring places, had a fresh coat of dark brown paint, a fence painted pale yellow, no grass, a small storm entry that opened into an area with the kitchen-pantry, a living room, and bathroom on the main floor. The overall dimensions of the building were eighteen by twenty-six feet. The second floor had three small bedrooms. There were kerosene lanterns, no electricity. The place looked new inside. The full basement had a concrete floor and tight stone walls.

"How much?" Bapcat asked.

"Six hundred an' fifty dollar. The commode, she got runna water, yes?"

"I'm buying for the State," Bapcat reminded his friend.

Vairo studied him, chewed his lower lip. "What you got to do with guvamint, Lute?"

Bapcat explained.

The Italian whistled and snapped his hand, making a sharp popping sound. "You gotta be crazy, game warden, Lute. Maybe house outside town be better, *si?* You live here, dey all watch you, know when you come and go, no?"

"They can watch all they want, Dominick."

"You don't like trappin' no more, Lute?"

"It doesn't pay. Beavers are down."

"This game warden t'ing, I t'ink not pay enough."

"Five-fifty for the house," Bapcat said. "Tops."

Vairo's shoulders slumped and his hands flew up, pleading. "You put me in poorhouse! I buy this place, fix up for profit, you understand? I want to throw away my money, I do better go play pool with Georgie Gipp."

"The offer stands," Bapcat insisted.

Vairo sighed. "Okay, you my friend."

The two men shook hands. "I'll bring a signed contract as soon as I get it from Lansing."

"No hurry. You wanna move in now, go ahead."

"Think I'll wait."

A large sign across the street proclaimed AHMEEK ATHLETIC ASSOCIATION. The wooden building was like an arena, but open to the elements. "What's that?"

"Croats and my pipples, we call it Cousin Jack House. The Cornwallers, they hold big wrestling games over dere."

"Against all comers?"

"No, just dere own kind. The rest of us prob'ly too dirty for dose damn Cousin Jacks," Vairo said sarcastically, referring to the Cornish, who still held the most powerful and lucrative positions in the mines.

As they headed toward the electric trolley station they saw George Gipp and two pals, all of them lean, muscled, and confident.

"Da muscatelles," Vairo greeted them, grinning.

"Yeah, Frenchmen like me," the tallest one said cheerfully, and extended his hand to Bapcat. "Chubb Chaput, ball player."

"Bapcat," the new deputy said.

"This is my pal, Dolly Gray," George Gipp said. "He's up from Notre Dame to play some summer ball with the Aristocrats."

"Ball players, dey t'ink kid games is work," Vairo muttered.

"I'm just here warming up for the Phillies," Chaput announced.

Aristocrats, Phillies, Notre Dame—Bapcat had no idea what these things were. And didn't care.

"Just kid games," Vairo said dismissively.

Chubb Chaput rubbed the tavern owner's back affectionately. "Hey, Dominick, it's the American game, not that silly cricket the Jacks play."

"Cricket, she's very old game," Vairo said. "Like bocci."

"And we're still a real young country," Gray said.

"You guys any good this summer?" Vairo asked Gipp.

"I'm bettin' on us," the young man said.

"You fellas help me convince your friend," Gray said. "George here is real good, and he belongs in college at Notre Dame. With me."

"He ain't finished high school," Chaput pointed out.

Gray dismissed him with a wave of the hand. "Guy can play ball like our Georgie, Notre Dame will figure a way to get him in. I've talked to Coach Harper about him, and he's a cinch. All he has to do is show up in South Bend."

All the talk about sport and baseball bored Bapcat. It had taken all his time and energy just to stay alive since he was twelve.

"We should be going," Vairo said.

"We come up to watch the Jacks grope each other," Gipp said. "You fellas want to join us?"

"Not me," Vairo said. "I get back to the saloon."

"I'll join you fellas," Bapcat said, wanting to get a better sense of this Gipp kid.

"We got good money on Roscopla," Gray confided as they entered the arena.

"Dolly does," Gipp said. "There's a new man here tonight. Thought I'd watch before I place any bets."

More cautious and calculating than he shows, Bapcat thought. Interesting.

"This Roscopla good?" Bapcat asked.

"Heavyweight, and the hill king here. Strong, big, tough, relentless," Gipp said. "And cocky."

"Hell, nobody's cockier than you," Chaput told his friend.

"I can back up the talk," Gipp said.

"So far," Chaput countered with a laugh.

The arena was about half full when the matches began. Unknown newcomer Harry Jacka took Kilty Roscopla apart like an overcooked chicken. Chaput and Gray were morose about their lost wagers. Gipp watched the match quietly, studying, and afterward whispered to Bapcat, "Jacka's tough, but his balance to his right side is poor. He wrestles one-sided. Not a strength issue to beat him. It's all about speed and leverage."

Gipp sounded pretty sure of his analysis.

During the final match Bapcat spied Captain Madog Hedyn in the stands with a retinue of people, including Cornelius Nayback.

"Who's the potentate across the way?" Bapcat asked Gipp.

"Cap'n Madog Hedyn. A little man physically, but one of the Copper Country's most important and feared men. Works his people like slaves and cuts miner contracts to his benefit."

"Cheats them?" Bapcat asked.

"Nothing that obvious. He just measures the day's digs close, cuts no slack for the miners, not even his own kind. Rumor is he hauls in a hundred thousand dollars a year, same as MacNaughton at C and H, but Hedyn's is all underground, just like the copper he and his men chase."

"He takes a cut from the wrestling promoters," Chaput chimed in.

"Why?" Bapcat asked.

"No cut, no wrestlers," Gipp said. "Hedyn controls everything the Cornish and Cousin Jacks do, and he always makes sure he profits off the top."

"I'm surprised everyone goes along," Bapcat said.

Chaput said, "Word is that a local minister wanted new music for Sunday services, but Hedyn's wife didn't. The minister ended up with two broken arms, resigned the church for medical reasons, and promptly left town. A new minister came in. The old music stayed. The new minister was kin."

As they left the stadium Gipp asked, "What's with your interest in Cap'n Hedyn?"

Gipp was remarkably observant for a young man. "We once had an awkward meeting."

"I'm just a kid, but I know there ain't no odds in stirring up poisonous snakes."

Bapcat took note that Cornelius Nayback was close to Hedyn and had whispered frantically at him throughout the matches. All the while Hedyn stared malevolently across at him. *The house across the street won't do*, he told himself.

The three boys headed for a pool hall in Laurium and Bapcat went back to the boardinghouse to find Zakov still on the bed, a pair of revolvers in his lap. "I have no plan to abandon this bed," the Russian announced.

Bapcat put up his hands and smiled a conciliatory smile. "For now," he said.

The house in Ahmeek village won't suffice, Bapcat thought. Hedyn and Nayback had both seen him, and would be asking around. *We need more space, some elevation, something to provide early warning, good high ground, like we had in Cuba.*

16

Bumbletown Hill, Keweenaw County

MONDAY, JUNE 9, 1913

Vairo seemed unsurprised to see his friend the following morning. "I figure maybe that place, she won't do," the tavern owner greeted him. "What exactly you want?"

"No neighbors, nearby firewood, a good well."

"How many rooms—five?"

"One large one is enough if we're on a hill and there's woods and a good well."

"Okay, I bought four log shacks from one of the mines. Not too good shape, but solid, okay? Top of Bumbletown Hill. Can almost see both sides Keweenaw on clear day, eh. No cellar, though."

"How much?"

"Got cabin, not justa one room, but *quattro* rooms, storage shack; call it all a hundred and it's yours. You want me to show you?"

"No need for you to go along."

"Okay, I got Mass, the wife and bambino, yes?" Vairo drew a rough map. "Heard there was dump where this place she got built. Mebbe some rats. You mind rats?"

"Not as long as they mind their own business."

Bapcat took the electric trolley to Allouez and traipsed west out of town a half-mile up a long hill until he found the log shack. There was a hard-rock outcrop nearby, and he could see where loggers had cleared forests for underground shoring. In the distance he could see mine structures and towns: Allouez, Ahmeek, Copper City. At night he guessed he'd see Red Jacket with all its electric lights. A couple small rats watched him as he studied the building. Opening the door to the snow room sent more rats scuttling. Four rooms, no cellar, but a privy and a small storage shack to the north. *This will do. The woods are close and thick, and it will be easy enough to walk up the hill from the electric.*

Back in Red Jacket he sent a telegram to Harju in Marquette and Chief Oates with details of the place, including the cost, and promised to send a contract at first opportunity.

He was back in the rented room by midafternoon. Zakov was still on the bed. "Did I mention Widow Frei requests your presence?" he said.

"No."

"My deepest apologies. I meant to, but all this anxiety over a domicile to inhabit has caused my thinking to become somewhat distended."

"I can imagine," Bapcat said, suspecting the scheming Russian did little by accident. "You can relax now."

"You are accepting our living arrangement?"

"Until I can dispose of you."

"*Dispose.* There are many layers of meaning in that one small word."

"Pick the one you like," Bapcat said. "Where, east of Bootjack?"

Zakov explained in a way only another outdoorsman could understand.

Bapcat got out a crude map Harju had given him. The electric trolley would take him from Laurium to Lake Linden, and he could hike south from there.

"Are you abandoning me again?" the Russian inquired.

"Mrs. DiSilvestro is around."

The Russian sighed heavily. "Clearly this woman does not like me and is not *sympatico*."

Bapcat said. "You should be used to it."

17

East of Bootjack, Houghton County

MONDAY, JUNE 9, 1913

Bapcat knew the upper Keweenaw well, but Houghton County was relatively unfamiliar. Wondering why the Russian got run off, he wanted to look over the lay of the land, see what was there. A good two hours remained until summer sundown. Zakov's shack was along the creek, whose clear moving waters were tinted orange. *Mostly woods, first growth, little sunlight penetrating. Deer would be on the edges near fields.* He pasted his exposed skin with creek mud to ward off mosquitoes and other insects.

Despite a careful search he found little sign—virtually no pellets, few tracks. *The does should be throwing fawns by now. Where are they?* There was a small hill just north of the shack, and beyond that, a much larger one. *Impossible to guess distance.* Mainly he wanted to find the edges of hardwoods and look for sign. He crossed a trail showing heavy wagon use, about a half-mile north of McCallum Creek. Just east of there a less-used trail pointed north, eventually leading him across a brushy, muddy creek, a half-mile from the hill. Here he stopped to reapply mud. He half expected to find deer sign on the new trail, but it seemed barren. *Strange.* He'd always heard that deer were abundant in this area. *If so, where are they?*

Just before sunset he moved into the hardwoods on the big hill. Mosquitoes and blackflies swarmed until he sat still and stopped perspiring. He made camp and settled in for the night.

• • •

Morning came gradually, as it tended to do in summer. His mud cake had dried and cracked away. He had a can of beans in his ruck, so he made a tiny fire, heated the can, and poured them down his throat once they had cooled. Late morning he found several hunting blinds made of windfalls, and below on the edge of a big field, the remains of an old Indian deer fence—evidence there had been deer here, but neither deer nor Indians were here now. The fence funneled animals through a few narrow openings where hunters would wait to ambush them.

Unlike some rich white men who hunted for sport, Indians hunted only for food, and their ways tended to be practical and lethal. Down by the field he found four deer skulls, old, no flesh on them. This was clearly not a winter yarding area where multiple remains could always be found. The remains here were close together, which told him hunters had been sloppy in their bloodlust, paying no attention to wounded animals.

Bones close to each other. The wolves haven't gotten to these carcasses. Conclusion: No hunting here, just mass killing. No wonder Zakov had been run off. The question was, why so much carnage when deer around here had been so plentiful in the past? *Something feels wrong,* he thought, *something I can't yet name.*

18

Bumbletown Hill

FRIDAY, JUNE 13, 1913

The rat was cat-size, gray, edgy, sizing him up eye to eye. Having lived so long in the boreal forest at the tip of the Keweenaw, Bapcat had become an experienced rat killer, one or two daily, sometimes as many as six. There was a poison he could get from the county health department, which apparently thinned the animals' blood and shut down their organs in twenty-four hours. But other creatures fed on rats, and he feared the poison would work its way from animal to animal; as a consequence, he chose to depend on his seven-foot-long fish spear.

Rats never looked in the direction they would flee. This one glared at him and then to the right, toward a wood pile. Bapcat guessed it would go left.

When it scampered, he skewered it with one thrust of the spear.

"My sweet dear old da, he hated the rats down in the mine," a voice said from the side of the house. "Name's O'Brien, and you, I presume, must be Deputy Bapcat."

O'Brien the circuit court judge; what the hell could he want?

"Aye, I'm Bapcat."

"If ya don't mind me sayin' so, you don't look like a killer," Judge O'Brien said. He had fair hair with a reddish tint, and a fedora tilted rakishly on the top of his head.

"You want to come inside, Your Grace?"

O'Brien laughed enthusiastically. "It's not Your Grace, son. It's Your Honor. I'm not no fookin' Cousin Jack or a bloody Pommy, boyo. Being a lowly Bark, I truly appreciate the invite, I do indeed, but best for the two of us we remain in the shadows whilst I have my say. You mind?"

"No, sir, Your Honor."

"You forty yet, Bapcat?"

"No, sir, thirty-five, thirty-six—I'm not exactly sure."

The judge grunted. “Me da, he died down in the mines, fell in a hole in C and H in 1899. Predictably, me ma got nothing from the bloody buggers. I was studying for the law at the time, come back here in ’01 and started representin’ miner claims in accidents. Didn’t make the local company boys happy, but the people elected me judge last year, so I guess at least they were pleased. Fook the owners and moneymen, I say. You think it’s important to keep people happy in your line of work?”

“What work would that be, Your Honor?”

“Don’t dissemble, Bapcat. Chief Deputy Jones is an old chum. Sent me a letter, said you’d pick the time and place to announce yourself. You’re a game warden, Bapcat. Who will you labor to keep happy?”

“The chief deputy and his boss, justices of the peace. Your Honor, how did you know about this place?”

O’Brien chuckled. “This is the Copper Country, Bapcat. I’m a judge, and people tell me things all the time, hoping to curry favor. Sometimes I hear drivel or things I never want to hear, but I didn’t come here to lament. Listen, Deputy, everybody dies with shit in his britches, no exceptions, even the rich and powerful and famous. As soon as we die, we’re all equal. You hearing rumors of trouble brewing?”

“Some.”

“Mark my words, there’ll be a strike, and she’ll get nasty fast. If the union delivers strike benefits, that should keep it more or less orderly, but if not, those miners and strikers will flood the woods, trying to feed their families. Are you taking in what I’m sayin’, son? In their place you’d do the same thing, and so too would I. My advice: Catch ’em, tongue-lash ’em good, and let ’em go. You do that, and word will get around that the new warden’s a fair man, not one of Cruse’s sycophants—like the last one.”

“But the law—”

“The dear old law’s not an iron bar, Bapcat. She’s flexible, and men on the bench like to interpret statutes, try to use judgment and common sense. I’d advise you to do the same. Fight the big fights, not every fight.”

Bapcat listened.

“You try poisoning your rats?”

“Just the spear.”

“Jones said you once was an undergrounder, a beast of burden like me da.”

"Yessir, three years tramming."

"Rats?"

"Everywhere."

"But you couldn't see them most of the time."

"Right."

"It's the same aboveground, Deputy. There are rats all around us, and I do not refer to the kind you skewer with that fish gigger. Think about what I said, Deputy, and best of luck in your new job. To start, you might want to ghost on down to Bootjack and have a look around. I hear there's a lot of deer down that way."

"Yessir, Bootjack, Your Honor." He didn't tell the judge he'd already been there and that he hadn't found any deer.

"One final little suggestion, if you don't mind: Big Jim MacNaughton runs Calumet and Hecla up here, and all the other mines' managers *and* their owners take their lead and marching orders from him. He was raised here, and he rules with an iron hand. I've known him a long time. Big Jim wants to be liked and admired and feared and respected, but not at the cost of compromise. C and H has only one way of doing things, and that's *his* way. They look benevolent. They're not. If you cross swords with MacNaughton, expect the worst, but expect it to come at you indirectly."

The judge paused before speaking again. "One way or another, C and H touches everything in these parts. It owns everyone, lock, stock, and barrel."

"Not everyone," Bapcat said.

"There's a fine sentiment to embrace, boyo. Be sure to hang on to it. You'll be a bloody legend if you can."

A moment later the judge was gone, leaving Bapcat wondering why he had come so far out of the way to talk in darkness.

19

Bumbletown Hill

FRIDAY, JUNE 13, 1913

The automobile looked like a jury-rigged contraption, its fenders black and muddy, the motor sounding like trapped rats scurrying inside a tin can. Deputy Horri Harju stepped down to the dirt road and surveyed the log building as he stretched and yawned. "You probably should have the owner pay the State for this ramshackle disaster," Harju said, grinning.

When Harju extended his hand, Bapcat drove his fist into the man's chin from below, lifting and dumping the muscled Swede onto the ground, raising a puff of dust and sending two large rats scampering for cover.

The still recuperating Zakov sat watching from a small bench on the front porch. Bapcat had made the bench of birch stumps and a rough-hewn board. "I shall never adjust to American greetings," Zakov announced. "You are all insane, and while our new abode is hardly a manse, it serves," he said, his voice thick with disapproval.

Harju rubbed his chin and let Bapcat help him up. "Never saw it," he admitted. "You got a damn brick in that hand?"

"The automobile overflows with treasure," Zakov announced, using a crutch to stand. "I have great hopes some portion of the contents are edible. My esteemed friend has us living on rabbits and squirrels, and other pedestrian and largely indigestible fare."

"You don't refuse any helpings," Bapcat said.

"A starving man must eat to heal," the Russian replied.

"You're not starving," Bapcat said. Then to Harju, "Meet Zakov."

"His reluctant wife," the Russian said with no hint of a smile.

Harju looked to Bapcat for an explanation. "He's a wolfer driven insane by his poisons," Bapcat offered.

"I use no such things," Zakov said shrilly in his own defense.

"Well, he sure *sounds* wifely," Harju said.

"He does nothing but sit around, grow fat, and complain," Bapcat said.

"My observation stands," Harju said. "Shall we unload?"

When the vehicle was empty Harju said to Bapcat, "She's all yours now."

Bapcat stared at the odd vehicle. He had never ridden in one, much less driven one. He'd never had any interest in owning one, as he preferred walking to riding in any conveyance.

"I thought I was supposed to provide my own transportation."

"Well, I guess your President Roosevelt changed that. Was him arranged this contraption for the department, under the stipulation you be the one to use it." Harju held out his hand and gave a small box to Bapcat. It contained a small bronze badge, a circle wrapped around a small five-point star. "A gift from your colonel," Harju explained.

"Ah, now we shall travel in style," Zakov said.

"Think there's room for a coffin in that thing?" Bapcat asked Harju.

"Sure. Just chop him in half and put one half on top the other," replied the officer.

"You are silly, mindless children unworthy of serious attention," Zakov carped, going into a pout.

"What is this thing?" Bapcat asked his colleague.

"Model T Touring Car chassis. Mr. Ford tried to sell this as a delivery truck last year, but without much success. Now he sells the frame and the buyer arranges to have a top installed. This one is a gift to the department from President Roosevelt. Oates and Jones decided that, given your connection to the president, you should be the one to use it—at least initially. Most roads up here are far better and newer than in almost any other location in the state."

Bapcat struggled with his thoughts and finally admitted, "I don't know how to operate one of these things. Do better in your hands than mine."

Harju laughed. "I'm new to it as well, and if I can drive one, so can you."

"And I shall serve as his mentor," Zakov declared.

The two game wardens ignored him.

Later in the afternoon they loaded Zakov in the rear and drove to a stretch of the Gratiot River, a mile from the hill cabin, and caught enough brook trout for dinner.

Bapcat boiled potatoes over the fire and fried the trout in a new black iron skillet Harju had brought with some other equipment, all from President Roosevelt.

"Judge O'Brien of the circuit court visited me," Bapcat told Harju. "He knew my job and where I live."

"Not from me," Harju said.

"He claims Jones is a chum."

"Take the man at his word, Lute."

"I don't like surprises," Bapcat said.

Harju changed directions. "You've not yet announced yourself and your appointment?"

"The judge knows, Nayback knows, my friend Dominick knows, and I have a feeling so do plenty of others, but for now I don't want to just put it out there for everyone."

"What's to know?" Zakov inquired, and again the two men ignored him.

"Have you patrolled any?" Harju asked.

"Bootjack, mainly," Bapcat said, and he explained what he had seen to the Russian and the other warden, adding that the judge had also suggested he visit the same area. "Not much to see at present."

"Market hunters won't get serious until after Independence Day," Harju said.

Bapcat knew venison tasted best July through September, when the animals' coats gleamed red instead of winter gray.

"You should get to know the railroad people," Harju said, "get a sense of meat and fish shipments in past years, unusual cargo requests, things that are out of the ordinary."

"Suggesting the railroad people are in cahoots with market hunters?"

"No, I'm only suggesting your prospects for information have to be carefully nurtured and developed, and railroads are a good starting place. If your investigations point toward railroad men, so be it. Tell me about Mr. Cornelius Nayback."

"He denies receiving money from Bestemand."

"Evidence contradicts him."

"I'm not so sure," Bapcat said. "The checks were made out to Bestemand, who cashed them. There's nothing to show the money got into Nayback's pockets."

"You believe the man?"

"No, but without some access to Nayback's finances, I don't see a future for this."

"What of our local scouts?"

"I doubt any exist."

"Will you pursue establishing a chapter?"

"Not with a lot of enthusiasm; I've already got enough to deal with."

"And your dear acquaintance, Cap'n Hedyn?"

"I saw Nayback with him at the Cornish wrestling matches."

"That's all?"

"I'm guessing Hedyn's having me watched."

Harju nodded. "What of your newest acquisition?" he asked, with a nod toward the Russian.

"He has skills, and knows the land around here."

"Your call," Harju said. "Jones and Oates have a target on Hedyn's back; any idea why?"

"The department's new. It needs big marks?"

"*Lufda*, you're a sharp one."

"Why? Hedyn's hundreds of miles away from Jones or Oates."

"There are telephones, telegraphs, letters, messengers," Harju said.

"The judge?"

"Somebody far away has no love for Hedyn is all I know," Harju said.

"Are we returning to our Kremlin tonight," Zakov asked, "or do we plan to live rough to provide the carnivorous insects their nourishment? I am an ailing man."

"You sound more like a pain in the extremes," Harju said. "What in dickens is a Kremlin?"

"A fortress."

Harju laughed. "That's a good one." He turned to Bapcat. "Want your first driving lesson?"

"Will there be more than one?"

"Two. You can drive me to Red Jacket tomorrow. That should suffice."

They stood beside the vehicle. "The motor runs on gasoline. There is a transmission, which has two speeds forward, and one in reverse. There are three pedals on the floor. The throttle is this lever here." He pointed at the steering column. "The starter crank is in front. It can break your arm. You turn the crank until you have ignition. The hand lever goes in to release the parking brake and engage the gears. You step on the pedal and use the throttle to move. What could be more simple?"

"Walking," Bapcat said.

"Walking wears out boots. Leave walking to the Indians."

Passing through Allouez, Bapcat was shaky on the gears, making the truck buck, jerk, and convulse, and causing Zakov to cry out in fear as much as pain.

"You could get out and walk," Harju carped at the Russian.

"My leg is broken," Zakov said, glowering.

"Just like a wife," Harju told Bapcat.

20

Laurium

SUNDAY, JUNE 15, 1913

Bapcat's operation of the Model T continued to be so erratic that Harju had decided to remain another day to help Bapcat polish his driving skills. The day before they'd driven up to Eagle River to visit Sheriff John Hepting, who admired the unusual vehicle and proclaimed, "Someday I can see every policeman in America in one of these contraptions." They all laughed at him, but he said, "I'm not joking."

Hepting looked at Bapcat's new badge, smirked, and raised an eyebrow.

"Something amuse you, Sheriff?" Harju asked.

"I'm just thinking that after that weasel Bestemand, there's a large adjustment ahead for Deputy Bapcat. When did this become official?"

"Three weeks ago," Bapcat said. "I took the oath in Marquette."

"Why has it been kept quiet?"

"Biding his time," Harju said. "Eventually, people will know."

Hepting nodded once and asked no further questions.

At noon on Sunday, Harju loaded his bags. Bapcat left Zakov with the rats and drove the other officer south six or so miles down to Laurium, less than a mile from Red Jacket proper. The other deputy obviously wanted to talk.

"Are you certain you want that crazy Russian wolfer with you?"

"He'll be all right," Bapcat said.

"He's no physical help until he heals. You need someone to help you until the Russian's healthy. And it takes two men to operate the Ford."

Bapcat said, "I know." He pulled up to the Red Ball Pool Hall in Laurium, parked, left Harju alone, and went inside. It was dark with a single light suspended over each table. "George Gipp live around here?"

A man with a bushy mustache and a cigar stuck to his lower lip stood with a pool cue in hand. "If he's not here or playing ball, he'll be fast asleep at home. Hecla Street, number 432. Don't rub his old lady the wrong way; her tongue's sharp enough to skin a trout."

Hecla Street was a block south of the business district, and the house at 432 Hecla Street was one and a half stories, with a gabled front, narrow lot, closed-in porch, shingled sides. It was painted, nice, but basically a lowly miner's house given some attention. There was a girl on the front porch, blonde, young, blue-eyed, ten or so. Bapcat was uncomfortable around children.

"George Gipp here?"

"Do I look like a boy?" the girl shot back.

"Does he live here?"

"Who wants to know?"

Bapcat held out his badge and let her look at it. "Is Georgie in trouble?" she asked.

"Should he be?"

"He's sleeping. My brother's always asleep, or he's not here," she added.

"Wake him up."

"He won't like it."

"But I will," he said.

The girl shrugged, slid inside.

Gipp shuffled onto the porch a few minutes later, barefoot and shirtless, suspenders over muscled shoulders, yawning. "Deputy?" he said.

"You find a job yet?"

"Like I said, I'm a ball player."

"A real job."

"Not yet."

"How'd you like to drive for the State, for me?"

Gipp looked at the truck. "You mean that contraption?"

"Yep. You'll have to bunk with us up near Allouez. Your schedule will be erratic."

"Nothing new," Gipp said. "My life's always that way. What's this so-called job pay?"

"Dollar a day, and you can use the Ford to get to your practices and ball games."

Gipp grinned and nodded. "You got yourself a driver, boss."

"Pack a bag for a couple of days," Bapcat told the boy. "You can come back later for more."

Harju showed Gipp how to drive, and the eighteen-year-old took to it immediately, his superior coordination letting him master all the skills effortlessly.

The Marquette deputy warden had some final words for Bapcat. "Squeeze Nayback and stay on that Bootjack business. The judge wouldn't have pointed you in that direction without a reason."

"I'm taking orders from you now?" Bapcat challenged.

"For a few months. Jones says he's too far away, but I can get over here pretty quick. You need anything, wire me. The phones at my end are unreliable—too many ears." The two men shook hands. "The kid there, you think he's up to this?" Harju asked.

Bapcat nodded. "Pretty sure."

"Don't let your wife order him around," Harju said. "And leave the wolfer out of the reports for now."

"Yes, sir." *What reports?*

Bapcat and Harju shook hands and Gipp helped the deputy carry his bags into the station to await a trolley going south.

En route to Bumbletown Hill, Bapcat asked Gipp if he could write.

Gipp smiled. "How much extra does that pay?"

Bapcat liked the boy, sensed toughness mixed with playfulness, a lot of self-confidence. In some ways Bapcat envied the young man who just wanted to be a ball player.

21

Bumbletown Hill

TUESDAY, JUNE 17, 1913

"I am telling you he's out there again," Zakov said, looking down the hill behind the cabin.

"Who is out there?" Bapcat asked.

"A little man, a troll perhaps, or an Arab *djinn*, a real American *manitou*—any of these creatures, all of them. I saw him loitering several times on Sunday."

Bapcat looked down the hill. "It's Nayback," he said. "Why didn't you say something before?"

"Must I report every individual I observe?"

Bapcat picked up his Krag, loaded it, put extra cartridges in his pocket, slung the rifle, and went out the front door. He ducked into the high grasses near the boulder field and worked his way down the hill through cover, to just north of where he had seen Nayback.

He came up behind the man. "Is there a reason you're hiding in our woods?" The rifle was un-slung, but at his side in one hand.

Nayback was startled, jumped, and clutched at his chest. "Where in blazes did *you* come from?"

"From the very place you've been spying on for the past two days."

"I've been waiting to see you," Nayback said.

"We have doors."

"I can't be seen with you, but I need to talk."

"Talk," Bapcat said, wondering what all the mystery was about and guessing Hedyn was somewhere in the mix.

Nayback held out an envelope. "One hundred dollars."

"The hundred Bestemand gave you?"

"Yes," the man said, looking down.

"Your eyes suggest differently. Whose money is this?"

"I just told you."

"No, you haven't. Why did Bestemand give you the money?"

"To establish a local Forest Scouts group."

"Which you failed to do, then lied about."

"He promised to help and then he disappeared. After that, there seemed no point, so I kept the money."

"Which you denied having."

"I know; I'm sorry."

"Do you know what happened to Bestemand?"

"Put his nose where it didn't belong."

"Care to be more specific?"

"Unless you are expressly invited, one must avoid a certain captain's swamp."

Bapcat didn't understand and didn't press. The man was shaking.

"Earlier you told me you never got the money."

Nayback's twitch began to intensify.

"An error in judgment, a lapse I cannot adequately explain. You said the State wants its money back, and now you and the State have it. I'm sorry for what I said about your birth status. I would like to put this thing behind us and get on with educating youngsters."

Bapcat weighed his choices, best as he could figure them. "You can't commit a crime, say I'm sorry, and escape justice. It doesn't work that way."

"Justice . . . *here?*" the man sputtered. "We're all slaves to the barons of copper. I just want done with all this," Nayback insisted, his voice reedy.

"I'll have to talk to my superiors and give you a receipt for the cash."

Nayback's face was flushed, flashing panic. His hands came up and he backpedaled away. "No receipt, no record; I know nothing of that money."

Which suggested to Bapcat the hundred was not the same that had been given to the man by Bestemand. It wasn't hard to figure out where it had come from, or why. *Hedyn wants me to back off Nayback. Why?*

Gipp and Zakov were waiting on the porch. "It was Nayback," Bapcat said. "How well do you know Captain Hedyn?" he asked Gipp.

"Only of him. I guess everybody in Copper Country knows who he is."

"Nayback was with the captain at the wrestling match."

"Hedyn likes to keep track of things . . . personally."

"You ever hear of Hedyn and Bestemand being tight?"

“Everybody said Bestemand was Cruse’s boy, but Hedyn keeps track—and score, I hear.”

“Score?”

“Anybody crosses him gets paid back.”

“A perfectly understandable and advisable trait in a toy czar,” Zakov announced.

22

Upper Black Creek Canyon, Houghton County

WEDNESDAY, JUNE 18, 1913

John Hepting appeared without warning at Bapcat's cabin. "I've got a situation that might interest you," the Keweenaw county sheriff told Bapcat.

Bapcat gathered his equipment and climbed into Hepting's Model A Ford. "Where we going?" He rode with the butt-end of his Krag on the floor between his legs.

"Upper end of Black Creek Canyon, camp of a fella named Enock Hannula. I've got a warrant."

"Stumper Hannula," Bapcat said with a sigh.

"You know him?"

"He used to trap beavers south of Copper Harbor, over in the Breakfast Lake area."

"Used to?"

"I had to teach him about stealing my traps."

"Have a little talk?"

"Not many words, and no conversation, but he got the point. Haven't seen him since."

"I've dealt with him a time or two myself."

"What's the warrant for?"

"Secreting property. Hannula ran up substantial debts, the court convicted him of same, and sentenced him to sell his belongings to settle the debt, but the booger moved all his belongings out of the county."

"Big debts for what?"

"Supplies and so forth—from your own Widow Frei. We arrested him for constructive larceny, and he was released on bail."

Bapcat shrugged. The widow wasn't his.

Hepting said, "The widow waited a year with Hannula promising he'd pay. Finally she swore charges, we made the arrest, and he was found guilty. That's when we learned he'd cleaned out his house at Copper Falls."

"And moved them up the Black River?"

"We don't know exactly where he took them, but his wife sent me a note saying he's got a shack up the canyon, barely into Houghton County."

"His *wife* turned him in?"

"Unhappy wives help us make a lot of cases. Hannula's a Church Finn and partial to the Book."

"Book believer or not, Hannula isn't the kind to come along peacefully," Bapcat offered.

Hepting furrowed his brow. "That's why I asked you along. Think Deputy Valo would be worth anything in a scrap?"

"He's *your* deputy, John."

"Correction: He's my *inherited* deputy. His old man's on the county board. I don't have a single deputy I hired. They're all holdovers, and mostly worthless when the chips are down."

"Get rid of him. Get rid of all of them."

Hepting glanced at him. "You've got a lot to learn, Lute. Politics steers a lot of things. Ain't right, but that's how she is."

"What if Hannula's not there?"

"We'll wait for him. Got something better to do?"

"I might," Bapcat said.

The sheriff laughed.

Bapcat asked, "Is there more to this than you're telling me?"

"In addition to telling us where he might be, his wife mentioned he's getting an early start on venison."

"She say more than that?"

Hepting looked at Bapcat. "Up here somebody telling the sheriff *anything* is by itself a whole lot!"

There was no sign of Hannula at his shack, but there was some evidence he had been around recently: semi-warm coals in the fire pit, a couple of partly burned cigarettes. One window in the shack was curtained over. The sheriff stepped into the woods and found a place to sit and watch, slapping mosquitoes.

Bapcat and Hepting circled the cabin slowly, and within a hundred yards, just beyond a sharp bend in the creek, they discovered a cellar storm door in the side of the hill. Bapcat tugged it open and found six deer on a bed of dry ice. No heads, just bodies, skinned, no hides in sight.

Without the heads, there was no way to judge how long the animals had been dead.

When Hannula showed up he was dragging another deer, freshly killed, his arms and clothing bloody.

Hepting stepped out to the Finn and touched his arm. "You're under arrest, Hannula. The charge is secreting property."

Hannula released the carcass. "What the hell's that mean, Sheriff?"

"Means larceny."

The Finn wiped his hands on his shirt and leered. "This is because that Jezebel keeps a house of ill fame for prostitutes. I want the strumpet arrested on morals charges."

Hepting said, "That business would be between you and your lawyer, Enock, not me. You and me got different business. Are you intending to come along peacefully?"

The man seemed to be weighing his chances with the sheriff when Bapcat stepped out. "What's that damn trapper here for?" Hannula asked, taking a step backwards. "Two against one ain't fair."

"Deputy Bapcat's the game warden now."

"*Him?*"

"That deer's illegal," Bapcat said. "New season's August one to December fifteen."

"A man's gotta eat."

"There's six more on ice down the creek."

"Not mine," Hannula said, with enough conviction that it gave Bapcat pause.

"You knew they were there."

Hannula gave him a cold stare. "Prove it."

"Don't have to. They're on your property. That makes them yours."

"It's not *my* property," the Finn insisted.

"Prove it," Bapcat played back at him.

"My property don't reach down that far."

"That *far?* Meaning, you know where the carcasses are."

"I said they ain't mine is all I said, eh."

"You said your property doesn't stretch that far. I just said there are six more iced down the creek, not where."

Hannula sighed, hunched over, and clenched his fists.

Bapcat knew the man was going to fight and bent his own knees, but Hepting wasn't waiting. The sheriff swept the man's legs from beneath him, smacked him in the head with a sap—a small fold of leather filled with lead—pinned him to the ground with his knee, and handcuffed him.

"The whore," Hannula hissed.

"Which one?" Hepting asked.

"All of them," Hannula shouted, "all of them!"

Bapcat helped the sheriff get the dizzy prisoner to his feet. "You saw he was going to bolt," Hepting said.

"Back, knees, fists."

The sheriff smiled. "You learn fast, Lute. Next time don't give him the chance to act. Strike first and hit hard! What do you want to do about the carcasses?"

"Can we tie them to your Ford?"

The sheriff poked Hannula. "You got rope in your camp?"

"Not for the likes of you," the man shot back.

"Break down the door," Hepting said.

"You can't do that," Hannula protested.

"When did you become a goddamn lawyer? I have a felony arrest warrant for your apprehension. We need to search for stolen goods. You emptied your place in Copper Falls. And you just resisted arrest."

"There ain't nothing in there."

"Open it," Hepting told Bapcat, who kicked near the handle and shattered part of the door inward.

The prisoner was morose, but he was partly right. There were no stolen goods in the shack, but plenty of rope.

• • •

The Eagle River justice of the peace was Hyppio Plew, a small, nervous man with a meticulously groomed beard and a silvery striped vest. He studied the warrant.

"I want bail," Hannula announced.

"And God wants a land free of sinners. Neither of you is getting your way. You want the same lawyer you had last time around, Enock?"

"I guess he didn't do me no good first time, did he?"

"That's your problem, son."

"This ain't no damn death case," Hannula muttered gruffly.

"Ain't nobody said it was, son. But fact is, you're a convicted felon, Hannula, and knowing a little law is like knowing a little medicine—it just makes things worse, so you'd best be still. Sheriff, lock him up until we can perform the examination tomorrow at ten in the morning. Unless, of course, the prisoner waives examination and stipulates to charges."

"What's that mean?" Hannula asked.

"We review the warrant and the arrest and the two officers here tell me what happened and then you tell me your side."

"Will that get me bail?"

"That's not in the cards," Plew said.

"What's the point then?"

"We're a country of laws, son, not a collection of howling damn heathens."

"But I'm going to jail either way?"

"Until the circuit court can schedule a trial for you."

Hannula slumped his shoulders. "Then put me on in. I'm hungry; what's for supper?"

Hepting and Bapcat stifled smiles.

Plew struck his table with a wooden gavel. "Give Mr. Hannula some supper."

The Eagle River jailer's name was Taylor. "Jailer Taylor," Hepting said, handing the prisoner to him, "Mr. Hannula's hungry for his supper."

"We all got crosses to bear," Taylor said.

Bapcat waited until the prisoner was behind bars. "You've got bigger problems than deer," he told the prisoner.

"I got nothing to say to no damn game warden," the Finn grumbled.

Back at Bumbletown Hill Bapcat looked at the sheriff. "What was all that business about Widow Frei and a house of ill fame?"

"You don't know? You're kidding me, right?"

"It's true?" Bapcat responded.

Hepting stammered, "Well, yes and no. She isn't a working girl herself, and she don't directly run no string of whores or nothing like that, but she's built a big business provisioning such places."

"Provisioning?"

Hepting was smiling. "Say your establishment gets raided and the police confiscate all your stuff and close you down, arrest all your girls and such; well, you just get in touch with Jaquelle Frei and she'll outfit your business with furniture, beds, paintings of cavorting naked angels—even arrange new girls if you need them. She's sort of a wholesale outfitter."

"This was Herr Frei's business?"

"Certainly not. Hers alone."

"How'd she end up with Frei?"

"Life's full of imponderables, and the human heart's worst of all. She ain't a working girl, Lute. She's a businesswoman, maybe the greatest in the history of the Copper Country. 'Course, there ain't that many."

This was too much information to process. "Hannula's wife told you about the deer?"

"Claims it's a business he runs."

"Details?"

"You just heard everything I know."

"Be all right if I talk to the wife?"

"Let me run it by her first. She come to me confidentially, and Hannula, Bible thumper or not, ain't the real forgiving sort. His Good Book tells him women are the fountainhead of all earthly evil."

Bapcat got out of the vehicle, slung the Krag over his shoulder, took a deep breath, and went into the house.

23

Bumbletown Hill

WEDNESDAY, JUNE 18, 1913

"About time you decided to return to the hearth," Zakov greeted him. "I'm famished."

"There's plenty of food," Bapcat said.

"I am recuperating and in extreme pain."

"Your tongue seems to be in working order. Where's George?"

"Away, and he didn't say where." Zakov held up a large book bound in yellowish leather. "I find this tome both instructive and fascinating," the Russian said. "Almost one thousand pages in all, yet the stipulations that apply to your responsibilities comprise but a meager four pages under the uninspiring title, 'Game, Protection Of.' "

The book in the Russian's hands was *Tiffany's Criminal Law,* which Harju had given Bapcat, tutoring him through the high spots concerning arrests and warrants. The book was a sort of Bible for justices of the peace, whose jobs required as much understanding of criminal law as circuit court judges. The book covered procedures and defined crimes, and provided reporting and processing forms to be used. Bapcat could read, but had never been overly fond of the practice. "Put it down," he told Zakov.

"In this book resides the greatness of this country," Zakov said, brandishing *Tiffany's*. "There's no equivalent in Russia."

"No?"

"The czar is God on Earth. His minions determine what is legal or not, who lives, who dies. What may be legal today may not be tomorrow. It is capricious at best."

Bapcat wasn't sure what *capricious* meant. "I thought you were hungry?" He unloaded the Krag and set the carbine in a corner.

"*Da*, but I try keeping my mind busy to divert attention from my stomach. This shack has a subterranean cellar."

Bapcat looked at the man. "Vairo said it don't."

"Perhaps the Italian is unaware."

"That seems unlikely."

"Nevertheless. I placed my hat on the floor. Tap near it."

Bapcat did as he was asked and heard the hollow ring. "Not large," he told the Russian.

"As long as the wood isn't rotten, this should not concern us," Zakov said.

"Aren't you curious about what's below?"

"A Russian is immersed from birth in the ambiguous, unexplained, and imponderable. I don't *care* what is down there."

"I'm *not* Russian." Bapcat made a mental note to ask Vairo about the anomaly, and if the former owner's response was inadequate, he would pull up the floor to see for himself.

"In my country, God anoints the czar and he controls everything, even if he is an utter fool, as our dear, dear Nicky surely is. The czar's leadership was entirely absent in the war against the Japanese. I was at Mukden. Tens of thousands of my comrades died. I swear in the name of St. Nicholas the Wonder Worker, everything our dear pathetic Nicky touches becomes disaster. The day he was crowned, horses bolted, and more than a thousand citizens died for no other reason than he wanted a spectacle, a crowd of thousands to see him crowned. *This* is my Russia. And you, my friend, you have *Tiffany's*. In this regard I think you Americans have the better of it."

"Would you rather eat or discuss the state of the world?"

The Russian sulked.

"Peel potatoes," Bapcat ordered.

"I am invalided."

"Peel or starve."

"You have the emotional insensitivity of a czar," the Russian chirped, using a crutch to rise to his feet. "The boy should assist," Zakov said with a nod toward Gipp, who walked in, grinning.

"I don't mind helping," Gipp said.

Bapcat held up a hand. "You're our driver. Zakov can earn his own keep."

The Russian scowled. "At least fetch water to boil," he told the boy, who looked to Bapcat for a nod, which he got.

"Nicholas the First abolished serfdom in 1861, the year your own civil war commenced."

"You're not a serf," Bapcat said.

"Worse," the Russian keened. "I am a wife, the most powerless creature on God's Earth."

"You believe in God?" Gipp asked the Russian as he brought water from the well.

"Only if he believes in me, and so far there is no evidence to support such a conclusion," Zakov said.

24

East of Bootjack

FRIDAY, JUNE 20, 1913

Late Friday morning, Gipp dropped Bapcat along the road that ran south from Lake Linden to White City, a new resort town. "You want, go on down to White City and look around," Bapcat told the boy. "I'll meet you here around dark tomorrow night."

"Yes, boss," Gipp said, "but I've got a ball game in Red Jacket this afternoon."

"Take the truck and I'll see you tomorrow night, George."

Yesterday Bapcat had returned to the Eagle River jail to talk to Enock Hannula, who continued to deny responsibility for any deer other than the one they had caught him carrying. Hepting promised Bapcat he would be in touch if the Finn changed his story, or when the circuit court scheduled the trial.

No meandering this time. Bapcat made his way directly to the hill he'd found on his last visit, and situated himself so he could see the Indian fence below. There would be no fire tonight. He had cold potatoes and biscuits in his pack. He made a quick examination of the area and found no fresh sign other than what seemed to be abundant deer sign not in evidence last time. He made a place for himself at the edge of the woods and sat back.

Two hours after dark-fall he heard what he took for activity in the field, just over a slight rise north of him. *Wheels needing grease?* No voices, no motor, just a low-grade squeal and rock crunching. He was tempted to drift into the field toward the sound, but held tight. Harju had emphasized this: "When you decide to sit on a situation, stay still, and use your eyes and ears, not your legs. You're not going to make arrests until you have evidence. Patience, thought, and careful observation lead to evidence."

"Not even if I see a crime being committed?"

"You have to ask yourself if the violation you see is as important as what led you to be there in the first place. It's like that Jesus thing, you know:

Feed yourself once, or set up something longer-range and farther-reaching, to feed multitudes."

The point had eluded him.

That was training, and now he was on his own. Hearing the sounds, he was at a loss as to what to do, and sighed. He'd been hunting almost all his life and he knew this: It was usually best to let the prey come to you.

Several torches suddenly glowed just over the field crest, but he couldn't make out any more than vague blobs of moving light. There were no shots, no sign of illegal activity, nothing to show for a night of sitting and waiting.

Early Saturday morning he made his way to where he had heard sounds and seen light, and on the other side of the hill found cart prints and boot prints, nothing conclusive. The wheel tracks were indistinct. Had they been draped with cloth to make them quieter? Waste of damn time. He followed the cart track north until it joined a larger wagon trail which led north and westward toward Lake Linden, blended with other ruts and tracks, unfollowable.

George Gipp was waiting for him as arranged that night.

"You look hot," Gipp said as Bapcat slung his gear in the truck.

"Let's stop in Red Jacket," Bapcat said.

"Kind of late."

"Still," Bapcat said.

"Okay, you're the boss."

25

Red Jacket

SATURDAY, JUNE 21, 1913

Dominick Vairo was looking nervously at a corner table in the small tavern, which was half full, when Bapcat came in and stood at the bar and ordered a beer.

"The cabin, Dominick—you said there's no cellar."

"*Si*, got no basement," Vairo said.

"Which mine owned the place before you bought it?"

"Hell's Creek."

"Never heard of it."

"Never got past exploration, yes? They builda cabins, coupla buildings, but not mine, 'cause no good rock."

"Miners' shacks?"

"No, for their *capitanos*. The mines they plan make for short-time bunkinghouses." Vairo glanced at Bapcat and averted his eyes.

What the hell is he so jumpy about? Why does he keep glancing at the corner?

Bapcat knew that captains ran operations for mine superintendents and rated far better houses than the miners they supervised. "So Hell's Creek isn't actually a mine?"

"They dig some holes, but no good, bad assays, no good, shut down before lose too damn much money making dry holes."

"Boston-owned?" Most of the area mines were built on money from East Coast, Boston-based investors.

Vairo shrugged. "I just runna tavern, that's all."

Bapcat grabbed his friend's sleeve and pulled him closer. "Something in the corner bothering you, Dominick?" Vairo turned red.

His friend was still sneaking peeks at that table. Bapcat snuck a surreptitious glance at where his friend was looking and saw a small man with shiny black hair sitting at a table against a wall in the shadows.

"Talk to me, Dominick. I'm your friend. Remember?"

Clearly exasperated and frightened, Vairo whispered, "Bruno Geronissi; he comes around, to sell birds."

"Like ducks?"

"No, little birds—robin, swallow, finch, like that."

"Songbirds?"

"*Si.*"

"For what?"

"For people eat. Back home in Old Country, they like little bird breasts, see?"

"Do you buy his birds, Dominick?"

Vairo seemed to lose his voice and Bapcat leaned closer. "No more, Dominick. You buy no more. Where's Geronissi live?"

"Rose's street, Swedetown."

"Your sister buy from him, too?"

"Everybody, dey buy from Geronissi," the proprietor admitted, recovering his voice.

"He comes around every night?"

"No, he take orders now, come back so many day, like this, like that, *uno, due, capisce?*"

"Next day?"

"Sometimes two day, three. Depends on time of year, what you ask for."

"Are there other suppliers?"

Vairo nodded. "Some. They hate each other."

"How much does he charge?"

"Two bits, one bird."

"All birds same price?"

"No; turkey, partridge, duck, pigeon, goose—they cost more, okay. All singers and woodpeckers, two bits."

"How many do you order?"

"Two dozen, *uno* week. I cook them, serve for shift change when miners come in. I make *polenta uccelli,* very nice, everyone like."

"Polenta?"

"Corn meal, very, very good, *si?*"

"Where's he hunt, this Geronissi?"

"I don't ask, he don't say. You must not tell my name."

"I won't have to if you tell me where he hunts. I'll grab him in the act."

"He go to jail? He got family, nice kids."

"I don't know about jail . . . probably not. The fine is five dollars a bird."

Vairo winced at hearing the amount. "Try out Traprock River where cross Copper-Gay Road. That's a lot of money."

"The State wants lessons taught, Dominick. Money is the best lesson for most people. Who was Hell's Creek's captain?"

"Don't think I ever heard."

"What's Geronissi do for a living?"

"Works the mine."

"Aboveground or below?"

"In the dark. Cornish make the money, Italians, Finns, what call B-O-B, beast of burden, *si?* Trammer-man."

"If you hear the name of the Hell's Creek captain, be sure to let me know, Dominick."

"*Si, si,* you hear about Georgie's balling game yesterday?"

"No."

"He got for his team three house runs."

"Home runs?"

"House, home—they are four baggings. Is confusing, this American game."

Bapcat took note of Gipp's modesty, and left the saloon.

"Vairo says you had three house runs?" Bapcat remarked with a sly grin, when he got into the truck. "You never said anything."

"Some fellas don't take the game to heart too fast. Some learn faster than others. And the pitchers, they weren't much to talk about."

Bapcat guessed that description would fit Geronissi equally well.

"Home?" Gipp asked.

Bapcat motioned forward.

"Will Mr. Zakov be with you for long?"

"I hope not."

"He seems real smart," George Gipp said.

"Books are one thing, life another," Bapcat said. "Remember that, George."

26

Kearsarge, Houghton County

MONDAY, JUNE 23, 1913

The house was built in a copse of paper birch along the course of the sluggish Slaughterhouse Creek, which was choked with tag alder. Clothes were pinned to a line suspended between two trees, women's clothes, no kids, no grown men. A woman alone, Hannula's wife. Hepting, as promised, had gotten in touch with Mayme Hannula, and she had agreed to talk to Bapcat—not at her home, but a nearby location along the creek, a small clearing you had to battle to find through a tangled trail. Bapcat saw no sign of human traffic, but a bear had left a sizable calling card a few days back.

She arrived shortly after he'd gotten into place. She was thin, attired simply in a baggy black dress, barefoot. "Mrs. Hannula?" The woman stared down at her feet and nodded. "I'm Bapcat," he added.

Met with silence. Bapcat said, "John Hepting said you would talk to me."

She looked up with intense, confused eyes, palpable fear. "It's dangerous talking to the likes of you. Ask what you got to ask, and then leave me be."

"You told the sheriff that Enock was getting an early start on venison."

Panic flashed in her eyes. "You din't found none?"

"We found them. What I want to know is, why? He do this every year?"

"First time ever," she said. "He goes by the Good Book, you know, but this is new. You know . . . the strike."

"There is no strike," he told her.

"Will be."

"How does illegally taking deer fit into the strike?"

"People gonna be off work, need to eat, feed their kids."

"He's going to give meat to miners?"

She rolled her eyes. "You a fool? Enock don't give nothing to nobody."

"But he goes by the Good Book."

"Parts he agrees with."

"Does he have more deer elsewhere?"

"Was me, I'd ask Laurium Ice Company."

"Ask?"

"They bring ice to him," she said. "He finds out I talked to you, he'll break every bone in my body. I heard him say plenty times, Good Book don't hold with game wardens. God's job to care for all the creatures he done made. You need to git," she concluded, sliding into the brush.

Two things were clear: She was scared, and there was more talk of a strike, just as Harju and the judge had said.

Laurium Ice Company. *Why didn't I think of that? I saw dry ice! God. Maybe I ain't up to this job.*

Enock Hannula was scared-dog mean. The woman had reason to worry. Might be time to revisit Houghton County sheriff Big Jim Cruse, show him his badge, tell him about the Hannula woman—how she needed looking after, urge protection. This was probably not the sort of splash Harju wanted, but the woman was in danger and deserved help.

Bapcat walked out to the Mohawk Road where Gipp was parked. "You want to drive, boss?" the boy asked.

"That's your job, George."

"I can't do this forever, boss. I think you need some practice."

"I'm sure you're right, George, but not today. Take us to Laurium."

"Where?"

"Laurium Ice Company."

Gipp grinned. "Sorry, boss, that's in Centennial, near the dam. They cut ice from Calumet Lake in winter."

"Laurium Ice Company is in Centennial?"

"Yeah, my Uncle Herman works there."

"Herman got an opinion on game wardens?"

"Don't everybody?" the boy said, deadpan.

27

Centennial, Houghton County

MONDAY, JUNE 23, 1913

They turned off the Mohawk Road past the looming Centennial Number 6 Rockhouse. "If you got to work underground, Centennial Number 6 is okay," Gipp said. "Good captains. People say they don't see Wop, Finn, or Mick, just how a man works."

"*People* say?"

"You play ball with fellas from all over, you can learn a lot."

"You hearing strike talk?"

Gipp grimaced. "The local boys are gonna demand a meeting with the companies and present what they call their demands. No meet, they'll strike, and the Colorado big shots won't have no choice but to pitch in."

Gipp acted like he cared only about playing ball, but he had a good mind and was a lot deeper than most people might suspect. "Tell me about your uncle Herman."

"Quiet little fella, works hard, got a big family—spends a lot of time out in the woods."

"Maybe I should talk to him alone. No sense linking you to the game warden."

Gipp laughed. "Boss, I been driving you all over. People already know. I'll go with you. Herman trusts me."

Smart and mentally tough. Good kid, but does he trust Herman? Not the time to ask.

Uncle Herman was a bocci ball with legs and sported a white walrus mustache. Most of his hair was reduced to diaphanous strands that moved when he moved, like ghostly little worms vying to cover his ears.

"Georgie boy," Herman warmly greeted his nephew.

"Unc, this is Deputy Bapcat, the game warden."

Herman looked at Bapcat and winked. "I told him: Georgie, no deer for another month."

Uncle Herman liked the role of joker, one Bapcat didn't care for. "This isn't about George," Bapcat said. "I need help from you."

"Like what?" *Still smiling, the grin losing some traction.*

"Ice deliveries."

"Georgie not pay his bill? Shouldn't the sheriff be here?"

"It's not about a bill," Bapcat said.

"C'mon, Unc," Gipp said. "He's okay."

"Customers ain't my job," the older Gipp said. "You need ta talk ta Ogden, da sales manager."

"Is he in?"

"Guys who wear ties don't talk ta guys who don't wear ties."

Celt Ogden wore a shiny grayish suit, had thinning pink hair, and what Bapcat assumed to be a perpetual smile.

Bapcat showed his badge.

"Have we met?" Ogden asked.

"I doubt it. We're trying to determine if ice deliveries have been made by your company to a certain individual," Bapcat explained, but not amplifying the *we.*

"Who?" the sales manager asked.

"Enock Hannula."

"No," Ogden said.

"You don't have to look at your records?"

Ogden tapped his forehead. "Records are all up here. I know every customer the company has ever had."

Thinking quickly, Bapcat asked, "How about deliveries to the upper Black Creek area?"

Ogden crossed his arms. "Where exactly is *that?*"

"I think you know." Bapcat pointed at his own head. "Up there."

"We have customers everywhere up here. You'll have to be more specific."

Stonewall. "Thanks for your time."

"Don't mention it," the man said.

Uncle Herman met them at the truck. "You get what you needed?"

"No," Bapcat said.

"Ogden's *asino buco,*" Herman said. "What you need?"

"Deliveries to Enock Hannula, or to the upper Black Creek area."

"Hannula, da one people call Stumper?"

"That's him."

"Everybody knows Stumper. Man's crazy. When you need ta know?"

"Anytime soon; a few days?"

"Okay, anyt'ing for my favorite nephew Georgie."

Bapcat and George Gipp drove away and Gipp said, "I know Unc can be a little strange with all the jokes and stuff, but you can always count on him. Is this important?"

"I honestly don't know," Bapcat admitted.

28

Bumbletown Hill

TUESDAY, JUNE 24, 1913

Gipp was gone, had taken the truck to a game for the afternoon. Bapcat tore at the wood floor, finally revealing a hole with a narrow ladder. Zakov puffed up with pride. "You see, it is just as I said."

Bapcat went outside, fetched a large bucket of birch bark into the house, and started wrapping the bark around sticks to make torches. Birch ignited gracefully and noiselessly, even in the rain.

Zakov asked the deputy as he looked into the hole, "What do you expect to find?"

"Chinamen."

Zakov snorted. "An Occidental myth of ignorance."

The hole under the floor had been hacked through solid rock and seemed stable, but within minutes Bapcat found his heart racing. He was having trouble catching his breath. He knew the cause and tried to fight it, but surrendered within minutes because of the terror growing inside him.

"Looks like you encountered Mongoloid ghosts instead of Chinamen," Zakov quipped when the deputy climbed out and sat with his unsteady legs dangling in the opening.

Suddenly, a woman's voice said, "You seem to have taken complete leave of your senses, Mr. Bapcat. I do swear." Jaquelle Frei stood at the front door, arms crossed. She was dressed in a nondescript frock and riding boots. "I'm speaking to you, Trapper; cat got your tongue?"

"Why're you here, Jaquelle?" Bapcat managed to say.

"Don't you dare use my given name in public, Mr. Bapcat. We are not familiars, you and I. Let us not misconstrue our relationship with loose etiquette."

"Sorry, Mrs. Frei. Yes, ma'am."

Frei smiled. "See how easy it is to keep things on the high road, which makes me wonder why on earth you are up here in a hovel on a baby hill, living with the pitiful Borzoi. I must say, I am deeply conflicted by what I see, sir. Much confounded and greatly disappointed."

"It's not a hovel," he said.

"There is a gaping *hole* in your floor, sir."

Zakov stared at the front door screen and announced, "The screen is turning red."

"The process is called oxidation," Frei said, "you Russian baboon."

"How do you know that?" Bapcat asked her.

"I am an educated woman, sir. I read, I think; I control my own destiny."

"But why are you here?"

Frei glanced at the Russian. "It's in the way of a . . . private matter."

"About?"

"A certain account in arrears."

"Or what, you'll make an accusation as you did against Enock Hannula?"

The woman's eyes narrowed. "What do *you* know about Hannula?"

"I helped John Hepting arrest him."

She clapped her hands together. "Finally there will be justice." Her face hardened as quickly as it had lit up. "Hepting and you; are you his deputy, sir?"

"No, I'm a deputy state Game, Fish, and Foresty warden for Keweenaw and Houghton counties."

"Since *when?*"

"Marquette."

"But you went for the former president's trial."

"That's what I thought, too, but I had no role in the trial."

"When word came that he won, I assumed it was you who had helped him, but I never saw your name on witness lists or in newspaper accounts."

"The summons had nothing to do with the trial."

"It was about this so-called game warden position, and I suppose this was offered by the State on the strength of the former president's say-so?"

"It was. The colonel gave me the rifle I used in Cuba."

"The one you used to dispatch Spaniards?"

When he remained silent, she pressed on. "Wouldn't suit a state deputy to be known as a deadbeat." He thought he saw the hint of a smirk.

"So which part of your business am I indebted to—the wilderness outfitter, or the supplier who brings sporting houses back to life?"

"I *beg* your pardon, *sir*," she said sharply, clearly surprised by his question.

"The thing about law enforcement, Mrs. Frei—it's a kind of brotherhood. We talk to each other, share information."

"I have no idea what you are referring to, and I find your insinuation patently offensive."

"I'm saying face-to-face only what others say behind your back, Mrs. Frei."

"You will surely hear from me again," the widow said. She gathered up her skirt and petticoats and flounced to the front door, where she stopped. "Debts left unpaid too long can become malignant."

"Malignant?" Bapcat asked when she was gone.

"Cancer," Zakov said. "She acted like I'm not even alive."

"I think she pretty much decides who lives in her world, and who don't."

"Like a czarina. Women do nothing but complicate men's lives."

Young Gipp returned just as the widow drove away.

"Who was that? She looked real mad."

"Mad, happy—it's impossible to sort out such emotional attributes among females," Zakov said.

29

Traprock River, Houghton County

THURSDAY, JUNE 26, 1913

George Gipp's next contest was not scheduled until Saturday, and Bapcat had him along, not certain why. The boy was his driver, not a fellow warden.

They stashed the Ford a half-mile east of the river and walked back through the woods. Gipp was quiet and appeared uneasy.

"I may need your help, George."

"You need another lawman? What can I do?"

"You're calm, you listen, and you pay attention. You've got courage."

"Courage in games. This doesn't feel like a game."

"Sometimes it feels like a game to me," Bapcat said. "But I'm still new." *This will change*, he told himself. "Don't worry."

"I'm not worried. I'm scared, boss."

"Of what? You don't even know where we're going or what we're up to."

"I gamble, boss; I know when stuff starts to turn sour."

"You know a Bruno Geronissi?"

"Sure. Everybody calls him Birdman. He comes into Vairo's saloon."

"Just Vairo's?"

"Other joints, too, I guess, but I don't know for sure. Why?"

"You know what he sells?"

Gipp shrugged. "Birds."

"You think that's okay?"

"I like partridge and goose."

"What about Keweenaw canaries?"

"Too small to eat."

"Then why does Geronissi kill them?"

"People are different. They do stuff in countries where they're born, and then they try to do the same things here. You can't blame them."

"Even if it's illegal?"

"How they gonna know the law, boss?"

"That's a good question," Bapcat said.

The Traprock River was heavily wooded along the banks, and there were a few mallard ducks around, but no songbirds. Bapcat and Gipp sat on a boulder under a tree and did not speak or move. After a while, Bapcat asked, "What's wrong here, George?"

"All I hear are bugs and the river," Gipp said. "No birds."

"I've seen a few over the trees," Bapcat said.

"Not close, though," the boy said.

"When we go into the woods, we push a sort of wave of sound and scent," Bapcat explained. "And wildlife can see us, feel our footfalls, sense our presence. But when we sit quietly like we've been doing, the wave settles, and animal life should return to normal."

"Not today," Gipp said.

"Right. They seem so leery the alarm doesn't wear off. Why do you suppose that is?"

"What's that tell you?" Gipp asked.

"I don't know, but let's go have us a look."

A mile north Gipp was walking five yards to the left of Bapcat when he cursed quietly. "Damn!"

"What?"

"Not sure."

"Stay put—don't move."

Bapcat found the boy with a yard-long shaved stick clinging to his shirt. "I'll have to rip my shirt to get this off. What is it?"

"I don't know. Relax and stay here. I'm going to look around."

Gipp stuck his finger on the stick. "This thing is real sticky."

Bapcat sniffed it. "Plums?"

"Got me," Gipp said.

"I won't be gone long."

Bapcat wove his way through the trees and found a half-dozen more of the strange sticks, most of them with feathers on them. He managed to get one down from where it had been set as a perch between branches, wrapped it in young ferns, and checked around the ground. There were boot prints where he found the feathers. *Fresh. This morning's tracks.*

Gipp tore his shirt getting loose. They took both sticks with them back to the Ford. "Do you know what's going on now?" Gipp asked.

"I'm not certain. Let's head for Vairo's."

Dominick was in his apartment behind the saloon. Bapcat knocked on the door and asked his friend to walk out to the Ford, where he showed him the two sticks. "You know what these are?"

"Back in the Old Country, you buy them everywhere cheap."

"For what?"

"See feathers? Bird thinks is safe place to land, but is glue. Can't get loose, and when bird fights, he hang himself upside down. Some choke, others wait till somebody come breaka their neck."

"Glue from what?"

"Kind of a plum."

"We found these along the Traprock. Lots more there. Geronissi's work?"

Dominick whispered, "I pay the man. I don't watch him work. His birds never got no shot in them, *capisce?*"

"You're sweating," Bapcat said.

"You no *capisce* what you got here, Lute. You like that damn bull in Chinese shop."

"China shop."

"You got piece of paper?"

Bapcat produced a pencil and a fold of thin paper and Dominick wrote *Mano Nera*. He added quietly, "You gotta swear I never said them words out loud."

"You didn't."

"Swear!"

"I swear."

"On your mother's life."

"Absolutely. What's it mean?"

"Ask Sheriff John. I gotta work."

"Dominick."

"I don't want to be seen with you, Lute. Not good for me, for you, for nobody." Vairo took a step but turned back. "You be damn careful, watch the *Lupara*, okay?"

Bapcat looked at Gipp. "What do you think?"

"Only that he scared me."

Bapcat showed Gipp the paper and the words, *Mano Nera*. "Mean anything to you?"

Gipp shook his head. "The Italians, they got their own ways, and they know how to keep secrets."

30

Eagle River

FRIDAY, JUNE 27, 1913

Gipp and Bapcat drove to John Hepting's house, which was across the road from the county courthouse and its one-cell jail. It was midmorning; it had rained all night, and the roads were all rough and pitted and slippery. But it had been dry in the traprock River country.

"Lute," the sheriff said, opening the door.

Bapcat handed him the paper Vairo had written on. "Know what this means, John?"

"Where'd you get this?"

"That's not important."

"Like hell it ain't. Any Italian says them words out loud pretty much signs his own death warrant."

"Nobody said nothing. I found it."

"I doubt that. It says 'Black Hand.' "

"What's it mean?"

"We ain't Italian, so we have to guess, but it seems to refer to an Italian organization that sort of keeps watch on other Italians."

"Like police?"

"Not quite. They force every Italian to belong. You object, you get hurt or dead. Once you belong, the groups needs something, you fork it over and keep your mouth shut. If you need something, these people, they get it for you. It's like a series of continuous favors and obligations."

"Sounds complicated."

"Byzantine, secret, complex, and deadly. No Italian dares talk about it."

"The word *Lupara*—you heard that one?"

"Something to do with wolves, and how guinea wolfers used to refer to the sawed-off shotguns they use to kill wolves in traps. What's going on, Lute?"

Bapcat explained it all: bird sales, the glue sticks. He left Vairo out of the telling.

"You think Geronissi has himself a little business?"

"It feels like something more."

"Couple of sticks and two words on paper aren't what a judge would call evidence, Lute."

"I know. Has Widow Frei been here?"

"Was she supposed to?"

"Heard she might, is all."

"Haven't seen her. You want to know if she does?"

"No, just curious."

"Your mind sometimes wanders," Hepting said.

"I know," Bapcat said, wishing it didn't.

"You talk to Mayme Hannula?" the sheriff asked.

"She said Enock's getting ready for the strike, and that I should talk to the Laurium Ice Company."

Hepting grunted. "Who?"

"Fella named Ogden. He wasn't real helpful."

"A worm, that one," Hepting said.

"Is the strike thing real?" Bapcat asked.

"All rumors say so."

"You'd think the mine owners would want to stop it."

"Yes, if they thought short-term profits were more important than crushing a union."

"You mean they *want* a strike?"

"More like both sides want it."

"Sounds like trouble."

Hepting said, "Sounds more like war, and that's exactly what it could turn into. These miners are tough customers, but so are the operators, and they have resources . . . *deep* resources."

"You ready for a strike?" Bapcat asked.

"Hell no, not even close. Most of my deputies aren't suited to breaking up dogfights, much less normal police work, never mind a strike that could blow up into a civil war."

"What about Cruse?"

"Fat Jim's less competent than his men, but he's in the owners' pockets. Whatever they want, he makes sure they get, but he won't take any personal risks. You can bet on that."

"Aren't we lawmen not supposed to take sides?" Bapcat asked.

"In theory. The practice is different," Hepting said.

"Is that a joke, John?"

"Attempted. If your man Geronissi's in Cruse's county, you'll get no help from Cruse with whatever you plan. You're on your own."

"Aren't we all?"

"Some more than others," Hepting said, "Especially you game wardens. When you make your move there's likely to be nasty backlash. Change ain't welcome here unless the powers that be sanction it."

"Meaning I should back away?"

"Didn't say that. Just know there's a lot goes on around here that's not strictly by Hoyle. Most of your laws have never been enforced around here. It will be a rough adjustment for a lot of people who don't like change they don't pick."

"But I can count on you?"

"Me, certainly. My men, not a chance. You want some lunch?"

"Thanks. I sort of lost my appetite."

31

Traprock River

SUNDAY, JUNE 29, 1913

Horri Harju had a hard-to-decipher look, and deputy warden Aldrick Tassone looked half asleep as they dragged into the cabin on Bumbletown Hill. Bapcat suspected trouble from the illegal birders, and had telegraphed Harju for advice. Instead of advice, Harju and Tassone had shown up yesterday.

The three game wardens left Gipp at the cabin with Zakov, and headed southeast long before sunrise.

Bapcat picked a new location to hide the Ford and the three walked briskly cross-country to the river through black spruce swamp and hardwood forests, staying way clear of the road bridge over the river. Tassone had explained the night before how he had engaged songbird hunters in the Ishpeming area, but that time the hunters had carried shotguns and made drives through heavy bird areas to flush the quarry to shooters on stands. Glue sticks were new to Tassone, who admitted he had been hired in part because he spoke Italian and could deal with the large Italian population in Marquette County. "Some of the Wops, I heard them talk about lime sticks, but I never knew what they meant," he said. "Maybe these?"

Tassone had been a deputy warden for three years and seemed pleased to come along with Harju to help.

At the river, which angled northeast, Bapcat left Harju and Tassone on the east bank, made his way down the rocky wall to the river bottom, and crossed the river to find the area he and George had seen Thursday. It didn't take long to locate the spot and get back to the others, who were waiting on the riverbank. Last night Bapcat had visited Vairo, who told him reluctantly that Geronissi had been in again. Geronissi had suggested the saloon owner place another order before the birds dispersed more than they already had, forcing the hunter and his people to the mode they called *caccia vagrante*, which Vairo translated as wandering the woods with a shotgun.

"Geronissi says I get the birds fresh Sunday afternoon," Vairo explained. "They always work mornings, first light."

"You placed the order?"

"Would look bad, I didn't. *Capisce?*"

The first thing the wardens noticed were birds skittering nervously through the trees. Only a few, but clearly spooked. Very quickly they heard some sort of tinny pounding, and hundreds upon hundreds of birds swarmed through the trees and shrubs, endlessly fleeing the noise. Bapcat could hear the birds' wings hitting leaves as they fled, and when they got tired and landed on lime sticks he could hear them begin the frantic sounds of entrapment as they struggled without hope to free themselves from the glue.

Over the next thirty minutes they heard human voices and saw men in the wake of the fleeing birds. They watched as they picked frantic birds off the glue sticks, squeezed their heads with a crisp snapping sound, and dropped them into cloth bags they carried.

Harju touched Bapcat's arm and nodded. "Follow them?"

Bapcat nudged Tassone. "There's a clear area south of us. Stay on this bank, and work your way south. If you see them gathering, cross the river; if they don't gather, keep going until you hit the road and the bridge. We'll follow and flank them on the other side."

Tassone nodded once and slid away. Bapcat and Harju crossed the gravelly river and angled into the brush. Harju kept on the man they had watched. Bapcat angled west before turning south, and soon saw men ahead of him passing a wine skin back and forth. All of them carried shotguns slung across their backs. Three of them stopped to strip birds off capture sticks and drop them in burlap sacks, all the time talking softly and animatedly, laughing, nudging each other.

As the terrain began to open up Bapcat saw more men, as many as twenty.

Harju looked over at him and Bapcat hand-signaled that they should sit down. *Three against twenty, all of them armed, most of them drinking—not the best situation.* Bapcat assumed Geronissi was somewhere in the group, and though all the men were involved in the hunt, he had in mind that Geronissi was the boss and organizer, the man in charge.

Bapcat tried to think. They were at least six miles from Allouez, eleven or twelve from Swedetown where Geronissi lived. It would be safer to confront the leader when he was alone, but the truck was at least a mile away, and it was a two-man job to start the damn thing. *Bad planning*, he chastised himself. An option was to intercept Geronissi at Vairo's saloon, but that might implicate his friend and reduce the number of birds he could charge Geronissi with. *Better confront them here with the full take in their possession*. Harju and Tassone were here and ready. The course was clear: It was time to act.

Bapcat waved Harju left to the river and signaled he would move right to the edge of the river plain and keep moving south. He assumed Tassone had seen the hunters congregate and had crossed to this side of the river.

The group eventually emerged into a clearing. They showed no anxiety, seemed quite relaxed—like getting birds was as easy as collecting eggs from a chicken coop.

Bapcat saw a line of tag alders that reached close to the gathering and slid his way through as quickly and quietly as he could manage, now and then pausing to see what was happening in the clearing, where more men continued to filter in and gather. They were piling their cloth bags on the ground. Standing next to the pile was Bruno Geronissi, gesturing animatedly with a black cheroot in hand, a prince holding court.

Reaching the end of his cover, Bapcat unslung his rifle, quietly slid a round into the chamber, and walked quickly to Geronissi before anyone could react. As he moved, he saw Harju and Tassone converging from the south side.

"Bruno Geronissi, you're under arrest for illegally killing songbirds." Bapcat firmly grasped the man's arm to signify arrest. Geronissi leered at him.

"Who are *you?*" the man asked.

"Deputy State Game, Fish and Forestry Warden."

"I don't hear no fucking nothing about birds in them words."

"Trust me, Bruno. It's there."

Harju moved close to the main gathering and Tassone hung back. "I want every shotgun on the ground right here!" Harju ordered, pointing. "Do it slowly, one at a time. When your weapon is on the ground, step back and put your hands on your head. Now!"

The men all looked at Geronissi, who nodded when Bapcat nudged the leader's chest with his Krag to start the process. Geronissi complied meekly and the others followed suit.

"This here's okay, boys," Geronissi said theatrically, putting his hands on his head. "Just a little misunderstanding. There no need you game wardens do this thing. All legal, by the book, you Americans say, *si?*"

"Legal?" Bapcat said.

"Law, she don't apply to guys collect birds for *prelievo*, take for science, *si?*"

"*Si, si, raccogliendo raccoglundo campioni scientifici,*" someone shouted.

Geronissi said confidently, "What we do here perfect legal, *Quello che stiamo facendo qui, so perfettamente legale.*"

A man growled, "*Non potete arrestore perquesto!*"

Bapcat said, "Tell your people to shut up!"

All talk stopped.

"We're confiscating the birds and taking you up to the JP in Copper City."

"You waste your time," Geronissi said. "How much your damn fine? *Quanto e al tuo bene maledetto?*"

"Five dollars a bird," Bapcat said. The forest became still and silent, the words met with a collective gulp.

"*Malle detto qioco operai!*" one of them shouted angrily.

Another man asked, "*A vete sentito della Mano Nera?*"

Mano Nera. Bapcat knew these words, which were never to be spoken aloud, but they *had* been spoken and everyone had heard them and stiffened like statues.

Deputy Tassone said, "These fellas aren't so pleased with us."

"So I gather," Bapcat said.

"*Questa dovrebbe essere una terr ade leggi, noni vero?* This is supposed to be country of laws, no?" Geronissi said, quickly piling English onto Italian.

"It is, and it's against the law to kill these birds."

"For science," Geronissi said, nearly hissing the words. "Is okay for science."

"Tell it to the justice of the peace," Bapcat said.

"*Ella, dichiara di puttane,*" the man closest to Geronissi said through clenched teeth. "*Figlio de una cagna!*"

Tassone laughed. "He says we're state whores and you are a son of a bitch."

"The second part would be accurate if he called me a bastard," Bapcat said.

Tassone translated, and all the men, including Geronissi, laughed.

"*Senzai fucili il sino fighe,*" Geronissi said.

Tassone put his shotgun on the ground and used his hands to invite Geronissi forward. "He says without guns, we are cunts."

Bapcat held up his hands. "Back off."

"I must protest," an exasperated Geronissi said.

"Your choice, your right—but first you are going to carry all the birds out to the road."

"Too many," the leader protested.

"Jesus bore his cross; consider the birds yours. Make as many trips as you have to. Deputy Tassone will accompany you."

"I am scientist," Geronissi, said, "*il dottore!*"

Tassone growled, "We don't care if you're da Vinci or the last Doge of Venice. Tell your men to sit on the ground and keep their damn hands on their heads. *Subito!*"

Geronissi mumbled some words and his men sat. When Geronissi had finished moving the birds, they made him carry all the shotguns. Harju picked up cartridges and put them in his kit bag.

"We'll count the birds out on the road," Bapcat said.

When the count was complete they had 224 birds, more than a thousand dollars in fines. Bapcat hoped the JP would levy all of it and not turn soft.

Bapcat stayed with the main group of prisoners, and Harju and Tassone went to fetch the Ford. When they got back, they loaded the guns and birds and lined up the prisoners in front of the vehicle. Bapcat said to Geronissi, "*Harch, il dottore!*"

Bapcat noticed several men smiling at this.

He made them march to Copper City a couple of miles from the arrest site, and by the time they reached town they had collected a large group of onlookers who yelled all sorts of insults at the Italians, who yelled back vociferously at their tormentors. Was this a large enough splash to announce his job? Word of mouth would carry the news all over the Copper Country, and beyond.

Justice of the Peace Alley Pahl came out of his office to look at the prisoners. "Bail 'em?" he asked Bapcat.

"Two hundred and twenty-four birds at five dollars each. That pushes it to felony level."

"Okay, then, I set bail for the leader, release the rest on their promise to show in court; that okay with you, Deputy?"

"Nossir. None of them will confess to any birds, and the main man here claims they're collecting them for science. I want them all on bail. That only seems fair."

"You're a hard case, eh, son?" the JP said. "It's Sunday, and I got no time for these piles of Wop-crap. Bail for the lead man, and the rest can go." Pahl barked at the Italians: "Listen up. Arraignment at ten tomorrow morning in Ahmeek. You all better be there, Johnny on the spot, or we get warrants for all of you. *Capisce?*"

"You got their names and addresses?" Pahl asked Bapcat. Tassone held up the list he had made and translated the JP's words. The men nodded and dispersed.

"I am *dottore*," Geronissi tried on the JP.

"You can tell me all about it tomorrow, *Dottore;* now step inside and let's see what kind of bail you can come up with. Some folks go to church on Sundays, not out killing pretty little singing birds and drinking wine."

Bapcat smiled inwardly, looked at Harju. "This the sort of public splash you had in mind?"

32

Bumbletown Hill

SUNDAY, JUNE 29, 1913

Harju and Tassone were asleep on the floor. George Gipp stared down into the hole. "Why do you keep going down there?"

"I need to know where it leads."

"I could do it for you. Dark doesn't bother me."

"You could, and thanks, but no thanks."

"You are both unbalanced in complementing ways," Zakov said.

"Did you notice the front porch?" Gipp asked Bapcat.

"Same as always," yelled back.

"Not really. Somebody left a message."

"Bring it inside," Zakov said.

"It's not that kind of message," Gipp said. "You have to look."

Bapcat came out of the hole and they all went outside and saw black handprints on both sides of the door and one on the porch floor.

"You know what this means, George?" Bapcat asked.

"Not what it says, but who sent it."

"*Mano Nera*," Bapcat said.

"There is no such creature as Black Hand," Zakov said. "This is a chimerical myth created by Italians to frighten their enemies."

"Maybe so," Gipp said, "but all the Italians I know think it's real, not a fairy tale."

"My boy, you must learn to demand evidence," Zakov said.

"Evidence?" Gipp countered. "How about the building called the Società Italiana di Mutua Benificenza? It means—"

"I *know* what it means. Make your point, boy," Zakov said.

"The Italians never say the words you said. They call it *the group*, or *the society*. You say the actual words out loud, things go bad for you."

"Myth," Zakov said dismissively.

Bapcat knew that the building Gipp was referring to was the same building in which Dominick Vairo had his saloon. The so-called Italian Hall was upstairs. Bapcat had never ventured up there. Vairo told him it had meeting rooms, an auditorium with a stage; it was used mostly for parties.

"Società Italiana is the same as *Mano Nera?*" Bapcat asked Gipp.

"That's been my impression according to what gets said and not said around town."

"*Mano Nera* owns the building?"

"Not by that name. Officially there's a society with members, and they meet at the hall, but I heard my old man say that nobody knows for sure who actually and legally owns the place."

"What do townspeople say about black handprints put on somebody's house?" Bapcat wanted to know.

"Some kind of message," Gipp said. "Not good."

Bapcat understood who it was aimed at, and why. He got more torch materials and headed back down the ladder.

"Why do you persist in that nonsense below?" Zakov challenged.

Bapcat pointed at his belly. "A feeling in here."

"A result of less-than-gourmet fare," the Russian grumbled.

"Okay if I tag along?" Gipp asked. "He's kind of cranky today," he added, with a nod toward Zakov.

"Get torch makings," Bapcat said. Gipp's help was welcome, though he didn't care to admit it. "Lots of them."

"If my injuries were healed, I would no doubt volunteer to lead this underground expedition," Zakov declared.

"You aren't healed, and no, you wouldn't," Bapcat said as he disappeared down the ladder.

One hour later the two men had moved a large rock aside and had seen a hint of light. Gipp started to excavate loose dirt, but Bapcat grabbed his arm. "Let it be for now."

"Why's this tunnel down here?" the boy asked.

"Storage, escape; no way to know. What's important is that we know it's here."

"It's not a mine."

"No, but I saw some copper seams when we were pushing back this way. I guess you can find copper just about anywhere in the Keweenaw."

"Do we tell the Russian?"

"No," Bapcat said. "Thanks, George. The dark unhinges me. I couldn't have done this without you here to steady my nerves."

"I didn't do nothing, and we've all got things we're afraid of," the boy said.

Bapcat wondered what sort of demons haunted young George Gipp.

33
Ahmeek

MONDAY, JUNE 30, 1913

Justice of the Peace Alley Pahl was at his table just before 10 a.m. as the tiny room filled with people. Bapcat saw sheriffs John Hepting and Cruse along one wall. Geronissi had hired a lawyer named Bally. Bapcat wasn't sure what a lawyer's role would be at an arraignment. At ten sharp, Justice Pahl read the indictment for illegal bird killing and threatening a peace officer.

Bapcat looked at his colleagues. None of them had asked for the second charge. *Why is it there?*

"Bruno Geronissi, how do you plead—guilty, or not guilty?"

"My client pleads not guilty by reason of misidentification," Attorney Bally said.

"Put that in plain English," Justice Pahl said tersely.

"Mr. Geronissi was collecting scientific specimens, not hunting. The statute clearly and specifically exempts scientific collectors."

The JP squinted at Bapcat. "How many birds these boys take?"

"Two hundred and twenty-four, sir."

"Thank you, Deputy. Counselor, I know fimble-famble when I hear it, but if your client, the *alleged* scientist, can give me the Latin names of any five species of those birds he and his chums slaughtered and had in their possession, I'll declare him a scientist, dismiss all charges, and release him, free as a bird—excuse the poor pun."

Bally whispered to his client, Geronissi, whose face flushed.

"Your Honor," the lawyer said, "my client wishes to change his plea to guilty on the bird charges, stipulating that he was unaware of any statutes governing songbird protection, but he pleads not guilty to the assault charge."

"You don't say," Pahl said. "He was unaware of statutes but knew there was an exception for scientific collectors? Best you keep your mouth shut, Bally. Okay, the assault charge is dropped, which is by far the most serious, and your client pleads guilty to all the bird charges and will pay the fines.

All the others here, charges and fines are dropped, but maybe they can help share *Signore* Geronissi's financial burden. Questions?"

"No sir, none," the attorney said.

"Let me say welcome to Sheriff Cruse, who met with me in private chambers and tried to convince me that this arrest was made in his county, and because Mr. Geronissi has been of great assistance in the past to him and his deputies, that I be lenient in this case. Now, *Signore* Geronissi, I surely commend you for you civic-mindedness. Maybe you and your chums threatened the game wardens, maybe not, but we'll overlook that based on your history of civic-mindedness, and you can thank Sheriff Cruse for stepping up on your behalf. Your past good behavior notwithstanding, you owe the county two hundred and twenty-four times five dollars, payable in full today. If you can't pay today, you will be incarcerated until such time that you can."

Geronissi's only response was a nod, and he and his lawyer left to arrange for the fine payment.

"Deputy Bapcat, come with me," the JP said, and took him into a cluttered office.

"You think I let them off light?"

"Mr. Geronissi sells songbirds in local establishments."

Justice Pahl coughed. "Hell, he sells to upstanding citizens too, some of them in high places. You know about *Mano Nera?*"

"I'm learning."

"Add this to your education: Bruno is one of the top dogs in the society, and his little bird-hunting sideline is one of the few the society doesn't have its hands into. It's all his, and he's likely to defend it to the death. You leave here, go to Kallio's Funeral Parlor, and tell Dutu Kallio that I sent you over."

"Dutu Kallio, yessir."

"You made one hell of a fine first case here, Bapcat, and all your game warden pals will be proud. Other badges will be jealous, and our many violators, mad as hell. You wonder why I threw in the assault charges?"

"I did."

"To give us some space to bargain. By taking those away, I can get Geronissi to go along with the fine on the birds. I take something away to get something bigger, see? Now, this may be one hell of a start for you, but from here on out, they'll be watching your every move."

"I'll keep that in mind."

"Don't care if you do or don't. We got a damn strike looming, and I don't want or need any tangential fireworks to set off some sort of public bloodbath."

"You expect violence?"

"Hell, thanks to you, we already have it. Go see Kallio. I've got a full docket today."

Sheriff Cruse was waiting on the sidewalk. "I declare, *Deputy* Bapcat. Never thought I'd see you again after we let you loose. You seem to have a talent for irritating important people. What fool went and made you a game warden?"

Bapcat gave Cruse a steely eye. "Don't take after what you can't handle, Sheriff."

Cruse stepped aside. "Songbirds? Who gives a damn? That ain't real law work, son—it's nothing."

The funeral parlor was less than a block from the JP, and attached to an old stable. Dutu Kallio was built like a blacksmith and had corn-yellow hair. He opened a wooden coffin for Bapcat. "This fella was found hanging from a tree this morning."

The man looked vaguely familiar. A testicle hung out of his mouth. Bapcat looked at Kallio. "His name?"

"Bruno's nephew, Aldo."

The one who had shouted *Mano Nera* out loud. "The sheriff got any leads?"

Kallio chuckled "I just clean 'em up, box 'em, and plant 'em. The sheriff pretty much lets the Wops police themselves."

"That what this is—self-policing? Where was the body found?"

"Right beside the road from Copper City to Allouez, so nobody could miss him. His balls and pecker are in his mouth, which means he said the wrong words out loud. Do that, and this is what they do to you. Doesn't matter if you're blood kin or not. The guineas put top value on privacy and secrecy. Their business is theirs, nobody else's."

"Pahl wanted me to see this?"

"Alley's a fine man. I'm guessing he just wants to raise your awareness."

He's done that.

It would be some time before Bapcat could erase what he had seen.

Returning to the cabin, he looked at his list of names from Traprock River. Aldo Geronissi had been one of the men—the one who went out of bounds, Bapcat assumed. Now he was dead. Whatever else it might or might not be, Italian justice was as swift as it was brutal.

"You know that myth we talked about the other day?" Bapcat said to Zakov.

"My memory is substantial."

"A body was found hanging, mutilated."

"Body?"

"One of the men we arrested."

"So he is dead, and there are messages on our cabin walls."

"We might assume they'll come after us, as well."

"Better to plan for the worst and hope for the best," Zakov said.

"For once, we think alike."

34

Swedetown

THURSDAY, JULY 3, 1913

George Gipp stopped the truck in front of Vairo's saloon, and Bapcat came out to join him. "George, I'm sorry, but your services are no longer needed."

The young man furrowed his brow. "I don't drive good enough?"

"No, you're a real good driver, George, but my job is going to drag me down into some pretty nasty business, and I don't want you to get caught up in it. I don't know what your life or mine holds, but mine feels less than comforting, and your ball playing seems pretty promising. You need to be out of this."

"You're firing me?"

"You know Bucky Root?"

"Know who he is—Copper Lode Taxi Service."

"Dominick and I have talked to him. He'll take you on as a taxi driver for the summer and manage your work around your practices and games."

"I don't hold much with practices," Gipp said with a smirk.

"I heard," Bapcat said. "Job sound all right to you?"

"Can I still bunk with you and Mr. Zakov?"

"No, George, it's not safe with us."

"Mr. Zakov isn't exactly mobile, what with his leg and arm."

"He'll heal."

Gipp shook his head and looked at the ground. "Okay, thanks, Deputy."

"Call me Lute. Root's expecting you around eleven this morning."

"That gives me time to shoot a little pool," the boy said.

"Just don't be late. Dominick and I vouched for you. Now help me get this damned jalopy started."

"Yessir, Lute."

• • •

Geronissi's house looked like all the others in his Swedetown neighborhood, except for a newly shingled roof over the front porch and several automobiles parked out front. There were no cars at nearby houses. A black-and-white cow stood in an intersection, tail up, liquefied shit spurting on the road.

The Italian's porch was crowded with men dressed in black. No women.

Bapcat inhaled deeply, opened the front gate, and marched down the narrow walk to the porch, feeling all eyes burning into him.

Geronissi came out of the house, wiping his hands on a towel. "You got the balls coming here, game warden."

"At least there are no bodies hanging in the neighbor's trees," Bapcat said.

Several men surged toward him, but Geronissi said, "Boys," and they all froze or turned away. "You don't belong here, Deputy."

"I mean no disrespect, but you and I need to talk—alone."

Geronissi studied him, then said, "Give us space, boys," and just like that the two men were alone.

"I saw your nephew Aldo," Bapcat said. "In a box in Ahmeek. I'm sorry for your loss."

"*Grazie*," the man said, "Can you imagine a young guy having such a terrible accident?"

"Accident?"

"Sure. What else could it be?"

Is the man stupid? "You know where I live?"

"Top of the big hill; what of it?"

"I wouldn't want any accidents up there."

"Shoulda maybe thought about that before the bird business."

"There's nothing personal in what I do, Geronissi."

"It feels personal to me—more than a grand's worth of personal."

"Threatening a law officer is a felony. You could be locked up for what you're saying right now."

Geronissi laughed. "Down here in Houghton County? You joking, Deputy."

"Your nephew was with you on the river. The way I see it, that makes you responsible for what he did."

Geronissi arched an eyebrow. "How you figure?"

"It's an uncle's job to teach his kin what to say and what not to say. I don't think you did such a good job."

"You think what you want."

"Just telling you what I think."

"Why would I care? You're not one of us."

"It's one thing, troubles happening to your own tribe. When it slops over to others, it becomes something else."

"You think I got the power or the balls to erase my own nephew, my own flesh and blood?" Geronissi asked, tears welling.

"All I'm saying is, keep it contained."

"You know the word *vendetta?*"

"No."

"It's like a grudge, leads to what Americans call feud."

"Not up here in Copper Country."

"Look, you, if you don't break up our hunt, my nephew, he don't lose his temper or his life."

"You actually *believe* that?"

"How it was," the man said. "Truth."

"Are you threatening me, Geronissi?"

The man put up his hands. "Good citizens don't threaten *polizia*."

"And you're a good citizen."

"I pay my fine, don't even flinch, more than one grand gone," the man said. "Be seeing you," he added, and walked inside.

35

Copper Harbor

THURSDAY, JULY 3, 1913

For reasons he couldn't understand, Bapcat had not been able to get Enock Hannula out of his mind. Surely the iced deer he'd found were the Finn's, but something more gnawed at him. Also lingering in the back of his mind was Horri Harju's advice about making judgments between immediate and longer-term justice and returns.

Last night, Bapcat had parked the Ford at the hill house, said nothing to Zakov, took his pack and rifle, walked down to Allouez, and caught the electric north to Mandan. From there he walked down the hills toward town—not on the road, but through the woods, skirting his old stomping grounds. He spent the night alone outdoors, unbothered by mosquitoes, happy for the solitude. It had been a long time since he'd enjoyed such peace.

Widow Frei's store and Copper Harbor were decked in red, white, and blue bunting, and there were signs posted about a town picnic to be held on the grounds of old Fort Wilkins. Lots of people were in the village, and though Jaquelle Frei saw him when he came into her store, she didn't acknowledge him. He knew they couldn't talk until her customers had cleared out, so he went back outside into the sunshine, rolled a cigarette, and sat on a wooden chair on the porch.

When she finally emerged, the widow glared at him. "Come to your senses?"

"We need to talk."

"I have been talking all morning, sir. Talk is the currency of commerce."

"We need to talk about Enock Hannula."

"*Pish*. I have no need of that. Justice will be done. It's your debt and fate that concern me, Mr. Bapcat."

He saw several people passing by, all staring at him and the attractive widow. "Could we talk inside?"

"I prefer fresh air," she said officiously.

"We arrested Hannula on certain charges relating to you, but he was also in possession of illegally killed deer."

The woman laughed. "I care not about mere deer, Mr. Bapcat. My only concern is settling debts, keeping my business healthy, sailing ahead full steam into a bright and shining economic future."

The way she poured out words made him dizzy. "Hannula is engaged in something bigger."

She stared at him. "Such as?"

"He won't say."

Widow Frei issued a burst of indistinct sound. "What is it you want here, sir? I have a picnic to attend, and little time for intellectual shilly-shallying."

"Drop the charges against Hannula."

Frei gasped dramatically and immediately slapped at him, but he grabbed her wrist and turned her aside, maintaining his grip. "Whoa."

"You would surely ruin me, sir," she said sharply.

"That's not my intention. You *know* that. But I need a way to bargain with Hannula."

"And you think I should finance this questionable activity on your behalf?"

"I'm just trying to find a way, Jaquelle."

She pulled her hand free and rubbed her wrist. "All right, let us step inside, and negotiate like civilized adults."

"I appreciate this."

"Do you?" she said, and went through the front door, talking over her shoulder. "Most men think women are too soft for the rigors of commerce," she said as he stepped in behind her, only to have her turn around and press a small revolver to his midsection.

"A gut shot's a horrible wound," she said. "It bleeds you slow from the inside and eventually kills you, but not until you have suffered excruciating pain. It's the same with debt," she concluded, pulling the pistol aside and tucking it into a fold in her dress. "Are you asking me to gut-shoot myself thusly, to suicide my business, as it were, to undo all I've worked to build?"

"You know that's not what I want."

"I know no such thing, sir, and I've seen neither hide nor other parts of you—especially certain other parts—going on fifty days. My dear Mr. Bapcat, I have labored under the impression that we have a subtle—but substantial—personal connection, a bond which our little debt-settling charade makes a truly delicious game. But fifty days, sir! Fifty! I swear, I am beginning to believe that I, who have unerring judgment in all things, have misled myself in this matter of the heart."

What is she saying? He was unable to respond, and suspected that anything he might say would only inflame her more.

"Thus, I conclude that I must put our relationship on a more-formal basis."

"Actual money—"

"Lord in God's Heaven," she said. "Your mental prowess makes me think your career in quasi–law enforcement will be short-lived. I certainly do *not* mean to terminate the form of payment. Rather, and quite to the contrary from your puny ways of thinking, I mean to formalize it, and put it on a rigid schedule, which will compel you to make regular deposits on account."

"But—" he said.

She held up a forefinger. "In the matter of one Mr. Enock Hannula, I will inform my attorney to tell John Hepting that if Hannula will agree to repay a percentage of said debt, I will accept that as a finalized deal, and shall abide by it."

"That's—"

"On the other hand," she said, poking his chest, "I shall add the reduced portion of Hannula's debt onto yours, which I will then expect you to work off on a schedule I establish, and that you will adhere to with great diligence. Do you understand and agree?"

"You're going to get your money, one way or the other," he lamented.

"I do not recall *mon père*," she said, "only *ma chère maman*, and she always said to me, 'Jaquelle, *jamais arriére*.' You know these words?"

He shook his head.

"*Jamais arriére*—this means, *Never retreat.* You understand?"

"I'm sure your mama would be very proud," he said.

"Do not attempt flattery, dear sir. I offer a contract to satisfy both of us. Accept or reject?"

He understood she was tightening her noose, which on the one hand he found constitutionally disagreeable, but on the other hand, it was a way to get what he thought he needed. Had it really been fifty days since they'd been alone together? Without understanding why, he felt an urge overtake him, and decided that as pressing and overwhelming as it seemed, it was not all that unpleasant. He looked at her and nodded.

"You accede, sir?"

"If that means yes, I guess so."

She slid to him and rubbed his face gently. "You are a project, sir, but my heart insists you are a worthy one. Let us proceed upstairs forthwith."

"What about your picnic?"

"They have watermelon and games. Our venue is here, our recreation of a more intimate kind."

"How about I take on all of Hannula's debt and John lets him go free and clear?"

"Suit yourself," she said, shaking her head.

36

Eagle River

MONDAY, JULY 7, 1913

John Hepting looked irritated when Bapcat showed up unannounced at the lawman's house.

"Bad weekend?" Bapcat asked. He had been at Jaquelle's since the third.

"Miners are voting on the strike," Hepting said, "demanding a meeting with the operators. If the mine operators refuse, the strike will be on. There are notices in union halls everywhere."

"Predictions?" Bapcat asked.

"No damn way the operators will meet, and if the miners go out, the operators will try to use the strike to break the union. This is going to be for all the marbles, and I'm thinking the miners are not in the position of strength."

"Sounds like a lot of ifs."

"Not ifs, Lute—just whens. What brings you here?"

"Hannula. I can't decide if he's lying about the deer."

"Follow your hunches and intuition."

"He doesn't strike me as the talking type."

"Chilly says all the man thinks about is money."

Jailer Taylor's nickname was Chilly. He'd once been a miner, but had lost a hand in an accident.

Bapcat looked at his friend and colleague. "Do you care whether the Hannula case goes to court?"

Hepting cocked his head and raised an eyebrow. "What the widow wants would seem the more germane point to raise."

"She and I have an agreement."

Hepting gave a thin smile. "Big gamble for you. I hope it pays off."

"You want to be there when I talk to Hannula?"

"To verify you're serious?"

Bapcat nodded.

"Okay, but I can't stand that self-righteous pig, so I might not stay the duration."

Before going to the jail they stopped to visit Justice of the Peace Hyppio Plew to explain the plan and seek his support, which he willingly gave after listening to it. The air was still, heavy rain clouds looming north over Lake Superior.

They found Hannula in his cell, fanning himself with a hat.

"Visitor, Stumper," Chilly Taylor shouted.

"There ain't but me in here," Hannula grumped. "And I ain't blind."

"Thought we might talk," Bapcat said.

"Got tobacco?"

Sheriff Hepting gave the prisoner a pre-rolled smoke and a match.

Hannula exhaled smoke gaudily and waved a hand. "Talk."

"You've got a lot of charges against you," Bapcat began.

"Because of that whore," Hannula complained.

"You want out of here, we can offer you a way. But if all you want to do is rant, forget it."

Hannula's hands went up. "I'm listening."

"I want the name of the person you were going to sell the deer to."

"I only shot one," the Finn retorted sharply.

Bapcat stood up and turned away.

"Wait!" Hannula yelped. "What do I *get?*"

"If you give me honest, verifiable information, all charges will be dropped and you'll be a free man."

"Bail?"

"No bail. Released, free and clear."

"Of everything?"

"All of it, lock, stock, and barrel, my charges included."

Hannula looked at Hepting. "Is he serious?"

"He is."

Hannula slumped on a bunk and shook his head. "You're asking a lot. What's the catch?"

"There's a lot at stake for you."

"You don't understand," the man said.

"Educate us," Hepting said.

"It ain't that simple. Stuff goes on hereabouts that the law don't know nothing about. *Lots* of things."

"Such as?" Bapcat asked.

"Certain captains you have to pay to get paid."

"Or no work?" Bapcat said.

"That's how it is," Hannula said.

"Everybody knows that," Hepting said.

"You a union man?" Bapcat asked.

Hannula said, "No, some of the boys can get away with that. Others—well, a rock falls on their head, or they trip into a hole. Accidents happen underground every day. Nobody pays attention, or cares."

"What do miners have to do with deer?" Bapcat asked, trying to steer the conversation.

"If there's a strike, some people won't have money to buy at company stores. But they'll still need to eat."

"So you sell the deer to the strikers."

"No, you don't understand. The deer don't go to nobody. They get left to rot and hunters get paid for each one they shoot."

"Someone pays hunters to kill deer so others can't kill and eat them?"

"Right—three dollars a deer, which is a day's wage underground."

"You have such an arrangement?"

"I was told to go out and do it, otherwise, no job underground anymore, no pay."

"Why you?"

"I'm a good hunter is why, a real sure shot."

"They have to see the deer to pay, or do they take your word?"

"Nobody takes my word. You show the heads to collect."

"How long after you make the kills?"

"Soon as possible. I get the feeling they're keeping count."

"Do they expect you to dispose of the carcasses?"

"No, they just don't want them used by others. In this weather, day or two, heat, wolves and eagles and little critters, the carcass is finished."

"But yours were on ice," Bapcat said.

"Waste not, want not. I'll use that meat."

"What happens to the proving heads?" Hepting asked.

"They take them."

"And dispose of them?"

"I ain't never asked that. Not my business."

"Any idea where?"

"Heard there might be an old mine hole somewheres, and they dump 'em down that."

"Which mine?" Hepting asked.

"Don't know, but I heard some mention of bats."

"Which captain hired you?" Bapcat asked.

"Can't say. That's too much."

Jailer Taylor said, "Shunk came by to see Stumper."

"Tristan Shunk?" Hepting asked with obvious distaste.

"The one and only," Taylor said.

Unfamiliar name. "Shunk?" Bapcat asked.

"Kearsarge man, topside captain, hard-nose even by Cousin Jack standards."

"Your deer contact?" Bapcat asked Hannula. "You didn't tell us. We guessed."

"We just know each other."

"Cousin Jack captain and a squarehead trammer," Hepting said. "That pairing's a little hard to swallow."

"He ain't the one," Hannula insisted.

"Shunk's dumb as a sack of rocks," Jailer Taylor said. "Cap'n Hedyn pulls all of Shunk's strings."

"Hedyn's not at Kearsarge," Hepting said.

"That don't matter," the jailer said. "All things here are run by Big Jim MacNaughton, and Madog Hedyn runs the show for MacNaughton."

"Hedyn works for MacNaughton?" Bapcat asked.

"No, technically they got different employers. But Hedyn knew Big Jim when they was growing up in Calumet."

"Hedyn's your deer man?" Bapcat asked Hannula, trying to sort out what he was hearing.

"I don't know," the Finn said. "I really don't know."

"What did Shunk want when he visited you?" Bapcat asked.

"Told me to keep my trap shut."

"You tell him why you were arrested?"

"He already knew. I told him I'm innocent, that I'd be out soon."

"You're a glorious optimist, Enock," Hepting said.

"I don't know them words," the Finn said. "Cap'n Shunk told me, 'Do right and ye'll be taken care of.' "

"Did he explain what he meant by 'right'?" Hepting asked.

Hannula hung his head.

"Shunk the one who pays you?" the game warden asked.

"No, a Wop called Cornelio Mangione picks up the heads and pays."

"How many have you killed so far?"

"Twenty, but I only been paid for fourteen."

"Shunk ask if you have more?"

"The cap'n never mentioned deer when he visit."

"Mangione one of Shunk's men?"

"Don't know."

"You're not giving us enough," Bapcat said.

"I give you everything I got."

"How does Mangione get ahold of you?"

"Bar in Ahmeek, Golden Eagle. He comes in, asks how many beers I had, and I say. He writes down a time after my next shift, and he shows up out to my place and we take care of it."

"At your house?"

"In the woods, not inside."

"But you and Shunk never talked about deer," Hepting repeated.

"No."

"Shunk finds out about this, what happens to you?" Bapcat asked.

"Like I said—accident," the miner said. "Fatal."

"Will they smell something if you get released?" Bapcat wanted to know.

"I told Shunk I was gonna get out."

Hepting looked over at Taylor. "Our story is that I'm not happy because our green-behind-the-ears game warden here made some mistakes and we ended up with no case against Hannula. We had to apologize and let him go. Make sure people hear it that way, Chilly."

"Yessir, Sheriff. You can count on me."

"You tell the same story to your wife," Bapcat said to Hannula.

"Just like that?"

"No," Bapcat said. "Go shoot more deer. When Mangione makes contact and sets a pay time, send me a message. You know Gipp, the ball player?"

"The big Kraut kid? Sure."

"He drives a taxi in Red Jacket. Get word to him. Stephenson's Pool Hall."

Hannula looked at the jailer. "Open the damn cage."

Bapcat squeezed the Finn's arm when he stepped out. "Double-cross us and you'll end up the same way the others would have it."

"Youse just be sure word don't get 'round I talked, or God help me, I'm a dead man."

Chilly Taylor laughed. "You're a miner, Stumper. That's the same as dead. You just don't got a date on your death certificate."

The Finn shuddered and left in a hurry.

"You trust him?" Hepting asked the game warden.

"Stakes are too high for him to not contact us."

"I could try to put somebody on him."

"I thought all your deputies were bad."

"Chilly can do it."

The jailer complained immediately. "I'm just a one-handed jailer, not no gun-totin' deputy."

"That might have to change," Hepting said.

"Let's try it this way first," Bapcat said after weighing the options. "You're sure Shunk is Hedyn's man?"

"Common knowledge. It's also commonly assumed that MacNaughton and Hedyn have spies all around the place. Paid informants, everywhere."

Hepting looked at the jailer. "You on their payroll, Chilly?"

Taylor held up his stump. "What do you think, boss?"

37

Bumbletown Hill

MONDAY, JULY 7, 1913

Bapcat had not been back to the hill since his time with Jaquelle Frei, and as he trudged toward home this time, he veered north into the forest and circled to the high grass hill by the outcrop. Down below he found the impression that marked the rear entrance hole, pulled dirt aside, and slid into the opening, no idea why he was taking this route. He and Gipp had left several torches near the rear opening and he found them, lit one, and headed toward the opening under the house.

He paused when he saw dim light ahead.

"It is I, Zakov," a familiar voice sang out. "I, Zakov, living like Job's turkey, gone to ground like a rat with the other rats. If you stayed away any longer, my four-legged companions might have declared war. Rats and man both must eat; this is a law of your so-called God, and nature's imperative."

"Why are you down here?"

"Some of your Italian associates attempted to exsanguinate yours truly, but I know a modicum of that fine language, and managed to get down the ladder before the barrage commenced."

Barrage? Exsanguinate? The Russian's crazy! "When was all this?"

"When is now? The thread of time eludes me."

"Monday the seventh."

"On Friday, the day you revolutionists celebrate independence from your British masters."

"You've been down here for three days?"

"They came late, after dark, and I took refuge down here. I have climbed up briefly each day to avail myself of the larder, which I must report, desperately begs resupply."

"There was a barrage?"

"At least twenty rounds in or through the structure, no doubt intended for you. My presence was incidental, which made me expendable—a reality I resent."

"Could you identify anybody?"

"Too dark, and I was scrambling to get below."

"They've not been back since?"

"I feel certain they are satisfied with the results of their initial effort, but it is possible they have left watchers. To my knowledge no one has breached the structure."

Bapcat climbed the ladder, found holes everywhere, shafts of late light cutting the interior devil's smiles. "Twenty shots?" he said into the hole. *Bad shots taken in a hurry.*

"We are not in the mood or mode of pedestrian accounting," Zakov said below. "This number is in the way of a very coarse estimate."

Off by at least half. The truck was untouched, and parked where he had left it.

"Looks like they left the Ford alone," Bapcat called down to Zakov.

"Perhaps they worship technology over human life."

Bapcat surveyed the house damage. *They didn't know if I was here, meaning the attack was probably spur-of-the-moment.* "No visitors since?"

"The silence has been truly tomb-like, an apt metaphor given the circumstances. Where is young Gipp?"

"He no longer works for us."

"How will we get about?"

"You will start walking to build leg strength."

"This has to do with the little bird killers, *da?*"

"*Da,*" Bapcat said.

"Who will transport us?" Zakov asked.

"We will. You will drive. You don't need both feet for that. And I will turn the crank of the starter."

"I am not some mindless aristocrat's chauffeur," Zakov complained.

"And I'm no aristocrat." *Whatever that is.*

"No, you are purely proletarian," Zakov said somberly.

"Is that a good thing?"

"Such a conclusion remains to be seen," the Russian said. "Zakov is hoping for hot food. He will even willingly assist in preparation."

"Better if you stay out of the way," Bapcat said.

"I have been practicing this skill," Zakov said. "I intend to arm myself for all future forays into the hostile environment beyond our sanctuary."

"It will cost a lot of time and money to fix this place," he told the Russian.

Zakov held up his hands. "Do these look like the claws of a mere peasant?"

"Pissant?"

"Peasant, uneducated one. Perhaps you should employ me to educate you. You have a disturbingly narrow mind, Deputy."

"I'm a peace officer, not a philosopher."

"As is painfully evident," Zakov said.

38

Red Jacket

TUESDAY, JULY 8, 1913

It was clear that Zakov relished his new role as driver. His initial pose of being offended had something to do with his sense of control, the sort of mind-thing Bapcat had no interest in unraveling. People were people. It was hard enough to track their doings, much less their reasons, real and imagined.

They parked outside the *Società Italiana di Mutua Benificenza* building, where Dominick Vairo's saloon sat on the first floor, next to the corner stairway that led to the inner workings of the Italian Hall above. The Atlantic & Pacific Tea Company sat adjacent to the saloon on the first floor, and filled a larger space.

Zakov began to dismount the Ford, but Bapcat waved for him to wait, this earning a frown from the Russian.

Vairo wasn't in the saloon. His partner Frank Rousseau looked at Bapcat, and jerked a thumb toward the back of the building and Vairo's family apartment.

Bapcat went outside and around the building to the back door. Vairo's wife looked out at him, said something to her husband in Italian, and Dominick stepped outside onto the back stoop.

"Georgie-boy come by," Vairo said. "He likes drive the taxi, lots of time to play ball."

"Have you seen Geronissi around?"

"He don't come by no more, I think."

"Some of his friends showed up at our place and shot it up. The Russian got to cover safely. I wasn't there."

Vairo cringed. "*E'un uomo difficile,* a difficult man, *si?* His boys, *lo fanno cose folli, che grappolo,*" Vairo said, touching his temple and making a snapping motion with his fingers. "Bruno is smart guy, but sometimes not all his boys. Boss lets them take risks."

Bapcat had already guessed as much. "What's the point? He kills me, the heat goes up for him because of people a lot more powerful and vengeful than me."

"You t'ink with logic mind, Lute. Geronissi, he t'inka wit' his nuts, okay?" Vairo cupped the front of his pants. "What you gonna do?"

"Not sure yet. The name Cornelio Mangione mean anything to you?"

Vairo was visibly shaken. "*Lue, e il diavolo deporee le uove*, the devil's spawn, yes. Don't go near this man, Lute, don't *dire il name del mostro ad alta voce*. This man *e peggio di una male dizione*—worse than a curse, okay?" Vairo looked to be near tears.

Overreaction? "What're you saying, Dominick?"

"*Persone vicine asparire lui*." Vairo made a sound, *Pffft*, and snapped his fingers. "Like-a that, here, then gone. *Pffft*."

"Dominick?"

Vairo leaned close, whispered, "*Lui e un assassino professionista, hai caputo*? Kills for money." Vairo vigorously rubbed his fingers together.

"Who does he work for?"

"Himself and anybody got . . ." The saloonkeeper made the money sign again. "Why you want to know this *animale?*"

"Heard the name, wondered. He work only for Italians with money?"

"He don't care, that one."

"Any names come to mind?"

"I never think about those things, Lute. *Never*."

"Just one?"

Vairo stepped back against the door. "I guess."

"Tristan Shunk," Bapcat said.

The blood seemed to immediately drain from Vairo's face. "*Capitano* Shunk?"

"*Si*, topside captain at the Kearsarge."

"Listen," Vairo said emphatically, "I don't know nothing this man."

"If people don't talk, things don't change," Bapcat told his friend.

"I gotta t'ink about family, capisce? I am dead, what happens to wife, *bambino?* You not married, Lute. Me. I got *familia*."

Vairo had a point.

"One more thing," Bapcat said. "Shunk and Mangione, people say they do business together?"

Vairo leaned against the house wall. "I don't wanna hear this kinda t'ing. The unspeakable one, he is from south, okay, *Napolitano,* involved in societies—you understand what I tell?"

Black Hand.

Vairo said, "Yes, he and Geronissi, these two names I hear together. They *hate* each other."

"I know where Geronissi lives, but where does he hang out?" asked Bapcat.

"Roma Saloon, in Lisa Block, Sixth Street, corner of bar, his place of business, okay?"

Bapcat thanked his friend, who said, "You talk to boss Italians, call them *dottore*, okay, Lute. Sign of respect. Very important."

"Even if they're not doctors?"

"Please, you just do like your friend Dominick ask, okay? For your own good."

How much do Geronissi and Mangione hate each other? he wondered as he walked back to the Ford.

"Where to next, Your Excellency?" Zakov wanted to know.

"Your sarcasm is wasted."

"Zakov is surprised His Excellency understands the concept."

"I also understand the concept of good manners."

"There is no need to berate your unpaid personal serf."

• • •

It was midafternoon, the Roma almost empty of patrons, but Bapcat saw Geronissi at a table along a dark wall and approached him, taking the back of a chair in his hand.

"I got your message, *Dottore*. Thought we should talk." *If they wanted to kill, they would have rushed the house and killed Zakov. The bullets were a message.* "Now a good time?"

Geronissi motioned for him to sit. The Italian said, "*Stai cer cando di suscitore una guerra?* You trying to stir up a war?"

"I could ask you the same, *Dottore*. It's not so smart to shoot up a lawman's house."

"You ain't no real lawman, Deputy, just a game warden, and I don't know nothing about shooting no house."

"Cornelio Mangione says differently."

Geronissi blinked hard. "Everybody got opinions in this country."

Bapcat started to stand. "Not being a real lawman, I guess I don't have to act like one and follow the law—is that what you're telling me, *Dottore?* Maybe one night you head for home and there's an accident." He knew he had Geronissi's attention now.

"So what's this Mangione say about me?" the Italian asked.

"I never said he mentioned you. Why do you assume that?"

"What is it you want, Deputy? I'm in no mood for word games."

"Word is going 'round that you and Mangione don't see eye to eye."

"The man's a pig," Geronissi said, adding, "We all got opinions, *si?* America! Opinion is in the air here."

"Most people don't fear pigs," Bapcat said.

"Who says Bruno afraid?" Geronissi asked, thrusting his chin forward.

"Not you. I'm referring to a general statement of how things are around here. But things never stay the same, Bruno. One day maybe someone sees to Mangione's downfall, puts him in jail for a long time."

"Why they do this?"

Bapcat shrugged. "You know the man and I don't. You *do* know him, right?"

"I know who he is, but he's not my friend."

"Of course he's not. You two are in different businesses."

"What's that mean?"

"You're the birdman, *Dottore.* Mangione's got deer."

"I don't know about no deer."

" 'Course you don't, because it's *his* business. You get nice profit from birds, but deer, the profit there's gotta be huge. Big animals, big money, right?"

"What you want, game warden?"

"Me, *Dottore*? Just thinking out loud."

"Talking about things not your damn business, and you know nothing about."

"Maybe there are things you don't know about either, *Dottore.* No disrespect, but Mangione pays hunters to kill deer so strikers can't feed their families."

"There ain't no strike!" the man insisted.

"They're voting right now."

Geronissi's face became passive. "How much this man pay these hunters?"

"Three dollars a head is what I heard—a miner's wage underground for a day."

Bapcat could see Geronissi trying to process the information, making calculations.

"Bullshit. That don't make no sense."

"Crime's never logical," Bapcat countered.

"You can't kill all the deer," Geronissi said. "Too damn many."

"You don't have to kill all of them; just enough to make the meat scarce and hard to obtain."

"Who pays this Mangione, Mr. Big Shot *Ingles* McNaught"

"Mangione isn't saying."

"Big Shot got his hand in everything around here. What I'm supposed to do with this information?"

"Do? Whatever you want. I just thought you should know, *Dottore*, on the off chance you didn't."

Geronissi said, "Maybe I know a lot, mebbe not. Why you tell me?"

"A trade. No more visits to my place."

"What's in it for me?"

"You stay alive, *Dottore*, maybe inherit a new business or something."

Geronissi smiled slyly. "Okay, Deputy, we got a deal—my word."

"Get in touch if there's ever anything you think I ought to know," Bapcat said.

"You want *gnocchi, vino*?" the man asked, pointing at a bowl.

"No, *grazie*, I've got to move on."

"How you know about strike vote?" Geronissi asked.

"You got your sources, I've got mine," Bapcat said.

"*Ciao*, Deputy. Nice talking to you."

Zakov was snoring in the Ford and startled awake when Bapcat returned. "*What!*"

"Home, sleepyhead."

"I was meditating, not sleeping. What have we been doing today?"

"Setting traps with poison."

"Which one?"

"Greed."

After this Geronissi would be sniffing out what Mangione was up to. More importantly, the *dottore* would take the gun sights off him and Zakov—at least for now.

39

Kowsit Lats, Keweenaw County

SUNDAY, JULY 13, 1913

The brooding Zakov parked the Ford a mile north of Seneca Lake, where Bapcat was hidden away on the edge of a pastoral expanse Finnish locals called Kowsit Lats, convoluted Finglish for Cowshit Flats, meaning grazing fields. George Gipp had heard talk in a pool hall about some deer being shot at night on the Lats, and had passed word to Bapcat. The night shooter was alleged to be the infamous Frenchman, Joseph "Sneaky Joe" Painchaud, a Lake Linden native and well-known year-round hunter of anything he could peddle. Zakov said Painchaud had been a sometime competitor in the wolfing trade, but had been "easily dissuaded." Bapcat sought no details.

Right at twilight there had been a single shot northwest of Bapcat, who moved steadily toward the sound, but there had been no more shots so he'd taken a knee and listened and moved ahead a few feet at a time. Eventually he heard what he took for heavy breathing, and chopping sounds. He stepped into a clearing where a man knelt beside a deer.

Bapcat had known of Painchaud for years, and had met him once in his days as a miner.

"Hey, Joe, why don't you light a lantern before you cut off a finger?"

The Frenchman jumped to his feet. "*Who da hell?!*"

"Game warden, Joe."

"We ain't got one, no."

"Now you do, yes."

"Dis ain't how it look, no. Somebody shot dis guy. I just put him out of his misery."

"Finish what you're doing, Joe."

"Dis ain't fair," the man complained.

"Think how the deer feels."

Painchaud laughed out loud. "Deer, dey don't feel shit! What dis cost me, hey?"

"The deer, to start with."

"Start?"

"Good information and I'll not take you to the JP."

"Okay, I give you money direct, *oui?*"

"No, Joe, no money to me. Just information."

" 'Bout what?"

"Who're you hunting for?"

"Me. I eat dese deers."

"It's customary to gut a deer before you butcher it, Joe. You're cutting off the head."

"I guess you got here too damn quick—din't give me no time get done my work, you."

Bapcat moved closer, saw exactly what the man was doing. "You want the horns? You can't eat horns, Joe."

"You din't let me finish."

"With the deer, or the shit you're telling me?"

"I din't do nothing to you."

"You killed my deer."

"*Your* deer?"

"My deer, everybody's deer. The people of the state own these animals, Joe, and you've got a hatchet in your hand, not a knife."

"Ain't no law against no hatchet, hey."

"You chopped into the skull, pulled off the horns, haven't gutted the animal, which you are going to leave here to rot."

Painchaud said, "You din't let me finish. What dis cost me? *Allez*, make number."

"Information: the name of the person who pays you for heads and horns."

"Can't say dat."

"Your choice, Joe. No name now, we'll let the JP decide."

"Jerko Skander," Painchaud mumbled. "Goddamn Croat."

"Jerko Skander pays you—that's what you're saying?"

"I said da damn name, didn't I?"

"How much does he pay you?"

"T'ree bits."

"What about the meat?"

"He don't want no meat, just heads, horns."

"Others work for Skander?"

"Don't know."

"Who does Skander work for?"

"Himself."

"Joe, you may be sneaky, but you ain't real smart. What fool's gonna pay just to have a deer shot and left to rot on the ground?"

"I just told: Skander."

"But *why*. What does *he* get?"

"You wanted name, you got one. Now what?"

"How do you get paid, Joe?"

Painchaud described a process similar to what Hannula had described.

"You give him just the head and horns?"

"*Oui*."

"What if someone pays him two or three bucks for the same head and horns?"

"Who do dat?"

"I'm asking you, Joe."

"I don't know nothing, dat stuff."

"Where's Skander live?"

"Don't know."

"No idea?"

"None."

"Get the hell out of here, Joe. Next time I catch you, there won't be a deal, but you know I'm going to have to make it known that you told me Skander's name."

"Dat ain't fair!" the man complained.

"Unless you tell me where the man lives."

Painchaud started to pick up the antlers.

"Drop them, Joe."

"Dey're mine."

"Walk on home, Joe, while you're still ahead."

"I don't feel ahead. I feel behind, me."

"See, every minute we live makes us smarter. Maybe someday they'll call you Smart Joe instead of Sneaky Joe."

"*Who* call me dat?"

"Everybody, Joe. For years. Hope to see you around, but if not, good luck in whatever place fate takes you," he said, as Joe took off.

Sneaky Joe was a major violator, and had been for many years. Like all good ones, he didn't blab about his work, but Bapcat felt certain Painchaud would spread the word that the game warden was afoot. *Too bad the man didn't tell me where his buyer lives.*

Bapcat looked around the area to see what else might be there, and after awhile, made his way back to the truck and threw the antlers and head in back. "Bait or harvest tonight?" Zakov asked.

"Bait, maybe."

"I think it worked. There's a man by a tree over there, says he wants to talk to you."

Bapcat found Painchaud waiting. "Skander lives over Atlantic Mine, him."

"Miner?" Bapcat asked.

"Pump-house gang."

"Thanks, Joe."

"You won't say my name?"

"Not if this checks out."

Bapcat put his rifle in back of the truck and stepped up into the passenger seat.

"You seem pretty elated for being empty-handed," the Russian said.

"The race goes to those who are patient," Bapcat said.

"There is no race," Zakov contended.

"There is always a race," Bapcat said. "Drive us home. For once, I'm hungry."

40

Kearsarge

MONDAY, JULY 14, 1913

It was close to a mile from Bumbletown Hill to Enock Hannula's cabin on Slaughterhouse Creek, on the northwest corner of Kearsarge. The air was choked with thick red and yellow smoke, all sorts of dust hanging, making breathing difficult. Bapcat waited for dark before visiting. He went on foot, leaving Zakov back at the hill. Hannula had not called since his release from jail. Had Cornelio Mangione and Tristan Shunk smelled trouble and backed off? It had been a week since union members had started voting. The deer-kill scheme should be at full boil, but not a word from Hannula. Something was wrong. He could feel it.

Bapcat watched the house from cover and saw Hannula's wife Mayme, but not her husband. He made sure Mayme saw him before he approached the house. She had stepped onto her small porch to smoke her pipe.

"Evening," he whispered.

"He ain't here," she said. "He come back one night, had what he wanted, told me next day he's going hunting, and he ain't come back since. I asked him, Ain't you had enough trouble? 'Course, he just swore at me, told me to mind my own woman business. I told him I guess my woman business was good enough last night when he was atop me."

"Did your husband say where he was going to hunt?"

"Got only the one place I know of, over to Black Creek Canyon. Case you care, he ain't took a rough hand to me since he come back. 'Course, was just one night, and he got something he likes real good. Truth is, me too. Don't know what you done said to him, but for now, it works good."

Mayme Hannula had once been an attractive woman. Did her husband beat her to make her unattractive to other men? Had she given him reason? Or did he think the Good Book told him to beat her? *Not important. Keep your focus.*

He considered fetching Zakov and the truck, but decided to walk to Hannula's camp, which was less than five miles away.

• • •

There were squirrel and hare bones in a cold fire pit outside Hannula's cabin. The door was open, but there was no sign of the Finn. Bapcat checked the cache of deer along the creek, smelling it because of the humidity and heat. Ungutted, they had bloated and would no doubt explode. *Something wrong here. Wait for light. Get help.*

Arriving back at the hill around 3 a.m. Bapcat saw a Model A parked behind the truck and stepped inside the house to find Jaquelle Frei drinking tea, while Zakov snored in a chair, looking like he would fall over at any moment.

"Good God, do you always keep such dreadful hours?" the widow demanded to know.

"Sometimes I'm out all night."

"Good thing we are not knotted matrimonially or I might well be harboring jealous notions. Your schedule is not good practice for the enhancement of connubial bliss."

"Like you said, good thing we're not married. What do you want, Jaquelle?"

"I have to go to Chicago for a spell, so thought I would pay a visit on my way south. You know, assist you in erasing some debt."

Bapcat pointed at the Russian and gave her a look meant to say, Are you serious?

The Widow Frei smiled. "Sleeps like he's dead, 'specially with what I put in his tea."

"There ain't even a real bed here, Jaquelle."

"Oh hell, Lute—floors been around a lot longer than beds." She was already undressing and looking for a place.

"What's in Chicago?" he asked.

"Suppliers' meeting," she said kicking off a shoe. "The vote is in: The miners will strike if the operators refuse to meet. I'm hearing it's a sure thing, and I'm also hearing the big union is against the strike, but it will happen despite what the national boys in Denver want. My suppliers and vendors need to understand there will be some dark times in these parts—no more business as usual until this thing runs its course. I'm a major client for some of these people, and I'm going to call in a few favors to keep my business afloat."

"They'll go along?"

"There's no right or wrong in business," she said. "Just profit or loss."

Later, entwined with him and sweating profusely, she said, "I always told myself I could take or leave this, but by God, Bapcat, I believe you have awakened in me a hunger of immense proportions, and some days I can think of nothing else. Care to offer an opinion on what that might mean?"

"I'm sure I don't know."

She bit his earlobe hard. "Oh, you bloody well know, sir. You just ain't come to grips with the enormity of it yet. When do you have to go back to your work?"

"Early," he said, trying to keep his breath even.

"Sakes alive, I'd better turn the crank on your motor and get us back to business," she said, breathing heavily.

• • •

He dozed afterward, wondering why it bothered him that she was going all the way down to Chicago. Just before giving in to deeper sleep, he admitted to himself that despite her difficult manners, this was a real nice way to relax and hit the hay, even if a man didn't have debt to work off.

But this was not a thought he'd allow himself to explore at length. His mind turned back to Enock Hannula. *Where is he?*

41

Upper Black Creek Canyon

TUESDAY, JULY 15, 1913

The Borzoi severely angled an eyebrow as Widow Frei sashayed out the front door and Bapcat set a cup of hot coffee in front of the Russian. "Your vigilance leaves something to be desired," Bapcat told the man, who looked bored.

"I find no intellectual fulfillment in trivial and mundane tasks," Zakov countered.

"We've got work today."

"I am not your lackey."

"Hepting is going to meet us at Black Creek Canyon. I walked down to Allouez and used the telephone in Petermann's store. The sheriff's bringing a new deputy."

"For what purpose is this exalted foray?"

"Not sure yet." He hoped Hannula had not met with foul play, but he refused to speculate. Saying or thinking things sometimes caused what you were thinking about to happen. He knew this was pure superstition, but you couldn't change how you felt.

• • •

The new Keweenaw County deputy turned out to be Chilly Taylor, who looked extremely nervous about his new promotion and badge.

Bapcat explained that according to Mayme Hannula, her husband had gone hunting a week ago and had not come home.

"If you hadn't stopped at the house, would Mayme have reported this?" Hepting asked.

Good question. The game warden shook his head. He'd not thought of it, and had no way to know. Off to the side Zakov and Taylor were involved in quiet conversation.

They spread out, and it was the gingerly moving Zakov who found blood spatters near the cache. The Russian was using one crutch now and getting around all right most of the time. Bapcat was once again impressed with the man's toughness. A hundred yards farther downstream Taylor found a deer carcass stuck in a logjam. It had been shot once in the head, was bloated and putrid, sloughing off flesh and fur.

The four men sat on the rocks at streamside. "Carcass intended for the cache, you think?" Hepting posed.

"Let's look around carefully between the blood and where Chilly found the deer," Bapcat said.

"If he needs only the heads to get paid, why does Hannula keep the rest of the deer parts?" Hepting asked.

"Could be that before we arrested him he planned to play both sides of the game; why else bring ice to the cache? Shoot the deer, get paid for their heads, then maybe sell the meat to those who'll pay? Claimed he'd eat them, but it wasn't convincing," Bapcat said.

"That fits Hannula," Hepting said.

"There will come a day when we will be able to examine blood and not only determine if it is animal or human, but from which exact human or animal," Zakov declared.

"You damn fool," Hepting said.

Chilly Taylor slapped his leg. "Steer clear of the breaky-leg, son."

"It is a matter of prognosticating a future from the possibilities and probabilities now at hand," Zakov insisted.

"Does the man talk this way all the time?" the new deputy asked Bapcat, who nodded.

The Russian said, "I think you are all sadly unfamiliar with Mr. Darwin's theories of natural selection, and what evolution portends for all living creatures."

"Darwin," Taylor said. "That damn fella who says we was once all monkeys?"

"A gross oversimplification," Zakov said. "My point is that all species develop, and we are all different. I have no doubt there will come a fine day when lawmen depend more on science than their eyes, or those of faulty witnesses."

"Darwin said all that?" Hepting asked.

"Mr. Darwin's seminal work has catalyzed my own original and inspired thinking."

"He talking monkey or Russian?" Chilly Taylor asked.

"More nonsense than either," Bapcat said.

But Hepting responded, "I guess I wouldn't be so fast to write off what the man thinks."

"Thank you, Sheriff," Zakov said. "Innovative thinking draws criticism the way feces draw flies."

Chilly Taylor said, "And here I thought my whole life it was plain old shit brung flies."

The men all laughed. "Let's get to it," Bapcat said.

Hepting said, "That Zakov has lots of theories; how about you, Lute?"

Bapcat took a deep breath. "It could be that Hannula was dragging a dead deer up to the cache and someone did something to him. Might be useful if we can find where the deer was shot."

"Might have been in the river," Taylor said.

"Let's move," Bapcat told them. "Evidence first, then guesswork."

Hepting smiled. "Seems you're getting a handle on this police business."

"New paint on an old building don't make it stronger," Bapcat said. "I'm trying."

"Don't underestimate yourself," the sheriff said. "The last man in your job rarely left the confines of Red Jacket or Houghton."

It was an hour later when Bapcat found a splatter of dry blood and followed it west to the road, where the trail disappeared.

The others gathered to look at the terminus. "Ideas?" Hepting asked.

"This isn't the deer," Bapcat said. "I'm wondering if maybe there was a head shot and Hannula got dragged up here where he got dumped into something to haul him away."

"Head shot?" Taylor asked.

"So much blood where this starts. Head wounds bleed, even lethal ones."

"What next?" Hepting asked.

"I need time to think." Bapcat looked at the sheriff. "We don't tell Mayme anything yet, right?"

"Nothing to tell," Hepting said, agreeing. "All this is speculation."

• • •

Instead of Bumbletown Hill, Bapcat had Zakov drive them to the icehouse in Centennial. Taylor and Hepting headed for Eagle River.

"Look at any wagons here," Bapcat told the Russian before going inside.

"For what?"

"Dried blood, anything not right."

Bapcat asked a clerk inside if he could talk to Herman Gipp, but the clerk fled, and in his place, sales manager Celt Ogden appeared.

"Mr. Gipp is no longer employed by this establishment," the man said gruffly.

"Since when?"

"That's not your business, young man."

"There's no call for your tone of voice, Mr. Ogden."

"I simply convey information. If you disapprove, that is, of course, your right. Now please leave this place of business; you're interfering with legal commerce."

Zakov was beside the Ford with one crutch.

"Anything?" Bapcat asked.

"Not exactly. A young man out back said a wagon got demolished late last week. They'll use the wood to rebuild other conveyances."

"Why break up that one?"

"The youth simultaneously proclaimed ignorance and his own suspicions. He insists the wagon wasn't old or broken—in fact, it was fairly new and in good repair, to his knowledge."

"Who broke it up?"

"Ogden and another man, with black hair and a silver streak in back."

"What day?"

"Wednesday or Thursday, he isn't entirely certain."

"Did he show you the woodpile?"

"Says it's not on these premises. He says Ogden and the other man took the pile to the business's repair shop."

"Which is elsewhere?"

"The boy told me Ogden's brothers also have an interest in this business, but they don't get along with people, so this Ogden runs things. The brothers build wagons at their place on the Heights, up Bumbletown Road, which, fortuitously, is on our way home."

"Let's find a telephone," Bapcat said.

He called Sheriff Hepting's house from the Centennial post office, but his wife said he was still out.

Ogden's brothers' place consisted of a pedestrian house, several outbuildings, and a large barn. Chickens wandered the grounds, as did two large brown hogs. Two black-and-white cows were tethered near the unpainted barn. Two large wagons were parked between the house and barn, and near the latter was a large pile of shattered wood fragments. No point searching without a warrant, so Bapcat got back into the Ford.

"Where to now, master?"

"Home."

"You seem somewhat disquieted."

"How I seem is none of your damn business."

"I rest my case," Zakov said with a cackle. "What every husband says to the spouse when he is frustrated."

Bapcat slammed his door after turning the crank and setting the Krag in his lap. "Shut up and drive."

42

Laurium

WEDNESDAY, JULY 16, 1913

Herman Gipp's house was immaculately kept, and his wife was as rotund as her husband. When asked where her spouse was, she told Bapcat sarcastically that if he wasn't out in the "bloody woods," like he was every day, then he was at work at the icehouse in Centennial. The game warden saw no reason to change her view of the facts and left her staring at him as he let himself out of the house.

Bapcat telephoned Copper Lode Taxis from Vairo's. Buddy Root said George was out on a run and due back anytime. Bapcat asked the cab company impresario to have the boy meet him at Vairo's.

Gipp soon arrived. Zakov welcomed him, saying, "It is time for the midday repast." Gipp was immediately surrounded by older men, all singing his praises as a ball player. No sign of Dominick.

Bapcat pulled the boy aside. "Everything okay?"

"Swell."

"Do you know that your uncle Herman got fired from the icehouse?"

"When?"

"Sometime after we were there."

"Not the first time he's lost a job. Herm isn't so good at taking orders, and he doesn't care much for indoor work."

"The timing doesn't bother you?"

"Should it?"

"His wife thinks he's still working at the icehouse."

Gipp frowned. "That part's *not* normal. Herman usually tells the old bat everything."

"Still not bothered by the timing?"

"You want me to help you find Unc?"

"Think you can?"

Gipp laughed. "Fig Verbankick. Everybody calls him that, but his real name is Jimmy. He and Unc grew up together, but Jimmy never married. You can bet Fig knows where Herman is."

"How do we find this Verbankick?"

"He's got what he calls a camp near Spider Pond."

"Bodie Creek," Zakov interjected, eavesdropping. "Are we eating or not?"

"Good hunting?" Bapcat asked.

"Nah," George Gipp said. "Its biggest selling point is that it ain't in town."

"Show us the way?"

"Not for free. I'm a hack now. That's what they call cab drivers in Chicago."

"We'll take the Ford. The Borzoi will drive."

"Him?" Gipp said, turning up his nose.

"There is no need for this boy to join us," Zakov said. "I know this place, I am going without food, and am in no mood for your sarcasm, Mr. Gipp."

Gipp was clearly amused. "How do you get to it?"

"From the Tobacco River Trail," the Russian said.

"You *could* go that way."

"Stop it, you two," Bapcat admonished. "How would *you* get there, George?"

"Me, I'd drive up to Phoenix. The West Branch of the Eagle and Bodie come together with the East Branch of the Eagle. It's about a mile and a half south, and relatively easy walking from there."

Bapcat said, "Call Bucky, ask for the afternoon off."

"No need. I'm done for today. Got practice this afternoon, but I wasn't planning on going."

"Think you could guide us?"

"Is Herman in some kind of trouble?" Gipp asked.

"I honestly don't know, George."

43

Spider Pond, Keweenaw County

WEDNESDAY, JULY 16, 1913

The camp looked like it was inhabited by savages, filth and refuse everywhere, fish bones, discarded bottles and rusted cans, toppled firewood piles, two crude chairs.

Fig Verbankick was a slight little man with an enormous head, shriveled skin and walleyes—one of the most physically disturbing people Bapcat had ever met. He had thick legs and drooled while maintaining a blank stare and a mostly toothless grin.

When they walked into camp Herman was urinating by a tree. "Georgie!" he yelled. "Sophie send you?"

"No, Unc. Deputy Bapcat wants to talk to you."

Herman Gipp looked at the deputy. "What about?"

"Your wife thinks you're still working at the icehouse."

Herman grinned. "Never liked dat damn job. Me and Fig are vacationating, right, Fig?"

Verbankick nodded enthusiastically and shouted, "Hooray!"

"You having fun, Fig?" George Gipp asked the strange man.

"Hooray! Ask Herman!"

"You feeling shy today?" George asked.

"Ask Herman."

Bapcat realized Fig Verbankick was "not right" in the head. "You going home nights?" the deputy asked Herman Gipp.

"Nah, we stay right here in camp, don't we, Fig?"

"Hooray—camp!" the little man said.

"She acts like you come home every night and that everything's normal," Bapcat said.

"Sophie? She don't like Fig. She knows I took vacationation." *Fig seems touched, and this man's language alone is unique: vacationating?*

"You weren't fired?"

"Was mutual. Ogden din't want me, and I din't want him or da damn icehouse."

"But you didn't tell Aunt Sophie," George reminded his uncle.

Herman shrugged. "I'll have a new job by da time she knows."

"Tramming?" George asked his uncle.

Herman turned serious. "I been underground and I ain't never going back. Fig will get us somet'ing."

Bapcat wasn't sure what to make of this. "What did Ogden say when he fired you?"

"I quit," Herman countered.

"Okay, when you quit."

"Hooray!" Fig shrieked.

"Ogden said dere's a strike coming, and dey din't need my services no more."

"Other people let go at the same time?" Bapcat asked.

"Just me dat I know of."

"Had you heard talk about this possibility beforehand?"

"Ogden don't talk ta working people except ta hire or fire."

"You know his brothers?"

"Carpenters. Dey make wagons."

"Are they like him?"

"Pretty much, I guess."

"You have anything to do with wagons in your job?"

"Every day."

"You hear any talk about junking one of the newer wagons?"

"Not likely. Ogden's cheap, and da wagons are in pretty good condition."

Fig nodded agreement, said, "Frugal!"

"Frugal," Herman agreed, "not cheap. Right word, Fig."

The little man grinned.

Bapcat turned to Fig. "Where do you work, Mr. Verbankick?"

"Ask Herman," Fig answered.

"Herman?"

"Fig does small jobs in Red Jacket—cleans floors, washes windows, cuts wood."

"Scrub-scrub-scrub, chop-chop-chop," the man said happily.

Fig didn't look strong enough to lift a mop or an ax, much less wield either. "You know Dominick Vairo, Fig?"

"Ask Herman," Verbankick said.

"Sure he knows Dominick, and his partner Frankie, too."

Bapcat switched directions suddenly. "Is it normal for Ogden to discard wagons in pretty good working condition?"

"Only old rotten ones," Herman said. "Dem Ogdens always reuse as much wood from da old ones as dey can."

"If Ogden personally pulled apart a newer wagon, what would you think about that?"

"Ogden don't do no real work. I'd say something was pretty fishy, right, Fig?"

"Hooray."

"How friendly are Ogden's brothers?"

"Less den him," Herman said, "which is why dey do all da wagon work."

"Thanks, Herman. Sorry to bother you and Fig."

"Hooray!" Fig shouted.

"Fig's sort of simple," George explained as they hiked north. "But he ain't as stupid as he likes to make out."

"Your uncle takes care of him?"

"Much as he can. Mostly Fig's pretty easy to lead around. Whole town takes care of him."

"Fig ever been in trouble?"

"Nothing like that. But people sometimes use him, see, treat him like a joke or something, because he don't seem to understand everything that's going on."

"Born so?" the sweating Zakov asked.

"No. His old man beat him with his fists every day till he died underground."

"Does Fig have a woman?" the Russian asked.

"No, Fig's real shy around girls. Spooked by them."

"You see," Zakov said. "Darwin, natural selection. He will not breed and thus, his line will end with him."

"He can't help how he is," George said in the man's defense, chastising the Russian.

"I assure you, Gipp, this was not meant as criticism. It is no more than an astute scientific observation, nothing more."

"Could be you won't be no breeder, either," George Gipp said angrily.

Bapcat laughed. The Russian sulked.

44

Bumbletown Hill

FRIDAY, JULY 18, 1913

Horri Harju came knocking as the sun was setting, a long hour before midnight. Bapcat met him at the door and showed him in. "Did I miss a telegram?" Bapcat asked. Harju had previously indicated that all visits would be announced by telegrams.

"I was in Ontonagon hiring a new deputy, and decided to swing up and see how you're doing."

"Hungry? We've got some eggs and spuds."

"Always."

Bapcat made breakfast and Zakov suddenly drifted in, sniffing like a dog.

"How much time have you spent south of Houghton?" Harju asked.

"None."

"My old chum Yary Nordson is undersheriff over in Ontonagon County. His sister Elena Ongin is writing him letters, reporting that she and her husband have been finding dead deer in their fields."

"Where?"

"Their farm is two or three miles southwest of Chassell."

Bapcat told Harju about his experience with the mine operators' possible scheme to deny strikers food, noting carefully that this was unproven. Harju listened without interrupting and concluded, "Seems like the whole thing is more than localized, and that might carry some implications."

"All the mine operators working together?"

"Wouldn't be the first time for collusion among big shots."

"My main witness has disappeared," Bapcat admitted. "I arranged to have charges dropped and for him to be released from jail. But now he's gone." Bapcat continued relating the whole story, including the disassembly of the ice wagon.

"No evidence, and if you got the charges dropped and he walked, that could show poor judgment on your part."

"Is that your only response?"

"I'm just explaining how things can get viewed at the state level, which is why we have to be real careful which cases we choose to intervene in. The ice wagon could be strictly coincidental," Harju concluded.

"Or a red herring," Zakov added, uninvited.

"Explain," Bapcat told the Russian.

"As a matter of survival in Russia, all must learn the art of avoidance, misdirection, we say *maskirovka*—disguising, if you will."

"And?"

Zakov made a dismissive gesture with his hand. "Your wagon man had to assume Hannula's absence eventually would be noticed by someone. Thus, perhaps he disassembles the conveyance to make it seem as if it carried the body."

"The blood trail ended at the road," Bapcat reminded him.

Zakov said, "It's possible the wagon went only a short distance, or they stanched the blood flow when they noticed it."

"And dumped the body there, assuming the law would take the bait?" Harju asked.

"*Maskirovka* seems provident," Zakov said.

"Seems too complicated, a lot of unnecessary trouble," Bapcat said.

"The simplest explanation is usually the best one," Harju said.

Zakov said: "The mine operators and local businessmen have woven a very tight web to control local peoples. They pay millions of dollars to shareholders each year. Such high stakes make it essential that all threats be taken seriously and dealt with severely and quickly."

Bapcat asked, "On what basis do you make this conclusion?"

"The *Rodina*, my motherland."

"This ain't Russia," Bapcat pointed out.

"*I* have seen both countries," Zakov said. "There are too many parallels to list."

"Hannula was my link to Mangione," Bapcat pointed out.

"What about the man called Painchaud?" Harju asked.

"The name I got from him was Jerko Skander, a Croat."

"But the setup described was similar?" Harju asked.

Bapcat nodded. "Different people."

"Two schemes, similar, almost identical," Zakov said. "This suggests conspiracy or collusion at another level, which is typical behavior of ruling classes in all countries."

"We don't have classes in America," Harju said.

"Really?" the Russian shot back. "Who holds the best-paid jobs belowground, and who serve as the beasts of burden?"

Harju looked at Bapcat. "Find Skander, see what he has to say."

"What about Painchaud? I told him I'd protect him."

"Which you now must make every effort to do. Go at this Skander at an angle. Tell him something like, 'I know *you're* not the kind of man to be involved, but I'm also told you're a man who knows what goes on.' Stroke his ego. Praise him for supporting the law, and make sure you tell him how the law takes care of citizens who cooperate."

"You see," Zakov said brightly, "this is identical thinking and tactics of the czar's secret police."

"Eat," Bapcat said. He could almost admire the Russian's mind, but had no plan to admit it. The man was difficult enough to live with as it was.

"The strike is a certainty," Bapcat told Harju.

"When?"

"Soon."

"You're going to get very busy with miners making illegal kills and operators trying to deny food to them. It could get bloody for man and animal alike."

"You predicted the former, not the latter," Bapcat said.

"Variety in human behavior, that's what we learn to expect—the unexpected."

Zakov said, "Stress is the mother of all surprises."

"Your Russian pal is pretty smart," Harju said.

"When he's not sulking, complaining, or whining," Bapcat said.

"I complain only when I am treated with disrespect. And I never sulk. Such behavior is beneath my dignity."

45

Red Jacket

MONDAY, JULY 21, 1913

Dominick Vairo's partner, Frank Rousseau, knew of Jerko Skander.

"Some call him Rat Dog, but he don't come around towns so much," Rousseau explained. "Works underground in Allouez Number Four, over to Ahmeek. Heard he's a trammer, but his real job is to kill rats down below. Some say he eats 'em."

"How do we find him?"

"He's supposed to have a shack somewhere out Seneca way."

"What's he look like?"

"Skander, or the shack?"

"Either, both," Bapcat said.

"Never seen the shack, but the man you'll know by his nose."

"As in?"

Rousseau laughed. "Don't need to paint no picture. You'll know, eh?"

"He ever come into Red Jacket?"

"Long time back. Not so much no more, and not that I seen," Rousseau said. "People don't like to be around the man, and he don't like to be around no peoples either."

Zakov said nothing until he was outside with Bapcat: "The longer I am in this place, the more I think of Babel and its tower to Heaven, and how God was displeased and intentionally damaged the speech of every working man. Unable to communicate, the building of the tower stopped."

Bapcat wasn't certain of his companion's meaning. "Are you saying God isn't happy with this place?"

"There is no God," Zakov said. "I am only pointing out that this stewpot of humanity makes if difficult to get anything done."

"They seem to get copper out of the ground just fine."

"*Da*, until the strike; then you will see."

Bapcat had no idea exactly what the Russian was thinking, but it occurred to him that the Borzoi, given the circumstances and his behavior when they had first met after the theft from his camp, and the Russian lay injured and defiant in a hole, might very well be mentally unbalanced.

46

Seneca Location, Keweenaw County

MONDAY, JULY 21, 1913

Zakov found a drunken cripple in Ahmeek, a man who spoke to Zakov in Russian, and learned from him that Jerko Skander lived between Seneca Lake and the Gratiot River, a marshy area edged by hulking piles of poor rock dumped from nearby mining operations. Zakov did not tell Bapcat who his source was, which led the deputy to think it might be a blind alley.

Bapcat looked out at the soft terrain and told the Russian, "You'd better stay here."

Zakov said, "Nonsense. An injury should be exercised, not rested." He brandished his crutch.

"Meaning you're bored?"

"I'll allow that element."

"How many languages do you speak?" Bapcat asked his companion.

"I've never found reason to inventory them."

The only shack west of Seneca Lake was made of logs caulked with yellowing mosses and chinked with pale red mud. There was a small fire pit outside and a young blonde girl sitting on a split log, tending a metal grill, set on stones over a small fire. A pot of coffee was brewing, and several lumps of gray meat were on the metal grate over the fire.

"We're looking for Jerko Skander," Bapcat told the girl, and thought he heard coughing inside the cabin. "Is he here?"

The little girl, whose age Bapcat couldn't guess, looked up. "There is no one here but me," she said earnestly, her green eyes sparkling.

"I heard coughing in the shack," Bapcat said, examining a small morsel of meat on the grill.

"Not coughing," the girl said matter-of-factly. "You hear rats screaming for help from others of their kind." A smile crept over her face. "Rats *never* help other rats."

Bapcat leaned closer to the grill. *Not venison.* Several rats had been beheaded, skinned, split in half, spread flat like chicken breasts. "That's a lot of meat for a little girl."

"It's not just for me. Father is fishing in the river and will return soon."

As predicted, the man arrived with an unwieldy string of trout hanging down his back, suspended by a forked stick—so many fish that the man needed two hands to manage the load.

"Luck was with you," Zakov greeted the man.

"Until now," Skander said coolly, glaring at them.

Where his nose should be was a piece of copper hammered and folded to resemble a nose, held in place by strips of leather tied behind the man's head. Skander dropped the fish, nodded to the girl, and said in crude English, "Do work. Pour coffee." Then, to Bapcat, "Who you?"

"Deputy State Game, Fish and Forestry Warden Bapcat, and my associate here is Zakov."

The man waggled his finger at the child. "Talk for us, girl—not that Russian bastard."

The little girl moved to stand next to the man with the copper nose, who said, "*Moja kcer ce govoriti za mere.*"

"My father, he says I will speak for him. My name is Draganu Tihan Skander. This means in English language, 'beloved quiet one.' It is a beautiful name."

"Why does your father speak so badly of Russians?" Zakov asked.

The girl looked past him to Bapcat. "I not talk to Russian, okay?"

Bapcat smiled at his colleague's ire. "Your father?" Copper Nose looked too old for a daughter so young.

"Yes, my father."

"Where is your mother?"

"Gone to heaven. Consumption, doctor called it. She coughed blood and died." The girl seemed unmoved by the death.

"How old are you, Draganu?"

"Eleven."

She looked small for her age. "And where do you live?"

"Here," she said, in a tone that blended pride with defiance.

"This is a hunting camp."

"This our home, Mr. Sir. There are few houses for Croats, and those they would give cost much and need fix. Here we are warm. Father built this house for Mother and me. It is a good house."

"You go to school?"

"Ahmeek. I walk road. Not far, only two miles."

"Long walk in winter," Bapcat said.

"I have snowshoes," the girl said. "I have never missed school except when Mother died."

The older man grunted and whispered something to her.

"Father wishes me to clean the trout and asks what do you want. We have work."

"How many fish does he have?" Bapcat asked.

When asked, the man scratched his head and mumbled and the girl reported, "He doesn't keep count. He says only that today was a good day."

Zakov stood over the dead fish. "I count at least one hundred," he said to Bapcat.

"Does your father know he can keep only thirty fish each day?"

The girl talked to her father and turned back to Bapcat. "What fool says this?"

"It's the law."

The girl translated for her father, who let loose with angry gibberish.

She said, "Father says there is no damn law on our river."

"Tell your father we are going to take his fish," Bapcat told her.

Before the girl could translate, Bapcat found a revolver pointed at his belly—not by the man, but by the child.

"*Our* fish," she said ferociously. "You go, they stay."

"Point the gun away from me, please. The fish belong to the people of the state. Does your father have a rod license?"

The pistol didn't waver in her small hand. "No license here, no law here—our fish," she insisted.

"May I address you as Draganu?" Zakov asked.

"You even *smell* Russian. We do not like Russians. Remain your mouth shut."

"Brat," Zakov mumbled.

Bapcat remained calm. "If your father talks to us about deer-killing, we may let him keep the trout."

She translated and listened to the man's reply. "Father says we already have the fish, and if you try to take them, he says I should shoot you in guts."

Decision time. "Please put the gun away," Bapcat said. "Keep the fish. We just want to talk."

Hearing this, the man pushed the girl's pistol aside, nodded, and indicated the two visitors should find a place to sit. The girl brought tin cups for coffee, and wooden plates. The man nodded at the rats and Bapcat speared one with his knife and put it on the plate. Zakov began to reach, and Skander put a knife to the Russian's throat. "*Nyet!*"

Zakov glared, but sat back. Skander gestured for Bapcat to eat. "*Covjek mara jesti*," he said.

"All men must eat," the girl translated. "Father is a great *lovac*—hunter," she added. "We eat much."

"Rats are not proper food," Zakov criticized.

Skander mumbled and the girl said, "What would a Russian know about food? You are all savages. We eat everything that crawls, swims, runs, or flies," the girl announced proudly. "As God provides."

"*Ovo je moj kamp Nemate dop ustenje,*" Skander said forcefully.

"This is our camp. You are not allowed here," the girl said.

Bapcat nibbled the rat meat and found the flavor bland, the texture stringy. "A bit like pork," he told Zakov, who rolled his eyes.

The girl looked at Zakov. "You may eat now, Russian."

Zakov speared the meat, took a bite, chewed, smiled. "Not pork—partridge. My compliments to the chef," he said grandiosely.

The girl ignored him.

Bapcat told her, "Tell your father thank you for the food."

Before she could translate, Skander said, "*Sam ubiti stakar au tarai zenlje. Mina ce ubiti sue nas.*"

"Father says he kills rats in the darkness of the earth, but the mines will kill everyone and everything."

"Ask him why he is killing deer, whose meat he doesn't eat."

The girl asked the question.

Skander said, "*Kapetani su poput boja. Marams napraviti ono sto smo rekli da ne.*"

"Captains are like gods. We must do what we are told," the girl translated.

"The captains ordered him to kill deer?"

She relayed the question and her father replied slowly, almost cautiously. The girl said, "He does not kill these deer you talk of."

"But he knows who does," Bapcat said. "He pays them to kill the deer and bring him their heads or antlers."

"Who tells this lie?" Skander demanded to know, his English suddenly improved, understanding more than he had been letting on.

"You pay hunters three bits, turn the heads and antlers in for two dollars, maybe three."

"*Zvijer tereta*," Skander said.

"Father says he is a beast of burden, a rat dog among beasts and men."

Skander spouted a stream of words and his daughter nodded as he spoke. "Father says to tell you that a man who would be a true man first takes care of his family."

Bapcat responded. "Tell your father we agree with him. Which captain pays him?"

The girl translated, and the man mumbled and turned his head away.

"He does not know. It is a different person each time, never a captain, though only captains would have so much money."

"How does he know if he is talking to the right person?"

The girl nudged her father, who pointed at his eyes.

"Their eyes tell," the girl said.

"Are these men from a captain he knows?"

She asked her father and he said, "*Tuje kapetan kapetani, cudo viste, ug lavni.*"

"He says, 'There is a captain of captains, the big boss of bosses,' " she said.

"What name?"

The Croat shrugged and nodded. The girl waggled the gun at them. "It is time for you to go and leave us alone."

"Tell your father if he remembers a name to get in touch with the game wardens on Bumbletown Hill."

"Go away," the girl said wearily.

"She should have been born an aristocrat," Zakov complained as they walked away. "Her heart is already black and her tongue sharp."

"She's just a little girl."

"I saw a tail on her."

"Wait!" the girl called out, her father talking to her with his hand on her small shoulder. "*Kapetani su poput boga. Maramo napraviti ono sto smo nekli da ne*," the man said.

"The captains are like gods," the girl said.

"He is repeating himself," Zakov said, cutting her off.

"*On ce me staviti u rure stakara I da nece biti poratka*," Skander said.

The girl translated, "They will push him into the hole of rats and there will be no return," she said with a flat voice.

"This has happened to others?" Bapcat asked.

"*Previse* . . . too many," Skander said quietly. "*Volim moja kcer. Shvacate li sto to zrace?*"

"Father tells you he loves me. Do you understand what this means?"

"*Ako umrem, one ce umrijeti*," the man added.

"He says if he dies, I die."

Cold-eyed, emotionless voice. This child is tough beyond her age, Bapcat thought.

"I understand," Bapcat said, knowing that he really did not. This bond of child and parent had never been his, and while he could pretend to imagine it, he could not know the feelings involved. What was clear was that the man was desperate and feeling threatened.

"Tell your father the next time he is called, to let me know so I can watch."

The girl translated and the man stared up at the sky, saying nothing, betraying nothing.

47

Pike River, Houghton County

TUESDAY, JULY 22, 1913

They had made their way south to Chassell the day before and had slept under the truck last night, hearing sporadic rifle reports throughout the night.

In the morning at first light they made their way to the farm of Elena Ongin, the Ontonagon County sheriff's sister, and her husband Olaf, who met them outside their small log house. Olaf had fresh blood on his hands and boots.

"Bapcat, Deputy State Game, Fish and Forestry Warden. He's Zakov," he added. "We heard about the letters to your brother."

"It's terrible," the woman said. "A bloodbath."

Bapcat looked at Olaf. "You're bleeding?"

"Dey shooting our milk cow," Olaf said. "Bastid."

"Where?"

"Behind barn," the woman said. "Look south pasture."

What they saw when they got into the field were ten deer and two cow carcasses.

"You see the shooters?" Bapcat asked the couple when he got back to the farmhouse.

"We go root cellar," Elena Ongin said. "Too dangerous above the ground at night."

"How long has this been going on?"

"May," the husband said. "Late May."

"Every night?"

"Not every. Sometimes, then nothing," Elena said. "Last night was worst. It is getting worse, we think, because of strike. We heard last night, neighbor come over, say strike start today."

"Where?" Bapcat asked.

"Everywhere, all copper," Olaf said. "Will be bad for all dis."

"You need to file a report on your cows with Sheriff Cruse," Bapcat said.

"Da mine owners' lackey? He don't care," Olaf said.

"He's the sheriff."

"Only for certain people in this county. Not for the likes of us," the woman said. "All these deer, you think everybody suddenly go crazy?"

Olaf laughed. "I tell you, mine operators, dey hire boys shoot dose deer so strikers can't eat."

"How do you know this?" Bapcat asked.

"I got eyes," Olaf said.

"Me, too," his wife added. "I mebbe can't to vote, but I damn sure got a brain and the ability to reason and think. It's not landowners and sportsmen do this. Thugs for pay, and you need to stop this, Mr. Deputy," she concluded, brandishing her forefinger like a rapier.

"Did you know the last game warden?" Bapcat asked the couple.

Olaf spat. "Wort'less, dat one."

"He got hurt down this way," Bapcat said.

"Takes no brain know you don't t'reaten t'ugs. Got big fellas hire dose t'ugs," Olaf said.

"Care to proffer a name?" Zakov asked.

"Dead cow iss one t'ing," Olaf said. "Dead me or dead Elena is whole nudder t'ing, eh."

"Is there anyone down this way who might be willing to help us?" Bapcat asked.

"Matti Karki, timberman over Champion Mine, Painesdale," the wife said. "Brings his wife and kids down here to fish, hunt—told Olaf he knows captain paying men to kill deer, seen where they throw heads and horns."

"Karki?" Bapcat said.

"Nice man," Olaf said. "He all fed up, says lots of da men wit' families feel same way as him," Olaf said. "But don't go tell him we tell you his name." The man's wariness was as palpable as his frustration.

"Thanks for your help," Bapcat said.

"This Karki fellow won't talk," Zakov said as they got into the Ford.

"Won't know unless we ask," Bapcat said, thinking the Russian was probably right.

48

Houghton

WEDNESDAY, JULY 23, 1913

They drove west along an impostor of a road to Painesdale, the road not much more than a deep-rutted cow path in places. They took a room at a small hotel run by a woman named Cekola who wore an eye patch and was missing two fingers on her left hand. They slept in the same bed, boardinghouse style, and had a meager breakfast. Over coffee, Cekola told them where Matti Karki lived, and she tried to pry out of them why they were interested, but Bapcat said nothing and the Russian followed suit.

They drove to the address the woman had given them, but found an empty house, the front door standing open.

A man stood by an unpainted fence next door, arms folded, watching them.

"Matti Karki live here?" Bapcat asked the man.

"Gone."

"To work, for the day?"

"Mebbe forever, the strike and all. Been gone mebbe one hour, I think."

"What about the strike?"

"Could get rough, no work. Matti talk about taking his family to Detroit, look for work there. We hear rumor Old Man Ford say he will pay workers five dollars a day." The man whistled. "Don't seem possible."

"He's driving to Detroit?"

"Matti got no car. Take family on train from Houghton."

"What's Karki look like?"

The man laughed. "Just another roundhead. You never find him in big crowd," the man said, pointing at other houses where carts and wagons and even some automobiles were being hastily overloaded.

"All rats jump ship," the man said. "Get out now while they can."

"But not you?"

The man held up a revolver. "All I need," he said.

Zakov walked toward the Ford, muttering, "*Et slishkom mnogo fignya*, this is too much bullshit. *Yebatz etot idot*. Fuck this fool."

Outburst complete, the Russian brooded in silence as they made their way toward Houghton, where they found hundreds of people in and around the train station.

"They act like an invasion is imminent," Zakov said. "Or a revolution. Sniff the air, you can smell their fear."

Bapcat approached a man with red dust on his hands and face. "The strike on?" he asked the man.

"Some places this morning," the man said nervously. "Will spread everywhere tomorrow."

Bapcat watched the man bull his way through the crowd of families and board a passenger car by shoving people aside. An engine wheezed in anticipation. Steam and sweat hung in the air. People were shouting, crying, surging left and right. Several dogs ran loose, snarling and barking frantically. A goat wandered by itself, unnoticed.

"John Milton," Zakov said. "*Paradise Lost.* But only now do I finally understand something of this country. A job is just a job. Why risk one's life for mere recompense?"

"Soldiers do," Bapcat said.

"And you are a fool," the Russian said. "There is seldom any choice involved in serving as a soldier. When you are there you risk your life for yourself and your comrades, not for rhetorical pap. Smart soldiers, like these miners, leave when the risk of remaining outweighs the uncertainty of leaving."

"The way you left?"

Zakov nodded solemnly and held out his hands. "I understand these people here today."

49

Red Jacket

WEDNESDAY, JULY 23, 1913

Dominick Vairo was nervous and pensive, rubbing his hands together repeatedly. It was late afternoon, the saloon full of sullen men with tired eyes. Ribbons and carnival tents had been pitched in the fields near the Italian Hall.

"No good," Vairo told Bapcat. "Feel how tense?" He rubbed his chest.

Bapcat felt it.

"Men in street, firemen from all over."

"Firemen?" Bapcat said.

"Tournament next three days," Frank Rousseau added. "Lotsa men stayed away from work this morning. Tomorrow, all the mines, they be shut tight."

"The miners are not all union men," Zakov said.

"Ones that aren't will sit back, see what happens," Vairo said. "Stay home, sniff wind, *si?*"

"*Daily Mining Gazette* saying one hundred fifty miners have been made special deputy by MacNaughton," Rousseau said. "He gave them badges, revolvers, billies."

Bapcat said, "Civilians can't deputize men. Only sheriffs can do that."

"Happen down Painesdale, paper say," Rousseau said. "Paper say Sheriff Cruse gives permission."

No wonder people are clearing out, Bapcat thought.

"How do special deputies differ from Cruse's minions?" Zakov asked.

Bapcat had no idea. "Can only say what paper say," Vairo said apologetically.

A man walked into the bar and shouted, "They got guns, and they're marching on Centennial! They're gonna shut down engine houses."

Bapcat understood that engine houses at mines contained the pumps that kept water out of the mines' deepest levels. Without pumps, many mines would fill with water and quickly become unworkable. Anyone trapped below would drown.

"Big Jim is making more deputies," the latecomer yelled. "He's gonna make every man take a side—no watchers, and no fence-sitters."

Which Big Jim? Bapcat wondered. MacNaughton or Cruse? Surely this referred to MacNaughton, who appeared intent on creating a private army. Bapcat left Vairo's, walked to the telegraph office, and sent a wire to Harju in Marquette:

> CHECKED SHERIFF'S SISTER'S PLACE NEAR CHASSELL. STOP. SAW SAME THING AS HERE, MAYBE MORE. STOP. STRIKE ON AS OF THIS MORNING. STOP. MINE OWNERS SOMEHOW HAVE AUTHORITY TO APPOINT AND ARM DEPUTIES. STOP. THINGS HERE TO GET COMPLICATED, BUSY. STOP. MAY NEED HELP. STOP. BAPCAT.

He read over the wire and added NOW after MAY NEED HELP, and gave it to the operator. He wished he could describe the kind of help he needed, but that was impossible. He had seen the chaos and fog of war in Cuba, and hoped this would not be like that. Once in a lifetime was enough of that.

Back at the saloon Zakov was holding court with some Frenchies from the Lake Linden Fire Company.

"Revolution cleans the air," he expounded, taking a dramatic deep breath. "Look at France, America—brothers in arms, where revolutions and forward-thinking men freed nations of the tyranny of leaders claiming God's appointment."

Bapcat took the Russian's arm and led him outside. "Out, now."

"*Ya vash rabotyaga, a ne vashi sert.* I am your dogsbody, not your serf," the Russian barked. Glowering, he pulled his arm away.

How much had the man consumed? "I want no trouble," Bapcat said.

Zakov grinned. "It is good you recognize I am a force to be reckoned with."

Bapcat punched Zakov on the chin and sent him down on his back in the street. He then loaded the drunk Russian into the Ford and asked a young passerby to turn the crank for him.

It is a sunny day. Why does it feel so dark?

50
Bumbletown Hill

THURSDAY, JULY 24, 1913

Bapcat answered a knock at the front door early the next morning to find a stranger, fortyish, blondish, wearing a black trilby. "Looking for a game warden," the man said. "Believe his name's Bapcat."

"That's me."

"J. W. Nara," the man said. *Faint accent: Finnish?* "I got a studio up Fifth Street. Take pictures. That's my brother Frank outside," the man said, pointing at a man in the automobile. There was a tall lump in the backseat, covered with canvas.

"What can I do for you, Mr. Nara?"

The man fidgeted, as if trying to decide something. "Show you something?" The man carried a fat leather bag.

"Come on in," Bapcat said, swinging open the door.

Nara looked around. Zakov nodded a silent greeting. Bapcat didn't introduce them. "Coffee for our visitor, Pinkhus Sergeyevich?"

"Yes, Your Excellency," the Russian said obsequiously.

"Russians," Bapcat said, earning the hint of a smile from the Finnish photographer.

Nara took a package out of his bag and carefully untied the string around it.

"I travel all around, you know, Copper Country, see this, see that, take pictures, make a record." The man placed a photograph in front of Bapcat. It showed a stack of headless deer.

"When was this?" Bapcat asked. "And where?"

"West of Ojibway, in the oaks on the high ground, two weeks ago," Nara said.

There was a cloudy haze over the pile. Bapcat touched the area with his finger.

"Flies," Nara said, and put another photograph on the table. This one showed eight wolves, each with a headless deer, standing over each carcass with what looked like conviction of ownership.

Bapcat called over the Russian, who bent down to look. "Anything jump out at you?" the deputy asked.

"Like the others, no heads. Wolves rarely bother with heads. I surmise they must have come upon all this meat, like finding treasure under the rainbow. Wolves do not arrange orderly piles like cordwood."

"Any people there?" Bapcat asked Nara.

"No, sir," Nara said. "Just what you see. We didn't touch nothing."

"This is why you stopped—to show me your pictures?"

"I would like to make picture of you and your servant," Nara said. "For history."

Bapcat said, "My partner, not my servant. Some other time, maybe; not today. You're on Fifth Street, you said?"

Nara nodded. "Okay, good. You keep pictures. I got more."

"I will. Mr. Nara, do you take pictures of miners down in their mines?"

"Sometimes, but operators sometimes nervous about this, you know?"

"But you spend a lot of time with miners."

"Yes, I guess."

"How long ago did you hear about the possibility of a strike?"

"Three weeks back, maybe. Certainly not before that."

"What about miner complaints before that—you know, men who were mad, or scared, nervous about accidents and all the people being killed below?"

"The men same like usual, you know, they don't like nothing to do with bosses."

Bapcat watched the man leave and rubbed his face vigorously. "God, we should be out in the bush tonight, but where?" he said out loud.

Zakov shrugged. "You didn't want coffee, you should have told me," he growled, then softened. "Thank you for making me more than your servant."

"Don't sass," Bapcat said.

"Why did you ask him about the possibility of the strike?" the Russian wanted to know.

"The way I see it, this deer-killing fandango didn't get thrown together overnight. It seems like a grand plan, like an army likes to have, you know; if our enemy does A, we will do B, or if the enemy does B, we'll do C."

Zakov blinked. "In Russia the only strategy is to overwhelm enemies with people, and who cares how many die—a hundred, a thousand, a hundred thousand, it doesn't matter. Soldiers are supposed to die."

"Your view of life is dark, Zakov."

"I lack a Widow Frei," the Russian grumbled. "*Mne puzhn zhenschina somnitelinoi nravstvenmosto I nizk oi tseroi.*"

"In English, please," Bapcat said.

"I need a woman of questionable morals and low price," Zakov explained.

Bapcat laughed. "You think the two things are linked?"

"Inevitably, in my experience. Are we venturing out this morning?"

"Let's stay near Allouez and Ahmeek and watch what happens. If we hear shots we'll investigate."

"You know," Zakov said, "I am performing my dangerous duties without pay."

"You get room and board, and you're fulfilling your civic duty."

"Who will bury me if said civic duty kills me?"

"The State, and me."

Zakov said, "The same as Russia, where they would dig large hole and fill it with dead."

"You will have your own grave," Bapcat said. "I promise."

"Ah, I had only to move thousands of miles to be buried alone. America is truly great."

Bapcat chose to ignore the Russian's sarcasm. "Let's collect our gear and see what's happening down the hill."

51

Allouez, Keweenaw County

THURSDAY, JULY 24, 1913

Unbearable humidity. Bapcat felt the sweat rolling off him. They parked near the bottom of their hill in the woods and watched a line of miners carrying signs, all of them wearing suits and ties, marching silently on both sides of the main street in town.

"*Lumpenproletariat*," Zakov muttered.

"What?"

"The underclass of Cimmeria."

"What in blazes are you talking about?"

"Ulysses ventured into a foggy, dark land where there was, according to Homer, never any light . . . a land of perpetual darkness."

"Ulysses—you mean General Grant?"

"No, the Greek adventurer."

"But it isn't dark. The sun's up. It will be a nice day."

"You are far too literal. I refer to Russia."

God, the man can be annoying. "We aren't in Russia."

"No, the czars here are capitalists, but will step on the uprising with no less savage force."

"Looks peaceful so far," Bapcat said. "Orderly."

"*Pentimento*," Zakov said. "This word means 'what lies underneath the painting our eyes can't see.' "

The man was impossible to understand sometimes. "Let's get closer to the mine," Bapcat said.

Later, in the shadow of Ahmeek's Numbers Three and Four Shaft Rock-house, there erupted what Zakov would refer to as a scuffle, but bottles and rocks quickly arced through the air from disorderly strikers toward non-strikers, who had dared cross the lines to report for work. Behind their salvos of projectiles the strikers swarmed forward, clubs in hands, wood and pipe; the morning was pregnant with hate, frustration, fear, and the slight metallic scent of blood.

"Do you miss war?" Zakov asked. "The immediacy of blood boiling, the impending clash of forces?"

"No." *My blood never boils.*

"When the moment of truth came, our charge to destroy the Japanese usurpers, I went the other way," Zakov said, "past our artillery, far to the rear, there to take a portion of accumulated treasure and pay my way out of all of that, to here and now, where I see mankind once again at its most basic, monstrous self. My heart is pounding, Deputy, pounding."

"We need to stay clear of this," Bapcat declared, as serious fistfights raged nearby. "This ain't our fight."

"You, who are sworn to uphold your precious laws and peace?"

"I'm sworn to specifically protect game, fish, and forests."

"A legalistic ribbon wrapped neatly around a moral conundrum," Zakov said, retreating gingerly.

"Talk less, act more," Bapcat admonished.

"Faced with *Gotterdammerung*, we turn tail?" the Russian asked. "My friend, I had begun to see you as a heroic figure, and now I see you as discriminating. Some might characterize this erroneously as cowardice, but I see a full measure of unanticipated wisdom, action being the last option, not the first."

"Shut up and get in the Ford," Bapcat said.

A man ran up beside the Ford, blood streaming from his head, a torn lip flapping, laughing demonically and shouting, "We've won, we've won! The owners have canceled the second shift!"

Zakov peeled the man's hand off the car and pushed him, sending the man bouncing along the side of the road like a marionette shorn of strings.

52

Red Jacket

FRIDAY, JULY 25, 1913

Harju had arrived the night before with a game warden named Sander Sandheim, out of Alger and Schoolcraft counties, a tall man, clean-shaven, stooped of back, hands raw and red, plate-sized.

"Eastbound trains are overflowing with people," Harju reported. "A conductor told us there's already been violence here."

"We saw it yesterday in Allouez," Bapcat said. "Fists, projectiles, and clubs, but no guns—so far. Word is going around Houghton that the National Guard has been called out by Governor Ferris—the entire state militia from armories all around the state, twenty-five hundred strong, including artillery, not just a company or two for show."

"We talked to some soldiers on the trolley," Sandheim said. "They'll set up strategically with companies in Ahmeek and Allouez, stretching all the way south to Painesdale below Houghton."

Bapcat wanted to talk to John Hepting, but guessed his friend's plate was full enough with the strike. *Guard coming to Keweenaw County? Not like John to ask for such help, even with incompetent deputies.*

The four men drove into Red Jacket first thing in the morning. The firemen's carnival tents were gone. Instead, men from all over the state were scurrying like ants to muster, all of them moving north, qualified martial law already imposed, saloons to close if full martial law got declared. Bapcat had no idea what *qualified martial law* was.

He took his companions to Vairo's and they stood outside the front entrance, watching the guardsmen scurry about. An army band was playing loudly, and soon a brass band came booming and tooting down the street, the usual martial music—heavy on percussion and blare, massive manufactured noise from the two units. The strikers were marching down the street in white shirts and dark ties, and the soldiers watching from the sidewalks kept their own counsel, each maintaining decorum. Some of the strikers carried signs: WE MEAN WHAT WE SAY: NO CAPITULATION.

Zakov stepped toward passing strikers. "How many of you speak English—one out of ten? Less?"

A man elbowed his way over to them. "Army's got instructions to shoot; no orders needed. They all got told this on the way up here. We have to be careful. They want to kill all of us!"

Bapcat and Harju exchanged glances and Zakov said, "In the czar's army, perhaps. Here, no. You Americans worship order from law, a thing that would be classified as fantasy everywhere else in the world. Draco the Greek would prosper in this country."

The men went inside. "John Hepting been around?" Bapcat asked Vairo.

"I ain't seen him for a long time. Too busy, I t'ink."

"Cruse?"

"T'ings too hot here for fat man. He sticks to cover till it's safe to be out," Vairo said with undisguised disgust. "Strikers beat hell out of a lot of company deputies, I heard. We seen none of Cruse's reg'lar deputies anywhere—so far."

Bapcat stepped outside again. The strikers were parading in single file on both sides of the street. At the front and between them a band marched, followed by women in flowing white dresses, red Western Federation of Miners sashes draped diagonally over their bosoms.

"Hey, Big Annie!" Vairo shouted at a giant woman carrying an equally outsized American flag, whipping and snapping in the morning breeze.

"Big Annie?" Bapcat asked.

"Anna Clemenc, wife of miner we don't see so much, on account he got no balls. Annike, she's tough gal; crossing her is a big mistake."

Bapcat watched the woman, over six feet tall, straight-backed, iron-jawed; other women clustered around her like peeplings, as did dozens of children, all the girls dressed in virginal white.

"This many women here yesterday?" Bapcat asked Vairo.

"I think not so many."

"Dangerous if it turns ugly."

"Dose girls hold dere own, you see," Vairo said.

"Do Russian women march like this?" Bapcat asked Zakov.

"Our Russian flowers protest on their backs with their legs spread, protest by prostration, an old and revered civic skill, taught by Genghis Khan and Napoleon."

The striking miners seemed wary of the soldiers' combined power.

"What would your Colonel Roosevelt do here?" Harju asked.

Lute Bapcat didn't know, and oddly enough found himself thinking of Jaquelle Frei, who had not yet returned from Chicago.

J. W. Nara came to the saloon and stopped as his brother marched on beside the demonstrators. Bapcat looked at the photographer, dressed in a black trilby, dark suit, string tie, and polished black shoes. *He looks like an undertaker*. The man's shoes were beginning to turn red from the dust raised by the marchers.

"You know Caledonia Car Camp Fourteen, up Gardner's Creek?" Nara asked Bapcat.

"I know it," Zakov volunteered.

"Night before last a woman named Norma Polo heard a whole bunch of shooting. Yesterday morning she went down to the creek for a look and found twenty dead deer, maybe more."

"Headless?" Bapcat asked.

"Some, I believe."

Bapcat grimaced. "You talk to her?"

"Let's just say that the information came to me. What I heard is, Norma saw a man named Arven Lammie with a shotgun."

"Someone she knows?"

"I don't know. Old Man Polo, Norma's grandpap, owns the camp. This Lammie fella, he used to work at Caledonia Car Camp Fourteen. Now he's a timberman at Ahmeek Seven."

"She's sure of the man's identity?" Harju asked.

"Supposedly she told him, 'Arven, why you out there shooting at night?' and he told her to mind her own business or he'd teach her a lesson."

"Ahmeek Seven."

"Yeah, bad bunch in that outfit, a blackguard captain named Madog Hedyn."

"Heard that name," Bapcat said noncommittally.

"Makes being mean a hobby," Nara said. "You might want to step easy around him."

"We appreciate the information, Nara. Will Miss Polo talk to me?"

"Girlie lives out there among all them loggers. They eat, work, sleep, drink, fart—not much on talking. She's happy to talk."

"Use your name?"

"Suit yourself."

"Hedyn," Bapcat said, drawing in a deep breath. "Arven Lammie," he said to Vairo. "Know him?"

"Russian-Finn," the Italian said. "Mean son of a bitch." Vairo slapped his hip. "Carry two guns, holster there, 'nother down his right boot. Kicked out of most saloons in Red Jacket. Don't hear where the man drink no more."

"Perhaps he's on the wagon," Harju offered.

"Snakes see, snakes bite; all snakes can do. God made them one way."

Harju grinned as the four men trooped out to the Ford.

"Something funny?" Bapcat asked.

"Got people comin' to you with information already. *Knew* you'd be good at this job."

"We don't have much to show for it."

"Patience, Deputy. Patience is the cardinal virtue for all game wardens."

"I thought it would be the ability to shoot fast and straight," Zakov offered.

53

Caledonia Car Camp Number 14, Houghton County

FRIDAY, JULY 25, 1913

When J. W. Nara had talked about a car camp, Bapcat had had no idea what the man meant, but now as he looked at four railroad cars sitting on a hundred yards of track that connected to nothing, the meaning seemed clear. Ladder steps led to a short platform where a woman stood smoking a small black cigar. She wore a pressed gray apron over a black dress, black leather shoes with low heels, revealing her ankles and nothing more. Her hair was packed in a bun, her hands red and rough.

"We're looking for Norma Polo," Bapcat said.

"You ain't alone," the small woman said, deadpan, with a growly, gravel voice. "I heard there was a time she was the most looked-for woman in the county." The woman smiled. "I'm her. Least, I usta be before my grandpa got me work up here in this bloody camp. Usta have beaus piled up in the parlor, could just take my pick, like a whole pack of yammering beagles. Now all I got is a buncha Bohunk Eye-tie jacks that'd rather make love to forty-rod than a woman with hot blood."

Zakov nudged Bapcat, who started to introduce him, but was cut off. "Pinkhus Sergeyevich Zakov," the Russian said, bowing gallantly. "We are most apologetic for interrupting your meditation."

The woman eyed him. "You Polack, Bohunk, Croat—what?"

"Russian," Zakov said. "Of esteemed ancestry."

"You like one a them tin stars the mine bosses got running around?"

"Czars," he corrected her gently. "I am a military man."

"Like a general or a skunk-low private?"

"I was advancing inexorably upward before the war injured me," he said, taking a step to show off his limp.

"J. W. Nara told us you found some deer," Bapcat said, cutting off Zakov.

"He ain't been around, J. W. hasn't."

"Maybe Arven Lammie said something to him," Bapcat tried.

"Don't make sense he would," the woman said, "but Lammie ain't got a whole lot of sense."

"Did you or didn't you find deer and see Lammie with a shotgun?"

The woman stared over Bapcat's head. "I seen what I saw and heard what I heard," she said. "You want to see them deer?"

"Your courage is duly noted," Zakov told her.

"I had twenty by my count, but the wolves got at 'em pretty good last night."

Fifteen minutes later they stood on the killing ground, and surveyed the carnage.

"You heard the shots?" Bapcat asked.

"I did, and I looked out at one point and saw lights, too, miners' lights—on their hats." She touched her forehead.

"Was Lammie wearing such a hat when you saw him?"

"Nope, but he had it in his hand, like he was trying to hide it. I reckon I seen enough of them in my life to know one when I see it."

"You talked to Lammie?"

"Don't nobody talks to that one, eh. Told me it was none of my business. I told him I work hard, and he and his buckos woke me from a fine dream, so I guess their shooting all night concerns me, all right."

"Did he threaten you?"

She chuckled. "Said he'd strip me, use me, and throw me down a hole. I told him if he tried, I'd be the last woman he touched." She held up a sawed-off shotgun, not more than a foot long. "This ain't no damn ladylike thirty-two. This here's for turnin' people to mush. I said, 'Arven, you no-good skunk, you got doubts what I'll do, you might want to talk with Old Man Polo, but he'll do the same thing I will, so I think you're shit out of luck, chum.' "

"Well put," Zakov said. "Eloquent, simple, and to the point—the zenith of pointed rhetoric."

"What do I care what some uppity Russian thinks?" Norma Polo countered.

"You should report Lammie's threat to the sheriff," Harju told her.

"This here's the woods," she said. "We don't need no lard-ass sheriff waddling around out here like an overstuffed tom turkey. We can take care of ourselves, thank you very much."

"Lammie's at Ahmeek Seven?" Bapcat asked.

"Timberman aboveground, topside, first cap'n's favorite pet. Lammie got in good with the Cousin Jacks, but not enough to get underground where the good pay is. Others trap him down there, he won't never come up again. Good Book says you reap what you sow, and I guess that's true."

"You know where he lives?" Harju asked.

"Across the street from Allouez Four, miners' house, though he don't qualify."

"What does a captain's favorite do?" Harju asked.

"Whatever the cap'n wants done, and don't be using the name of a particular cap'n out loud. The Indians say everything got long ears in summertime. And memories, too. Mostly, a favorite kisses his cap'n's arse."

"You'll let us know if you hear from him again," Harju said.

"Next time he shows, I'll blow his head off," she said.

"What we meant is, if you hear any more shooting?" Bapcat corrected.

"Goes on all the time in the deer fields and along the creek."

"All the time, and you never reported it?" Harju said.

She shrugged. "Like I said, we got our own law out here."

"Meaning?" Harju pressed her.

"Could come a day when a blind eye might be a good thing for a lawman to have."

"Silence as needed," Bapcat said.

The woman pursed her lips and nodded resolutely, lines forming where her mouth was drawn.

"Might I have the honor of calling upon the lady sometime?" Zakov ventured.

The woman said, "I ain't no lady, and you come sneaking 'round here, I'll blow your head off, just like Lammie. I don't like no Russians, silver-tongued dandies, or the like."

54

Ahmeek Location

SUNDAY, JULY 27, 1913

It had been a long, peaceful night on the hill, the usual lights and fires from mining operations gone black, giant mine pumps and engines silenced—"A preview of the end of the world," Zakov called it. After his rebuff by Norma Polo, the Russian had been quiet, and only seemed to revive early this morning when Bapcat began to replay events for Harju and Sandheim.

The facts were disjointed, only loosely connected by the seeming rash of dying deer.

Jerko Skander, poacher for pay, rat killer extraordinaire, claimed pay from mine operators for dead deer, perhaps more details to follow, but the man would go only so far in talking about his employers. Enock "Stumper" Hannula had admitted a similar arrangement, and Bapcat had arranged to have charges dropped so Hannula could be released to resume his work and act as an informant. But Hannula had disappeared, perhaps without a trace (or not). There was blood at his camp, but whose? Or had Hannula run away? No way to tell yet.

Fig Verbankick and Herman Gipp seemed incidental, though the Laurium Ice Company letting Herman go after Bapcat had talked to the owner-sales manager seemed more than a coincidence. The destruction and disappearance of what was said to be a perfectly functional ice wagon seemed suspicious and begged for follow-up.

Bruno Geronissi and his songbird killers appeared to have Sheriff Cruse's protection, at least for the moment, the reason far from clear because the sheriff seemed no friend of foreigners. If *Mano Nera* had a role in all of this, that role was far from evident or clear, but Bapcat had it in the back of his mind that the Black Hand was in some way an instrument of the mine operators and political power brokers. Maybe.

Bapcat plodded methodically through what they knew, or thought they knew, and Harju, fighting sleep, occasionally asked for clarification of this point or that. Deputy Sandheim made no pretense of participation and only halfheartedly fought sleep.

Only Zakov seemed entirely alert.

After multiple cups of strong coffee and Bapcat's voice straining to the brink of failure, Zakov fully came alive. "The month of April—this seems to be most relevant. This is when the deer-killing seems to have begun. There is evidence of long-standing conspiracy and preparation by mining capitalists. In Russia the czar's control people were his secret police, who in turn paid or extorted other citizens to spy on their neighbors, colleagues, and relatives."

"We ain't Russians," Harju said.

"Hear me out," Zakov said. "Those who have power will do anything to keep it. You cannot retain power without information about your enemies and their intentions, and the most effective way to do this is to find enemies who will take pay and betray those they pretend loyalty for."

"This is *not* Russia," Harju repeated.

"The mine operators and owners are the equivalents of our aristocrats and nobility. They will use spies. They have no other option. This is true across the world, and the mine owners have the sort of money needed to do this. In Russia, of course, the regime can go further: read correspondence, arrest without cause, all of that and more. In this regard, America is not Russia, but we are not talking about your country and its values; we are talking about a class and its values, the most important of which is to keep getting rich on the heads of the poor, and the mine owners will do anything to continue this."

"What are you driving at?" Bapcat asked. Hepting had already told him there were spies for the mine operators. "As I have said, the deer-killing appears to have begun in April. When did talk of a strike begin, and among whom? It seems foolish to strike now, looking into the mouth of the long winter. It would make more sense to strike in March or April and have summer and six snowless months ahead. Why now? And why not eat the deer they are killing? Who would want this?"

Bapcat was listening. The Russian's logic and questions made some sense. "Assume you're right," he said. "What's that to us?"

"The longer something exists in secret, the more vulnerable it is to discovery."

"The deer-killing is no longer a secret," Sandheim said, his only words in hours.

"We need evidence to connect the deer-killing directly to the companies," Bapcat said. "If it's true."

"We can't compete with money," Harju pointed out.

"Pay is an ambiguous and expansive topic," the Russian said. "The secret police began under Ivan the Terrible as the *Oprichnina*. They wore all black and carried the emblem of a dog's severed head. This gave way eventually to the czar's Third Department, a bland and ambiguous title, and this was in turn replaced by the *Okhranka*, the so-called Guard Department. All of these had the same charge: to become experts in what motivates men, be it money, power, women, other men, whatever."

"Other *men?*" Sandheim asked, coughing.

"When the business is survival, you use what opportunity presents," Zakov told them. "Staying alive isn't for the squeamish."

"Unless one is morally opposed to using poison to kill wolves," Bapcat reminded the Russian.

"Point conceded," Zakov said. "Nonetheless, mine holds."

"Do these Russian guards get physical and use force?" Harju asked.

"Yes—torture, beatings, starvation, isolation—every form of intimidation is employed."

"Not here," Harju said. "We have limits."

"Do the opponents know these limits?" Zakov asked.

"Their lawyers will," Harju answered.

"I don't have experience," Bapcat said, "but even lawyers may not have a specific notion of our limits. In most ways, game wardens are a new thing, yes?"

Harju nodded. "Relatively new, yes."

"We should find Mr. Arven Lammie," Bapcat said quietly, "and help him to decide what's best for his future: cooperation with us, or blind obedience to his mine bosses."

Which was how the four came to visit the house of Arven Lammie and were waiting for him when he came stumbling home drunk in the early hours of Sunday morning.

Zakov pushed a stick against the stumbling drunk's back and ordered him inside. The house was unexpectedly clean and well-furnished. Lammie was a stocky, wide-shouldered man with squinty, puffed eyes, his brain soaked in alcohol, not quite connecting.

Harju smacked him hard in the back of the head with a weighty sap and ordered him to lean forward and place his hands flat on the kitchen wall. Harju then slipped a hood over the man's head.

Bapcat tried to pull off the hood, but Harju grabbed his arm. "Trust me with this."

Zakov began to talk in Russian.

"What're youse spoutin', ya heathen foreign mongrel bastards!" Lammie shouted.

"You are killing the state's deer for money," Bapcat said, slapping the man's head again to get his attention. The slaps were not hard, only meant to frighten and disorient.

"I got nothin' to say to heathen scum."

Harju kissed him with the sap, buckled the man's legs, and ripped off the hood. He soaked his hair with forty-rod, and lit a match.

Lammie sputtered. "Go ahead, ya dunna have it in ya, laddie."

Harju touched the match to the man's wet hair and a plume of fire erupted. Harju immediately smothered the flame with the hood.

"Next time," he said, "your whole head goes. Who pays you?"

"I say a name I'm a dead man. I don't, I'm dead. It's Hobson's bloody choice."

"Now is now," Harju said. "I think you know that if we want the information, you'll give it up. The only issue is, how much pain and permanent injury you can absorb. And in the long run, if you don't talk, we can damn well convince your bosses you did, which would put you right back into the whole pickle brine again."

Lammie sighed, breathed deeply. "If youse're already knowin' the name, why do I have to say it?"

Harju sapped the man again and growled. "You don't get to ask the questions."

Silence from Lammie, now on the floor trying to lift his head. "We get out of here, I find you, youse're dead men," Lammie threatened.

Harju struck the man again. There was blood now. Two trickles threatening to become more.

"The name," Bapcat said, grabbing Harju's wrist.

"Hedyn," Lammie said. "You already know he's the boss."

Zakov pressed close to the man on the floor. "Norma Polo—if you threaten her, I will cut off your head like a deer."

Moments later they were outside the house and running. Zakov gimping along with his crutch, a combination of ineffective running and desperate hopping.

"Hedyn," Bapcat said, when they were a half-mile away.

"You know the man?" Harju asked, breathing heavily.

"We met once."

"You propose we go after him now?"

"What do you think?" Bapcat said.

"One of the operator's big men, is he?"

"That's how it seems."

"Best gather multiple witnesses and evidence to put together enough of a case that his employers will cut him loose to cut their losses. They always do when it's the survival of the organization against that of an individual."

Bapcat said, "Okay," but he was not so sure Hedyn would ever capitulate. "Can we find Hannula?"

"Is he even alive?" Harju asked the obvious question.

"Gentlemen," Zakov said dramatically. "Assume the most severe actions on the part of your foes. Your country is founded on ordinary people, *narodny*, and your system controls government excess on behalf of all. This is not so? You have corruption for a long time, collusion, deception, greed. People must decide who is the least evil. No mistake, these enemies we face will do whatever they think necessary to keep what they possess. Capitalists are fueled only by greed."

Bapcat looked at the Russian. "You think Hannula's dead?"

"*Nyet*, but I would assume so and look for his body."

Harju said, "This Russian's got a good head on his shoulders."

Zakov continued, "What exists here is not your ballyhooed democracy, but mass entrapment of foreigners serving the capitalistic monopoly and its greedy stockholders in defiance of law and fair play."

Bapcat admonished quietly, "We have the picture," and then he pushed Harju against a tree. "You ever treat a prisoner like that again, you'll get the same from me. You told me when we started out to avoid unnecessary harshness in making arrests."

"No arrest made here; we're just talking plain to the man. Belligerents like this, you have to calm them down to get their attention."

"I don't like it," Bapcat said.

"Your approval ain't my concern," Harju said.

55

Bumbletown Hill

SATURDAY, AUGUST 2, 1913

Deer continued to be killed and found headless, the meat left to rot. Bapcat, Zakov, and the two state deputies staked out likely areas and some nights chased after shots, but they caught no violators and made no arrests. The hours were long and sour, the payoff nil, prospects for success never high.

A weary and concerned Sheriff John Hepting dropped by the house on the hill and railed under stress. Citizens of Keweenaw County, he insisted, sympathized with the strikers, including his worthless force of goddamn deputies, all of whom had relatives on the strike lines.

"I told Cruse when he asked the governor to send the Guard, not to send them here, that we would be just fine, that bivouacs close to the county line would suffice, but some of the county board forged my signature and requested our mousy governor send troops into Ahmeek, Mohawk, and Allouez. I'll be goddamned if this is not going to blow up on us. I *told* the bastards! The air's full of blind hatred now. I've got locals and soldiers yelling at each other and making fists and threats, all that schoolboy crap, and the Finns and Italians are by damn far the most militant."

"Such behavior in these circumstances is *de rigueur*," Zakov observed, and the others stared at him.

A meat market at Centennial had been burned, and there was daily violence in Wolverine, arrests made. Two groups of businessmen had petitioned Governor Ferris, one group demanding guardsmen be removed, the opposing groups insisting they remain, despite the army deployment costing Michigan citizens more than ten thousand dollars a day.

Some stability from the army's presence had made it possible for the mines to deploy small workforces. Pumps were going again, water levels dropping, and the tens of thousands of rats first driven aboveground by rising water and no human food scraps to sustain them had begun to disappear back into the deep holes in the earth. It was also being whispered that at least two thousand miners and their families had fled the Keweenaw for safer pastures.

Hepting's opinion: The fighting and rock-throwing would turn to shooting, and then the real massacres would begin. Hepting had no word on Hannula, but promised to visit his wife again to check on her.

Early that day George Gipp showed up, smoking a cigarette and looking for coffee.

"You lost, George?" Bapcat asked.

"No, sir." He handed a small envelope to Bapcat. It read, "*The Widow Frei requests the presence of Trapper Bapcat's company, Noon, August 2, 1913.*"

"You read the note, George?"

"No, sir. She called the cab company, asked for me, and told me to hand you that note personally. She's at the Hotel Perrault on the top floor."

The note inside also said, "Make a payment; ask for me by name."

Gipp said, "I drove all the way up here from Lake Linden on her orders, my meter running the whole way. She said she'll double it if I fetch you back by noon. She said to fetch you right back, Deputy Bapcat," he said, holding open the door.

The Russian said, "The flamboyant wood tick Norma Polo, who resides in a railcar, rejects Pinkhus Sergeyevich Zakov, and the stunning Widow Frei summons you, and you wonder why I doubt the existence of a supreme being?"

"Maybe he's got a good sense of humor," Bapcat said, picking up his coat and .30-40 Krag. "Or maybe it's simply justice for former colonials."

"Mr. Zakov doesn't believe in *God?*" Gipp asked, his mouth agape.

56

Lake Linden

SATURDAY, AUGUST 2, 1913

The Hotel Perrault was a solid brick building on a corner from which you could see Lake Linden, which was no more than the upper end of Torch Lake, itself connected to Portage Lake, which led past the Dreamland Resort to Torch Bay. A turn south from there took you into Keweenaw Bay and Lake Superior.

"How's your team doing?" Bapcat had asked Gipp as they drove.

"Deputy, sir, I need to concentrate on driving if we're going to make it by noon," his young driver said. "No offense."

"Loosen up, George. You'll get your pay."

"I'm not tight, but a man has debts."

Man? "You're how old?"

"Eighteen," Gipp said.

"Stop gambling."

Gipp gawked at him like he was crazy, and when they pulled up to the hotel he shadowed Bapcat to the front desk, where a sleazy man with a bow-tie stood, arms crossed.

"Mrs. Frei," Bapcat said quietly.

"Whom may I say is calling?" the man asked.

"Deputy Bapcat." He plunked his rifle on the front desk and the man took a step backward. "I doubt you'll need that in this establishment," the clerk said.

"It goes where I go. What room's she in?"

"Please just go upstairs, sir."

"The fare," Bapcat said, but the officious desk man said, "Tut-tut," waved at the stairs, and held an envelope out to Gipp.

"Want me to wait?" Gipp asked Bapcat.

"The gentleman will notify your employer if and when your services are needed," the desk clerk said.

The last thing Bapcat noticed was a huge grin on Gipp's youthful face.

Standing at the top of the stairs was Jaquelle Frei, dressed in a silk frock, open to just above her navel and hanging precipitously at each shoulder, a long necklace of red stones, sparkling in the light, her hair pulled back and glistening, a red ribbon woven into her hair. "How fortunate, Mr. Bapcat. You are one minute early. I like men early in most of life's endeavors. Cat got your tongue, sir?"

The widow, he knew, favored plain clothes that covered as much skin as possible and almost reached the floor. Or no clothes at all. He had never before seen her dressed so . . . memorably. Zakov had once called her stunning, but even that word now seemed inadequate.

"I asked which room," was the best he managed to say.

"Not a room, sir. A floor, all of it just for us, each room as long as it pleases us, and pleasing us surely is on the agenda, *n'est-ce pas?*"

"I reckon," he said.

She smiled. "So quaint, so Western, so cowboy," she said, holding her hand out to him. "Come hither, sir."

Which he did.

• • •

One of the rooms had been configured as a parlor. The widow lay unclothed on a divan, a glass of red wine in hand, her hair ruffled and disordered, the red ribbon long gone.

"Ah," she said, offering him a cheroot, "I swear, you do know how to sink a woman into ecstasy. You have the mystic powers of the great Dionysus himself."

He did not like being compared to anyone, especially somebody he'd never heard of. "You were gone a long time," he noted.

"Thanks to you, but a settling smoke and my good Madeira will bring me back until we descend into our incandescent coupling fires again."

"I just meant you were out of town a long time."

"Nineteen days at the Palmer House," she said, "Not a stinky miner in sight, or smell. Did you miss me?"

"I was busy."

"Yes, the strike has been predictably ugly, and will no doubt be more so in the future, I fear. My God, Lute, were we ever in the Palmer House together, I am certain we would ignite another conflagration sufficient to raze that great city again."

He had no idea what she was talking about, other than the tone of her voice, which rarely changed when the mood for love swept over her.

"Your Russian's the real thing," she added, abruptly changing mood, voice, and direction.

"He told me he was a soldier in some war with the Japanese."

"More than a mere soldier, my dear. He was a colonel, a much decorated and celebrated officer with a reputation for high intelligence, refinement, and concern for his men—the latter, I'm told, being a particularly un-Russian viewpoint. Officers above looked down on him with suspicion; those below held him in awe."

"Claims he ran away."

"Perhaps, but only after his commanding general ordered a needless suicidal frontal attack, and Colonel Zakov calmly walked said general across the field at gunpoint until an enemy bullet killed the general and wounded him. His men then spirited Zakov away from the field to safety, and eventually out of Manchuria. He was known as king of the army."

"*Our* Zakov?"

"One and the same."

"How could you know this, Jaquelle?"

"I know a certain charming Russian *chargé d'affaires* in the Chicago consulate, who shared information with me." She took his chin in her hand. "Look at me, Lute. I am not that simple widow of Copper Harbor. I have connections, know things, can make many things happen."

"I see," he said.

"But you surely don't, dear Lute. The WFM didn't want the locals to strike. Not enough money in the national treasury, wrong time of year, nothing was right about it. They wanted to wait for a year to build the union war chest, but the locals had no patience. Fools! Calumet and Hecla by itself has more than a million dollars in ready cash, not to mention other deep and easily disposable assets. The owners wanted this strike, Lute. They schemed for it, had inside information and sources, urged it forward. They wanted it, and now they have it."

A million dollars? His mind couldn't process that many zeros. "Sources here?"

She nodded solemnly. "Here, Denver, everywhere. The miners can't make a move the operators don't know about before it happens."

"You mean they have paid . . . spies?"

She smiled. "What's money for if not to advantage one in life's great struggles. The mining scene looks crude and messy, but it's a money factory for a small number of East Coast investors, and everyone involved plays to win."

Bapcat considered what he'd heard and thought a long time before speaking. "And you have your own sources."

Her answer was a come-hither smile. "I tire so quickly of commercial banter," she whispered. "A woman of means requires diversions. Care to divert me, Trapper?"

Bapcat wasn't entirely sure what *divert* meant, but her look and tone of voice were unmistakable. "I'm looking for someone," he ventured, wanting to tell her his feelings for her were deepening, but unable to find the right words. Their relationship had begun as a convenience, but it was changing in ways he could not explain.

"You've found me, dearest Lute. Now shush and come hither."

57

Bumbletown Hill

MONDAY, AUGUST 4, 1913

"All hell's loosed," Zakov exclaimed when Bapcat returned from Lake Linden, depleted, certain that one more call to action by Jaquelle Frei would have crippled him. During one of the interludes between their spells of ardor he explained what was going on: Hannula missing, the link of Arven Lammie to Captain Hedyn, Jerko Skander the rat killer, how they'd roughed up Lammie in the night, the Italians and their birds, the attack on the house—everything.

Despite all this, Frei had evinced little interest in his business until he was dressing to leave. "Enock Hannula?"

"Yes."

She then dismissed him without further comment or discussion, and he had no idea what she was thinking.

Harju and Sandheim were with Zakov when he returned.

"Deputies had a hellacious fight at a Hunky boardinghouse," Zakov reported. "One General Abbey summoned operators to a meeting with union representatives, but they refused to come; said they wouldn't meet with the WFM under any circumstances. MacNaughton is supposed to have told a newspaperman he'd see grass growing in the streets before he'd meet anyone from the WFM, but you know how your newspapermen are with hyperbole."

Hyperbole. How can someone foreign-born know so many words in English?

Harju said, "Army patrols go out every two hours in Red Jacket, but from what we hear, the real frictions and troubles are here in the far north, and down in the far south ends of the copper range. Hell, the union's got some old woman named Mother Jones coming in today to stir the cesspool. Calumet and Laurium and Red Jacket have all put commercial enterprises on half-days, and local businessmen are in evil moods. Yesterday there was an anonymous threat that the Calumet Dam would be dynamited. The Guard deployed troops, but nothing happened except some rifle and pistol shots."

"*You* heard shots?" Bapcat asked.

"Me and Sandheim sat on different fields," said Harju. "The shots were mostly in daylight, and pretty much all around us. The Russian stayed here."

"I heard shots as well," Zakov said. "It's better, I think, to hear gunshots by day than by night."

"A bullet's a bullet," Sandheim countered.

"But in daylight you can intentionally hit or miss your target. At night, without light, every shot becomes random, and therefore uncontrolled."

Bapcat understood. "I would think most daytime shots are meant to scare."

"Or annoy," Zakov said. "In the light, they avoid killing. In the dark, they don't care."

"As when you were visited at night," Bapcat said.

"There was intent to kill that time," Zakov said through gritted teeth.

"We saw Sheriff Hepting near Mohawk," Harju said. "He said he directly wired the governor to demand troop removal from his county, but he doubts he'll even get the courtesy of a reply. What did you hear where you were?"

"I heard the operators have spies everywhere, paid informants."

Zakov perked up. "Just as I predicted. Did you hear shots where you were?"

Bapcat said, "No," which struck him as odd. Was Lake Linden exempt from the violence happening elsewhere, and if so, why?

"Hepting said he visited Hannula's wife. She's still not seen him; she's afraid, and packing up to leave the state," Harju reported.

"Without knowing her husband's fate?"

"She appears to be assuming the worst."

Hannula had now been free for twenty-eight days. "We're also going to assume he's dead and out of the picture," Bapcat told the others.

They all looked at him. "Hannula told Hepting and me that deer heads got dumped in a mine hole that attracts bats. He said a man called Cornelio Mangione paid him, but a Captain Tristan Shunk of Copper Falls visited Hannula in jail at Eagle River and warned him to keep his mouth shut."

No questions. He continued. "Shunk's a Kearsarge man, tough as hell, but Chilly Taylor claims Shunk walks in Captain Madog Hedyn's shadow."

Zakov's eyes flared. "I should have known," he said. "Everything seems to point to this Hedyn, Knight of St. George, madman of the worst kind, he who looks respectable but is despicable."

"*You* know Hedyn?" Bapcat asked the Russian.

"Only in whispered stories."

"If there's a bat hole, we should be able to find it," Sandheim offered.

"Better bet when the snows fly, if they keep dumping heads. I'd rather follow and catch someone with evidence in hand," Bapcat said.

Harju said, "One disposal site for so much activity has to be noticed by someone."

Bapcat suspected Harju was right. "I don't want us caught. I want us to find this place and appear there out of thin air."

"Abracadabra," Sandheim said.

"There are Arabs who are true magicians," Zakov said.

"Thank you, Colonel, that will be quite enough," Bapcat said.

The Russian smirked. "A colonel once, but no more. May I guess your source? More importantly, you might want to consider that bats hibernate in winter and don't come out again until spring," Zakov pointed out.

"You didn't know that?" Bapcat asked Harju, who nodded.

"Forgot."

"I never knew," Bapcat said, shaking his head and taking a deep breath.

"Something we need to know?" Harju asked.

"I want to hire Zakov as a deputy. Who needs to approve it?"

"I can do it, and swear him in. I'm comfortable with him."

"You've not asked me," Zakov said to Bapcat.

"*Would* you serve as deputy alongside me?"

"Will it be dangerous and poorly paid?"

"Yes," Harju and Sandheim said in unison.

"Is there a badge, and can we forgo any nonsense with a Bible?"

Bapcat nodded, and handed him his own badge. "Until we can get you your own," he added. Badges were not issued by the state of Michigan. Deputies could purchase their own, if they wished. Roosevelt had given Bapcat a badge as a gift and now that Zakov was a deputy they would need a second badge and Bapcat had in his mind to have the person who made his badge in Marquette make one for his colleague—at Bapcat's expense, and to give it to the Russian as a gift. Until he could make the arrangements, they would have to share and make due with one.

"Do we remain married?" the Russian asked Bapcat, who nodded.

"We do."

The Russian smiled and raised his right hand. "I do."

58

Red Jacket

WEDNESDAY, AUGUST 6, 1913

Bapcat thought it could be useful to go where strikers would congregate in numbers, so he and the Russian could watch, listen, and observe. Normally an ice hockey arena, The Palestra was teeming with people when Bapcat and Zakov made their way into the giant building and found a place to stand where they could see the stage. Bapcat saw George Gipp in the crowd, who winked at him.

A tiny woman with snow-white hair ambled across the stage to the rostrum. "I am Mary Harris Jones. I've lived eight decades on God's great Earth, and I have come here to raise hell on behalf of my brothers of the Western Federation of Miners."

The crowd murmured and she continued: "Now, boys, some people say to me, 'Mother, why don't you just stay home in your rocker and take life easy?' You know, we drove over here today from the train, and one of the soldiers your governor sent up here called me a mouthy old bitch. I told the boys to stop the car so I could knock that whelp in the green monkey suit on his arse, but the boys reminded me that all you folks were waiting."

There was enthusiastic applause this time.

"Instead of just that one soldier, I want you to help me kick the arses of General Manager MacNaughton and his money-grubbing minions and stooges. Yes, brothers and sisters, your mother is an agitator—and damn proud of it! Together we are going to win this righteous fight, and ultimately bring justice to this place. If your mother says it's so, believe it!"

The crowd erupted in wild celebration, screaming, waving placards, whistling, dancing around.

When the cheering subsided, the woman said, "Don't get me wrong, friends. I want you all to find peace and fairness and contentment, but more than that, I want to raise hell with the mine owners, and I want those bastards to know that my only home will always be wherever there's a fight."

She paused to catch her breath and her voice went up. "As a girl in Ireland I watched soldiers of Queen Victoria march past my home with severed Irish heads on their bayonets."

The crowd hushed, waiting for more.

"They hung me dear father and dropped his body in front of the house."

A long howl of sympathy and anger ripped through the crowd. "And that very day, I swore to fight for little fellas everywhere, and to fight the bastards with bayonets and bullets if that's how they want it!"

The resultant cheering and chaos lasted for ten minutes before tapering off, and all the while the little woman in black stood on stage, smiling innocently.

"In Russia, the czar's men would put a bullet in her bonnet before she left the stage," Zakov said.

Mother Jones held her hands over her head like a triumphant fighter, and waved for the audience to be quiet.

Bapcat was astounded by the number of women and small children in the ice hockey arena.

"No one-man drills," Mother Jones shouted, and the crowd took up her chant, roaring.

"The poor dig copper and die while the mine operators play golf!" she yelled.

"Golf!" the crowd chanted.

"You don't need a vote to raise hell, ladies!"

"Hell!" the crowd roared.

"I'm told the operators said they would blow my brains out if I came here—that they didn't want to see me." The crowd awaited her next words. "Well, here I am. I didn't come to see them; I came to see and find solidarity with you!"

The cheering was louder than anything Bapcat had ever experienced.

"A lot of you here are immigrants, new to America, just as I once was. You came here dreaming about streets of gold and opportunities without limit. Instead, you found streets of mud and holes a mile underground. The mines kill and maim you every year, and the operators treat you like slaves—no, worse—like pieces of equipment. This country fought a war to free the slaves, but here you are still shackled by the greed of insatiable capitalists."

The crowd buzzed. "The Russians freed their serfs just as our own beloved Abraham Lincoln freed all slaves, black, white, red, green, short, tall, Greek, Italian, Finn, Austrian, Slovenian, Croatian, Irish—not just *some* slaves, but *all* slaves. *All slaves are free!*"

The crowd roared and surged and Mother Jones continued, screaming, "Brothers and sisters, we are strong united, weak alone! Every inch of progress made by man has come at a cost, often the ultimate cost. We have here injustice on an unprecedented scale. I ask you now to stay the course. Stay the course!"

"Stay the course!" the crowd thundered. "*Stay the course! Fight fire with fire!*"

The audience chanted on, and Bapcat felt the building trembling under the noise and size of the crowd. As he studied the red-faced celebrants he saw Fig Verbankick jumping up and down in the front rank, screaming, his face flushed red, eyes bulging, veins sticking out on his scrawny neck. Bapcat nudged Zakov and pointed at the gnome-like man.

"Born follower," Zakov said dismissively.

Verbankick seemed to be screaming the same word over and over, but Bapcat couldn't quite make it out, and after a while, he looked around the arena to see what was happenng. He saw people screaming and demonstrating with signs, and waving placards, and breaking into smaller groups.

After the rally, the crowd followed Mother Jones en masse as she rode in a car to the union hall, two thousand people cheering, clapping, and marching behind her in two lines, on both sides of the street. Right behind her car marched Big Annie Clemenc, carrying her giant American flag, which snapped in the breeze like a bullwhip.

Soldiers silently watched the demonstration. But eight C & H special deputies rode behind the marchers on black horses that whinnied nervously and dropped horse apples on paved streets. The deputies wore dark navy peacoats, dark pants bloused in knee-high boots, star-shaped badges over their hearts. None of their caps matched. The horses' shoes echoed hollowly on the paved streets.

"Remarkable country," Zakov said. "In Russia, the army would shoot demonstrators without discrimination."

"We're not savages," Bapcat said.

"No, you're slaves," the Russian said. "Did you not hear what the *babushka* had to say?"

"You think the strikers can win?"

Zakov sighed. "Not the slightest chance. It's summer, and warm now. Let winter come and see what happens. Wars are often lost in winter. Ask Napoleon."

"You escorted a general to his death," Bapcat said, changing the subject suddenly.

"You're misinformed, Lute. I escorted a butcher to a hero's end he did not deserve. What more could a true general ask?"

"The stories you told me were untrue."

"Only in facts, not spirit."

"You cut some fine distinctions."

"In time you may find the wisdom to emulate my ways."

59

Mohawk, Keweenaw County

MONDAY, AUGUST 18, 1913

John Hepting and Deputy Taylor met them at the general store in Mohawk. The day was cool and foggy. "Seeing some leaves start to change," the sheriff said. "Anything yet on Hannula?"

"Nothing," Bapcat said.

Hepting said, "I went to see his wife, but she's gone, cleared out. The neighbors don't know where."

There had been no word from Jaquelle since Lake Linden, and Bapcat reminded himself that perhaps her connections were not as muscular as she had made out, or maybe he had misunderstood. It had been a little more than two weeks since he had seen her at the Hotel Perrault.

"You hear about Seeberville?" Hepting asked.

"Conflicting details," Bapcat said.

"Croatian boardinghouse, and five fellas from there marched over to South Range to check on strike matters, and drink some beer in a park. When they headed home, two men stopped at a candy store, and when they came out, they decided to take a shortcut to catch up with the others, but the route was past Chapin Mine's Dry House, which is off limits to anyone without an official pass. The soldiers stopped patrolling the day before, so it was special deputies who took over and challenged the men."

"*Company* deputies?" Bapcat asked.

Hepting nodded. "A deputy challenged the men, who basically told him to go to hell and kept walking. Then a Waddie showed up."

In the newspapers Sheriff Jim Cruse had repeatedly denied hiring any Waddies—Waddell-Mahon agency strike-breakers—from New York.

Sheriff John Hepting said, "The guard told the Waddie what had happened. One of Cruse's real detectives arrived and got his dander up, enlisting more Waddies and special deputies. Another Cruse deputy and the whole mob joined forces, caught up to the two men, and tried to grab them, but the pair fought, escaped, and went into the boardinghouse. Some soul came outside the house, hurled a tenpin, and hit a Waddie, who took out his revolver and shot the owner of the boardinghouse, who happened to be outside at the wrong moment. All sorts of shooting commenced from the operators' men. The mob left without checking for wounded or dead, and later the Waddies and deputies all swore they'd been ambushed, but no guns were found in the house. Two dead. The prosecutor ordered Cruse to take badges from all those involved, but Cruse has refused. Where *were* you fellas yesterday?" he concluded.

"Boots in the dirt," Bapcat said. "The usual."

Said Hepting, "Yesterday the strikers held a rally at the Palestra. There were five thousand mourners and strike supporters. They brought a train through all the towns from Painesdale to Red Jacket. It was one heckuva show. Finnish band, little blonde girls in white dresses carrying bouquets and wreaths, American flags draped in black. One of the dead men was supposed to get married, so ten girls in white with bridal veils marched behind the hearse, like virgins on a death march."

"Arrests?"

"Two Cruse deputies on Saturday. But the Waddies have disappeared. I heard they sent word through an emissary that they'd surrender if charges got lowered, but the prosecutor refused."

"With blood in the water, the sharks will feed now," Zakov said.

"You fellas making *any* headway?" Hepting asked.

"Nothing yet," Bapcat said.

"The mines got their pumps running again," Deputy Chilly Taylor volunteered.

Harju said, "We heard there was a compromise on that with the strikers. Fire departments depend on the nearest mine pumps for their water. The fire at the meat market was cited as an example of what can happen without water access. Strikers depend on the stores, and I guess they decided it made sense to compromise."

"Any compromise in this thing is a loss," Hepting said. "The operators are dead serious."

The mine operators' iron resolve supported what Jaquelle had told him.

Taylor asked, "Why is it mines have hoses going out all over the place, stuck in the ground?"

"What?" Bapcat asked.

"I just said, all those hoses we're seeing."

Bapcat had no idea what the man was talking about and had a more pressing question. He turned to Hepting. "You think the charges will stick with the Waddies and Cruse's people?"

"Would never bet against Tony Lucas," Hepting said. "Besides, he hates Cruse's guts." Lucas was Houghton County's prosecutor.

Hepting headed north on foot, Harju and Sandheim east toward the Traprock River country, and Bapcat, puzzled by Taylor's odd comments about hoses, took Zakov with him to find a pump house, to see what they could see.

Leaving the Centennial pump house, they noticed hoses stretching from the center like legs of an octopus. The two men sat on a boulder and lit cigarettes and said nothing. Bapcat noted there were no trees in the immediate area. Off in the distance he saw a boy with a rifle. The two men ran after the boy, yelling for him to stop. He came back reluctantly and walked toward them, eyes down.

"Game wardens, boy," Zakov said.

"I don't see no badges," the boy retorted defiantly

Zakov flipped up a collar to reveal their shared badge.

"Hunting?" Bapcat asked.

"Not 'round here," the boy said. "This here's like the Suharry Desert."

"A desert has no water," Zakov corrected.

"And it don't got much wildlife neither," the boy said, "like rabbits, foxes, woodchucks, even squirrels. The mines got people cuttin' down all the trees on their property. They run hoses down all the animal dens," the boy said.

"The water will be good for fish," Zakov said.

"Could be if mines didn't dump big cans of white stuff in creeks."

"White stuff?" Bapcat asked.

"Barrels full. Got dead fish floatin' everywhere."

"Which creeks and what's in the barrels?"

"Upper Seneca, Quince, Brown's Run—all the little ones. Don't know what the white stuff is, but it sure kills fish fast."

"Show us?" Bapcat asked the boy.

Quince Creek was no more than a trickle, clogged with dead, rotting brook trout.

Zakov keened, "Evil ditches, Dante's eighth circle of Hell."

"Have you seen eagles eating the fish?" Bapcat asked the boy, trying to ignore his Russian partner's ravings.

"Ain't nothing eats such shit," the boy said bitterly.

"Who dumps this stuff?" Bapcat asked.

"Who do you think?" the boy answered. "The mines."

"You've seen them?"

"No they do it only at night."

Zakov knelt by the stream, sniffing. "An acid, perhaps."

"Which kind?"

"I doubt that it matters to the fish," he said.

"Deer, dens, rivers—they're trying to kill everything," Bapcat said. "We need to move around, see how widespread this is. What's your name?" Bapcat asked the boy.

"Jordy Kluboshar," he said. "I am a proud Croatian."

"How long has this been going on?"

"Past week or so," the boy said.

Zakov said, "Good for you, Jordy Kluboshar. Run along now. And thank you for your help."

"You men gonna do something to help us hunters?" the boy asked.

"We hope to," Bapcat said.

"Can't eat hope," the boy countered, and marched away.

"Should we inform our colleagues?" Zakov asked.

"When we know more."

"Come winter," Zakov said, "this will have severe consequences."

"I expect that might be exactly the plan," Bapcat said.

60

Baltic, Houghton County

TUESDAY, AUGUST 19, 1913

Bapcat and Zakov checked mine properties and creeks all the way south to just north of Hancock, and saw nothing resembling the disruptions in the northern reaches of the strike zone. They crossed the ship canal into Houghton and worked their way south through Atlantic Mine, South Range, and Trimountain, to the village of Painesdale, where they found numerous guards patrolling the streets. The weather was sweltering again. Last week thermometers had climbed above 100 degrees, and tonight felt like 90. Rather than take a room in a hotel or boardinghouse, the two men found a field near the Pilgrim River, parked, and put their bedrolls under the Ford.

Bapcat said, "When I was a boy at the orphanage, we sometimes went camping by the Pilgrim River. It was rich in brook trout. I remember a lot more trees then."

"Mines require timber shoring," Zakov reminded him.

"Shoring requires large timber, not the small trees that were here."

"Time passes; trees grow, and some die. Like people," the Russian said philosophically.

"They don't grow to the size mines need—not in that short a time. The big trees come from far up the Keweenaw."

"Do you ever think about *food?*" the Russian asked.

"Not the way you do."

"I am hardly a glutton."

"We'll find food in the morning."

Bapcat could smell death, and knew the Russian smelled it, too. At first light they saw the source, and both men lost their appetites. Dead fish were everywhere in the discolored water. Trees were gone, and up the road at the Baltic Pump House, hoses were stretched out into the surrounding area, flooding animal dens, turning the entire area into soft red muck.

"We see the octopus," Zakov said. "In military terms, this is a siege we are looking at."

"I don't follow."

"Is there more violence and disorder at the extreme ends of the strike area because of sabotage, or more sabotage because strikers on the ends are more militant and violent? Is it better to weaken your enemy through starvation and thirst than through direct fighting? The question is not entirely rhetorical."

"I don't know," Bapcat said, having only a vague notion of what a rhetorical question might be, and reminding himself how badly he needed more education. *You can't talk to people if you don't understand them.* In some ways, his own native English sometimes seemed like a foreign language to him. Such deficiencies notwithstanding, he knew that even though his ability to think and figure things out was raw, it was solid. "Twenty-eight miles," he said. "And not all Calumet and Hecla properties."

Zakov nodded enthusiastically. "The word is *conspiracy*," the Russian said, "and there is little doubt that everything that happens grows directly or indirectly from what MacNaughton thinks and wants."

"Could be it's time we visited the man," Bapcat said.

"A military man learns that a well-executed ambush leaves fewer casualties and doubtful outcomes than direct frontal assaults can ever deliver."

"We should wait?"

"A mentor once advised me to never ask a question to which I did not already have the answer."

• • •

The Ford was parked near a branch of the Pilgrim that ran south from the west side of Baltic. Two deputies in dark coats on black horses approached, one of the horses nickering and snorting, and acting unruly. Both men carried long wooden clubs.

"You fellas got business here?" one of the men challenged. He had light hair and a bushy mustache.

"Our business is not your business," Zakov told the man.

"Says who?" the man said with a chirp as he dismounted, only to find the barrel of Bapcat's .30-40 pressed under his chin.

"Mr. Krag says," Bapcat growled to the man.

Zakov turned his lapel to reveal their badge.

"Sorry, boys; it would have helped if you'd shown a badge before," one of the horsemen said.

"Help is not in our brief," Zakov said.

"What the hell's that supposed to mean?" one of the company special deputies asked.

Bapcat wondered, too. "It means, keep out of our way and our business," Zakov said. "Our badge comes from state authority, not some damn trumped-up company costume game."

"Stay out of your damn way, or *what?*" one of the men challenged.

Bapcat poked the man's throat hard with the rifle. "Figure it out."

The man stepped back. "You can't challenge a deputy sheriff," the man said, glaring.

"Or what—you'll call the Waddies in to hold your hands?" Bapcat spit back. "You're not lawmen; you're night watchmen in costumes."

"Maybe we'll see about that," the man still on horseback said.

"Not here, and not now," Bapcat said. "We hear that the style down this way is bushwhacking houses and unarmed citizens."

The man glared, but remounted.

"Don't worry, Tom," the other deputy said. "They'll get theirs."

Zakov said, "Company deputies are a disgrace to all legitimate lawmen. You should be ashamed of this charade."

"You can bet Sheriff Cruse will hear about you two," the first special deputy said.

"Good," Bapcat said. "Tell your mamas too."

The men gone, the game wardens got into their truck. Zakov said, "Tell your mamas?"

Bapcat shrugged. "You're the clever one. It was all I could think of."

Both men began laughing.

61

Mandan, Keweenaw County

THURSDAY, AUGUST 21, 1913

Young Gipp arrived at 5 a.m., knocking urgently on the front door, and when Zakov answered, he pushed past him to find Bapcat. "Widow Frei wants to see you."

"Now?" Bapcat asked.

"She called my boss and he sent me to fetch you."

"Double if we hurry?"

"Yessir.

Bapcat took his rifle and a small bag with a shirt and put them in Gipp's cab.

"Where to?"

Gipp handed him a piece of paper with directions scratched in pencil. The destination showed only an "X," but, knowing the area, he was pretty sure he could decipher the destination as the Mandan Nimrod Club.

"You know the place?" Gipp asked.

"It's close to all my old traplines," Bapcat said, wondering what shape his old camp was in, and feeling a sudden and unexpected wave of sadness for having left the trapping life. "A man from Cleveland used to own the club," he told Gipp. "With a full section of land."

"You've been there?"

"Only seen the house from the woods."

"A game warden trespassing?" Gipp asked teasingly.

"Wipe the smile off your face, George. That was *before* I took the oath."

On a sharp curve between Allouez and Ahmeek, the Ford's windscreen shattered, raining glass on Bapcat, who heard a thump in the seat behind them. Gipp lowered his head, hunched his tall frame over as best he could, and sped up as Bapcat racked a round into the chamber of his rifle.

"Was that a shot?" Gipp yelled.

"Yes, George."

"Holy moly! What do we do?"

"Keep driving. If they wanted to hit us, they would have."

"I almost ran us off the road," Gipp said.

Bapcat knew this wasn't true. Gipp had driven on as if nothing had happened, calm the whole time. *The boy has great inner strength.*

"I heard some shots south of Allouez, too," Gipp said. "But nothing *that* close. Who's doin' the shooting?"

"Either side, both sides," Bapcat said. "Outside agitators; it's impossible to know, and it doesn't matter who's shooting if you get hit."

"The strike's getting *crazy*," Gipp said.

Bapcat didn't have the heart to tell him the situation would undoubtedly get worse as winter settled in.

The road to the club stretched south from the Mineral Range Road to Copper Harbor, and veered west to a ridge near Clear Lake. The Montreal River lay a half-mile south of the club, over several steep, razorback ridges and a dark, almost-impenetrable cedar swamp.

Gipp pulled up to the sprawling log building. Widow Frei came out and handed him an envelope. "Tomorrow morning at eight, George," she said. "You'll come and fetch me to Copper Harbor and then take the deputy wherever he needs to go. You have the key to my Copper Harbor store in the envelope. The upstairs apartment is yours. Help yourself to the food."

Frei looped Bapcat's arm and watched Gipp drive away.

"What happened to the windshield?" she asked.

"Bullet," he said. "You know the owner of this place?"

"Intimately," she said, steering him inside. The interior was large, but not fancy, a well-equipped hunting club like those he'd once worked for in the Dakotas.

"Sit down, Lute," the widow said, waiting for him to sit down on one of the chairs. Then, "Hannula's gone."

"Gone," he echoed.

"Dead, Lute."

"You know this how?"

"Never mind that. I know he's dead, and that's what you needed to know."

"You know more than you're saying."

"A lot more, but I don't wish to follow Mr. Hannula, nor do I want you to emulate him."

"I can protect you," he said.

She laughed out loud, and caught herself. "I beg to differ. Your protection did Mr. Hannula no good that I can see, and the window in your Ford got shot out."

"We did it the way Hannula wanted," Bapcat said defensively.

"Good. Then you won't mind doing things my way as well, and if something goes wrong, it will be on my head, not yours."

"You got me all the way out here to tell me Hannula's dead?"

"You asked me to find out, did you not?"

Why—and how—did she always find a way to twist him?

"I just meant that a message would have been enough."

"But a note wouldn't take care of me, dearest. I need you here—in the flesh."

"Working off the debt."

"However you wish to characterize it." Frei sucked in a deep breath. "Do you have any idea what you've latched on to? *Do* you?"

"We know," he said.

"I seriously doubt you do, Lute. MacNaughton and his cronies, both in Boston and here, are serious men. Dangerous men."

"We're also serious," he countered.

"You're professionally serious," she said. "They're kill-the-opposition-for-money serious, huge stakes, millions of dollars. *You* follow the rules, Lute, and serve the rules. They don't, because money can make its own laws and change them when and how money wants and directs. The only law they recognize is the law they pay for, and which directly benefits them and their investments. They own miners' houses, churches, schools, the library, the police, politicians, newspapers—all of it, and more. In their minds a simple game warden lacks gravitas," she said. "They don't even recognize you as a serious foe."

"They killed Hannula?"

She stiffened. "I did not say who killed him. I said only that the man is dead."

"Two plus two," Bapcat said.

"No, Lute. Don't be so damned literal. In their game they define the sum and others have no say. If they focus on you, they'll treat you as no more than a minor impediment, nothing more than a pesky fly to be swatted dead."

"I took an oath," he said.

"Quit the job and join me, dearest. Let me take care of you," she countered, in a tone he had never heard before.

"I'm not the quitting kind," Bapcat said.

"You have to trust me, Lute. You really do."

"I do," he said.

"This thing you're in, it can't end well. It just can't."

He stood in front of her. "The mines are cutting down trees, pouring water into animals' dens, poisoning streams to kill fish, paying people to kill deer to deny meat to hungry miners," he said. "The operators are trying to crush the strikers' resistance with starvation. If they go out, they can't use company stores, and they won't be able to live off the land because there won't be anything left to live off of."

She looked at him and folded her hands in her lap. "You have evidence of all this—witnesses?"

"Hannula knew."

"Hannula's gone," she reminded him.

"It's happening at both ends of the district, where there are more foreigners and stronger support for the union. In the middle, miners seem more in tune with the owners." Zakov had offered these observations, which Bapcat decided were accurate.

"That's opinion, not evidence," she said.

"You're not a lawyer."

"For God's sake, Lute, neither are you, and I suspect you can barely read."

"I don't have to read like a lawyer or schoolteacher to know what I see, and to be able to tell right from wrong."

"Sometimes insisting on right *is* wrong."

"You sound like the Russian."

"Good. Perhaps he and I can persuade you to employ some discretion and common sense."

"And if I don't?"

Jaquelle Frei pursed her lips: "I prefer not to consider that path." She stood up and held out her hand. "Come, there is a lovely back porch. I am cooking dinner for us tonight, and we'll talk more when we are more relaxed."

"I damn well intend to see this thing through," Bapcat declared. "Wherever it takes me."

She sighed. "I pray it doesn't take you where Hannula went."

"You know more than you're telling me."

She smiled. "Alas, I suspect this will always be so."

The night, he noted, seemed to pass with far less urgency than in the past, and he was not sure why. Over coffee the next morning, he gave her a hard look.

"You're close to the owner of this place? He just lets you borrow it?"

Frei tilted her head and smiled. "Are you *jealous*, dearest?"

"No, I'm just asking a simple question." *Not entirely the truth, but it was all she needed to know.*

"Then you shall have your answer. I am as close as one can get to the owner, and have been for a long, long time."

Bapcat gulped and went silent.

George Gipp knocked on the door at precisely 8 a.m. All the way to Copper Harbor, Widow Frei was friendly but reserved, having put on her public face. At the store she gave Gipp another envelope and he returned her key. She whispered something to him and he said, "Yes, ma'am," and drove away.

Bapcat didn't look back.

Around Phoenix, Gipp looked over at Bapcat. "She said to tell you she's the owner, and she said you'd understand."

Bapcat shook his head and laughed, as much from relief as from the humor of it. He wanted to think about her, but his mind was locked on acid in Quince Creek. The boy Jordy Kluboshar had asked, "Are you fellas gonna do something to help hunters?"

"Where to?" Gipp asked.

"Back to the hill."

Bapcat noticed a large number of blue-coated special deputies and National Guardsmen all together in Mohawk as they drove through, and wondered why.

62

Bumbletown Hill

FRIDAY, AUGUST 22, 1913

A nervous man called Bartlow came to the house late Friday morning to report a riot under way in Allouez, and the fact that no special deputies or army men were there to restore order. Bapcat had doubts about intervening. Harju and Sandheim had not come back last night and were out patrolling somewhere. But after some urgent pleading, Bapcat and Zakov followed the man down the hill into the village, which initially looked quiet.

Soon they saw two men hurrying to catch the electric; they were being chased down the street by a dozen women and girls wielding buckets and brooms, swatting wildly at their prey, who tried to defend themselves using cylindrical lunch pails as shields. The swats from the women eventually knocked them to the ground and the women swarmed, raising a scream that made the hair stand up on Bapcat's arms and the nape of his neck.

Paulie Pelkow, who managed a small boardinghouse in town, stood on the side of the street, watching. "You fellas gonna help them boys?" he asked Bapcat, who felt no need to answer. He had already decided the two men were not in any real danger and were on their own.

The victims missed their trolley and fled north on foot, their distaff assailants breaking off the chase. When the women marched triumphantly back, Bapcat realized the buckets they carried contained shit.

Zakov asked one of the women where she had acquired her ammunition, and she laughed at him. "The one thing we got plenty of hereabouts is privy holes."

"What is this tactic supposed to accomplish?" Zakov pressed.

"We like to see scabs run with tails betwixt their legs. Some men *they* are," she said. Zakov thanked her and stepped back to Bapcat. "Pyrrhic," the Russian said. "A tactic without value, an outcome without significance."

Bapcat had a different view. "You think the other scabs will let those men into the dry house, much less into the cage to go down into the mine?

Those men will have to clean up and get other clothes. Once shifts start they don't take late arrivals underground."

Zakov said, "You loathe everything mining. I hear it in your voice."

"I have nothing against miners; it's the black holes in the ground and the operators I have little use for."

Harju was making coffee when Bapcat and Zakov got back up the hill.

"Anything last night?" Bapcat asked.

Harju shook his head. "Nope, cold ground."

Sandheim came in from outside and yawned.

"Hannula's dead," Bapcat told his companions.

"How—when?" Harju asked.

"I know only that he's dead."

The four men stood silently until Bapcat said, "I've been thinking."

Harju swigged coffee. "We're listening."

"I want to spread the word among the miners that they won't need a license to hunt deer this year, and that we won't enforce the shortened season. In fact, I want us to encourage them to go out and hunt, starting immediately."

"You have no authority," Harju said. "We can't do that."

"I don't want to change the law, Horri. I just want to ignore it this year. How will Jones and Oates react if we ask them?"

"Easier to ask forgiveness than permission," Harju said. "Oates and Jones are dedicated but practical men. They'll understand, but they shouldn't concern us. The mine operators' reaction is what concerns me. Have you considered that?"

"I *want* them to pay attention to us," Bapcat said. "They want to starve people this winter. This can help prevent that."

"You're taking sides," Harju said.

"I'm for the things we protect. The operators think they can do whatever they want, and I want them to stop and wonder what we're doing, and what we might do next about their plans."

"This could be putting targets on our backs," Sandheim said.

Zakov grinned. "In war, the combatant who can do what the other side doesn't expect is likely to shift the fortunes and outcomes of the conflict. Even better is to do something the other side cannot conceive of."

"Such as lawmen encouraging people to act unlawfully?" Harju said.

"It's sure not something I'd think of," Sandheim said.

The Russian looked at Bapcat and bowed. "Unexpected, sneaky, underhanded, brilliant."

"How do we spread the word?" Harju asked.

"I have some ideas along those lines," Bapcat said.

"Why ain't I surprised to hear that?" Harju asked.

Bapcat looked at them. "We may all lose our badges over this."

Zakov said, "Not our badges as human beings.

63

Red Jacket

MONDAY, AUGUST 25, 1913

Bapcat waited in the Model T down the street from where Cornelius Nayback rented a room. When the man came hurrying past, Bapcat jumped out and steered him by the arm behind a nearby lilac hedge. The blood immediately drained from Nayback's face.

"I told you we can't be seen together," Nayback whined. "It's not safe."

"It's almost dark."

"What do you want?"

"Seen Cap'n Hedyn lately?"

"We don't grace the same social circles," Nayback said.

"Not even wrestling?"

"There are exceptions. Don't make more of that than what it was."

"Tell me what it was."

"There's a wrestler at the high school. Hedyn's interested in seeing an exhibition, schoolboy against a Cousin Jack. I told him the boy's too young to wrestle grown men."

"He accepted this?"

"Not happily."

"We need your help."

"I can't imagine what I could do."

"If we have certain handbills printed, could you see to their distribution?"

"Handbills about what?"

"Hunting," Bapcat said. "There's information we need to get out to people as fast as possible."

"When?"

"Get them to you next week, before the last day of August, put them out Labor Day?"

"You can't bring them here—not to my place."

"Where, then?"

Nayback pointed at the truck. "Spiro's Blacksmithy in Tamarack, west side of Tamarack Hills, right after dark, August thirtieth, I'll open the door. Pull your Ford inside, unload it, and get out."

"Right after dark isn't specific enough," Bapcat said. "Let's make it ten. It will be dark by then."

"All right, ten. I have to go. You don't know what you're asking me to do."

• • •

Zakov went up to the front door of Circuit Judge Patrick H. O'Brien's house. The judge himself answered, his red hair mussed, sleep in rheumy eyes, his gigantic ears sticking out like wings.

"Your Grace," the Russian greeted him.

"I know you not, sir," O'Brien said, not bothering to mask his irritation. "State your business. It's nighttime, and my court's business hours coincide with the sun's passage."

Bapcat stepped out of the shadows. "Your Honor, I thought we'd return the favor of a visit."

O'Brien shook his head. "Inside, you damn fools."

The house was massive and handsome, paneled in masculine, dark wood. The judge's office had floor-to-ceiling bookshelves, all full, more books than Bapcat had ever seen in one place. It was intimidating. The judge also had a nickel-plated revolver on his desk.

O'Brien grinned. "It seems sometimes that all a judge really does is read. Libation, lads?" he asked, lifting a decanter. "Genuine Oyrish, right from the auld sod—puts hair on a man's jewels, it does indeed."

Bapcat smiled.

Drinks poured, the three men sat down. "Neither hear nor see much of you, Deputy."

"That's probably about to change, Your Honor."

"Give it air, son."

By the time Bapcat finished explaining, the judge's mood had shifted from almost amused to something heavy and dark. "Two comments, Deputy. First, the scheme is so bloody damn crazy, I'm certain nobody will have predicted it. Second, because they won't have predicted it, the mine operators won't react well. That, I am absolutely certain of." Judge O'Brien looked up at a bookshelf. "I doubt I could find a precedent for what you propose; in fact, I am almost certain that what you intend to do is entirely illegal on several levels. Will your names be on the handbills?"

"No, Your Honor."

"Good, leave it anonymous. Printing to be done hereabouts?"

Before Bapcat could answer, the judge said, "Make sure it's not. Pretty hard to track game that leaves no tracks, eh?"

Bapcat nodded.

O'Brien drained his glass. "All right, I never saw the two of you, so get the hell on out of here and disappear into the night like the scallywags you are."

"You sympathize with the strikers," Zakov said, his first words.

"I am not so much for the strikers as I am against the operators. I know it's a fine distinction, and no doubt un-judgelike, but there it is. The operators are a pack of greedy, foul bastards, no matter how pressed their white shirts and polished their leather shoes. Good luck to you fellas, whoever you are. Let me give you one wee piece of advice an Irishman always passes along to those who would fight the powers that be: Don't get caught, lads; don't get caught."

Back in the Ford, Zakov said, "Judges in Russia are extensions of the czar. Here, they are—."

"Their own men," Bapcat said.

64

Red Jacket

SUNDAY, AUGUST 31, 1913

It was the day before Labor Day, and the Palestra was festooned with red, white, and blue ribbons and multitudes of American flags, but there was no sense of celebration, or hope. The whippet-like, sad-countenanced Charles Moyer, national WFM president, had come to town from Denver to address the local brotherhood.

The union gate-guards hesitated when Zakov flashed their shared badge for admission, but relented when the two state deputies glared at them and went on inside, where they stood watching the crowd and listened to warm-up speakers, waiting for Moyer to take the podium. It appeared to Bapcat that the women in the hall were more agitated than the men, and he was again surprised by how many women were present. Everyone in the Palestra knew the mines were open and again producing—not at the output level they were at before the strike, but operating nonetheless, despite the walk-out, using supervisors as workers and bringing in scabs from other places. Not a lot of ore so far, but definitely on the increase, rumors contended. The strike was losing force.

The handbills had been hurriedly printed for free by a union man in the village of Diorite, between Champion and Marquette, and Harju had taken a train east to fetch them, returning last Thursday with three thousand copies. Most of these had been left for Nayback at Spiro's Blacksmithy the night before, in Tamarack. This morning the game wardens had seen handbills tacked up around town, and now there were stacks of them in the Palestra. People were picking them up and reading them, paying little attention to the speakers on the stage.

The crowd applauded politely when a dog-faced man with a droopy mustache made his way to the podium. He had a high, shiny forehead, mournfully lidded eyes, and he wore a baggy dark suit that hung on his spare frame.

"Gentlemen," Moyer began, but a stentorian female voice quickly rang out, "It ain't just men in this brotherhood, Charlie-boy!"

"Gentlemen *and* ladies," Moyer said, beginning again. "I assure you it is with a great deal of satisfaction that I have come here to the front lines to report to you that despite all efforts by mine operators and the state and federal governments to destroy us, we remain not only afloat, but steaming full speed ahead in our righteous battle to ensure a living wage for all workers, and conditions that nurture rather than main and kill. You are not alone, brothers and sisters; you are not alone."

There were lukewarm cheers and applause, and the union man let them peter out. "The WFM is now in productive preliminary discussions with unions across this great country, and I can report to you here today that there is strong support for your brave efforts—for example, from Mr. Gompers, of the venerated American Federation of Labor."

The audience clapped politely.

"To support our fight, your brothers and sisters in other states have volunteered to be assessed ten dollars a month. The Illinois District of the United Mine Workers has loaned us one . . . hundred . . . thousand . . . dollars, and the United Brewery Workers of America have given us another twenty-five thousand."

Cheers blended with ragged applause.

"But we still ain't working, by God!" a voice rang out.

"You leading this meeting, or are you some facking bookkeeper?" another voice shouted at the first.

Moyer plowed on. "Yes, brothers and sisters, the mines are trying to operate again, but in a much-diminished capacity, and we—you—must step up all activities. And mark my words, dear friends, the operators will bring in more outside workers—true scabs, some just off the boat from those same countries you left for the promise of America. That the operators have to reach so far to find help tells us that we . . . are . . . winning!"

It seemed to Bapcat the resultant applause was not so enthusiastic.

"Hey, Mr. Big Shot," someone yelled out. "When are we gonna get that pay you promised us?"

Another person held up one of Bapcat's handbills. "And what about what these here papers say?" a man shouted.

Moyer looked baffled. "I'm sorry, I don't know what that is. Can you please pass it forward?"

The man made his way to the stage and handed it up to a local official who handed it to Moyer, who looked it over and told the crowd, "We'll need time to look this over and study it. It could be a trick by the operators to put you afoul of the law. Let me repeat: We are at a critical juncture in our holy war. To relent now will sink our ship. You must remain strong. Double, triple your efforts. The WFM and our brother unions are in your corner. Strike pay will be distributed; I repeat, *You will be paid, as promised. You will get your strike pay*. That is my promise to you, and as you know, Charlie Moyer always honors his promises."

A nearby man said loudly to another, "I thought the national WFM had a treasury and a strike fund. Why the hell they gotta borrow money to pay us?"

Others nodded agreement.

Moyer held up his hands. "I know there's been violence here, and that people have died. As in Colorado and Montana years ago, the military and police are but weapons in the mine owners' hands, and it is politics that arms operators against labor. Remember, there once was a time when Russian citizens bowed at the feet of the czar and were shot dead by the czar's Cossacks. If we concede . . . nay, if we bow our heads even a little, they will destroy us!"

The cheers were louder at the end, and Bapcat saw many people reading the handbills.

Zakov looked smug. "This man is of course not exaggerating about the czar and his cavalry. I think so far your militia is well-disciplined and even quietly supportive of the people gathered here, and walking in parades. I suspect this confounds the capitalist owners. I also think our Mr. Nayback has done a commendable job of distribution."

A parade assembled outside the Palestra and a man came up to Bapcat with a handbill and asked, "Is this for real, or is it a joke?"

"Is what a joke?"

The man waggled the handbill. "This."

"I haven't seen it."

"Here," the man said, handing it to him. "Read."

Bapcat pretended to scan it.

"True?" the man asked.

"Looks that way to me. Why are you asking me?"

"You two are our game wardens. You gonna arrest or not?"

"No; not until orders change."

"A lotta people here t'ink dis damn good t'ing," the man said, moving toward the organizers.

Bapcat felt uneasy. How had the man known who they were? But it also occurred to him that Harju had once told him that locals always knew who the local game warden was, and where he lived. They had shown the one badge between them to get into the building, but the badges were not commonly exposed. "I hope we've done the right thing," he confided to the Russian.

"The right thing here is not the law, but how to help people not starve. If this works, it is the right thing. Sometimes fate presents no reasonable alternatives."

"Like walking a general at gunpoint onto a battlefield?"

"I must admit that the event you speak of felt eminently reasonable to me," Zakov said, holding a hand in the air. "Is it me, or does the air seem prematurely cold? I think I smell snow."

"You can't *smell* snow."

"A Russian can."

"The question is not if snow will come, but how much, and when," Bapcat said.

"If winter comes early and stays long, many are going to suffer terribly," Zakov said.

• • •

When they stopped at Vairo's saloon, Dominick was reading the *Calumet News*. A large headline proclaimed GUARD ANNOUNCES WITHDRAWAL PLAN; COUNTIES TO TAKE OVER.

Vairo looked at Bapcat. "Don't mean counties; it means the bloody companies. They always the ones control t'ings."

65

North Kearsarge, Houghton County

MONDAY, SEPTEMBER 1, 1913

Harju and Sandheim reported considerable deer sign along Scales Creek, near the north Kearsarge mine. The morning after the Palestra assembly, Bapcat and a crutchless Zakov went south to the area, to have a look around. They were along the creek bottom in heavy tag alders when a shot rang out. Bapcat immediately charged toward the sound with the Russian trailing behind him.

The amount of gunfire was astounding, and Bapcat lost count at thirty rounds as he burst out of the creek bed and saw several deputies with sun-shaped badges firing revolvers at a group of women and children. A few soldiers stood nearby, watching. Without thinking, Bapcat charged into the deputies, began grabbing weapons and punching men, screaming, "Cease fire, cease fire!" Every time he heard another shot he pivoted and smashed the man with the butt of his Krag, and eventually a mine captain in a white smock, with a sun-shaped badge and blank eyes, pointed a revolver at him.

"Stand back, you! Put down that rifle."

"Those people are unarmed," Bapcat said. "There are kids!"

"These *creatures* are in violation of the law, unlawfully assembled, seeking to prevent citizens of the United States from working, and they attacked us. My men are shooting over their heads."

"Attacked with what? Their fingernails, buckets?"

Zakov caught up, and without pausing, clubbed the captain to the ground, kicked him in the face, and picked up the man's revolver. "I have seen this thing myself, and will swear in court that you and your swine fired at unarmed women and children!"

The shooting stopped, and Bapcat saw dark-coated deputies running away.

The captain moaned. "Court? You think the court will bother with this scum?"

Zakov hit the man in the mouth with the butt end of his own revolver. "*Da*, I do, you disgusting pig," the Russian said.

A man from the crowd came over to Bapcat. "Sirs, you better come quick."

Zakov kicked the captain one last time and followed Bapcat.

They saw a small figure on the ground, and nobody trying to help. Bapcat knelt. A girl, thirteen, fourteen. Head wound, bleeding profusely. Bapcat looked up at a nearby woman. "Get some clean rags, and someone call a doctor."

"No doctor will come for this," a woman said with a shaky voice.

Zakov said, "Take me to a doctor, and I will make him come with me."

A woman began tearing up her petticoat. Bapcat stuffed pieces into the wound, his hands slippery with blood. He looked up to the man who had come to summon them; had never seen him before, but could see concern in his eyes, had heard it in his voice. Not dressed like a striker. "Keep pressure right there on the bandage."

Zakov had gone to get a doctor.

The captain, who had just regained his feet, walked over to join Bapcat and the girl. Looked down on her, the captain said, "I seen this before. She's a goner."

"You had better hope she's not," Bapcat said angrily.

Zakov appeared a few minutes later with a man who seemed red-faced and shaken. "I'm Dr. Jolly."

"Bleeding's heavy," Bapcat told him.

The doctor knelt beside the girl and examined the wound, slowly unpeeling the makeshift bandages. "We need to get her to the hospital. What's her name?"

"Margaret," a woman said. "Margaret Fazekis."

Dr. Jolly said to the girl, "Margaret, I'm a doctor. We're going to take you to the hospital, and you're going to be all right."

Zakov and Bapcat helped carry the wounded girl to the trolley station. They entered a trolley car and laid her on a bench, with the doctor and several women and kids in attendance.

The doctor pulled Bapcat close. "I've never seen anyone survive a head wound like this." Dr. Jolly turned to the women and children. "Does anyone know the mother?"

Several women nodded dumbly. "She lives in Wolverine," one of them said.

He said in a low voice, "Best find her quickly, and tell her to start thinking about a funeral."

Bapcat and Zakov exited the trolley car and watched as it headed south. As they returned to the scene of the shooting, Bapcat looked at Zakov. "You're covered with blood."

"This was an abattoir. How many more were hit?"

Miraculously, the girl seemed to be the only serious victim. The game wardens looked around and saw dozens of cartridges glinting in the sun. "Let's pick them up, make a count for a report," Bapcat said.

They collected eighty pieces of brass and two full cylinders that had been dropped in the fracas. Someone apparently had been excited, and in attempting to reload, had dropped the cylinders. "Company deputies," Zakov said disgustedly. "No training, no judgment, no discipline."

A soldier from the National Guard came over and said, "The deputies did fire over their heads."

"Not all of them. The whole mess keeps getting worse," Bapcat said.

• • •

They stopped at the telegraph shop in the electric trolley station and sent a wire to John Hepting in Eagle River.

The two game wardens then sat outside the station and smoked. The captain had disappeared with his men.

"People dying, and we're worried about fish and game?" Bapcat said, thinking out loud. It was an unsettling thought. He looked at his own blood-soaked clothes. They needed to get back to the hill, change.

"There is good news, albeit anticlimactic," Zakov said. "I found three viscera piles along the creek bed. It appears someone has taken our message to heart."

Gut piles meant the dead deer most likely had been taken for food, not pay. It seemed a small thing in comparison to the wounded girl, but a small thing was still something, and he was in a mood where he desperately wanted something to be positive, no matter how seemingly insignificant.

66

Kearsarge No. 4

TUESDAY, SEPTEMBER 2, 1913

Tristan Shunk was the embodiment of control and confidence, resplendent in an unwrinkled white captain's smock. His hair was combed over, his mustache trimmed precisely, fingernails dirt-free, skin glowing a supernatural pink. Two men in shabby black peacoats and sun-star badges stood back from the captain, next to a wagon filled with deer carcasses, heads, and the bloodied human bodies of Arven Lammie and Cornelius Nayback.

"My men here discovered the two men on the cart, shooting deer, and challenged them. The dead men began shooting and my people answered in kind."

Shunk had summoned the sheriff, who in turn had called Bapcat and Zakov. Bapcat had not anticipated this scene and guessed that his fellow lawmen hadn't either. Shunk's men looked nervous, their eyes dark; they were sweating heavily even though the day was breezy, with a cooling wind from the northwest.

"These men are?" Hepting asked Shunk.

"Lukevich and Pinnochi."

"They work for you?"

"They're new men; poor language skills, but diligent workers."

"Working at what jobs?"

"Cleanup," Shunk said. "Aboveground."

"Here since?"

"Early July, or late June. I would have to defer to our personnel department to secure precise dates."

"Do they have given names?"

"Lech Lukevich and Paolo Pinnochi."

"We'll need to talk to them."

"Quite right. I've already summoned translators," Shunk said, waving his arm flamboyantly.

Despite the facade, Bapcat saw that the captain was antsy.

"Alone," Hepting told the captain.

"They are my employees, Sheriff, my boys—dependents of the company. We have translators and interpreters to assist in matters of this kind."

Bapcat mused, *What's the difference between a translator and an interpreter?* And what does Shunk mean by "matters of this kind"?

"We'll let you know if we need help," Hepting said diplomatically.

"Suit yourself," Shunk countered, reluctantly.

"When did this happen?" Hepting asked.

"I was informed last night."

"By whom?"

"I don't remember which man told me, Lukevich or Pinnochi. One of them."

"So, last night they reported two dead bodies, claimed they had shot the alleged trespassers in self-defense, and you're *just now* getting around to informing me?"

"You're an exceedingly difficult man to locate, Sheriff."

"I was home all night with my wife," Hepting said. "And I have a deputy on duty at the jail at all times."

"Well, of course, we responsible men all have our deputies, but I prefer to deal with the top man, as I'm certain you do, as well."

Hepting coughed. "Where did these events take place?"

"On mine property."

"Where, exactly?"

"I can show you."

"You've been to the location?"

"Of course," Shunk said.

"We'll let your guides show us," Hepting said.

"We are allies, Sheriff, you and I," Shunk said.

"Do you feel I'm treating you otherwise?" Hepting countered.

"I simply want to emphasize the relationship between the company and county officials."

Hepting looked at the man. "I was elected, Captain—by the people, not a damn company, and you *weren't*. Care to explain why men with such poor English have been appointed special deputies?"

"As stated, they are reliable workers."

Both men had revolvers. "Chilly," Hepting told his newest deputy, "please relieve the gentlemen of their sidearms. They'll get them back when we're done here."

"They're legally entitled to carry," Shunk said.

"I'm not arguing that, Cap'n. I just don't want a tragic accident to happen. It's a question of safety, not legality."

Chilly Taylor took the weapons to the sheriff's vehicle.

Both men were disarmed uneventfully, and stared, dumbfounded. Hepting looked to Bapcat. "Which one do you want to start with?"

"Doesn't matter," Bapcat said.

"Take the Italian," Hepting said.

"Who're you?" Captain Shunk asked, stepping forward.

"Bapcat and Zakov, game wardens."

"I see no point in your being here, much less questioning my men."

"Your cart is filled with dead animals, Captain."

"I must protest."

"Sing a lullaby, if that's what pleases you. We couldn't care less," Bapcat said, taking the Italian's arm and leading him toward the cart. When they got close, Bapcat rolled and lit a cigarette for the man, who took it, and bowed his head. Bapcat lit it with a match. "Tell us what happened."

"*Non parlo inglese. Parli Italiano,*" the man asked, grinning, jabbing the cigarette like a maestro's baton.

"No *Italiano,*" Bapcat admitted thumbing his chest. *Shit.*

"*Tua madre i un cane,*" the man said. "Not talka."

Bapcat mimicked a gun with his hand. "You shot, bang-bang?"

The man said, "*No capisce.*"

Bapcat tapped the man's empty holster, pointed his hand at the dead men on the cart. "*Banga-banga, si?*"

The man exhaled smoke. "*No capisce inglese.*"

Bapcat pointed at the man's badge. "You're a special deputy."

The man shrugged, looked skyward.

"How'd you take the oath if you don't speak English?" Bapcat asked the man.

"*No capisce,*" the man said again.

"That's my point," the exasperated game warden said, and looked to his partner. "Ideas?"

"Seek assistance from an Italian speaker."

"No Italian for you?"

"Alas, it is not part of my linguistic armamentarium."

Hepting came over, leading the other man by the arm. "No language with this bird; nothing. You guys?"

"Same story here. Want to switch, see if it makes a difference?"

"Might as well. We don't get something out of them, I'm going to get a warrant and jail the whole damn lot of them, Shunk included."

"Grounds?"

"Who cares? Prima facie, they're in possession of illegal deer and two human bodies. Their employer informed us that his two men, these two, shot and killed the men during a trespass. What more do we need to hold them?"

"What about the Fazekis girl?" Zakov asked.

"Still hanging on, last I heard," Hepting said.

"It's your call what you do, John, not mine, but isn't this Houghton County?"

"Technically true, but Cruse don't pay much attention to things that happen this far north. I can't remember the last time I saw that arsehole up here. I want to take it, and he won't make a peep. Let's switch."

"May I?" Zakov asked Bapcat.

Bapcat stepped aside. "Please."

"*Jestes polska?*" Zakov asked as he stepped over to the man.

"*Tak, z Cracow,*" Lukevich said.

"*Weesz, dlaczego tu, jestes my?*"

"*Nie bardzo,*" Lukevich replied.

"This man tells me he is from Cracow in Poland, and he doesn't know why we are all here. I speak okay Polish," Zakov told Bapcat.

"Ask him about the deer?" Bapcat said.

"*Wedzisz wozek z umarlych i jelenie?*"

The man answered, "*Oczywiscie nie jestem slepy.*"

Zakov reported: "I asked him if he saw the cart, and he told me he is not blind.'"

"Ask him what happened."

Zakov thought for a moment, asked, "*Dia czego nie molznami co si stato?* I asked him to tell us what happened."

The man said without pause, "*Kapitan powiedzlat nam w zeszlym tygoodniu nie mamy juz miejsc pracy tutai.*"

"He states that last week the captain told him he no longer had a job here." To the man, Zakov said, "*To jest wazne. Moj polskinie jest tak dobry. Czy masz rosyjsku*?"

"*Nie wyhstorczy mowic dobaze.*"

"I asked Mr. Lukevich if he speaks Russian, but he tells me he does not know enough to speak it well." Zakov turned to the man, "*To jest wazne*—this is important."

"*Jesli nie dziataja, dikaczego nosi zltcak gwlazda?*" the man said.

"*Kapitan wizwat mnie ranok, powiedaiat mi umie scicgo ze moge muc nowa prace.*"

"Mr. Lukevich says his captain called him here this morning, told him to put on the badge, that he has a new job."

"What about the gun?"

"*Rewolwer*?" Zakov asked.

"*Wraz z odznaka.*"

"Came with the badge," Zakov translated.

"Did he bring the cart here from elsewhere?"

Zakov asked and listened to the answer. "*Nyet*, it was here when he arrived. He knows nothing about it."

"Ask where he was last night."

"*Gdzide byes ostatniej nacy?*"

"*Restauracje czteidziesci pret.*"

"*Zkim*?" Zakov asked.

"*Moja glowabol i*," Lukevich said.

"I know your head hurts. *Kimbylici?*"

The man said, "*Pijesam.*"

Zakov reported, "He says he was drinking alone last night."

"Tell him his captain told us that he and the other man shot the two men dead for trespassing."

Zakov translated and the man screamed, "*To jest zle, klamz! Klamca Damn!*"

"He says, 'This is wrong. Liar, damn liar!' "

"Why would the captain tell us this story?" Bapcat asked.

Zakov said, "*Dlaczdego kaptian nam to?*"

"*I powiedziec, zde klamie!*"

"He insists the captain lies," Zakov said.

"You believe him?"

"*Da*," Zakov said. "I do."

Hepting came back. "Chilly knows a little bar-side Italian, but our boy has lockjaw. Yours?"

"Zakov speaks some Polish. This man claims he was fired a week ago, called back this morning, given the badge and gun, and informed he has a new job. He says Shunk is lying about him shooting anyone."

"Shunk's gone," Deputy Taylor announced. "I saw him drive away."

Hepting and Bapcat exchanged glances. "This is crazy," the sheriff told the game wardens. "We need a coroner, and we need to take these men into custody." The Keweenaw County sheriff took each man by an arm and announced, "You are under arrest." Neither man resisted.

Blank stares reigned until Zakov and Taylor translated. "*Jestes wareszcie. Rimy to dja wlasnego bez pipczen enstwa.*"

Chilly Taylor proclaimed the arrest in his casual Italian.

Pinnochi sank to his knees, shaking.

Lukevich's face turned purple and he raised a fist, "*Klam cas Damn!*"

Hepting asked Bapcat, "Got anything to say?"

"None of this makes any sense. Does Shunk actually think he can set up these men so easily? And why—what's the point? Is Shunk stupid?"

• • •

Dr. Henrijk Hill, Keweenaw's part-time coroner, took two hours to arrive, looked briefly at the bodies in the cart, and pronounced, "Both dead, ostensibly of gunshots. Dr. Scanlan and Justice Carbolt are on the way."

"Our case," Hepting said. "Not Cruse and Scanlan or Carbolt. You and me, Henrijk."

"Not our county, John," the coroner said.

"You know Cruse don't pay no attention to things up here. We handle them."

"Apparently not this time," the doctor said.

"Shit," Hepting cursed.

Dr. Marcoach Scanlan and Justice of the Peace Hugh Carbolt arrived in a car driven by Sheriff Cruse, who slid clumsily out of the vehicle, hiked up his pants with both hands, and waddled through the mud toward Hepting and Bapcat.

"Boys," he said.

Hepting stepped forward. "My case, Jim. We were called into this."

"Far as I know, Johnny-boy, that's not what the law dictates or provides for." Cruse held up a bloated hand. "This is my county, which means my case, and Dr. Scanlan's."

Cruse looked at Pinnochi and Lukevich and flicked his hands. "You fellas are free to go, so git. Mr. Justice Carbolt will transport the deceased to the hospital in Red Jacket," Cruse concluded. "Mr. Carbolt?"

"Dammit, Cruse, this is my case!" Hepting roared. "There is some very slippery shit going on here. Capital crime suspects dismissed?" Hepting asked. "Captain Tristan Shunk fled the damn scene."

Scanlan said, "Seems open and shut. The two dead men were well-known WFM sympathizers and agitators."

Bapcat thought: *How does Scanlan know who the dead men are? He didn't even look at the bodies. Something very shady here.*

Hepting said, "These two men were given revolvers and badges just this morning. They weren't here last night. I doubt they've even been sworn in. Neither speaks English, Sheriff."

Cruse said. "If they're sworn deputies, they'll be on the master list. As you can imagine, it's of a size that won't fit in a pocket."

Hepting growled, "You could carry ten-pound hams in your pockets, Fat Man!"

Carbolt said, "There's no call for that sort of vitriol. All things will be sorted out properly in good time. It's my experience that foreigners tend to confuse things," the justice of the peace said.

Hepting shook his head.

Carbolt said, "Jurors will be called to convene at 10 a.m. tomorrow. Survivors and family members will be called to provide postmortem identification."

"What about the scene of the crime?" Hepting asked.

"A police matter," the justice said.

"Why do you need formal identification?" Bapcat asked. "Dr. Scanlan already said they're well-known union sympathizers, so he must know who they are."

"Who might *you* be?" Carbolt asked with a raised eyebrow.

"Bapcat, game warden."

"Human death is of no concern to a game warden, sir."

"Shunk told us he'd show us where the men were shot, but he skedaddled."

"I've talked to the captain. He mentioned no such thing," Cruse said.

Bapcat took a step toward Cruse, but Hepting blocked him with a leg, steered him away, and took both game wardens with him, saying little until they reconvened at Bumbletown Hill.

"It's a setup," Hepting announced. "They want Lammie and Nayback tied to the deer, and they wanted you to see that before the jurisdictional divide took them away."

Bapcat looked at the sheriff and winked. "I've got jurisdiction in *both counties*, Jimmy."

"Only for fish and game."

"In chess this might be termed a preemptive strike," Zakov said.

"I'm a checkers man," the Keweenaw sheriff retorted. "You take one of mine, I take one of yours, and on we go till just one of us is left standing. Why do they want Lammie and Nayback blamed for the deer? I don't get that at all."

"Maybe to back me off my case?" Bapcat ventured.

"Why is your case so damned important to them?" Hepting countered. "But maybe you're right, and they're hoping you'll walk away."

Bapcat rubbed his eyes. "Hope won't do them any good."

67

Laurium

WEDNESDAY, SEPTEMBER 3, 1913

Harju and Sandheim straggled in well after midnight, in the early hours of the morning. They stowed their gear, made coffee, and rooted around for food. Bapcat and Zakov joined them.

"Saw a dozen gut piles today," Harju announced. "Word's getting around."

Sandheim complained, "I want to be glad about it, but I'm not. We're not just allowing violations, we're encouraging them."

"Values change in wartime," Zakov said.

"We ain't in no war," Sandheim said.

"We may not be, but the people around here seem to be," Zakov countered.

Bapcat told the other two about their day. Harju just shook his head, stared into the distance, and looked weary.

• • •

It was 5 a.m., and Bapcat was knocking on Judge O'Brien's back door. Zakov had dropped him off and had driven to another location to wait.

O'Brien answered in a tattered blue robe and leather slippers. "Do you *ever* work regular daylight hours?" the judge asked.

"We need to talk," Bapcat said.

The judge let him in, rustled up coffee, and listened attentively as they sat at a small table in the jurist's study.

"Sounds like Cruse didn't think through the jurisdictional issues," the judge said after he had heard the tale.

"But I'm only empowered for fish and game," Bapcat said.

"True, but there were dead bodies among the deer, and that makes the bodies prima facie evidence in *your* investigation. Doesn't matter what laws you're empowered to enforce."

"Can I have the bodies quarantined—not release them yet for burial?"

"On what grounds?"

"I'm asking you, Your Honor."

"Think out loud, Deputy."

"To investigate bullet calibers in the bodies so they can be compared to the deer wounds, to determine if the same weapons were used, or if there is other evidence bearing on the deer case."

O'Brien smiled. "I'd grant an injunction on those grounds." The judge dug in his desk and produced some forms that he handed to the game warden. "Make damn sure you write precisely what you want."

"When I took this job, I never imagined anything like this," Bapcat confessed.

"You think it's any rosier or less surprising for a judge?"

Bapcat struggled to complete the forms, breaking into a sweat. When they were finally filled out, Judge O'Brien read them over and signed them and then Bapcat signed them. The bodies were to be held by the coroner until Bapcat had adequate opportunity—on his schedule, which would be binding for the coroner—to examine the bodies and extract evidence.

"You'll probably want this, too," O'Brien said, handing Bapcat a handwritten letter.

"What is it?"

"Your ticket to observe and participate in the autopsies and inquest. They're gonna scream bloody murder," the judge said with a hearty laugh. "Put the injunction in Carbolt's hands before proceedings begin."

"Thanks, Your Honor. Can I ask why you're doing this?"

"You can ask, but all I have to say is good luck. We'll all need it with that lot."

68

Red Jacket

WEDNESDAY, SEPTEMBER 3, 1913

The autopsies and inquest were conducted at the Calumet and Hecla Hospital. Justice of the Peace Carbolt read the injunction from Judge O'Brien, cursed softly, and handed it to Sheriff Cruse, who said to Bapcat, "You've got some nerve. When do you want to examine the bodies, Game Warden?"

"The injunction says it will be on my schedule, and this is between Dr. Scanlan and me, not you. Go ahead with the inquest. I'll observe."

Carbolt said, "Dr. Scanlan and I decide who other than our jury will participate and observe."

Bapcat handed the judge's letter to the justice of the peace.

Carbolt read it and said, "Disgusting." He handed the letter to Scanlan, who said nothing.

Bapcat stood with the jury to examine the bodies while the coroner took them through what he observed in the autopsy, concluding that each man had been shot once in the back, probably with a rifle. The inquest seemed concerned only with physical facts. The so-called jury, with heavy direction from Scanlan, agreed only that the gunshots were of unknown origin or caliber, and there appeared to be justifiable evidence for a verdict of foul play.

"Family?" Bapcat asked Sheriff Cruse. "I thought you were bringing family survivors here."

"Lammie, none. Same for Nayback. When you get around to finishing your hocus-pocus malarkey, we'll give these men a decent burial at the county's expense."

"Why isn't Shunk here?" Bapcat inquired.

"Don't see the need."

"I'll want to talk to him, as well."

"He a suspect in your so-called case?" the sheriff asked.

"Shunk reported it to Sheriff Hepting, and the animals and bodies were on his mine's property, and in his possession."

"You'll probably have to go through his lawyer."

"Just let me know," Bapcat said. "If I don't hear from you in a reasonable amount of time, I'll be back to *discuss* it with you."

"Is that a threat, Deputy?"

"Take it as a promise, Sheriff."

Bapcat cornered the coroner after the jurors were gone. "You can say for sure the wounds in the men came from a rifle, and not a revolver?"

"Can't say anything until I look for and find what's left of the projectiles."

"Let me know right away when you have something concrete."

Scanlan studied him, asked, "*Why* are you doing this?"

"It's my job, Doctor."

"These men were just foreign troublemakers."

"And that makes murder acceptable?"

"Nobody here has used that word," the doctor said.

"Maybe they should," Bapcat said, striding out of the morgue in the basement of the hospital. He stopped at the door. "Pretty unusual for the company to authorize the autopsies to be held here, isn't it? Neither of the dead men was an employee."

"It was approved is all I can tell you, young man."

69

Bumbletown Hill

FRIDAY, SEPTEMBER 5, 1913

John Hepting was slumped in a chair, wearily rolling a cigarette. "Shunk, Lukevich, and Pinnochi have all disappeared. None of them's been seen since Tuesday morning."

"You're still investigating?" Bapcat asked.

"Goddamn right. I don't suffer blindness based on potential political gain."

"The jurors at the inquest would agree only to probable foul play."

"Dammit, Lute, we know better. Each victim was shot in the damn back by a rifle. There wasn't no gunplay with special dicks wielding piddly-ass revolvers."

"It more than smells," Bapcat agreed. *Shunk lit out, Cruse dismissed the other two, and now all of them were missing. What the hell were they trying to accomplish?* "The jurors at least agreed that the fatal wounds came from a rifle, though no caliber has been specified."

Hepting grinned. "How the hell did *you* get into that inquest?"

"O'Brien," Bapcat said.

Hepting raised an eyebrow. "Our local Robin Hood in a robe. You're learning the unwritten rules pretty quick."

"We need to talk to Lukevich and Pinnochi. They were carrying company-issued revolvers. Did they even own rifles? Do the bullets in the deer match the bullets in the dead men? Hell, I just hope the coroner will preserve the evidence for me."

"Don't bet on it with Scanlan. He's a boyhood chum of MacNaughton's."

"I had the sense Scanlan will do whatever Cruse commands. Where do the two men live? Do we know yet?"

"Pinnochi lives in Raymbaultown in a boardinghouse, and Lukevich, on East Amygdaloid Street in Centennial. Captain Shunk's house is in west Wolverine."

Bapcat scribbled some notes to himself. He had begun this practice not long after the whole thing had begun, and now his notes were accumulating; he needed to find a way to organize them, another aspect of being a game warden he'd not thought about, even after his training with Harju.

Sandheim came in sweating and out of breath. "Horri says come quick."

"Where to?" Bapcat asked.

"To talk to the leper," Sandheim said.

The word sent a chill through Bapcat. He had seen lepers in Cuba, sloughing skin, noses, fingers, toes. It had been horrendous. Zakov showed no emotional response as he got behind the wheel of the Ford and Bapcat spun the crank.

The house was like hundreds of others constructed by mine operators: stick-built, two stories, just inside the Houghton County line, a mile and a half north of Centennial Heights. One among many identical places, except that this one sat alone, far from any neighbors.

Harju was sitting on the front steps with a man who had numerous small patches of light-colored skin on his face, and no apparent disfigurement.

"Meet Marelius Jensen," Harju said. "There's a pot of coffee inside, and don't worry about catching leprosy from touching stuff. It don't work like that."

"You live here alone, Mr. Jensen?" Sheriff Hepting asked.

"Wife and daughters live in town. MacNaughton arranged houses for us, got her a job. Kids still can't go to school, though," the man said bitterly. "Given the fate God put on us, things could be worse. If you believe in God, which I don't."

Anger barely contained just below the surface, Bapcat noted.

"Tell them what you seen," Harju said to the man.

"Lepers don't get no goddamn company," Jensen said morosely. "I hunt and fish, wander the woods. Don't see my family 'cept on some Sundays, so most nights, ain't no reason to come home. I sleep in the woods rather than come here. If I die out in woods some night, who the hell will care?"

"About what you saw," Harju prompted gently.

"Monday night I was up on Kearsarge land. Word's out it's okay to take deer now, so I was out looking. Wife will can the meat, so ain't nothing gets wasted by us, and if I can get real meat, we don't got to depend on the damn poorhouse for food. Anyways, there's a big stand of oaks in this one place, and the acorns pull deer in like magnets this time of year."

"Monday night?" Bapcat asked.

"I don't own a watch. Doctor said it could make my skin fall off, so yeah, Monday, though it might've been after midnight, which would make it Tuesday, you want to fuss over details. Anyways, there was a real good shooter's moon and I had me a good seat right next to the edge of an open field."

"Go ahead," Harju said, encouraging the man.

"Out of nowhere I hear these voices, two men, and they sound unhappy. One of them asks the other, 'How come we're here?' and t'other one says, 'I don't got no idea.'

"Then the first man, he says, 'Well, I got school to teach, and it's a long way home.' Soon as he says that, a light comes on and a new voice says, 'Okay, lads, I brought lights, so we can see what we're about.' "

Teach? Bapcat thought. *Is the man talking about Nayback?*

"Anyways, number three, there, he tells them fellers, 'Let's jest get these things loaded so we can run 'em out to the hole.' "

"He said *hole?*" Bapcat asked.

"I heard *hole,* so I guess that's what he said. My ears ain't sloughed off yet. I listened to them loading stuff, and after a while number three, he says, 'Okay, you two,' and then I hear two shots, *pow pow!* Nearly made me jump right outta my skin. There was jest one light on, and I heard the wagon move away and horses snorting, and that's exactly what I heard that night."

"Did you see the men?" Hepting asked.

"You deaf? Just heard, was like I jest tell you."

"Recognize their voices?" Harju asked.

"For sure? Can't say yes for sure."

"Tell them," Harju said.

"Okay, mebbe that number three, he sound an awful lot like Cousin Jack captain called Shunk."

"Shunk, of the Quincy mine?" Bapcat asked.

The leper cackled. "Only know one Shunk, and that be the North Kearsarge Shunk, and one's plenty enough, I reckon."

Harju said, "Marelius has volunteered to show us where this happened."

"When?" Bapcat wanted to know.

"Whenever you fellas want. Ain't like I got me a schedule to keep," the Norwegian said.

"Tonight? Now?" Bapcat asked.

"Long walk," the man said.

"We'll all be driving, not walking," Zakov volunteered.

"People don't let me in cars. I ain't never been in one."

"Nonsense," Zakov said. "Tonight's your night to ride in style."

Harju said, "Let's go."

Bapcat leaned in close to Zakov. "Is this safe?"

"It depends on one's irrationalities. Is it safe to be attacked by Italian bird-eaters in one's own domicile? Bullets are real, the spread of leprosy, also real, but rare and far less understood than high-velocity lead poisoning. You tell me the greater risk."

Would the Russian ever answer a question simply?

"Sit next to me, Jensen," Harju said.

"I'll hang on the back," Sandheim said. "No offense meant."

"Nor taken," the leper said. "You're just like most men."

Bapcat rode with Hepting. "Could we get as lucky as this?"

"Being that Shunk's disappeared, where exactly do you see this so-called luck?"

"If this is the place, there will be evidence."

"Four days old," the sheriff reminded him, looking up. "At least we have a clear sky.

They drove both vehicles into the fields where the events had taken place, but the sky suddenly clouded, the air thickened, the clouds opened, and hard rain pounded them with heavy, loud drops. "Case killer," Hepting said.

Zakov came over to them. "Russians say, Luck and bad luck drive the same sledge."

So much for evidence, Bapcat thought, but Jensen had said something interesting—that MacNaughton had arranged housing and a job for his wife. Why would he do this?

Bapcat approached the man, who had moved from the truck to the cover of a tree. "Did MacNaughton talk to you directly?" Bapcat asked.

"Never. Everything was through his people, not from His Highness Himself."

"More than one person?"

Jensen said, "Mainly one, and this ain't for public knowledge. His name's Lark, and I ain't s'posed to talk about him. I do, we lose everything, and we'd be put out on our own."

"Lark?"

"Loosemore Lark. He's a small-fry lawyer for the Calumet and Hecla legal office in Red Jacket."

"He made all the arrangements—house, job, poorhouse connections, everything?"

"He insisted MacNaughton personally dictated everything, but I never believed that. Hilarious now that with the strike, MacNaughton is sneaking around like a rat at night."

"What are you talking about?"

"You don't know? MacNaughton sent his family away, and he never sleeps in the same house for two nights running. He keeps moving around so no one can find him."

Bapcat looked over at Hepting. "Did you know that, John?"

"Nope."

"Did Lark come into your house?" Bapcat asked.

"No, we always talked outside."

"He afraid of the leprosy?"

"Real scared, I'd guess, but more scared to not do his job for MacNaughton."

"How long since you've talked to Lark?"

"Been at least a year ago."

"What's he like?" Bapcat asked.

Hepting said, "An eel."

"You know him?"

"We've had some dealings," Hepting said. "He once got a court order directing me to physically remove a man from one of the mines. The man had been fired and refused to leave."

"Did you move him?"

"Court ordered it. We don't make the laws, or even have to like them."

"Could we use him to get to MacNaughton?"

"Could try, but why?"

Zakov stepped up. "If you are at war, it behooves one to know the opposing commander."

Bapcat said, "If MacNaughton's calling all the shots here, I want to get a feel for him."

"Takes care of himself, his family, and his company, in that order—period," Hepting said.

"Man takes care of himself first might be prone to a weakness or two," Bapcat said, and despite questions from Hepting and Zakov, would say no more about his thinking.

70

Swedetown

MONDAY, SEPTEMBER 8, 1913

The four game wardens had talked to dozens of people on Saturday and Sunday, working hard to find anyone who knew or worked with Lukevich and Pinnochi, but to no avail. Nobody wanted to own up to knowing anything, and Bapcat had a feeling that showing a badge only made it worse; end of discussion, go away.

In desperation, Zakov took Bapcat to Swedetown to seek an audience with Bruno Geronissi, who greeted Bapcat like a long-lost brother, inviting him to sit on the porch and take a glass of chokecherry wine he had made.

"Long time," the Italian said. "You want bowl of *polenta uccelli?*"

The songbird dish.

"*No grazie, Dottore,*" Bapcat said. "Not fresh, I hope."

Geronissi smiled. "*Faccio il solletico le palle.* I tickle your balls, okay? *Il cazzo de francese*, those fucking French guys, they got this bird they call *ortolan*, little thing, *si?* They roast him and serve whole. You take it in one bite, really hot, tastes like *nocciole*, here you call hazelnuts. Eat the whole bird, bones, everything. *Il cazzo de francese, si?*"

"And *polenta uccelli* is different?"

"*Va bene, si*, Italian civilized, you know, from Romans. The French . . . pooh! They come from dogs, fucking frogs. But you no come talk food, *si?*"

"I'm looking for a man named Paolo Pinnochi, worked at North Kearsarge, but he seems to have disappeared."

"You asking a favor? What Bruno gets back, tit-tat?"

"I don't work that way, Geronissi."

"*Si, si uomo nero-blanco*, Mr. Black-White, but me, I'm *di uomo grigio*—you know, gray, *Dottore* Game Warden."

"Just game warden, *Dottore*."

"You show respect, this is good thing, but *noi abbaianio avuta un problema*, we got us a problem?"

"I came to ask for your help, *Dottore.*"

"This man's name Pinnochi?"

"Yes—Paolo."

"Okay, one favor me to you, no quid pro quo, I let you know. *Abbiamo un accordo* . . . a deal?"

Bapcat weighed what to do next. I *don't want to trade with this sonuvabitch, but I need help.* He stuck out his hand.

"North Kearsarge, *si?* I let you know. You and your Russian still up on the hill?"

"You know we are."

"Don't hurt to ask," Geronissi said.

• • •

Zakov pulled up in the street and Bapcat got in. "He know anything?"

"He'll look into it."

"At what cost?"

"The goodness of his heart, one-time thing."

Zakov laughed out loud. "Geronissi's *heart?*"

71

Houghton

SATURDAY, SEPTEMBER 13, 1913

Louis Moilanen lumbered down the street with a stiff, awkward gait, his massive shoulders yawing like a ship in dirty weather.

Bapcat saw the man ahead of him and sensed something was wrong. He hurried to overtake him, but before he could catch up, the giant veered into Guild's Tavern. Bapcat went in behind him to find the bar's patrons all cowering against a wall and Moilanen holding a thick piano leg in each hand, a two-legged piano on its chin on the floor.

Moilanen's voice seemed to rumble deeper than ever, words exploding like thunder in the room. "You people need my help, beat Legion outen youse, God tole me, 'Louis, go to Guild's—help them heathen unbelievers and hoors get free!'"

Bapcat gulped and took a deep breath. *Stay calm.* "Lauri, are you sure it was God who said Guild's?"

Moilanen turned around, slowly brandishing the clubs. "Nobody calls me that name."

"But that's your name . . . Lauri."

"Was Lauri over Finland, not here; new country, new name. Louis, Louis Moilanen, not Big Louie, not Lauri—Louis."

"Mr. Justice Moilanen," Bapcat said.

"Takin' dat away," the huge man said, and a blow from a club cracked the slate top of a billiard table, while a second demolished a Tiffany sconce, showering the room with leaded glass. Almost immediately doors opened behind Bapcat and city police poured in. Everyone began yelling as they threw themselves at Moilanen, who fought ferociously, smashing his clubs into the men, breaking arms and heads, but eventually the sheer mass of the attackers took effect and the giant sank to the floor under a pile of black uniforms and angry, bleeding men.

As the police officers unpiled, Bapcat knelt close to his friend, who vomited violently, spewing stomach contents and bile everywhere.

"My head, Lute, my head—it's gonna blow up. Lend me your gun, make it go away."

"Calm down, Louis." Bapcat tried to keep his voice soothing, to help his friend, but it was quickly apparent he was having no effect.

"They take my job, those devils and hoors! No more justice, just Louis, just Louis!"

"Please relax, Louis. We're going to get you help."

"Ones who need help is us," a cop with a bloody mouth said. "Big fuckin' Finnlander fuck."

A police sergeant showed up, ordered, "Lock him in the Penthouse. For his own good."

One of the cops said, "For everybody's good. Lucky he didn't kill all of us."

Bapcat showed his badge, which he had taken from Zakov today, and asked the sergeant, "Penthouse?" The shared badge was becoming a problem he needed to solve.

"Special cell in the county jail for lunatics."

"He's not insane," Bapcat insisted.

"We're gonna have six, maybe seven men off duty from fighting that big sonuvabitch. Officer Thurgood's leg is broken in five, six places. The hell he's not nuts."

"He's sick, not insane," Bapcat said. "I want to see him."

"Talk to Cruse."

Bapcat followed the procession of cops escorting the now-meek giant to the county jail. The police looked like goslings trailing their mama. At one point Moilanen stopped, looked back, and laughed maniacally. "I feel like that Gulliver fellow, Lute! Me and him both traveled the world and got stared at. I don't like being stared at, Lute."

Who the hell is Gulliver?

Cruse was in his office and kept the game warden waiting. When Bapcat was finally allowed into the inner sanctum, Cruse made a sour face.

"Damn disgrace, a public figure like that going off the deep end. No wonder they're removing him as JP."

"He's a sick man, Sheriff."

" 'Course he's sick," Cruse said. "The freak is what, eight, nine feet tall? There's something seriously wrong with that."

"I want to talk to him."

"No visitors, no exceptions."

"He won't hurt me."

Cruse grinned. "Your funeral, Game Warden. You look at them bodies yet?"

"When I'm ready."

"Do you want to see that damn freak or not?"

"That's how it is?"

"Way of the world, Game Warden. Get used to it."

"How about this tit for your tat: You knew the identities of the two dead men before you got to the scene, and that's the sort of fact to make people scratch their heads and ask questions. Am I clear on this? I met both men on cases, but you? I doubt it. There could be a lot of explaining for you to do, Cruse."

"That freak cracks your skull, it's your own damn problem," Cruse said. "The Barber will want to look him over first, but if you want to jump the gun, so be it. Get out of my sight."

• • •

Gray bars separated the two men. Moilanen was stretched out on the floor on his side, using his arm as a pillow.

"Louis?"

The big man opened his eyes to suspicious slits. "My head, Lute. She's gonna blow up."

"A doctor's coming to help you," Bapcat told him.

"God told me I'm coming to see him, praise be," Moilanen said. "Soon, Lute. The train's pulling out soon."

Bapcat found himself at a loss for words, slid the Bible through the bars, scootched it across the floor to his friend. "I guess you'll be needing that."

Moilanen pulled the book to his chest and wept. "They're driving out the demons, Lute."

"Who is?"

"You know. I heard 'em talk in my saloon one night. MacNaughton and them. No more demons, they said. Get rid of 'em, whatever it takes."

"Whatever it takes—they said that?"

"Ya, like that."

"Who else?"

"Didn't hear no names, Lute, but MacNaughton, he called 'em Cap'n this and Cap'n that."

"Hedyn?"

"Ya, I heard that one for sure. Don't remember no others."

The Barber turned out to be the county's official physician, who oversaw the infirmary and medical affairs at the poor farm.

"Who're you, and what the hell are you doing here?" the man challenged Bapcat. "No visitors allowed, dammit!"

"Game warden," Bapcat stammered.

"That don't make pickles into pancakes. I need to examine the patient first. That's how it's done. Could be dangerous—dangerous for you, for me, for the man behind bars—dangerous for all of us because you just couldn't follow the damn procedure. You hearing what I'm trying to lay out for you, son?"

"There's no patient here, just a prisoner. Look at him down on the floor there," Bapcat said sharply, tired of the man's officious tone of voice.

This seemed to render the man temporarily silent. "Let's start over. I'm Dr. Robair Labisoniere," the man said, holding out his hand.

"Lute Bapcat."

The man squinted. "You the one fought beside Teddy Roosevelt down in Cuba?"

"One of them."

Labisoniere smiled. "My granddaddy fought with the Michigan Fifth in the War between the States. He was killed in battle by the Rebels."

"Sorry to hear that," Bapcat said.

"Water over the dam. I hardly give it a thought."

"Who's the Barber?"

"Goddamn that Cruse!" the doctor yelped. "I graduated from high school and worked three years barbering to raise money for college. Sold my shop to my brother, moved down to Ann Arbor, and cut hair while I went to medical school. After graduation I interned at C and H Hospital in Calumet and barbered to make extra money, and that damn Cruse still calls me the Barber.

"You know this Moilanen?" the doctor asked.

Bapcat explained what he had witnessed, along with the big man's spell in May on the Montreal River.

"You say he was naked?"

"As the day he was born."

The doctor rubbed his jaw. "Man that tall's likely to have plenty wrong inside him."

"You know him?" Bapcat asked.

"No, no, just heard of him. Seen him at a distance a couple of times. Hard to miss him. Heard there's some sort of move afoot to remove him as JP. He been violent before?"

"Not that I've seen."

"Well, a man doesn't just turn insane like turning on a newfangled electric light. There had to be signs. It happens over time."

"He's real quiet and very clumsy. He seems to fall a lot for no good reason."

"Huh. Bad air up by his brain? That's a joke, Bapcat. You one of the county's orphaned bastard babies?"

"Yessir."

"Listen to me, son. Your service with Teddy—that's the only damn credential of legitimacy you'll ever need. Don't you ever forget it. You hear me?"

"Yessir."

"Good. Now I'm going to examine Mr. Moilanen, and if he needs it, which I'm sure he will, I'll transfer him to St. Joe's in Hancock. The nuns there can tame a raging bear."

The abrupt and voluble Labisoniere was an odd duck.

"We get him settled in over there, come visit. Man falls over the edge like this and crawls back, he needs all the friends he can get. And if you hear Cruse call me the Barber again, tell him I said he should go have carnal knowledge of himself, so to speak." The doctor held up a forefinger. "Truth is, I don't give that barber business a second thought, Bapcat."

Oddest duck ever, Bapcat thought. *But there's something about him I trust.*

72

Hancock

MONDAY, SEPTEMBER 15, 1913

Jaquelle Frei had showed up on the hill late the night before. "Word's going 'round that Big Louie's in the hospital," she said.

"He had some kind of fit in Houghton and a bloody fight with police. They put him in the county jail. I was there."

"No doubt the Penthouse," she said, demonstrating knowledge he'd not had until two days ago. "You think he's insane?"

"No. Dr. Labisoniere is moving him to St. Joe's."

"I heard that too. You met the Barber?"

"I did, and he doesn't care for that name."

She laughed. "He tell you his grandfather was killed by Rebels in the War between the States?"

"Water over the dam," Bapcat said. "He hardly gives it a thought."

Frei smiled. "His grandfather was a bank robber in Quebec City, and the Barber forgets nothing, which makes him a fine doctor and a misanthropic human being. Insult him once and it burns forever in an unholy place in his brain."

"Got a place like that in your mind?" Bapcat asked, jabbing at her.

"We all do," she said. "I have to go to Hancock on business. You want a ride?"

Bapcat looked at Zakov. "I'll be back; don't know when." He picked up his rifle and his pack, and Zakov winked.

They spent the night in the Hilltop Hotel, overlooking the Portage ship canal, and in the morning Frei's hired driver took them to St. Joseph's Hospital, on Water Street, not seventy-five yards above the canal.

The hospital, known locally as the "poor little hospital on Hancock Street," had a portico and entrance on one end and another portico in front, a ground floor. The building was less than a decade old.

The receptionist was an unsmiling nun, built like a trammer.

"Mr. Moilanen," Jaquelle said.

"He's in isolation, the poor brute. Family only."

"We are family," Widow Frei said. "And don't you dare call him a brute."

The nun bristled. "I certainly didn't mean it that way."

"Well, I took it that way, you poor brute, so let's get moving. He needs company from people who care, not someone who thinks he's an animal."

"I am not accustomed to being bullied," the nun said officiously.

Jaquelle Frei said, "You took the habit to dish it out, so you could use God as your damn shield. I spent years in a convent school, Sister, and I know your kind."

"You are a rude, crude woman," the nun said.

"And you are not a woman at all," Frei fired back. "Now show us the way before I stop being civil."

"I don't give guided tours," the nun countered.

"With your attitude, I'm not surprised," Frei said without missing a beat.

Another nun led them to a ward and a curtained-off area. Moilanen, who was too tall for regular beds, was stretched out on two mattresses lined end to end on the polished floor. He smiled when Bapcat pulled back the curtain. "Beat up on any cops lately?" he asked his friend.

Moilanen sucked in a breath and hung his head. "Jeepers, Lute. Dey told me, but I don't remember not'ing about it, honest I don't."

"I was there. It happened, but it wasn't you—it was your sickness."

"God keeps whispering t'ings ta me, Lute."

"You still going to meet Him?"

Moilanen tapped his Bible. "We all meet God," he said sincerely. "It's all in da Good Book. But I'm going to meet him sooner den you, or my ma, I t'ink."

"I never could read that book, Louis."

"You're a good man, Lute, always a good man. You don't need no book like da rest of us sinners. Hear dey make you da game warden. Dey give you dat badge, Lute. Dat says you're a good man."

Bapcat wondered if his friend thought this of everyone who wore a badge, because there were plenty he knew that didn't deserve such a pedestal.

"God made da animals and you ta save dem, Lute. Game warden—dat's a calling, same as a minister or somet'ing." Moilanen looked past Bapcat to Frei. "Who's da lady, Lute?"

"Louis, meet Jaquelle Frei."

"She your girl, Lute?"

Frei whispered behind him, "Answer the man, Trapper."

"I guess she is, Louis."

Moilanen smiled. "Dat's real good, Lute. A man ought ta have him a wife. God says so." Moilanen picked up his Bible and began to read silently.

When it became apparent the big man had mentally departed their company, Bapcat said, "Get some rest, Louis; we'll be back to see you."

Moilanen looked up from his book. "You're my friend, Lute. You never once stared at me."

Out in the corridor Frei said, "You love the man."

"I do," he admitted.

"And I'm your girl," she said, taking his arm and squeezing affectionately.

"I suppose."

"You going to argue with God, Trapper?"

He said, "If God thinks everyone ought to have a wife, how come *He* doesn't have one?"

She poked him in the ribs. "Blasphemer."

"No, it's a kink in the story. This isn't the time to talk about us, Jaquelle."

She pressed against him. "I suppose."

"He's going to die," Bapcat said.

"You have to believe he will be in better hands, dearest."

"At least God won't stare at him. I feel helpless," he confessed.

• • •

While Frei dropped him off and went about her business in Houghton, Bapcat telephoned the Barber. "I just left St. Joe's. Thanks for taking care of my friend."

"It's my job; I hardly give it a thought. You headed north?"

"Tonight, probably. You got time to talk?"

"My office is in the Masonic Building on Shelden. Drop by and we'll get some lunch at Spingo's."

"When?"

"Make it noon," the doctor said, and hung up.

• • •

The Barber was waiting in the Masonic Building entrance, which was emblazoned with Freemason symbols. The building was four massive stories of pink sandstone. Spingo's was a tavern also on Shelden, and filled with miners and some of the rougher denizens of the city.

Each man ordered a beer and a pickled egg, and the doctor asked for some fried hen's eggs, over easy, "not runny like snot." Bapcat ordered beef, well done.

"How's your friend resting?"

"Says God is talking to him—that he's soon going to meet Him."

"I'm guessing he knows better than us."

"What's wrong with him?"

"My guess? Advanced tuberculous meningitis. All his symptoms fit, but we won't know until we do an autopsy."

Bapcat felt a chill, talking about his friend like he was already dead. "You and Cruse don't much care for each other."

"I hardly give that bloated pig a second thought."

"There some history?"

"Not that it's any of your business, but when the county board appointed me physician, Cruse went to bat for another man—said he was more sophisticated than a mere barber."

That would do it.

"Not that I dwell on it," the doctor said. "I gathered from Cruse he doesn't much care for you, either, which automatically makes us friends, the enemy of my enemy being my friend, if you follow the logic. What did you do to step on the Fat Man's foreskin?"

Bapcat told him about the altercation with Hedyn and subsequent arrest by Cruse, who was forced to release him due to the Roosevelt connection.

"Yessir, Cruse doesn't like a man with more backroom clout than him." Labisoniere added, "Take care. The Fat Man doesn't do dirty work himself, but he'll hire it out to get done what he wants."

Bapcat nodded and they ate in silence. Eventually the doctor said, "It won't be long for your friend, a week at the most. Nature's in control now."

Bapcat felt heavyhearted and listless when he met up with Frei and they began the drive back to the hill.

73

Hancock

FRIDAY, SEPTEMBER 19, 1913

The call to serve as a pallbearer for Moilanen shocked Bapcat nearly as severely as his friend's death Tuesday morning. Yesterday, Jaquelle had come down from Copper Harbor driving a Ford, and Bapcat piled in with her. The funeral would be at nine this morning. They had spent last night in the house on the hill, and he had been nervous and in no mood to work off any debt. Burial at Lakeside Cemetery, two miles west of town, would follow the services. The cemetery sat on a hill overlooking the canal, and he hoped Louis would have a good view. He quickly chastised himself for such stupid thinking. Dead was dead, an afterlife a fool's fantasy.

The Finnish Evangelical Lutheran Church on Reservation Street was a three-year-old brick building that looked down on the canal, and Houghton on the other side. Reverend Pesonen greeted the eight pallbearers in front of the church.

"You fellas were each picked by Louis. The casket and Louis together, six hundred, maybe seven hundred pounds, so you fellas hang on tight and we'll give Louis a nice send-off to meet his maker."

A man next to Bapcat whispered, "Does that mean he's not already there?"

The coffin was plain wood, unadorned, nine feet long and three feet wide, the lid nailed down. People crowded around the street in front of the church and more milled around outside than came in.

"Gawkers," his fellow pallbearer said. "Ghouls."

A pipe organ was blasting away inside the church, ripping at emotions, and Bapcat wished someone would haul the organist away. *Buck up*, he told himself. *Your friend picked you.*

Reverend Pesonen stood at the church entrance as the organ reached yet another crescendo and then stopped. The air seemed to collapse under the silence. The air was hot and sticky, not normal for September. Bapcat could smell the bodies in the pews as he and the other pallbearers struggled with the enormous coffin. Pesonen followed the casket, clutching his Bible like a kitten.

The coffin was heavy and unwieldy, and Bapcat found his hands slipping. The cords in the necks of the seven other men showed similar strain and discomfort. Eventually they got to the allotted place and set the coffin on sawhorses painted white. The unpainted, plain pine box looked out of place. The pallbearers slid into pews, four to each side, and sat, sweating.

Most of the service was conducted in Finnish, and while Reverend Pesonen talked, the stone-faced congregation made not a sound, nor displayed signs of any emotion whatsoever.

"To the eight strong men who carry Lauri today, I say thank you from Lauri and his mother Annie. He was a large man in all respects, and he was lonely beyond words," said the reverend. Bapcat kept sneaking glances at the congregation. *Still no reaction.* He finally managed to locate Jaquelle and make eye contact. She responded by subtly raising one eyebrow.

Service done, Louis's tiny mother was escorted by Pesonen in front of the coffin, and the eight pallbearers hoisted their burden and reversed course, repeated the struggle, loading the casket onto a horse-drawn hearse. Bapcat went to find Jaquelle. They got in her Ford and drove to the cemetery with the other pallbearers to await the funeral procession.

"You think he got many women into bed?" Jaquelle asked.

Bapcat shook his head and began to laugh. "The things you think about," he said.

"Funerals are always stressful," she said.

"The reverend kept calling him Lauri. Louis hated that name. I hate funerals," he added.

Eventually the mourners arrived at Lakeside, their ranks swelled by the curious, who crowded into the cemetery and watched as Bapcat and the other men lowered the coffin on thick ropes into the deep hole.

Reverend Pesonen concluded the service with "Dust to dust," and the mourners turned and departed, leaving Bapcat and Widow Frei and two or three dozen people who all came up to the hole. Bapcat growled sharply, "Get the hell away," and the people scattered. The game warden grabbed a shovel from the dirt pile and began throwing the dark soil and sand into the hole, and when it was mostly filled, he threw the shovel away and stared down at the grave and said, "No more people staring at you now, Louis."

A man came down from a slight rise. He wore a black suit and dark fedora pulled low on his forehead. "Our friend, *il dottore,* he says you look for other man at the house with the star, Helltown, by the river." The man paused and took a breath. "Our friend, *il dottore*, says to tell you that this one is on the house; the next one will cost. *Ciao*."

Jaquelle asked, "What was all that about?"

"You ever hear of a Star House in Helltown?"

She acted huffy, as if insulted, and sucked in her breath before smiling. "Ulrick Moriarty."

"You know this person?"

"Irishman, Trapper. I know everyone in every aspect of a certain business in the Keweenaw, and most in the business in surrounding areas."

"Moriarty?"

"Typical Irish, hard as nails on anybody not of his tribe. Why?"

He told her about the events with Captain Shunk and his two special deputies. "I just got word to look for Pinnochi there."

Widow Frei said, "Let me check first, through my channels. They'll probably work better than a lawman coming through the front door in that town."

He held out his hands. "I'm at your mercy," he said.

She smiled. "And always will be, dearest."

Why didn't you tell her you know Moriarty?

74

Bumbletown Hill

MONDAY, SEPTEMBER 22, 1913

Judge O'Brien leaned against the side of the house on the hill, clearly suffering from an overindulgence in spirits.

"Come inside, Your Honor—drink some coffee?" Bapcat asked.

"If it's not too much trouble, I'd like to have my coffee out here in the lovely air under this beautiful night sky."

Bapcat went inside and brought out a cup. "It's fresh."

The judge raised his cup in salute. "*Sláinte.* May the devil . . . and all that Irish shit," he said, sniggering. "Dumb, greedy, stubborn bastards have lost it all."

"Who?"

"WFM, who else?"

"The strike's over?"

"Good as. Two days ago I signed an injunction for the mine operators. No more parades or pickets, and no harassment of men who want to go back to work. I'm for the miners, Bapcat—I'm of their kind—but this thing has to be done through negotiation and compromise, not brute force."

Bapcat was also wearying of the strike and all its twists and turns and violent outbreaks. "You ever hear of a Moriarty?"

"What bedeviled twist of fate could possibly lead you to be interested in that lowest form of so-called human life?"

"The Moriarty in Helltown?"

"Only one I know, which is one more than plenty."

"What's his business?"

"Whatever he can milk for money. Why are you asking?"

"Off the record?"

O'Brien laughed. "I *am* the record, Deputy. Talk to me, man."

Bapcat outlined the search for Pinnochi.

O'Brien sucked in a deep breath. "The Moriarty I know detests Wops and makes no bones about his druthers. Got a stink on it, that tip does, or so me stomach hints. Know why I'm here?"

"No, Your Honor."

"I like to ride trolleys. I like to get to places where stars shine and damn streetlights don't block my view of Heaven. I love the stars, Bapcat, white specks in God's great void, little marks of reality in all that unknown nothingness. The night sky reminds me that I took this job to find truth in reality, and to make sure people get equal treatment under the law. But when you act stupid, you can't expect even treatment, can you?"

"Whatever you say, Judge."

"You're no damn salve to my conscience, Bapcat. That's what I say."

Zakov joined them, lit a cigarette, and talked to the judge. "Are you intending to sleep here on our mountain tonight, or would His Excellency prefer a ride home to his own bed?"

"Some pair," O'Brien said. "A Russian and a bastard."

"We'll take that as a compliment, Your Excellency," Zakov said.

"Precisely as intended."

When they pulled up in front of the judge's house in Laurium, he got out and stood beside the Ford. "I can find my way from here, intrepid explorers of the night sky." He looked over at Bapcat. "Moriarty and your missing Italian, those two facts don't add up. Steer clear of Moriarty, but if you must go, take your guns, boys."

• • •

The next morning, early, Zakov went around the hill to go into the cave below the house. He was working on some sort of door in the field, something that could be securely locked.

Bapcat heard an automobile pull up outside and looked out to see Bruno Geronissi strutting toward the house. He invited the man inside and Geronissi asked, "Are we alone?"

Bapcat told the man they were, and the birdman said, "This thing you heard about the house with the star—it's no good, bad source. Pinnochi, who knows where?"

"Are you telling me to stay out of Helltown?"

Geronissi shrugged. "You want trouble bigger than Pinnochi, go."

"Talk to me, *Dottore*."

"I got a position, family, business, obligations—you *capisce?*"

"Not really," Bapcat said, trying to draw the man out.

"You remember a day when we talk, you and me . . . about some business with deer?"

"I remember."

"That man, you know his name, one of his people made it known that Pinnochi is maybe in Helltown. This person hear somewhere how Bruno Geronissi looking for information on Pinnochi for *dottore* game warden."

"Not what it was billed to be?"

"The information? Who knows? But it feels like *agita* . . . you know *agita?*" The man patted his stomach and made a circular motion."

"Pain."

"You know what deer man is, *si?*"

Professional assassin. "I've heard."

"Okay, *bene*. I keep after information, do better to check source, okay?"

"You're sure Pinnochi's not in Helltown?"

Geronissi leaned close to him and whispered, "Listen to me: The best way to kill your enemy is from blindside."

Bapcat processed the information as best he could. "As in, sometimes you go looking for one thing and find something entirely different?"

Geronissi touched a finger to the tip of his nose. "*Va bene, ti capisco.*"

"Is there more you're not telling me?"

"Ah, there's always more, *Dottore. Ciao,*" the man said. He stood up, tipped his hat, and walked out to the waiting automobile.

Bapcat opened the trapdoor and Zakov climbed up. "You hear any of that?"

"Enough."

"Opinions?"

"Geronissi's right about blindsiding your enemy."

"In other words, we need to learn more."

"Yes, of course, but the biggest pitfall sometimes is to want too much information, to want all information. One must learn to recognize when enough information is enough."

This made sense. Jaquelle was also doing some sort of investigation. "We'll wait," Bapcat said.

"Good. We were awake all night and I am tired. I intend to sleep. Where are our colleagues?"

"No idea," Bapcat said. "Both of them work like phantoms."

"Good-night, wife," Zakov said, yawning.

"Good-night, wife," Bapcat said. Uninterrupted sleep would be most welcome.

75

Clifton, Keweenaw County

THURSDAY, SEPTEMBER 25, 1913

The boy at the front door this morning had been holding the severed head of a seven-point buck in one hand and a Winchester .30-30 in the other. The deer's eyes were not completely glazed over with the gray film that started with death and typically ended twenty-four hours later. This deer was fresh. "Remember me?" the boy had asked.

"Jordy Kluboshar, right? *Your* deer?"

"Found it."

"Where?"

"Above the Cliff."

"When?" Bapcat asked the boy.

"I heard the shot yesterday afternoon and went to look and I seen this fella run away and I followed him for a while. He shot at me twice, but I think he just wanted to scare me off, not hit me, or nothing like that."

"Why didn't you stop?"

"Saw him cuttin' off the head."

Bapcat felt his heart racing. "Do you know who he is?"

"No," the boy said, "but I seen where he went."

Bapcat yelled for Zakov and the other game wardens and they piled into the truck with the boy. It was nearly eight miles north to Clifton, and the sheer four-hundred-foot-high bluff that had been the site of the first profitable copper mine in the Keweenaw. It had been abandoned thirty years ago.

"How did you get down here?" Bapcat asked the boy as the truck jounced along.

"Hiked over to Mohawk and took the 'lectric to Allouez."

"You carried the head on the trolley?"

"Conductor wanted to throw me off, but the other passengers wouldn't let him, and he let me ride in back."

"Why come to us, boy?" Zakov asked.

"People talk."

"Make sense, boy," the Russian said.

"People say how you game wardens are lettin' people kill deer to eat, but you're after those who kill deer and leave 'em to rot."

"People are saying that?" Zakov asked.

"I ain't saying who," the boy said defensively.

Zakov and Bapcat exchanged glances.

When they reached the abandoned mining village of Clifton there were few trees left from the mining days, the slopes denuded by the ravenous hunger for timber shoring underground. The ruins of an old stamp mill still stood, some of the old log miner cabins, and the frame of an old Methodist church.

"The deer was shot down here?" Bapcat asked. There were several old farms in the area with fruit trees, mainly apples, and the fields that sometimes attracted deer. Even so, the old mining town was now inhabited mostly by ghosts. There were only a few farm families doggedly hanging on, trying to grow root vegetables. More failed than succeeded.

"Up top," the boy said, pointing.

"Show us," Bapcat said. "What were you doing way up there?"

"Same thing he was—looking for meat."

The remains of the animal were a long mile north of the old mine site, the trail twisting along edges of natural canyons and drop-offs made from poor-rock piles from mining days.

Pausing at the body, Jordy Kluboshar pointed. "That way."

Harju and Sandheim stayed with the animal to look around the area, while Zakov and Bapcat followed the boy, who moved along steep trails like a mountain goat. After two hours they advanced up the spine of the Cliff Range past the old Robbins and Phoenix mine to where the steep hills dropped abruptly down to a rough road that cut north, the Eagle River flowing in a narrow chasm beside it.

Pointing at the river, the boy said, "He went down here. I couldn't see where he crossed, but this is where he climbed down." The boy showed them some disturbed ground and Bapcat saw that the boy was right.

"You followed him a long way," Bapcat told the boy, "especially after he shot at you. Where did that happen?"

The boy held out two brass cartridges. "Back up in the hills, but I picked these up."

Bapcat looked at them. "Thirty-forties; not many of these around here," he said, sliding them into a pocket.

"*You* carry one," the boy countered.

"Indeed I do." *The boy seems observant and reliable.* "We want you to go home now."

"My old man's a souse, my ma's dead, my sister's a whore, and I live on my own schedule."

"You go to school?"

"Only when the damn truant officer can catch me, which ain't that often, or when there ain't nothing to hunt or fish."

"You're supposed to be in school."

"Out here is where I belong."

"Go back to Harju and stay with him and Sandheim. Tell them to stay where they are until we get back."

"I can keep up," the boy said.

"I'm not saying you can't, but we need to keep our minds on what's ahead, not on your safety."

"I can take care of myself," the boy protested as he turned away. They watched him cross the road and reluctantly climb a path back the way they had come. Bapcat looked down at the Eagle River, which was as low as he had ever seen it. The two men descended to the riverbed, where Zakov went downstream, and Bapcat up, careful to maintain visual contact with each other.

It was Zakov who found something and waved for Bapcat. The Russian showed him faint scuffings on three rocks about six feet apart. "He's jumping from rock to rock, using the butt of his rifle for balance."

Bapcat studied the sign, saw Zakov was right, and also recognized that the boulder trail led to lava formations miners called traps on the other side. Bapcat began nodding. "He started climbing up here. You can stay on the traps for a long, long way. I used to hunt float copper over this way in summer. You can follow this lava ledge all the way to the Central Cutover Road, and if you drift north you'll strike Cedar Creek Canyon and you can follow the rim from there. Easy going either way, little soil to leave signs, firm footing for speed, and easy dragging if you've got a deer."

"Are we going to pursue?" Zakov asked.

"We know the man came across here yesterday. I'll follow. You get Harju, Sandheim, and the boy, and drive the truck up to Central Location."

Central was a largely abandoned mining community that had once been a stronghold for Cousin Jacks. There was a general store there where they all could meet up. "I'll stay on the track and meet all of you tonight at Stugo's."

Zakov said, "The ratting grounds are north of Central."

"Ratting grounds?"

"Old mine-shaft entrances and pits that connect underground in the area of Copper Falls Pond. In summer the area teems with rats, and wolf packs sometimes take their pups there to teach them to hunt."

"Wolves hunt beaves in summer," Bapcat pointed out.

"There are no beavers up there, just rats, and the wolves adapt, almost as well as humans. Bears, too. They take their cubs there for the same reason. I had some fair hunting up there. When snow comes, the area also seems to attract deer, though I have no idea why."

Ratting grounds. What else don't I know about this territory I'm supposed to protect?

Zakov took off and Bapcat readjusted his pack straps. Two summers ago he had worked his way along the confines of Cedar Creek Canyon, which lay ahead and north. He had fished holes all day, camped at the headwaters spring hole, eaten until he was full of fresh trout, and fished his way out the next morning. He had discovered Cedar Creek accidentally, and it reminded him that in the Keweenaw there were always surprises waiting for you if you got off the beaten path.

The deer killer had shot twice to warn the boy. *Strange behavior.*

No time to daydream; eyes down, move uphill, and don't stop until you are on top and have covered some distance.

Approaching the crossover wagon trail, Bapcat sensed again that he wasn't alone. He'd been feeling something dogging him for going on an hour. He saw a pit ahead and noticed that it ran like a trench up into some boulders to his right, through an outcrop of brown basalt. He jumped down, scuttled right as quickly as he could, climbed out, and circled back to behind where he had come from.

Just as he stopped to rest, a shadow passed him, and he reached out and grabbed Jordy Kluboshar off his feet. The boy was startled and dropped his

Winchester, which discharged, sending a bullet snapping around the stony surrounds. The boy tried to flail, but Bapcat held firm. "What the hell are you doing, boy?"

"I told you I ain't afraid."

"You're supposed to be with the others."

"Well, I *ain't*," the boy said defiantly. "You made me drop my goddamn rifle."

"You're the one dropped it, and I ought to wash your mouth out with soap. That bullet could have hit one of us."

"Well, it didn't, did it? And I ain't afraid."

Bapcat released the boy. "Climb down, get your rifle, unload it, and bring the bullets to me."

"They're my bullets."

"If I give them back. Boy can't keep hold of a loaded rifle shouldn't have it loaded."

"It ain't much good unloaded," Kluboshar said.

"That's the point here, boy. I don't want to get shot because you got spooked."

"Goddammit, you're the one who spooked me!" the boy protested.

"Get the rifle, Jordy, and shut up."

The boy shook his head.

"You follow the track all this way?"

"Didn't you?"

The boy hung his head.

"Fetch the cartridges."

Jordy Kluboshar did as he was told and handed the rounds to Bapcat. "It ain't fair."

"It ain't supposed to be," Bapcat said.

"I thought lawmen had to play fair," the boy complained.

"Not game wardens," Bapcat said. "We play to win, whatever it takes."

"We going to keep tracking?" the boy asked.

"Sure, if you can show me where the trail is."

The boy hung his head again.

"We're going to meet the others," Bapcat said.

"All the way back there?"

"They're waiting for us in Central," the game warden said.

"I'll just go on home," the boy said.

Bapcat pushed down a laugh. "From now on you'll be going where we take you, boy, until I can figure out what the story is with you."

"You ain't even gonna thank me for bringing that deer head?"

"What did it lead to?"

"I don't like you," the boy said.

Bapcat told him, "I ain't too sure about you, either."

76

Ratting Grounds, Keweenaw County

FRIDAY, SEPTEMBER 26, 1913

They slept all night on the ground behind Stugo's. Harju said in the morning, "Sandheim and I have to get back to our counties. This thing feels like it's slowing. I can jump back over here if you need me."

"Leave the truck back at the hill," Bapcat said.

"What about you two?"

"Hepting's not that far away. Take the boy with you."

"Where?"

"To his home."

The boy sulked. "You have my bullets."

"*And* your rifle. You'll get everything back if you behave, and before you start whining, I know—it's not fair."

Zakov and Bapcat watched as Harju and Sandheim drove away in the truck, Jordy Kluboshar their unwilling passenger. They bought food and tobacco plugs in the store and hiked north up the cutover trail.

"You didn't notice the boy wasn't with Harju?" Bapcat said sharply to the Russian.

"I saw the little sneak in the forest and knew he was shadowing you. That boy is trouble, I think."

Bapcat had similar concerns. "He has backbone."

"As do all vertebrates."

"Philosophy again?"

"Where are we going?"

"I found six or seven spots on the traprock formations—old blood."

"I don't understand why one would haul trophies across such a difficult path."

"Impossible to know. I want to get up to the top of the crossover and cut northeast."

"Small lakes and high swamps."

"I know. And the ratting grounds."

"That has nothing to do with what we are doing."

Technically, his partner was correct. "Still, I want to see."

"The wolves will be gone by now," Zakov said. "Wrong time of year."

"How long to get there?"

"Three hard uphill miles, then northeast to just this side of Madison Gap. Two hours, perhaps three. Are we working off the previous trail?"

"I'll take us to the last blood spot and we'll work from there, see how far we can follow it. Like you, I keep thinking if you need to get things up here somewhere, why not up the main road to the cutoff?"

"Secrecy," Zakov ventured.

• • •

They paused later at Indian Dog Cut, where legend had it a dog had once led some stranded redmen down to safety from a killer blizzard. Bapcat had found two more blood spatters, tiny specks on the traprock, but the formation had suddenly dipped underground and disappeared. Bapcat walked along, looking upward at rocky promontories and overhangs.

"The blood is on the ground," Zakov said.

Late in the afternoon they climbed up to a stone-and-grass benchland. On top they found scrub oaks and dozens of holes in a layer of blue-gray sand, the ground littered with countless piles of wolf scat and bear feces, dotted with fur and bone remnants.

"Here?" Bapcat asked.

The Russian nodded. "The rats come out to hunt at night. Our brothers in darkness."

They sat on a pile of rocks by some pin oaks to wait. A bear came out within twenty minutes and likewise took a seat to wait, ignoring them, its focus exclusively on the area with the holes. After dark they heard rats squealing in terror and running and the sound of the grunting bear cavorting in front of them, but only the one bear came, and after a few moments of noise, the night settled back to silence.

Zakov made a fire at first light and heated a can of beans for them to share. After eating and extinguishing the tiny fire, they continued hiking northeast.

Bapcat felt all day they were being watched, but the watcher was skilled, and careful, left little sign, allowed no glimpses.

As they circled around the area in expanding clockwise laps they came to an unexpected stand of giant white oaks. On the southern perimeter a hundred or more dyed squirrel tails had been affixed to the branches of a mature ironwood tree, hanging in languor until zephyrs from Lake Superior a few short miles away swirled up the bluff and animated the colorful tails like battle pennants.

The Russian looked around with only his eyes. "We are under surveillance."

"For some time," Bapcat said.

"I suspected as much," Zakov said. "Would you like to flush him out?"

"No," Bapcat said. "It's time we went back. The squirrel tails—you've seen these before?"

"Never, and I have no idea what they signify."

"That makes two of us," Bapcat said, turning back to the southwest.

77

Bumbletown Hill

SATURDAY, SEPTEMBER 27, 1913

Bapcat and Zakov threw their gear in a corner and collapsed onto the floor, both sighing deeply. "We'll worry about grub later," Bapcat said.

"*Da*, stop talking."

Bapcat's mind refused to shut off. Colored squirrel tails fluttered from tree branches near the ratting grounds. *Who else is carrying a .30-40 Krag? Where's the disposal site?*

Unable to sleep, Bapcat sat up and rolled a cigarette. The Russian was snoring a low buzz. *Why no word from Jaquelle about Helltown? Summer gone, no wood yet made for winter. We will need to see to that for a few days. Will be welcome, mindless work. So many questions, no answers.*

Suddenly and silently, Zakov got to his feet, shuffled over to the trapdoor, leaned over to listen, yanked it open, and reached down to haul up Jordy Kluboshar by the scruff of his neck.

"Boy!" Zakov said with a snarl, shaking him.

"Leggo!" the boy shouted.

Bapcat saw that the boy's face was red and swollen, with puffing around his eyes and a cut near one ear. "Pinkhus Sergeyevich," Bapcat said softly. "Release our guest."

The frightened boy tried to compose himself.

Zakov examined his face. "You've taken up pugilism since we last saw you?" the Russian asked.

"I'm Catholic, not whatever you said," Kluboshar said defensively.

"You're supposed to be home," Bapcat said.

"Them wardens took me there, but my old man didn't like it."

Bapcat went closer to the boy, looked at his face. "Your father did this?"

"If I wasn't so quick, it would be a lot worse," the boy said.

"Where do you live, boy?" Zakov asked.

"I ain't going back," the child said defiantly. "I want my rifle."

"Show us your house," Bapcat said.

The boy crossed his arms and set his jaw. "To hell with you."

"Stay with him," Bapcat told the Russian.

• • •

They had found the boy in the Centennial Mine area, two and a half miles south of the hill. Assuming the boy lived nearby, it could be Kearsarge, Wolverine, Centennial, Centennial Heights, or any of several other small mining villages. They had first seen him near the Centennial mine pump house, and this would be Bapcat's starting point again.

Few people seemed to be out and around, including strikers, though they seemed most active at shift-change times. Saturdays were workdays for miners. Smoke spewed from stacks, pumps ran noisily, chains and cables in lift houses clanked and squealed. Hoses still stretched from the pump house to animal dens, and the nearest creek oozed a malodorous yellow-white fluid.

The few people he found were in no mood to talk to him and brushed right by, even when he tried to show his badge.

He was close to giving up when he stopped on the edge of Kearsarge at a blacksmith shop run by a tall man with eyebrows so bushy they looked like woolly bears. "What you want?" the man asked.

"A boy," Bapcat said. "Information, on Jordy Kluboshar."

"Croatian, very spunky boy; we call him Little Nomad. He in trouble again?"

"I want to talk to his father."

"Then you be the one got trouble," the man said gravely.

"The boy trouble?"

"No, he's just a scalawag."

"They live near here?"

"Up toward Phillipsville, east side of main road, set back some. Old barn, log house. You sure you want to see this person?"

Bapcat showed his badge.

The man laughed. "Hope they give you gun, too. You mix much with Croatians?"

"No."

"Foul mouths, yes. If Andro Kluboshar say his cunt hurts, he mean he don't care what you are talking."

Andro. "Good to know," Bapcat said, thinking, *What the hell is going on here*?

Bapcat found the property, the dilapidated barn and cabin, dregs of a potato field, several chained hounds baying wildly. A man came out on the cabin porch with a two-bang shotgun, squinted at him, said nothing to the dogs dancing choke dances at the end of taut chains.

"You aren't inviting to here," the man roared, and leveled the shotgun at him. "*Jebe se!*"

"I want to talk to you about your son."

The man spit. "He is all shit, that one."

The man seemed unsteady on his feet, but the gun didn't waver, and Bapcat warned himself to move slowly and deliberately for the moment. "Put down rifle," the man ordered.

Bapcat said, "Game warden."

The man sneered. "I piss on you, Game Warden."

"Have you been drinking?"

"Fuck you, Game Warden."

Think. Get him in close. Make him come to you.

"Look, your boy dropped some money and I found it. I just wanted to bring it back."

"Give to me the money," the man said, staring, taking a step down. "How much is there you got?"

"Hundred dollars."

Kluboshar's eyes widened and he stepped closer, the shotgun now in one hand. "Show me," he ordered.

Bapcat put his hand in his jacket, made a fist, and caused the pocket to bulge. "Got a lot here, afraid I'll drop some. Spread your hands?"

The man clamped his weapon under his arm, the barrels facing to the rear, and greedily stepped forward with his hands spread open and waiting. Bapcat could smell the alcohol wafting off of him. Before the man could react, Bapcat took his rifle and ripped the barrel across the inside of the man's knee. The man fell into a heap. Bapcat grabbed Kluboshar's shotgun and windmilled it into the weeds as the man recovered and bounced up, swinging wildly.

Bapcat hit him in the cheek with his rifle butt and the man keeled over and was still. The game warden put his knee behind the man's neck, pulled his hands behind him, and handcuffed his wrists.

When the man began to recover he mumbled through a bloody mouth, "My boy's money, my money. Mine!"

"There isn't any money," Bapcat said. "You ever beat your son again, I'll be back, and it won't go this easily."

"My cunt hurts," the man said spitefully with a growling sound.

Bapcat stood, rolled the man onto his side, and drove his boot toe between the man's legs, causing an explosive loss of breath followed by violent gagging and moaning. "Touch that boy again, I'll use a knife next time."

"I calling sheriff," the man managed.

"My cunt hurts," Bapcat said, and walked away, careful not to turn his back.

Back at the hill Bapcat got the boy's rifle and ammunition and gave them to him.

"This is your home now, boy. Understand?"

"You can't keep me here."

Zakov said, "This is legal?"

Bapcat's intense glare silenced the Russian and the boy.

78

Eagle River

MONDAY, SEPTEMBER 29, 1913

The sheriff met Bapcat outside the county's white building on the hill. "Most of the National Guard's been withdrawn," Hepting reported. "I can't prove it, but most workers are back in the mines, all but Finns, Hungarians, and Croatians. The strike parades are shrinking, and with the army gone, the operators are about fed up." The sheriff handed him a white button with red lettering: ALLIANCE. "Won't nobody say so, but this is MacNaughton's work. Bet on that."

Finns, Hungarians, Croatians—no doubt all unskilled workers, trammers, beasts of burden, the bottom of every mine's pecking order. He didn't want to think too deeply about the strike. He had enough problems to contend with.

"You might want to have a talk with your lady friend," Hepting said out of the blue. "About scabs."

Bapcat wrinkled his brow and Hepting said, "Talk to her."

What the hell? "John, have you ever heard about squirrel tails up by Madison Gap?"

"Jesus, is he back?"

"He, *who*?"

"Captain Erastus Renard Webster, formerly of the Sixteenth Michigan Infantry, First Independent Sharpshooter Company."

"War between the States?"

"Four years, fought pretty much the whole shebang."

"He the one with the squirrel tails?"

"Got something to do with Genghis Khan and nomads, though I don't know zackly what, and don't much care. The man's not right in the head. Webster moves around a lot, and he's usually out in Arizona by the time the snow flies here. Far as I know, this is his first time up by Madison Gap. Most summers he's south along the Gratiot River. Got him a woman, too; she's always well-armed."

"What's he do?"

Hepting pursed his mouth. "Don't really know. He avoids towns and stays in the woods and that's fine by me."

"Dangerous?"

"Never broke laws here I know of, so I don't really know, but he's always struck me as desperate, and desperate usually means dangerous. Why?"

"Saw the tails in the tree, wondered."

"What were *you* doing way up there?"

"Looking around. Zakov showed me the ratting grounds."

"What the hell is that?"

"Long story. You ever cross paths with a man by the name of Kluboshar?"

"Good God," Hepting said. "You bump heads with that sonuvabitch?"

"He's got a son."

"You mean had one. His boy ran off years ago."

"His name is Jordy, and he's still here."

"The way that man beats on him, and he's still around?"

"He was, but now he's with Zakov and me."

"Kluboshar beat his wife to death, though we couldn't get enough evidence to prove the case. This was five years back. Whaddya mean, the boy's *with* you two?"

"His father beat on him so I went to see the old man."

"He come out fighting?"

"With a shotgun." Hepting snorted contemptuously. "Threaten to call the sheriff?"

"Something along those lines."

"Won't happen. He knows I want him for his wife's death, and he won't go to Cruse because Cruse hates the man. He's a lush and a WFM man, one of those natural loudmouths that weaker men are drawn to because they talk big."

"Strike *leader?*"

"Hell no, just a drunken agitator. If Cruse goes after him, it will only be under the banner of crushing the strike; otherwise the Fat Man don't like to personally get into potentially lethal confrontations. What other good news have you got?"

"We want the boy to stay with us—at least until we can find kin."

"None here; they're all back in Croatia."

"He can't live with his father."

"Then you fellas hang on to him. I'll tell the JP and the judge."

"I thrashed his father pretty good."

"Pardon me if I shed no tears."

"What about Jaquelle?" Bapcat asked.

"None of my business, but word's going 'round that she's sponsoring scabs."

"What the hell does 'sponsoring' mean?"

"I don't know the details. Ask her."

"Then you don't actually *know* anything."

"No need for that tone, Lute."

"John, you're pro-union."

"Officially, I'm neutral, but I'm also an honorary member of the WFM."

"It can't be that all operators are bad."

"Never said they were, but some want only money, and they don't much give a damn where it comes from, how they get it, or the costs others have to pay for their wealth."

"Meaning Jaquelle Frei?"

"Dammit, it's just something I heard, Lute. Don't take it so damn personal."

Switch directions. "What about Ulrick Moriarty?"

Hepting loosed a nervous laugh. "Shit, Lute. Kluboshar, Webster, and Moriarty; now *there's* a threesome."

"Star House," Bapcat said.

"Your proverbial den of iniquity: gambling, draggletails, the usual low-life menu."

"Some say he's hiding Pinnochi."

"*That* Mick protecting a Dago?" Hepting said with a snarl. "Not very likely."

"Tell me about Moriarty."

"Well, as I hear it, he's threatening to kill the next lawman who steps over his threshold."

"And he's still free?"

"All talk so far, and last I checked, the Constitution protects talk. You going up to Helltown?"

"Haven't decided yet."

"You decide to go, take an army."

"Including you?"

"Well, if you're that set on it—otherwise, I opt to leave that SOB right where he is."

79

Copper Harbor

FRIDAY, OCTOBER 3, 1913

Frei Dry Goods and Outfitters sat on the town's extreme eastern perimeter and overlooked the harbor, the last commercial enterprise before Old Fort Wilkins and the wilds that stretched out to Keweenaw Point, land's end of the seventy-mile-long peninsula.

Bapcat noticed that there was a door open to Frei's icehouse, a substantial structure added to the west side of the main building by Jaquelle's late husband. Seven or eight men were gathered on the front steps of the establishment, their haircuts and clothes identifying them at first glance as foreigners.

The game warden looked down at Jordy Kluboshar, his rifle slung over his shoulder. "Your weapon unloaded?"

"How many times you gonna ask that?"

"As many times as I need to in order to feel satisfied that the rifle is safe."

"It ain't loaded."

"Good. Wait out here on the porch," Bapcat said, and went inside. A bell attached to the door sounded his arrival. Jaquelle was talking to two women about a bolt of yellow cloth, but used her eyes to direct him to the tiny room she called her office.

"Good God and hallelujah, Mohammed's surely come to the mountain!" she exclaimed dramatically but quietly. She smiled seductively and looked him over. "Thought maybe you forgot how to get here."

"Helltown," he said.

"Good God, Lute. We women need foreplay, the music of language, songs of the heart, not just spitting out requests for information," she said, her voice on edge.

"Ulrick Moriarty?"

"What about him?"

"You were to get information for me."

"I have. Pinnochi's not with Moriarty and not in Wyoming," she said. "Your informant was wrong."

"And you know this *how?*"

"I believe I told you that I know Moriarty. I talked to him."

"There or here?"

"What difference does *that* make?" she demanded.

Her jaw was clenched, back straight, chest heaving, chin out, fists balled, ready to argue, and he had no inkling why. "Who're those men out front?"

"Men who want honest labor."

"Scabs?"

"I detest labels," she said. "They demean."

"They're foreigners," he said.

Which drew a snicker. "Good God, Bapcat, who in the Keweenaw *ain't?*"

"The operators have trouble getting strikers back to work, so they import workers? How many of them fellas even know they're walking into a strike?"

"What business is this of yours, Trapper?"

"Technically none, but a lot of my work has been directly because of the strike, and I guess that's *made* it my business."

"Mine are all here legally," Frei said.

"I didn't say they weren't."

"John Hepting made that same accusation to my attorney."

"I'm sure John's just doing his job the way he sees it."

"WFM people are watching trains from the East Coast, and when immigrants are recruited by personnel bureaus out east, strikers talk them out of coming. Some are threatened, and get off the train along the way. Others get to Houghton or Red Jacket and go straight to the WFM office to sign up as soon as they leave the station. It seemed to me there could be a more efficient way to handle the shortage. The mine operators asked me to look into alternatives."

"The men out front."

"My second group of ten. The first group's already working. The men come up the St. Lawrence to Montreal by ship, then by train to Soo, Ontario. They take a ferry to the Michigan side where Immigration checks them in and our people pick them up and bring them by boat to Copper Harbor. The WFM and their sympathizers are all looking south and back to the East. I'm bringing them in from the north—behind the lines. I also heard more are coming down from Minnesota."

"Got your own little military operation," he said.

"I suppose," she said, smiling.

He wasn't sure why he said what he said next. It just sort of came out, pushed by something deep and heavy inside him. "What's Moriarty's role in your little scheme?"

Frei was smart and seldom caught short, but he saw momentary panic in her eyes. "Why would you ask such an entirely *ludicrous* question?"

"I'm not sure," he confessed, "but whatever it is, it's also telling me to talk to Moriarty face-to-face."

"You are an unrepentant, willfully stubborn man, Bapcat. I say again: Pinnochi's not there and never has been."

He thought he detected a hitch in her voice. "Why're you trying to block me?"

"Not block—preempt," she corrected him. "Perhaps I'm trying to protect you, Deputy. Has that ever occurred to you?"

"I don't need *your* protection."

"Ordinarily I might accept your contention as true on a theoretical level, but in this case I do not. I contracted Moriarty to provide security for our new immigrants, and he's employed a number of crusty fellows."

"You mean thugs?"

"I mean, men who do difficult, often-unwanted jobs for fair pay," she said.

He thought for a moment. "Men with criminal records?"

"I prefer to think of them as individuals who deliver what they are contracted to deliver."

Thugs and criminals. "Did the operators come to you, or did you go to them?"

"That, I believe, is none of your business, Deputy."

"Jaquelle, I understand your interest in making money, and I know you're good at it."

She showed a sliver of a smile. "Then you will surely understand that I make such money by rendering wants into needs, and satisfying said needs."

Some things were still gnawing at him. "Your crusty fellows wouldn't include strike-breakers, would they?"

"My contract is limited to security and escort duties for newly hired miners."

Her contract? How many contracts were there, and between whom? "For twenty men so far."

"Yes, so far. I think of it as a pipeline, which is now built and ready for me to turn on the flow to match demand."

"Moriarty hires security men for you?"

"That's the arrangement."

"And you don't want me to visit Helltown."

"The place is a veritable hornet's nest, Lute. Why disturb the hive if it's isolated and not bothering anyone?"

"I take your point, Jaquelle. Let me show you something."

Frei followed him to the front door, which he opened. "Boy, get in here."

"I got a name," the boy grumbled as he stepped inside.

"Jordy Kluboshar, meet Mrs. Frei," Bapcat said.

"*Widow* Frei," Jaquelle corrected him gently.

Bapcat said, "What do you say, Jordy?"

"Pleasedtameetcha," the boy mumbled.

"Thank you for saying so, even if it's not how you really feel," the widow told the boy.

Bapcat said, "Go back outside, Jordy."

"Are we leaving soon?" the boy asked.

Bapcat pointed at the door and the boy stepped out. To Frei: "Zakov and I have taken him in. He's been living nearly wild. Mother's dead, father's a drunk who beats him. The boy's got good instincts and he's got courage."

"And you and that obnoxious Russian have taken a notion you can save this boy's lost soul?"

"We don't care about his soul, just his life," Bapcat said. "He stays with his father, sooner or later he'll turn up dead. I need your help."

He saw she was surprised. "I don't like kids, Lute. And they don't like me."

"This will help both of you."

"*This?* He's carrying a ruck and a rifle. Are you intending to leave him *here*, sir? *Here?*"

"Add it to my debt, and make sure he gets to school."

"This will cost you substantially, dearest."

"Everything with you costs me dearly."

"Why, Mr. Bapcat, you are manipulating us into having a family, and you have not even had the decency to ask for my hand in marriage."

"Do you think you can manipulate everyone in your life all the time?" he shot back.

She smiled. "Actually, yes, and I can hear acceptance of the family concept in your heart," she said. "I shall look forward to your proposal for my hand. Does the boy have good hygiene?"

"I'm sure he will when you're done with him."

She put her hands on her hips and swayed. "Agreed. It goes on the tab. You want to make partial payment now?"

"There's no time, Jaquelle."

He could see her mulling something over. "Lute, there's a man hanging around Moriarty's, Frank Fisher."

"Just one?"

"Dammit, you listen to me. Fisher is dangerous. Even Moriarty's petrified of him."

"He can fire him."

"Apparently Fisher's not the kind you can fire, and he doesn't work for Moriarty, he just seems to always be there."

"What about Pinnochi, Jaquelle?"

"Moriarty says he was never there, and he started to amend his statement with something about Fisher, but came up mute. This is why I don't want you to go to Helltown. Something's dreadfully wrong out there."

"I can take care of myself," he said.

"I know that, but a little insurance never hurts," she said, and stepped over and kissed him. "You're going to Helltown, aren't you?"

"Probably not," he allowed. "Fisher come in with your first group?"

"Just before that. On his own."

"But he's not one of Moriarty's security hires?"

"No, he's an Ascher Agency dick from out east."

Bapcat opened the door and called the boy inside. "Jordy, you're staying with Widow Frei. Do what she asks you to do and mind your manners. And before you whine, I know this isn't fair."

"It sure as hell ain't," the boy said.

"Is that rifle loaded?" Jaquelle Frei asked the boy.

"He asks me that all the time," the boy complained.

"Answer me," she said. "Is it?"

"No."

"No, what?"

"No, it ain't loaded."

"No, ma'am, it *isn't* loaded."

"I just said it ain't loaded," Kluboshar insisted.

"You'll learn to say it better. Do you have anything you need to tell Deputy Bapcat?"

"Yeah, them's all Croats outside and they don't speak no American . . . and *Goddammit, please don't leave me with her!*"

"This is for your own good, Jordy," Bapcat said, brushing his hand against Frei's thigh and stepping past the sputtering boy into the day.

80

Wyoming (Helltown), Keweenaw County

SATURDAY, OCTOBER 4, 1913

The town of Wyoming had been built in a clear field a mile or so south of the village of Delaware, on the south bank of the Montreal River. Bapcat had trapped all through and around the area for years. Wyoming had been one of the Keweenaw's original mines, established halfway through the previous century, but had been long since closed. All that remained were the rusted remains and stone walls of an old stamp mill and a half-dozen buildings, including a small general store and four taverns, which operated all day, every day, and attracted so many miners from nearby communities that it became known locally as Helltown. There was no law.

The first draw in the village was alcohol, followed closely by loose women—sporting girls called tumble-downs, meaning they had tumbled from sporting house to sporting house, each time descending to more-demeaning circumstances. Helltown was as low as a woman could fall. *Does Jaquelle supply women for Moriarty and the other bar owners there?* Bapcat wondered.

Some nights and days the town was wild with drunks and brawls and shooting. You could always gauge the mood by sitting in the woods and listening a quarter-mile out.

Moriarty's place was reputed to be the most depraved in town, and had held that distinction for as long as Bapcat could recall. Rather than frightening him, Jaquelle's worries about one Frank Fisher only served to make Bapcat curious.

Assuming Fisher might be as dangerous as Frei thought he was, Bapcat knew he should get Moriarty alone so there could be no interference. Such an opportunity might be rare, but Bapcat knew it was just a matter of patience and caution on his part, and the call of Mother Nature on Moriarty's part. When Bapcat got Moriarty alone, the man would not be happy to see him.

Late that night, the big Irishman came outside to his private privy, and when he opened the door to go in, Bapcat stepped up behind him, put the rifle barrel on the man's skull, and said calmly, "Don't even think of moving, Moriarty. Step inside."

"I'll be the picture of compliance. Who are ye?"

"Speak only when I tell you to speak."

"Yer fookin horse's arse."

Bapcat smacked the man's head with a short thrust of the rifle barrel. "Only when I tell you to speak, otherwise *listen*."

Moriarty whispered, "Mother of God, I know that fookin' voice."

"Pinnochi."

"Why're people so interested in a bloody guinea?"

"He was here."

"Yer mother's arse."

"I have it on good authority."

"Bollocks, who'd be spoutin' such shite?"

The strain in the man's voice said fear, lots of fear, torrents of it just under the surface. "Remember the lesson you got about poaching another man's trapline?"

"Swear to God, I don't even trap no more."

"I find out Pinnochi was here—ever—you know what will happen."

"I don't want *your* kind of problem, and now word's going around about how the Trapper's acquired a state badge."

"Who else asked about Pinnochi?"

"Widow Frei," Moriarty said.

Bapcat prodded him with the Krag. "And?"

"Not sure. I got patrons, they all talk shite and ask questions, you know, bar talk."

Switch direction. "Who around here carries a .30-40 Krag?"

Long delay in response. "Only one I seen."

"Name?"

"Frank."

"Frank Fisher?"

"Could be. Just Frank is all I know."

Bapcat slowly chambered a round. "Say your prayers if you know any."

"Yes, yes, Frank Fisher—Jaysus!"

"He works for you."

"More shite. He don't work for me. He come in here one night and that's all I know."

"Who's he work for?"

"Not me."

"He around tonight?"

"Ain't seen 'im."

"Why's he come to your place?"

"Best girls in town."

"Not much of a claim there, Ulrich."

"I think he's looking for someone."

"He mention names?"

"Not much of a talker."

"And no idea where he is now, or where he hangs out?"

"Nah, no talker, that bugger."

Bapcat made Moriarty squeeze around him and face the door.

"I ain't shat yet," the man complained. He was sweating heavily and shaking.

"Find another place to leave your brains," Bapcat said.

Silence again, more trembling.

"Someone out there, Ulrick?" a voice called.

"I don't know."

"Step out. It's time for you to depart the premises."

Moriarty put up his hands up, cried "Don't shoot!," kicked open the door, and stumbled outside.

Bapcat rolled out behind the man but immediately moved right into the dark and belly-crawled to a pile of wood for cover. He was prepared for a shot, but none came.

The game warden moved to another location near the river and settled in to watch Moriarty's place of business. Just as dawn began to suggest itself in the eastern sky, a figure in a dark shirt came out of Moriarty's and quickly walked to another establishment, where he opened the door and glanced back. For a split second Lute Bapcat could clearly make out the man's features, and sucked in a deep breath.

He was thinner and all gray and it had been seventeen years, but there was no mistaking Sergeant Frankus Fish. He was carrying a Krag carbine, and wearing a Rough Rider slouch hat. *What the hell is happening here*?

81

Sault Ste. Marie, Chippewa County

SUNDAY, OCTOBER 19, 1913

Michigan game wardens had been in the town that locals called the Soo for a week to train, get acquainted, and compete. For Bapcat and Zakov, who walked away with the two-man shooting competition, most of the rest of the week had been a strain, beginning last Sunday with a strange scolding by some mealymouthed lawyer from Lansing about them illegally subverting the laws of the state legislature in the suspension of the deer season, while Oates and Jones looked on without comment. As soon as the lawyer left the room, the diminutive chief deputy Jones put them in a brace, and gave them an ass-chewing "for being too damn involved in strike politics," a dressing-down Zakov later characterized as "legendary in tone, proportion, and duration."

Despite the heavy daily schedule, the two men got down to the St. Mary's River and found a sloop called *Angel Wind,* whose master said he had been contracted to carry immigrant miners to Copper Harbor. So far there had been but two deliveries, with no more scheduled. Further, the captain remembered a passenger named Frank Fisher, who had gone to Copper Harbor in July and whom he had not seen since. There was also another passenger slated for that trip, the man's name Rudyard Riordan, but the man had not shown up for departure, and had been left behind.

The two game wardens also learned from Deputy Harold Barothy of Schoolcraft County that a man by the name of Riordan had arrived in town sometime in July, and caught on with a logging company about eight miles north of town in the Little Fox River country.

"You're sure the man's name is Riordan?" Bapcat asked.

" 'Tis indeed," Barothy reported.

When the weeklong meeting broke up, Bapcat and Zakov intended to locate Riordan and question him.

Three full days of grinding through statutes and procedures in *Chase's Duties for Game Wardens* and *Tiffany's Criminal Law* left most of the wardens with headaches, and it hadn't helped that the presenting lawyer for the *Tiffany's* work had all the dramatic effect of stagnant pond water.

The night before there had been a group dinner at the old Fort Brady's officers' mess. The fort had been built to house soldiers guarding the Soo locks. Last night's speaker was an army colonel from Pittsburgh, who talked about the implications and safety issues involved in the shooting of antlered deer. After dinner, and clearly in his cups, the man lamented what he called the absolute certainty of a war in Europe within two years, a war, he said, which would draw in the entire civilized world. Bapcat had only a vague notion of Europe, but Zakov seemed quite grim all night after hearing the speaker.

At final assembly this morning after breakfast, Bapcat and Zakov received medals for their shooting triumph and kudos for their Italian bird case. Chief Deputy Jones asked Bapcat to get up and tell the other officers about the case, an order which made Bapcat's knees shake and heart palpitate. Talking publicly was a nightmare for him, one he had pretty much avoided his entire life.

Afterward, Horri Harju laughed and congratulated him. "Nearly canned, decorated, and complimented, all in the same week, Bapcat. Well done. They tell you to enforce the new law?"

"No, just chewed us out."

"They were both covering their potentially exposed political posteriors. Jones and Oates are both real good at that."

"Meaning, we just keep on?"

"Yessir, and if it comes up again down the road, our supervisors can claim honestly that they chewed your ass once before, and that will be that. Unless they decide to discharge you."

"Because it will then be my fault."

"Attaboy. That's how this business works, but neither Oates nor Jones has yet hung any of us out to dry."

"This sort of thing is worthy of the czar's convoluted court," Zakov said with a groan.

Bapcat said, "I never expected this job to be so—"

"Vague?" Harju said, finishing the sentence for him.

"Right."

"There are times when none of this seems real," Bapcat said.

"Stop and think. People have died because of the strike, and there have been mass violations of fish and game laws. That's as real as it gets, but even if it wasn't, who cares? Lansing has one reality and we have another. Lansing, where A can't ever relate to B. You going to need me back over your way?"

"We're not sure yet."

"Let me know."

That night in the barracks Zakov said, "I think I have a superb aptitude for the law."

"Most of us would prefer you mute," Bapcat said.

Zakov laughed and pointed a finger. "*Touché, mon ami.* Did you understand the significance of what we heard about Europe?"

"No," Bapcat admitted.

"It means that small political missteps could create a conflagration."

"Europe's across an ocean, right?"

Zakov rolled his eyes and sighed.

"Then what do we care about a war thousands of miles from us?"

"Because, *gospodin*, America's days of isolation from the world ended when you and your comrades fought the Spaniards."

Bapcat didn't understand how Cuba related to Europe, and didn't care. "Seney tomorrow," he said, and Zakov grinned.

"The reputation of Seney is the equal to Siberia," Zakov said.

"Siberia?"

"Across the Bering Straits from Seward's Folly."

"Seward?"

"Your secretary of war under your great slave-freer Abraham Lincoln, and his successor, President Andrew Johnson. Seward negotiated an obscenely small price for a land mass from Russia that is twice the size of your state of Texas. Another example of a czar being incompetent at things he should be strong at."

Bapcat knew about Lincoln, and even Johnson, but who was this Seward, and what land was the Russian talking about?

82

Seney, Schoolcraft County

MONDAY, OCTOBER 20, 1913

Zakov, Bapcat, and Harold Barothy got off the train with their packs and rifles and headed straight across the main dirt road to the Grondin Hotel, a white, three-story building that stuck out among all the other buildings painted in dark colors and tones.

Barothy's wife and kids lived in Manistique, in the far south of the county, and when he worked this part of the county he always took a room at the Grondin. The proprietor had once been a famous cook at a logging camp, had saved his pay and opened this business. He was successful right from the start because of his fabled kitchen.

Barothy guided them into the bar and pointed at a man at a side table. "Riordan."

"I thought he was a logger?" Bapcat said.

"I said he caught on with a camp, not that he lasted. He busted his leg real bad in the second week and now he's here for the winter."

Riordan was manhandling an oversize spoon in a large bowl of fragrant brown liquid with vegetables floating on top.

"Mr. Riordan?" Bapcat ventured.

Riordan kept eating, said nothing—did not even look up from his bowl.

"Are you Riordan?" Bapcat repeated.

"I am indeed, and who might be inquiring?"

"Why didn't you answer the first time?"

"Needed to know you were serious about talking. Phil Grondin himself makes this Mulligan, and there ain't a stew on Earth can match its flavor. Do yourselves a favor and grab a bowl—while it's still available."

"Not hungry," Bapcat said. "How's the leg?"

"A doc here wanted to whack it off like a dead branch, and I told him if he did, I'd put a bullet in his head."

"Is that how you settle things—with a gun?"

"At times," Riordan said, shoving more stew into his already-full mouth.

"Word is that strike-breaking left a bad taste in your mouth."

Riordan stared at him. "You some kind of law?"

Bapcat showed him the badge he shared with Zakov.

"Game warden? Why you sticking your nose in?"

"I heard you lost your nerve."

"More like I recovered my brain when I found out Frank Fisher was going to be my boss."

"Who's he?" Bapcat asked, playing dumb.

"Count your blessings you don't know," Riordan said. "The man stinks of hellfire."

Zakov sat down on the other side of the man. "A metaphoric fantasy I would like very much to witness as a phenomenon."

"Who the hell are *you?*" Riordan challenged.

"Zakov," the Russian said, and pointed to their badge, on the table. "Tell us about this remarkable fellow redolent of hellfire."

"One of J. J.'s lone operators."

"J. J.?" Bapcat asked.

"J. J. Ascher, president of the Ascher Detective Agency."

"Never heard of them," Bapcat said.

"I have," Zakov said. "Waddie competitors. I heard Cruse also hired some Ascher men."

"Your friend's right," Riordan said.

"You were headed over to the Keweenaw?" Bapcat said.

"I usually work alone—go in, gather information, and bring it out to pass on to my boss or clients. I don't get involved in nothing else, see? But I got out here and there's this Fisher, and he tells me, 'You're working the conflict lines,' and that's when I didn't bother getting on the boat. I gather information, nothing else, and I don't think everybody interested in unions is a flaming socialist. My specialty is information-gathering, not skullduggery or violence."

"Yet here you sit, broken leg and all," Zakov pointed out. "My deepest sympathies. I have myself recently recovered from a similar disability."

"I drown my disappointments in Grondin's fine menu."

"What do you live on?"

"Promotion. Each time I get someone to order a meal, I get a percentage of the price, and I talk up Grondin's all over town—or I will, when I heal sufficiently to get around better."

"Is Fisher armed?" Bapcat asked.

"Always, and you can bet his bloody Krag is never far from hand."

Krag. "He talk about his background?"

"Not to me, but I've heard he brags to some that he killed nineteen Spaniards at Roosevelt's side in Cuba."

Frankus Fish for sure. Why is he here? "Who does he work for in Copper Country?"

"Only J. J. Ascher. Who places the orders with Ascher, I can't say, and since I was never out there, I can't even venture a guess."

"Did he indicate where he would be in the Keweenaw?"

"Nothing specific, only that he had special business in the north."

"Of which county?" Bapcat asked.

"How many are there?" Riordan asked back.

"You took a ship, not a train."

"That's the order come down from New York, and when I saw Fisher he didn't bother to explain. If you fellas don't mind, the Mulligan's not getting any hotter."

Deputy Barothy came down from stowing his gear and took them to a small cafe near the railroad depot where they ate a logger's meal of fresh baked bread, beans and bacon, black tea, and vinegar pie with spice and raisins.

Barothy was an older man, a longtime timber cruiser who had gotten a political appointment as game warden in northern Schoolcraft County and demonstrated enough mettle and competence to be shifted to civil service this year. Harju told Bapcat that Barothy knew more about deer and their habits than all but a rare few outdoorsmen in the state.

Bapcat told Barothy about the Keweenaw and how deer seemed scarce most of the time.

The older warden said, "You cut down all the whites for your mines, and I mean pine, spruce, and cedar, not to mention hemlock. Take them down, you remove shade, and that lets the bright sun hit evergreen shrubs like Canady yew. Now, you ask a big old buck deer what his favorite vittles might be, and sure as blue vitriol kills blue jackets, old horny head will say, 'Apples, clover, and Canady yew.' I seen pictures of the mines over your way, and all those trees got cut down. Was me, I'd go look down in your gorges and deep canyons for yew, anywhere they can get good shade. Find yew, find deer, and that, my boy, is a fact of white-tailed deer life, not some city sport's fantasy."

"Is there yew around here?"

"Not much, but we've got a small stand over by the watering hole. Can show you fellas, if you want."

They walked west down the main street until they reached the Fox River, where it ran south past the west edge of the village, and Barothy took them to a place just north of the railroad trestle.

The yews were under a thick stand of white birch and ringed in by thick brakes of red willow. Bapcat remembered seeing what he now knew was yew in several places in the Keweenaw, places he and Zakov had not yet patrolled.

"The water here have something special that makes it good to drink?" Zakov asked.

Barothy chuckled. "Well, if it's good enough for speckled trout, it's surely good enough for mankind, but we don't call this the watering hole on account the water's particularly sweet. See, this has always been a lawless town, and for long periods there weren't no police or judiciary, so when somebody got himself out of line, citizens had to take care of it themselves. If the man did something, for example—say, took advantage of a lady against her wishes—the committee would walk him over here, make him strip, wade the river, and keep going. Men with bullwhips flogged him the whole time he crossed the river until he was gone, and he was told that if he ever came back, there would be a bullet waiting for him."

"What if he resisted the whipping?" Zakov asked.

"They shot him right here."

"This approach," Zakov said, "is something a Russian can embrace."

83

Marquette

TUESDAY, OCTOBER 21, 1913

The train hissed and jerked to a stop at the Duluth, South Shore and Atlantic Railway depot in Seney, and the two game wardens clambered aboard.

A short woman with an open face and clear voice asked, "If you gentlemen are hunters, shouldn't your weapons be safely secured in the baggage car?" The woman had a pad of paper and pencil in hand.

"Tools for your job?" Bapcat asked the woman.

She smiled, "I suppose they are."

Bapcat showed their shared badge and put the rifle between the seats. Bapcat reminded himself that he needed to have another badge made for his Russian partner.

"Is the weapon for dispatching wounded, sick, or wild animals?" the woman asked.

"All of those things, two-legged and four-," Bapcat said, sitting down beside her. The Russian had already slid into a seat by a ginger-haired beauty with far too much face paint.

"What's your work?" Bapcat asked the young woman beside him.

She had a small, fat leather briefcase under her legs and a lot of pencil graphite on her left hand. "I could say I hunt jobs," she said with a smile. "I work for Northern State Normal School in Marquette, officially the secretary for placement, which means I travel around the Upper Peninsula trying to arrange jobs for our teaching graduates. So far, every single one of them has been placed. Knock on wood," she added.

Bapcat liked her.

Zakov and ginger-hair were conversing with an overabundance of dramatic hand gestures. "Sounds like you're pretty good at your work," Bapcat said.

"I like to think so. Axelinavellimina Aho, but people call me Lina," she said, holding out her small hand.

Bapcat grinned. He knew only one Finnish phrase, which equated roughly to "How are you today?" "*Kuinka voit tanaan?*"

The Aho woman smiled. "*Hauska tavata.* How long have you been a game warden?"

"Six months." The words were out before they sank in. It seemed sometimes like he had always done this job. He could hardly remember working his traplines.

"Before that?"

"Beaver trapper."

"Schooling?"

"Grade seven, more or less." *Mostly less.*

She had a quiet, thoughtful manner. "Did you leave school for work?"

"No—to become a cowboy."

She chuckled. "Ah, a romantic's choice. How did that turn out?"

"Some of the time I was a big-game hunting guide out west, and later I was a soldier."

"Where?"

"Cuba."

She raised an eyebrow. "Rough Riders?"

He nodded.

"Surely that's something to be proud of," she said.

"Everything I've done seems like an accident," he confessed. "Just happens."

"And you think this is unusual? Do you have regrets?"

He whispered, "Sometimes I wish I had finished school."

"Why don't you?" she asked.

"I'm too old."

"Nonsense. How old *are* you—if I may be so bold as to inquire?"

"Thirty-five."

"There's no age barrier to finishing school."

It was his turn to smile. "Can't see me sitting in a classroom full of tykes."

"Neither can I," she said, "and that's not what I'm talking about. There are tests to help determine what level you're at."

"Then what?"

"A place like Northern State Normal would evaluate you on your tests, interviews, life experiences—of which yours seem numerous—and then we'd decide what level you should enter."

"Is this what you do, evaluate?"

"No, but there's a secretary who does that, and she's very good. She picks the students and when they graduate, I help them obtain positions."

"I have a position," he said.

"You anticipate never changing?"

"No, ma'am, probably not."

"Doesn't matter. More education and knowledge will help you do your job better. It always does."

"I don't know," he admitted. School seemed an unclimbable mountain, and after a while he tuned out the helpful woman, and thought about when he'd see Jaquelle and the boy again.

Upon their arrival in Marquette, Zakov and his traveling companion arose, and Bapcat realized that the two had made a connection. Zakov looked back at him and mouthed, *Brunswick Hotel?*

Bapcat nodded.

No stopover had been intended here, but it wouldn't hurt to see Harju again. Zakov went off with ginger-hair and Bapcat walked up the steep hills to Harju's green house on Rock Street.

"Didn't expect to see you again so soon. Where's our Russian?" Harju asked.

• • •

Two hours later Bapcat was smoking with Harju in the green house, helping the shaved-head Finn to clean and oil weapons.

"I don't feel like I'm making headway," Bapcat confessed.

"It takes time, and the stakes are high, Lute. If this thing doesn't work and the system reverts to the old political patronage, we might as well fold the whole bloody thing as unworkable. We can't have statewide protection of natural resources run on pinhead county-by-county rules. The people of this state deserve better."

• • •

Zakov was seated on the second-floor porch overlooking the street when Bapcat got back to the Brunswick Hotel.

"Where's your lady friend?" Bapcat asked.

"She is neither a friend, nor a lady, and our business has been successfully transacted."

"Did you even get her name?"

"To what end?" the Russian countered. "It was just business—pleasant and satisfying, but just business. Did you see Harju?"

"Briefly."

"There's a night train west," Zakov said.

"Let's stay the night and eat a good meal."

"No argument. All that disagreeable strike business seems a million miles away from here."

"I guess we'll be back in it soon enough."

"Don't remind me, *gospodin*."

"You've used that word before. What does it mean?"

"*Gospodin* means citizen. It's an honorific."

Good—explain the meaning of one word I don't know with another word I don't know.

84

Champion, Marquette County

WEDNESDAY, OCTOBER 22, 1913

The DSS&A train made the long, slow climb past Negaunee and Ishpeming, culminating in the long Superior Grade to Champion, where Bapcat saw two loggers get off the train and no passengers get on.

Zakov stepped outside and came back to report a wagonload of wooden boxes being loaded into the baggage car. "Caskets, it would appear," the Russian said, sitting down.

"How many?"

"I didn't make a precise count. Ten or twelve. What does it matter?"

"I don't know, but the Champion mine closed three years ago, and there aren't many people living around here anymore, so it seems odd to think of that many people dying suddenly."

Typhoid sometimes devastated mining communities, and TB was always lurking, as Big Louie's untimely death had proven. Even something called "fall influenza" sometimes swept through a town. But he had heard nothing of any outbreaks, and there had been no mention in the Soo papers. Such an outbreak was always covered by the news, because it could spread fast by ship or rail.

"Could be disease," the Russian suggested. "An epidemic."

Bapcat shrugged. "We would have heard." He put his head back and tried to sleep.

Zakov woke him, caught him in a groggy state.

"Where are we?"

"Chassell, taking on passengers. There are twelve boxes."

"You went back there?"

"The baggage man is Davidov, alleged son of aristocratic Russians. The boxes are labeled 'Ore Samples.' "

Bapcat rubbed his eyes and saw they were stopped again. "Ore ain't our business."

"Perhaps. But why not humor me? Let us visit *Gospodin* Davidov."

The train lurched out of Chassell moving north as they made their way through swaying passenger carriages, having difficulty maintaining their balance until they went into the fifth car in line, the one just ahead of the caboose. It was decorated outside with white ribbons. Zakov had pointed this out in Marquette, explaining that railroad men always marked the deaths of other railroaders with white ribbons on cabooses, a practice he had no explanation for.

Mines blow horns, trains decorate their cabooses, soldiers lower flags to half-mast. Why is it the start of life gets so little public celebration, only death? Perhaps finishing school would help me to understand. Do the decorations relate to the coffins? And if so, why do the boxes indicate they have ore in them?

Bapcat saw that the boxes were made of Norway pine, a poor choice for weight-bearing storage containers. They were stacked in four rows of three. Zakov introduced Davidov, who claimed Russian descent, but had been born and raised in America, spoke with no accent, and evinced little interest in Zakov's proclaimed genuine Russianness.

Zakov held out a plug of Spear Head and Davidov pinched off a jot and put it between his front lip and lower gum. "*Spasibo*."

Zakov and Davidov made small talk, and Bapcat thought about going back to his seat, but his partner clearly wanted him to see something, so he began to look around, careful to move his eyes more than his head so as not to be too obvious. Along the seam of a wooden box he saw hair, grayish-red, tinged with white, and he made eye contact with Zakov, who nodded almost imperceptibly.

"Mr. Davidov, do you know the people who shipped these boxes?" Bapcat asked. *Each box tag says the weight is one thousand, five hundred pounds. It took eight of us to carry Louis Moilanen's coffin, which weighed seven hundred pounds at most, and we had a helluva time with it.*

"Not personally. They belong to a company called Nesmith in Houghton."

"Regular shipments?"

"First one I seen."

"Ore, right?"

"That's what the bills of lading declare."

"Does the railroad unload them?"

"No, Nesmith's people meet the train in Houghton."

"Are there Nesmith people in Champion, too?"

"I suppose so, but it was our depot men who put this load on board."

"So the traffic is one way, Champion to Houghton?"

"How many men does it take to load these?" Zakov interrupted.

"Three," the trainman said. "Now, why are you fellows asking all these questions?"

Three men to move fifteen hundred pounds? No chance.

"Occupational curiosity," Zakov said.

The conductor said, "I've heard it said such a thing causes poor health in cats."

"Not to worry," Zakov said brightly. "We are people, not feline misanthropes."

The game wardens went into the nearest passenger car. It was practically empty. "Deer hair?" Bapcat asked.

Zakov reached into a pocket and pulled out tufts of hair. "In the box seams, just as you saw. Further, the boxes are extremely cold. I felt them. Iced, I'm guessing."

"Ore doesn't need cooling," Bapcat said.

"You Americans have peculiar habits and customs. Do you wish to challenge the shipment and Mr. Davidov now, or when it is picked up in Houghton?"

"I doubt we can get a search warrant that fast. Let's follow the boxes, see where they take us."

"It would be a small tragedy if a full box fell from the train and spilled its contents."

"I don't mind pushing rules," Bapcat admitted, "but it's a federal crime to disturb US Mail, and I don't know if a railroad shipment qualifies as US Mail." *Yet another example of my own ignorance—another reason to go back to school. Why are we even bothering with this?*

"All of this insistence on following the law seems to me to sometimes get *in the way* of enforcing the law. In Russia we open mail if that is what is needed. The czar's orders support such direct intervention. Power is what makes the police effective, not fair play and frivolous legal requirements."

85

Houghton

WEDNESDAY, OCTOBER 22, 1913

Three men wearing gray overalls came to the station with a tall wagon and four hulking mules.

"That should bear the load," Zakov said with grudging admiration. "But it now seems far too much wagon for too little weight."

Three men to load, three to unload. "You don't use Norway pine on heavily loaded boxes," Bapcat said, thinking the same thing. "This is for show." It was the contradiction between wood type and weight that made him look more closely at the boxes in the baggage car. They had gotten off the train, taken their gear, and set up to watch the baggage operation.

"For whose benefit?"

A sign on the side of the wagon read NESMITH VICTUALS—WHOLESALE RESTAURANT SUPPLIES FOR ALL UPPER MICHIGAN.

A victualer receiving ore boxes? Even more suspicious.

The three men transferred the dozen boxes with a minimum of strain and effort.

"Fifteen-hundred-pound boxes moved so easily?" Zakov said. "Eighteen thousand pounds in a quarter-hour? This strains all credulity."

"Shippers pay by weight, right?" Bapcat asked.

"In Russia, *da*. One might assume the freight men who loaded the boxes in Champion would question discrepancies in weight between the manifest and reality," Zakov said. "Is this the sort of thing working men would ignore?"

"I wouldn't," Bapcat said.

The Nesmith Company was downhill, a warehouse along the canal.

"Do we go inside and ask questions?" Zakov asked.

"No. We also can't sit here and wait forever. That's deer hair for sure."

"Perhaps you should call our young friend George and ask him to fetch some chums to help?"

Bapcat laughed. "Now *that's* a fair idea."

"Merely *fair?*"

Bapcat's mind, since Seney, had been turned to Canady yews, and the pine boxes felt almost like an unwanted diversion. It was difficult to sort out his feelings or make any sort of reasonable evaluation of priority. It made him feel like he was grasping at straws, and the feeling bothered him. Finding yews meant finding deer feed and presumably finding deer, which meant perhaps finding mine personnel in the process of killing the animals. He was having difficulty shaking the thought as they sat on the warehouse site.

He left Zakov watching the warehouse and walked up to Shelden Avenue and over to the impressive pink sandstone Masonic Building, found the Barber's office address on the marquee in the lobby, and walked up to the second floor to borrow his telephone.

The door was black wood with a smoky glass top half and the inscription LABISONIERE, MD, COUNTY PHYSICIAN, painted in gold capital letters. Bapcat knocked, got no answer, and tried the handle. The door was open.

Expecting to find a receptionist inside, he was surprised to see only piles of wooden boxes in a small room off the entrance, with narrow openings between the piles. The Barber stood off to one side, arms crossed, chin in hand, a pained look on his small face.

"Doctor?"

Labisoniere looked at him, puzzled.

"Bapcat, sir. Use your telephone?"

"Right, yes—yes, of course," the Barber said, waving permission.

Bapcat called Copper Lode Taxi and talked to owner Bucky Root.

"Buck, Lute Bapcat. Is George working today?"

"Ain't here no more. Sonuvagun quit for a construction job down to Hancock. Too bad; he was a good kid."

Damn. "Know how I can reach him?"

"Mike McGinn's Masonry. I don't got the number."

Bapcat thanked Root and asked the doctor for a telephone book. He found the number for McGinn's and called it.

"McGinn himself speaking, and who'd be callin'?"

Bapcat suppressed a laugh. Irish arrogance. "Deputy Warden Bapcat, State Game, Fish and Forestry."

McGinn grunted. “Bloody game warden. I ain’t even been out in the bloody woods this year. No time, when I’m tryin’ to make a living during this infernal strike.”

“I’m calling about an employee of yours.”

“Who might that be?”

“George Gipp.”

“Ah, the whelp himself. *Formerly* employed. Seems he decided masonry’s not his cuppa. ’Course, might be McGinn himself he decided against. Wouldn’t be the first cub to lack what it takes to stand up to the boss.”

“Any idea where he is now?”

“I hire ’em and fire ’em—I’m not their bloody da, but was me, I’d try Canal Snooker Parlor over to the Houghton side.”

Bapcat tried to find a telephone number for Canal Snooker, but couldn’t.

“Labor-saving device,” the Barber said sarcastically. “American named Bell claims he invented the infernal things, but I know it was some Italian, which just makes sense, them all filled with the need for endless gab. How’ve ya been?”

“You know, this and that.”

Labisoniere grinned. “Amen. Same here.”

Boxes. “Have you heard any recent talk of accidents or disease killing a lot of people in a short period of time?”

“Nah, all solos, and I’d know if something was brewing. Why?”

“Part of a puzzle. I’m just trying to find pieces that fit.”

“Something we share professionally,” the doctor said. “I sometimes think the only reason I became a doctor is because of the puzzle-solving required.”

“Canal Snooker Parlor?” Bapcat asked.

“Bit outside my sphere of interests. It sits west two blocks, and up the hill a block.”

“Thanks, Doc.”

“Anytime, my boy.”

The Canal Snooker Parlor was on a corner, and as Bapcat walked in George Gipp was on his way out, followed closely by three very unhappy-looking men.

“George,” Bapcat greeted him.

Gipp grabbed his arm and pulled him through the door to the street and pointed him downhill. “Got any tobacco?”

"Sure."

"Let's talk down on Shelden," Gipp said, looking over his shoulder.

Bapcat saw that the men had terminated pursuit. "Problem with those fellas back there?"

"I took sixty bucks off them. They're the ones with the problem. Thought *they* were hustling *me*, and they were a bit surprised at the reversal."

"Locals?"

"Never seen 'em before."

"Your chums still around?"

"Nah. Dolly's beat it back to college down to South Bend. The rest are practicing for hockey season."

"You play?"

"Great game, but I don't much like practices. The games help keep me in shape for baseball, assuming we'll have a spring."

"Zakov and I need some help."

"Does it pay?"

"Not much."

"You fellas been good to me. What do you need?"

Bapcat gave Gipp the tobacco plug and led him down Shelden Avenue, where they cut downhill to the canal. Across from the warehouse it looked like Zakov hadn't moved.

"Anything happening?" Bapcat asked him.

"Two men went inside. They're still in there."

Minutes later two laughing men came out. Both wore long, dark overcoats.

Gipp said, "Tall fella on the right is Chunk Raber, one of Cruse's deputies. The smaller gent is a Waddie, but I don't know his name. I gave him several rides up in Red Jacket a few weeks back."

"What do you know about Nesmith Victuals?" Bapcat asked.

Gipp shrugged. "Wasn't even here till this past spring, which was when I noticed them."

The game wardens looked at each other. "Perhaps we should pay a visit to this establishment and ask what they might do for our restaurant in Dollar Bay," Zakov said.

"What if they want to call for verification?"

"We are in the process of getting financing and will not open until next month."

"You two have a restaurant?" asked Gipp.

"Hush, George," Bapcat said. "We'll wait for you," he told the Russian, who walked down to the building and went inside.

Thirty minutes later Zakov returned. "For enough money, our new friends can supply—with no problem—all the fresh venison we need to sate the palates of paying customers."

"Did you ask about legality?"

"Of course. The man said brazenly, 'I presume your restaurant is designed to turn a profit, as is my business. The law is a matter of shades, not black or white, and in any event, there is so much confusion and lawlessness up north, there aren't enough lawmen to enforce trifling laws.' My newfound friend also informed me the word is out that the deer laws won't be enforced by game wardens this year."

"What prompts him to sell deer?"

"Because, dear wife, there are, according to said proprietor, no deer available. Someone has been killing them in droves to make them unavailable, and therefore pushing demand up as winter arrives."

"Where does he get his venison?"

"A great trade secret," the Russian said, putting his forefinger on his lips and adding *Shhh*. "But we might guess it is Marquette County."

Bapcat: "What about his visitors?"

"What visitors? He claims I am the first person on said premises today."

Bapcat looked at Gipp. "You know Raber, George?"

"Blowhard and a bully."

"Cruse will be of no help in our endeavors," Zakov said.

"What can I do?" Gipp asked.

"Nothing for now," Bapcat replied. "The deputy's involvement alters things—that, and the fact the businessman is denying anyone's been there. I'm sorry, George, I guess there's nothing for you here, after all."

"You fellas headed home?"

"We are."

"Mind if I tag along as far as Laurium?"

"We are always happy for your company," the Russian said, clapping Gipp on his broad shoulders.

86

Eagle River

THURSDAY, OCTOBER 23, 1913

Bapcat wanted to go into the woods to search for pockets of Canady yew and deer, but the whole Nesmith affair continued to weigh heavily on his mind, especially when he took into account the possible involvement of the two lawmen, Houghton County Deputy Sheriff Raber and the still-unidentified Waddell-Mahon man. Bapcat found himself anxious to talk to John Hepting, who usually served as a reliable compass.

Hepting greeted them at his house, which looked out on Lake Superior a hundred or so feet below the hilltop. The sky was spitting sleet and snow and the water looked the color of sludge as large yellow clouds scudded across the roiling sky.

"Haven't seen much of you boys," Hepting greeted them.

"Training in the Soo," Bapcat said. "Cruse has a deputy by the name of Chunk Raber. You know him?"

"One of Cruse's top muscles. You have an encounter with him?"

"Is he in Cruse's pocket?"

The sheriff answered with a shrug and listened attentively as the game warden related the tale of the boxes and their movement from Champion to Nesmith Victuals in Houghton.

"What're your intentions?" the sheriff asked after Bapcat finished the telling.

Bapcat had been thinking furiously about the situation since leaving Houghton. "We can't arrest him for shooting deer out of season. One, we didn't witness him shoot anything, and two, if others are doing it for him, we have to catch them in the act and have them point fingers at him. Thirdly, we aren't enforcing the law in our two counties, so we can't very well charge him on that, but we could charge him with the illegal sale of meat and participation in commercial hunting, and conspiracy."

"On what evidence—a few deer hairs?" Hepting asked, playing devil's advocate.

"We got hair off the wooden boxes, and my hunch is that railroad men, including the baggage-car man, Davidov, are part of the whole thing. We can arrest everyone and throw heaviest pressure on the lowest ones to force them to turn on the others with more to gain."

"That's a half-baked plan at best. What evidence do you have? A few hairs on boxes in a public baggage compartment aren't especially compelling. We need to get Hyppio Plew into this conversation. You're talking felonies in terms of scale, which will bump all proceedings into the circuit court. Plew will give us a reasonable evaluation of your chances in that venue."

• • •

Plew's ornate beard was neatly trimmed, and he wore a pressed silvery-striped vest over a white shirt.

Hepting poured whiskey all around and Bapcat retold his story, omitting nothing.

"If O'Brien's sitting, you might have a fighting chance," Plew said. "Any other jurist, your chances are remote at best. They have bigger fish to fry than deer, if you'll pardon my mixing of metaphors. The trick here is evidence. Houghton County has an assistant prosecutor named Echo. Ever heard of or worked with him?"

"No," Bapcat said.

"Exactly," Plew told them. "Roland Echo's a real backroom, keep-his-puss-out-of-the-papers man. He and prosecutor Tony Lucas were boyhood friends, went to the same law school, been together forever. Echo does the heavy lifting and thinking, and Tony works out front in the spotlight and takes the public heat. Echo has no design on Tony's job. When Tony leaves office, Echo will go with him to whatever is next, but Tony listens to everything Rollie Echo whispers in his ear, and if Echo thinks Tony can get something up on Fat Man Cruse or one of his thugs, he'll do it. Tony's the public face: Echo's the engine and brain.

"After the Seeberville killings, Lucas arrested two of Cruse's deps, but they made bail, and Cruse still has them on duty, and on the payroll. The Waddies involved disappeared. Tony Lucas was outraged at Cruse's utter disregard for the law, but you'll never hear him say so publicly. Mark my word: When all's said and done, justice will be served, and when that happens, you can bet your bottom dollar that Rollie Echo will have been the legal architect."

"Echo might listen favorably to a request for warrants?" Bapcat asked.

"Persuade him that it puts Cruse in a bad light, and he'll convince Lucas and you'll get your search writs. If your search uncovers good evidence, they'll authorize arrest warrants and look for a way to take the case forward. Neither Lucas nor Echo can tolerate the incompetent Cruse, and if they can nab one of his key cronies, they'll do it."

"Cruse sprang his deputies on the Seeberville murder charges," Hepting pointed out.

"He did indeed," Plew said, "and he may well do that in this case as well, but once you've got the county prosecutors in your corner, you can be sure that charges, and the case, will eventually go forward, no matter the resistance and shenanigans from Cruse. Meanwhile, what advantage does newspaper coverage offer?"

Bapcat had never considered such a thing, and Harju had never mentioned it. He had no immediate answer, but John Hepting did. "You file charges on Raber and the unidentified Waddie, if evidence warrants. But you leave the railroad men and the operator of Nesmith Victuals alone. At the same time you make sure the newspaper knows that the case is a lot bigger than it appears, and that you expect the ongoing investigation will identify additional conspirators and bring forth multiple arrests."

"This lets the free ones cook in the fetid juices of their own imaginations," Zakov said. "It encourages them to come forward with information in order to minimize their own roles and culpability. This is truly brilliant, Justice Plew."

The JP grinned and downed his whiskey. "Making the laws work is a hell of a lot more complicated than printing them on paper. You boys recognize, of course, that if you get the warrants and fail to uncover evidence, your case dies right there?"

Zakov said, "We are not enforcing the deer laws in these counties, but surely this is not so in Marquette County. The boxes were loaded there."

"All things are possible—with evidence," Justice of the Peace Hyppio Plew said. "I would advise you to move as quickly as possible for search warrants. Any delay enables the guilty to rid themselves of evidence. Time is the key to your success, lads."

Should have followed my hunch. Bapcat told Zakov, "We need to sit on Nesmith from now until we serve warrants."

"By *we,* you mean me, I presume," the Russian said.

"Get Georgie to help you, and tell him we'll pay him for his time and help."

"You?"

"I need to make another black-of-the-night visit. You and George can drop me and head for Houghton. I'll catch the electric when I'm done."

87

Laurium

FRIDAY, OCTOBER 24, 1913

Night had come, and Judge O'Brien was in a contentious, argumentative state and looked like he had been pulling hard on a bottle. He shook his head at the sight of Bapcat on his porch and said angrily, "Git your arse into me fookin' office."

O'Brien sat in silence, sullen, face dark, hair sticking out at angles. He was wound up like Bapcat had never seen before.

"Fookin' blind, greedy fookin' fools," he finally mumbled, taking a swig from a glass. "The operators demand an injunction, and I've no choice but to grant the bloody thing. The whole bloody lots are driving me to an early grave, they are, the whole damn buncha them, *both* fookin' sides.

"I've told them all, on numerous occasions, that I won't stand for no more bloody head-cracking, fookin' gunplay and such shite. They want this settled, they have to do it like civilized humans, not a bunch of two-legged hyenas. I want this settled with words, not guns.

"When the strikers began roughing up men, trying to go to work, the operators came to me. I had to give them the injunction against the strikers to stop the bloody harassment. What happens? As soon as the operators have the upper hand, they turn up the heat and start pounding on the strike parades. Result: I lift the injunction and the whining bastards appeal to the state supreme court, which takes it out of my hands.

"Two weeks ago, the State crowd overruled me, and reinstated the injunction in favor of the operators. Strikers can have their parades, but they can't stop men from working if that's what they want to do. How do the strikers react? They ignore Lansing and are at it again. Later this morning I'm going to have to order mass arrests in Allouez and Mohawk . . . Damn them all."

"Those are Keweenaw locations, Judge, not Houghton. Sheriff Hepting, does he know?"

"Nah, tomorrow's soon enough. John will be pissed at me because his heart's with the strikers, but I've got three Pullman cars being hauled out from Houghton to house prisoners and take them back to Houghton, to the jail."

"What about Eagle River?"

"What about it!" the judge howled. "It's a two-bit one-room jailhouse. Truth is, the damn place is no more than a lame joke. There's no damn reason for two counties up here; my circuit covers both." O'Brien ran his hands through his greasy hair. "This thing is ready to really blow—more guns, more fighting, more deaths. It has to stop *here*." The judge glared at Bapcat. "What in hell are you doing here? At night. *Again?*"

"Same as you—looking for peace and fair play."

The judge sneered. "I'm listening."

Bapcat laid out the scenario involving the boxes and Nesmith Victuals.

"For God's sake, boyo, the hairs could have come from anywhere, at any time."

"But the manifests say that each Norway pine box contains fifteen hundred pounds of ore. I personally watched three men lift each box easily, and all twelve in short order, so I am wondering why the manifest weights are so inaccurate. The railroad man who escorted the shipment seemed not the least bit concerned about the discrepancy."

"Norway pine?" the judge asked. "Worthless stuff."

"Exactly, and when we buried Moilanen, it took eight of us to carry his coffin and with him in it we're talking only seven hundred pounds. There's no way three men can handle fifteen hundred in Norway pine. If we search and find nothing, we can just say we're sorry and depart."

"You think Raber's part of this—whatever *this* is?"

"Speak freely, Your Honor?"

"You always do, Deputy. Spit it out."

"The mine operators are attempting siege tactics—poisoning streams, flooding animal dens, killing deer, and leaving them to rot. They want to starve the miners and their families."

"No chance that will succeed," O'Brien said. "The union opened a cooperative in Red Jacket. I think there are plans for a couple more in towns to the south."

"How long can they afford to operate?" Bapcat asked. He had very little notion of economics and money, and again felt a hole where knowledge ought to be.

"Keep going," O'Brien said, rubbing the stubble on his face.

"I don't know if Cruse is involved, but he damn well knows what the operators are up to. It could be that Raber is working on the sheriff's behalf with this Nesmith thing, I don't know, but it's also possible Deputy Raber has found a way to line his own pockets, independent of the sheriff. Frankly, Your Honor, I don't care what direction it goes, as long as we can get into Nesmith Victuals, the rolling stock, and the rail depot in Champion."

"That won't work. Champion's out of the question, as it's not part of my jurisdiction. It comes under the circuit court in Marquette. But I can order Echo and Lucas to issue a writ on Nesmith, and I'll sign it and make sure there's a second signature, which will allow you to enter at night. But you get nothing on the rolling stock unless you come up with something at the warehouse, understand?"

"Yessir. Can you call Lucas now?"

"Don't push me, dammit. Don't you have the slightest interest in the distasteful things I have to do today?"

"Honestly, Your Honor? I don't."

"God help me . . . an honest man," the judge said with a grand smile. "You're fast learnin' the unwritten rules," he added, pulling papers out of his desk and sliding them across. "Warrant forms." He took a pen and signed and held them out, then reached for the telephone and cupped the mouthpiece. "Take the forms to Lucas's office tonight. He and Echo can use your information to create the warrants. I'll dictate the language so you won't need to worry about it. Just get into Houghton as fast as you can get there. Now git!"

Bapcat heard the judge say into a telephone, "Tony, it's Patrick. I've got a little late-night work that might gain you some ground against a certain fat bastard with a tin star."

88

Houghton

FRIDAY, OCTOBER 24, 1913

Bapcat found the Russian and Gipp, and showed them the search warrant. "The boxes and any surrounding areas and any suspected or confirmed storage spaces or areas, attached and unattached. O'Brien and a JP named Peters signed the warrant, which gives us the power to go in tonight, right now. The prosecutor's already summoned Nesmith, who is on his way to open up."

"If he refuses?" Gipp asked.

"We break down the door," Bapcat said, adding, "but only if we have to." Assistant Prosecutor Echo had given him a thorough briefing on what he could and couldn't do, and having recently worked through *Tiffany's,* he felt almost confident.

The three men jogged down near the dark entrance and waited. There were street lamps up on Shelden Avenue and down by the rail depot, but few along the canal, and none in this area, which sat in total darkness. Snow was falling softly.

Nesmith arrived in a Buick roadster and centered his lights on them, jumped out, and shouted defiantly, "Nothing happens until my attorney is present, and he and I have the opportunity to read all paperwork!"

Bapcat said, "Just open the door," and handed the warrant to the man.

"Not until I can digest this in good light."

"Open the door and turn on the light," Bapcat said.

"I will not!"

"We're authorized to open the door by force if necessary."

"Like hell. This country's got a constitution. Who signed the damn warrant?"

"Judge O'Brien and Justice Peters."

Nesmith made a hocking sound. "Raging socialists, the both of 'em."

"Open the door," Zakov ordered sternly. The man sighed deeply and took out a key.

Bapcat stood while the man read the warrant and Zakov and Gipp went through the area, looking for the wooden boxes, which did not appear to be in the warehouse. What they found was a door to a room built into the back of the warehouse with the label COLD.

"What's in there?" Zakov asked Nesmith.

"Supplies."

"What about ore boxes?"

"I have no idea what you're talking about," the man said.

"We watched your men pick them up yesterday at the depot and we saw them delivered here," Zakov said. "Open the door to the room."

Nesmith's lawyer arrived looking sweaty and half-dressed, his hair tousled, eyes red. Deputy Sheriff Raber came in behind the lawyer, revolver in hand. "What's going on here?" the deputy shouted in a stentorian voice.

Zakov calmly showed him their shared badge while Bapcat presented the search warrant. "Holster your weapon, Raber," Bapcat said.

The sound of his own name seemed to deflate the man's bravado.

"Open the door." Zakov repeated.

Nesmith's attorney pored over the warrant. "There's no mention of a cold room in this writ," he said.

Bapcat said, "I quote, 'wooden boxes, surrounding areas, and all storage facilities, known or suspected on the premises or adjoining thereof,' end quote."

The lawyer, who gave his name as Elliott Fasman, took Nesmith's arm and said firmly, "Open the cold room for these gentlemen, Michael."

Inner door open, there sat the boxes, spread out, no longer stacked.

"Open them," Bapcat told the owner. "And turn on some lights in here."

"If you boys have everything under control," Raber said, backing out of the room and disappearing.

Dim lights came on. There were ice bins on the floor in several locations, filled with massive ice blocks that were covered with sawdust. They could see their breath hanging in the air. Shelves lined the walls, and packages wrapped in pink-brown paper were stacked on the shelves, the paper caked with frost. A metal table in the room had butchering tools, knives and grinders, cleavers, rolls of paper, balls of string, and the floors were stained with dark marks. *Blood.*

Nesmith said, "There are no box keys."

Attorney Fasman said sharply, "Michael."

Bapcat stepped up with his rifle and used the stock to strike the lock off the first box, metal bits skittering across the floor. He opened the lid and found meat, which looked hurriedly butchered, bones still in place, loose hair clumps here and there.

"Not mine," Nesmith said, raising both hands. "Don't even have keys. We store them for a client."

Fasman said, "Don't."

"Client?" Zakov said. "*Client* is by linguistic syllogism someone you have regular transactions with. What is your client's name?"

"We're paid by many to store their things," Nesmith said.

"Including contraband," Zakov said.

Bapcat left Zakov to question the man while he opened other boxes, eight of which also contained meat. The final four contained deer heads, which caught him by surprise.

Attorney Fasman started to walk over to Bapcat, who in turn went toward the lawyer to block his access to the last four boxes.

"My client wishes to cooperate," Fasman announced.

"He's got a funny way of showing it," Bapcat said.

"He's an honest businessman who has never been in trouble. He is nervous—a phenomenon I'm sure that you, an experienced lawman, can understand."

"We want information."

Fasman took his client by the arm and led him away. Once they had left the cold room, Bapcat showed Zakov and Gipp the boxes with the deer heads.

"Perhaps our entrepreneur is double-spooning," Zakov said. "He sells venison meat, *and* takes heads for bonuses."

"I'm not moving anything," Bapcat decided. "George, I want you to get over to the county building. Assistant Prosecutor Echo is in his office. Explain what we've found. Tell him we need a locksmith to seal the building, and we need to set up some kind of security arrangement."

"You want a locksmith to change the locks on this room?" Gipp asked.

"No, I want the whole building sealed off. We're confiscating Nesmith's entire operation."

"He'll fight," Zakov said.

"Let him explain that to the prosecutor when he gets here. Information can open minds, cells, and doors."

Zakov grinned. "Very poetic, not to mention truly philosophical."

"It must be the company I keep," Bapcat said. "Go find Davidov, and get heavy with him if you have to. Call Harju and tell him what we've found here, and that we'll need a warrant for the Champion depot. Are those Nesmith employees over there? Tell Harju we need him to rattle the cages of all the railroaders in Champion's baggage operations, to find out how they are connected with Nesmith and to Davidov."

"*Da*," Zakov said, and departed, limping slightly. He had been off his crutch for some time now, but soreness sometimes hit him.

Fasman soon came back, leading his sheepish client. "The meat belongs to my client," the attorney said. "The heads do not. We have no idea where they came from, or why."

"Who killed the deer?"

"My client."

"All of them?"

"Yes. He has an insatiable desire to hunt."

"And make money from it," Bapcat added. "There are laws against shipping contraband through the US Mail."

"There is no US Mail involvement here. The railroad is private and offers a private shipping service. A noble try, Deputy, but you have no grounds with that line."

Bapcat took a moment to clear his mind and focus. He had not mentioned the deer heads to Nesmith or his attorney, and there was no way they could have seen them, which meant they already knew what was in the final four wooden boxes before they were opened. Or at least Nesmith knew.

Gipp came back, followed ten minutes later by Houghton County assistant prosecutor Roland Echo, a locksmith, and a reporter for the *Houghton-Calumet Mining Journal*.

The reporter pompously introduced himself as Lars Allan Bernard Petersson, Esq. Following the plan he'd worked out in his mind, Bapcat told the newspaperman that more arrests were in the offing. On an impulse, he told the story of deer being killed and left to rot by persons—and reasons—unknown, which seemed a terrible and tragic waste of the state's resources, and that further, the State had credible information that certain persons were paying hunters to kill deer, solely to deny legal hunters the chance to hunt them—especially miners in need of food because of the strike.

The reporter was short and wide, with a square, bristling black beard and long, stringy black hair. "Who would author such a nefarious scheme?" the man asked.

"Well, we don't know for sure, Mr. Petersson, but the way we come at things like this is to ask who benefits most from a crime."

"Nobody benefits from deer left to rot," the reporter said.

"Really? What about someone who doesn't want others to have access to food?"

The reporter looked stumped, and Bapcat decided to say no more, although before parting, added, "We can't yet say who is responsible, Mr. Petersson, but we have some very strong leads, some growing evidence. A team of investigators from different agencies is working on this case, and anyone who comes forward now with new and relevant information will certainly find the prosecutor in a cooperative spirit."

"Will there be a reward?" the reporter asked.

"Yes, of course, but I'm not at liberty to reveal the source, or the amount. Let's just say that a wealthy, community-minded individual is appalled by the killing, and has stepped forward to provide an incentive to help us find the guilty parties and close the case."

It was noon by the time new locks had been installed and the building secured by a private guard brought in by Prosecutor Echo.

Bapcat said, "C'mon, George, let's head for home and get us some food."

"What about Mr. Zakov?"

"He'll join us later. George, have you seen your uncle Herman lately?"

"No, but he's working again, this time at Citizens Hardware in Laurium."

"Fig get him the job?"

"I don't know; why?"

"Let's stop and talk to Herman about deer hunting."

"Has he done something wrong?"

"Not at all. I just want to ask him something. He knows a lot about hunting, right?"

"Just about everything," George Gipp said.

89

Laurium

SATURDAY, OCTOBER 25, 1913

Citizens Hardware was less than six blocks from Herman Gipp's house. Bapcat wondered how Uncle Herman would escape to the woods from a job so close to home.

"Like your new job?" Bapcat asked Herman.

"Pays da bills, I guess," the man said.

"Where's Fig working these days?"

"Dunno. He sorta got mad at me and I ain't seen 'im for a while, ya know?"

"Nothing serious, I hope," Bapcat said. He hated making small talk, but was slowly learning to accept it as part of the job.

"Nah, Fig can't stay mad long on account he can't remember nuttin' dat long."

"Herman, you're a woodsman. You know what Canady yew is?"

"Yeah, sure, you betcha. My grandpa usta call it deer candy."

"Much of it in these parts?"

"Some, if youse know where ta look. Why?"

"Mostly curious, I guess. I like to know what's around me in the woods, don't you?"

"Yeah, sure, I guess."

"So?"

"You mean yew? Way up Lake Manganese ridges, ya know, 'round dere."

"How about around here?"

"Upper Owl Creek usta be good; Cedar Creek Canyon down low, and youse know, Delaware mine down ta Eagle River, all t'rough dose ridges an' deep cuts."

"Good deer hunting?"

"Can be, 'specially in winter when da deers yard up. Most head toward da bay, but lotsa dose big bucks, dey go west up into da yew canyons."

When did it become legal to hunt deer in winter, in their yards? "Don't hear much about that westerly movement."

"Most pipple lazy, eh. Won't work hard, which makes huntin' good for dem dat will."

"You ever hunt up there?"

"Not after all da wolfies come."

"Are you talking about the ratting grounds?"

Herman Gipp nodded solemnly. "Not no more so much, you know."

"But there are still some yews up that way?"

"Wun't s'prise me, but I ain't been up dere in years. Fig, he don't like it up dat place."

"How come?"

"Ghosts and spooks and stuff," Herman said nervously.

"Thanks, Herman."

The elder Gipp smiled and said nothing.

"See you, Unc," George told his uncle, and turned to Bapcat. "Get what you needed?"

"Could be." *Yew kills rats, but not deer. How come Herman knows yew attracts deer and I don't?*

"We done working?" George asked.

"Yes. How about you drop me up the hill and take the electric back?"

"Sure. You been to the ratting grounds?"

"Once, why?"

"Not a place people talk about. Spooks, ghosts, Indian *manitous*—all that crazy stuff."

"You superstitious, George?"

"Only when it makes sense to be. You?"

"Nope."

"Even when you were a kid?"

"Never." Being an orphan was all the monster a kid needed. You always felt like the world was out to get you, which was a mistake. For the most part the world didn't care if you lived or died. Either way, life—and what you did with it—was your problem.

90

Allouez

SATURDAY, OCTOBER 25, 1913

Mid-afternoon an agitated Zakov came stumbling and blustering into the house on the hill. "Davidov's gone. Nobody knows where, or why. I called and talked to Harju about Champion. There's big trouble at the depot down the hill."

Bapcat grabbed his rifle, Zakov got behind the wheel of the truck, Bapcat turned the crank, and they headed down the dirt road for town and the rail depot.

A few of the remaining National Guard soldiers were on the scene, but standing back from the action, which involved special mine guards and their sun-shaped badges and some of Cruse's full-time Houghton County deputies.

Bapcat had no idea what had precipitated the trouble, but all sides were brandishing weapons—rocks, bottles, and clubs—and lots of angry words were being shouted, including special deputies telling miners' wives they all belonged in whorehouses.

Both groups were rubbing and bumping, but there was no outright violence, save one example: Deputy Sheriff Raber was wading through the strikers with a sap, hammering anyone around him who was significantly smaller than him. Bapcat watched one small man lift his arm in defense against Raber, but it didn't offer any protection, as Raber came up with a sap in his other hand and drove it straight into the man's head, collapsing the victim. Bapcat thought he saw Fig Verbankick in the melee, but the scene was kaleidoscopic, shifting with wrestling and motion and an increased crescendo of noise, and he lost track of the odd little man.

"Where the hell is John Hepting?" Bapcat shouted over the din at Zakov. "This isn't Cruse's county." *So this is what O'Brien was talking about yesterday.*

Zakov pointed, and Bapcat saw that the special mine deputies were pulling out their revolvers, this action immediately dampening the crowd's fire.

Minutes later an army sergeant carrying a Springfield approached them and Zakov showed their shared badge. The sergeant said, "The specials got a hundred and forty-one for the lockup out of this mess, and another sixty or so up to Mohawk."

"To be taken to jail in Houghton?"

The sergeant looked surprised. "How'd you know that?"

"There's no space in the Keweenaw jail."

"Replacement workers are coming north on trains from Hancock today. Cruse and the mines have guards all along the rail route for protection, with more armed guards on board."

Feltrow, a clerk in Petermann's store in Allouez, came out on the porch. "Two weeks ago we had five hundred kids skip school and make a parade right here," he said. "It's a darn disgrace! Ignored school and come here instead. Lucky nobody got hurt.

"Last Tuesday someone over to Red Jacket tried to set fire to a house that boards forty guards. Kids come out of the house, yelling *Fire!* to get help, and the darn strikers mobbed the house and the firefighters, trying to stop them from putting the fire out. What the hell's wrong with people who think this way? Let a family home burn with kids inside? Good Lord.

"First of the month more than a thousand strikers jumped men trying to get to work; cavalry boys had to ride their horses into the melee to break it up. I'm telling you, when this thing got going, most folks were siding with the strikers, but now it seems they'd rather fight than go back to work. I just don't understand it," he lamented.

Zakov said, "Sometimes it takes violent acts to compel substantial change."

"Maybe," the clerk said, "but the jump between violent and tragic don't seem all that far, and that's what worries me. What if those strikers prevented that fire from being put out last week? There's some things that's just got to be off limits, even when you have a righteous cause."

• • •

Sheriff John Hepting stopped at the house on the hill late in the early evening.

"Looks like everything went swimmingly for you fellas down in Houghton," he greeted them, walking in. "I could sure do with a drink."

Bapcat told him about the deer meat and the heads, and Hepting took out a folded Houghton-Calumet Mining Journal from the day before and opened it. A banner headline read: GAME WARDENS FIND ILLEGAL DEER CACHE IN HOUGHTON BUSINESS; PROMISE MASS ARRESTS AHEAD.

"Cruse's men made a lot of arrests at the Allouez depot this morning," Bapcat said.

"Tell me something I don't know," Hepting said. "Our glorious governor has ordered all national guardsmen withdrawn, and has told the companies to defend their own property because the State can't take sides in such a dispute."

"What're sheriffs supposed to do?" Bapcat asked.

"Help the company side."

"And you?"

"Like the damn gutless State, I ain't taking sides neither. I heard Allouez didn't go that badly; mostly a lot of shoving and nasty talk. Up in Mohawk they came in so fast the strikers couldn't react, and they got 'em all locked up in a shed until a train could be arranged. You hear from Marquette yet?"

Zakov said, "I talked to Harju. Will take up to four days to get a search warrant for Champion."

Hepting grinned and tapped the newspaper. "Trust me; that story will move things along fast. That story will be all over the state. Government always reacts to newspaper reports. They got no choice. What's your next move?"

Bapcat said, "Let them all cook for a few days. We have the evidence secured, and Nesmith's business is closed for the time being."

Hepting said, "That will get the attention of a lot of local businessmen. Most of that crowd don't even start to think about things until money and profits are threatened."

"I'm going up to Copper Harbor for a day or two," Bapcat said.

"If she has a friend, send her this way," Zakov said.

91

Copper Harbor

SUNDAY, OCTOBER 26, 1913

The weather remained unseasonably mild. Jaquelle Frei's store was closed for most of Sunday, but she came downstairs to let Bapcat in, greeting him with an exuberant hug and kiss and leading him upstairs by the hand. Jordy Kluboshar was sitting by a window, reading.

"He likes school," Frei said. "Teachers not so much, but school, books, learning—these things he likes."

The boy looked up from his book. "I can read on my own. I don't need no teachers."

"We *all* need teachers," Bapcat told Jordy Kluboshar.

"Not you."

Bapcat laughed. "*Especially* me. How's your hygiene?"

"With *her* in charge?" the boy retorted. "*Her* rules, *all* the time," he said with a sigh.

"We haven't seen you in going on a month," Frei said.

"Training in the Soo, work in Seney, business in Marquette."

"We seen the paper," Jordy said. "About you and Mr. Zakov, and them deer you took down to Houghton."

"Did you see Moriarty?" Jaquelle Frei asked him.

"You didn't want me to."

She smiled. "It's good that you listen to your lady."

Bapcat smiled benevolently. *A lie, but not one he had a label for. Sometimes being uneducated could work in your favor.*

"Are you staying tonight?" Frei asked, hope in her voice.

"Can't."

Her disappointment was immediate.

"Thanksgiving," he said. "Thought I'd come back then, spend four or five days. When is it this year?"

"November twenty-seventh," the boy called out. "It was in the newspaper."

"That's good; just not soon enough," Jaquelle Frei said.

"Soon enough for what?" The boy asked.

"Read!" the adults said in unison.

"Sure about tonight?" she asked, rubbing against him.

"Duty calls."

"Lunch before you leave?"

"That would be good." It seemed forever since he'd had a good meal.

She pan-fried partridge breasts wrapped in bacon strips. "The boy shot them," she announced. "He's a fine little hunter."

"I ain't little," Jordy Kluboshar said.

"Deputy out of Houghton, name of Raber?"

"What about him?" she asked.

"You claim to know everyone up here."

"I do. Raber's been a roughneck all his life. Worked underground at the Quincy before Cruse hired him. His mother was widowed and she remarried well."

"Like, to a czar or something like that?"

"You spend too much time with that damn Russian. No, she married Philamon Hedyn."

"Kin to Madog?"

"The captain's baby brother, I believe."

"Also a miner?"

"No, a Methodist minister in Central. Cornish Methodist Church, big congregation. Got the job when the former pastor came to be at odds with the congregation."

A familiar ring to the story. "He ever work in the mines?"

"In Cornwall, maybe. I don't really know about here."

"Is he like his older brother, the cap'n?"

"Meaning?"

"Cock of the walk?"

She smiled. "No, that's Madog's way. The word is that Philamon will do anything for his elder brother."

"Anything takes in a lot," he said.

She countered, “Especially when blood’s involved.”

“Was Philamon a preacher in Cornwall?”

“I couldn’t say.”

“How long’s the younger Hedyn been here?”

“I don’t know that either, and you have become exceptionally inquisitive over the past six months. Do I look like the oracle of Delphi?”

He shrugged. “Do you?”

“Do you even know what Delphi is?”

Damn—caught. “Can’t say I do.”

“Think of a Greek gypsy with a crystal ball and more reputation than substance. I have a couple of errands the boy can run,” she said. “Two hours?”

“No time.”

“No time, or is it no interest?”

“There’s plenty of interest,” he said.

“Talk’s cheap,” she countered.

“Is Deputy Raber close to his stepfather? Does the reverend hunt?”

She sighed, and held her hands up in frustration.

On his way out he noticed dead birds hanging from wires in front of the store windows. “What’s that all about?” he asked, pointing.

“Jordy’s idea. It’s supposed to keep live birds from flying into our windows.”

“Does it work?”

“Seems to.”

Bapcat called the boy to the stairs. “You can’t kill songbirds. I’m the game warden.”

“I didn’t kill them,” the boy said in his own defense. “I found them out on the beach. Some of them fly across the big lake and get tired and die. You can always find them out on the flows.”

Exhausted from flying over Lake Superior? “Where did you get the idea?” Bapcat asked.

“Read it somewhere.”

Bapcat smiled. “Keep reading, and let me know what you learn.”

“I’d rather go hunting.”

“Thanksgiving we’ll go get a deer.”

The boy grinned and Frei kissed Bapcat good-bye.

He wondered how she'd feel about his notions toward his own schooling. Raber is Hedyn's nephew-in-law, if that's what it was properly called. Growing up without kin gave Bapcat little interest in such things. Central was a good location, Canady yew in the ridges to the north and west, big deer, all worth a look.

The newspaper article was much longer than he had expected. Was it too much? If not, he had a hunch that what lay ahead might come barreling right at him rather than him having to chase it down, and that maybe patience right now would pay off more than pursuit. Speed without direction didn't add up to much. He'd try to meet with Deputy Raber in a couple of days and see how he reacted. His appearance at the warehouse seemed to say a lot, especially when he saw what was happening and took off.

92

West of Madison Gap, Keweenaw County

MONDAY, OCTOBER 27, 1913

Bapcat hiked directly to the squirrel-tail tree, sat down, rolled a smoke, and waited. He wasn't crazy about tobacco, but it helped pass time and calmed his nerves. He knew the old man was near because all the birds and critters suddenly went quiet. After a while he saw the man sitting across a clearing, looking back at him.

Captain Erastus Renard Webster looked to be a hundred years old in wrinkles alone, but in full possession of mind and body if one ignored the dyed squirrel tails fluttering in the tree branches overhead, rifle across his lap. No sign of any woman.

"Captain Webster, Sixteenth Michigan, First Independent Sharpshooter Company?"

"Who be asking?" the man said.

"Corporal Bapcat, First Volunteer Cavalry, sir."

"You one of Roosevelt's boys?"

"Yes, sir."

"What want ye here?"

"Talk."

"Woman!" Webster called out. "Don't be bushwhacking this fine lad. We're brothers in arms." Webster looked over at him. "You *are* one of us, right? I can see it in your eyes."

"Right—yes, sir." *No idea what he's talking about.*

A woman appeared, tall and graceful, blonde hair in a long braid, buckskin pants and jacket, rifle with a telescopic sight.

"I'm Lute," he said, but she ignored him.

"You drink coffee?" the old man asked.

"When it's offered," Bapcat said.

"Come," the man said, popping to his feet.

They walked fifty yards to the lip of a steep ravine and angled down a narrow path to a cave opening about fifty feet below the lip. "Good place to hole up," the man said, waving with his hand for Bapcat to come inside.

"You're sharing your special place with me?"

"It's not so special, and ain't nobody just walks in the way you did. Me, I'm old. Me and Sue mean to get back to Arizona again, but I'm pretty certain this is my last time here. I got a feeling you'll take my place and become the guardian."

"Guardian of what?"

"Everything. I'm coming to the end of the line; it's time to join my comrades who fell while fightin' the Rebs."

"You seem pretty healthy to me."

"Looks don't tell it all, my boy."

"Why do you come here?" Bapcat asked as the woman named Sue made coffee on a small fire that just seemed to jump to life.

"Float copper. Still some good chunks here and there. Sue sells them in town. We do the same out to Arizona, but its gold out there, other minerals."

"You've explored this area?"

"Thoroughly as Sue's bubs, I reckon."

The woman blushed.

"I followed a blood trail up the lava flows," Bapcat said.

"Where'd it peter out?"

"This side of the cut-through, not far from here."

"We seen you and that other one," Webster said. "Told Sue then you'd be the one."

Sue said, "We seen that fella, couldn't figure out what he was up to."

"What fella?"

"Real short one with blank eyes, carrying a deer head."

"Seen him before?"

"No, not him."

"Others?"

"Sometimes."

"Others carrying heads?"

"Uh-huh . . . further north on the cutover road, there's a trail goes east, and we seen 'em up that way a few times."

"Not here?"

"Not so far."

"At the bat hole?" Bapcat ventured.

The woman said sharply, "Why ask if you already know? What's your game?"

"No game." Bapcat showed the badge.

"Lawman."

"Game warden."

The captain cleared his throat.

"Where's the bat hole?" Bapcat asked directly.

"Thought you knew," Sue said.

"Just want to make sure we're talking about the same place."

"I been soldiering going on sixty years," Webster said.

"The hole," Bapcat repeated, trying to focus the conversation.

"Up top on the ridge, between Owl and Copper Falls lakes."

"Deer heads are being thrown in there?"

"Can't say. We give that place a wide berth."

"For a reason?"

"None we'd say out loud until the hard freeze comes in, and none we'd whisper on account that would bring us too close, you being a stranger and all."

It was the old Chippewa belief that all things, even rocks, had spirits, and that all words spoken by humans could be heard by the spirits, remembered, and passed around. Only in winter when spirits slept were people safe talking outside.

"A mean snow sky by morning is a good thing," the old man said, looking at Bapcat. "How you can see little dark things against the dull light."

Bapcat understood. Webster had just told him the best time and conditions to look for the bat hole. They finished their coffee in silence, and when Bapcat got up to leave, he said, "I look forward to seeing you again, Cap'n."

The man cackled. "You do, 'speck we'll all be dead and huntin' on the other side."

93

Central Location, Keweenaw County

MONDAY, OCTOBER 27, 1913

When Central Mining Company had gone out of business years before, Calumet and Hecla had swept up its land and assets on the cheap. Bapcat remembered hearing about the events, and had wondered then why C & H seemed so intent on buying up tapped-out mine operations.

Back when Bapcat was just beginning to trap, the village was called Central Mine, and contained a couple hundred small wood-frame houses situated along narrow, well-maintained streets. The town in those days had a vitality and life, but now each time he saw it, fewer and fewer houses were occupied, and fewer people were about. You could almost smell the end in the air.

A man in a baggy dark suit stood on the porch of Moyle's General Store, smoking a pipe. A sign on the door said CLOSED.

"Reverend Philamon Hedyn?" Bapcat asked.

"Aw right, me 'ansum. 'Ere now, this pars'nage 'owse sit dreckly a-hind me 'ed is the church," the man said, chopping at a general direction with his pipe.

Bapcat hid a smile. Cousin Jacks were a cocky lot. They put down other immigrants for slaughtering the English language, even though they had their own peculiar ways of bending words, and there were plenty who were incomprehensible to all but their own tribe.

The " 'owse" behind the church was two stories, painted white, well cared for. There was even some grass in a small yard fenced in with black metal pickets.

A man in a suit came out the front door and to the yard gate. Small man, ruddy face; Bapcat immediately saw a likeness to Captain Madog Hedyn. The game warden presented his badge.

"Sorry to disturb you. Are you Reverend Hedyn?"

"Say yer piece, man."

"Your stepson is a Houghton County deputy named Raber; is that correct, or have I been misinformed?"

"None of yer business, you."

"Is he here?"

" 'Ere? *'Im?*" the man said, nearly spitting out the words. Dangerous to interpret, but Bapcat wondered if things were not so good between stepson and stepfather.

"You saying he doesn't come around much? That must bother your wife."

The man stared skyward and sucked in a long, deep breath before letting it out slowly.

"You are Reverend Hedyn, yes?" Bapcat said.

"Wasn't more important business for the Laird, I'd open da gate and give you a proper t'rashin'," the man said in a growly voice.

Way too aggressive too quickly. Touching some soreness here, but what?

"Your brother tried that once, and it didn't go all that well for him. Turns out his mouth's bigger than his fists."

The reverend looked to be seething, but made no move to open the gate.

"If you see your stepson, you might want to let him know that we will be talking to him about some illegal deer. I just thought he might be here, and that might save us all some trouble."

"Ain't 'ere, you," the man said, clipping his words again.

"All right. Sorry to have disturbed you, Reverend, and my apologies to your wife. You do hunt deer, don't you?"

"Get on wit' you," the man said.

"Wouldn't look good, a man of your station mixed up in illegal activities." Bapcat saw that the man was on the verge of exploding, and knew it was time to back off.

"Again, I'm sorry to have disturbed you, sir. Perhaps we'll meet again under better circumstances. In fact, I'm sure we'll see each other again."

The man hurried up the walk, across the porch, and slammed his front door with a report that swept over the village like a rifle shot.

94

Houghton

FRIDAY, OCTOBER 31, 1913

Assistant Prosecutor Echo got a subpoena, but Deputy Sheriff Raber came in voluntarily, accompanied by a lawyer who introduced himself as an attorney with the firm of Rees, Robinson, and Petermann.

Zakov examined the card and looked over at the lawyer. "Your firm works for the mine operators, yes?"

"The firm does some work along those lines, yes," the man said.

He had a shiny face, like it had been waxed. Bapcat instinctively didn't care for him, or the self-assured way he presented himself.

"Why are you here with Deputy Sheriff Raber?" Zakov asked in a tone suggesting impropriety. "Can it be that this illegal deer-killing case involves the mining companies?"

"Nonsense," the lawyer said. "Friends of Mr. Raber asked me to advise and assist him."

"Assist him with what?" Bapcat asked, speaking for the first time. "No charges have been brought. We just want to talk to Mr. Raber."

"It's a man's constitutional right to legal representation and advice," the lawyer countered.

"At what price, and who pays for you?" Zakov asked.

"This is none of your business, sir, and if you insist on this childish wordplay, I will advise Deputy Raber to leave this meeting."

"There is a subpoena extant," Prosecutor Echo said from behind the table.

"I come in willingly," Raber said.

Echo placed the subpoena on the table. "Until now this was informal. But now you've been legally served, and this is now a formal interview."

"It's a non-distinction," the lawyer said.

"What do you advise the deputy to do?" Echo asked.

"We'll listen to your questions," the man said, sitting beside the deputy.

Zakov took out the October 24 edition of the *Mining Journal* and spread it out so that the men across the table could read the substantial headline. Zakov said nothing about the newspaper, and instead said, "You paid Mr. Nesmith to store wooden boxes containing ore."

"I certainly did *not,*" Raber said. "Did he tell you that?"

Zakov said, "Our information tells us that you sell the meat and heads to Nesmith, and he turns around and resells the meat to other customers, and delivers the heads to those who have put out a private bounty on deer."

"That's a lie," Raber whispered in a low voice. "I was just visiting Nesmith in the line of duty."

Zakov said, "Which time—the morning we served the search warrant, or the previous afternoon, right after the boxes had arrived from Champion? We saw you both times."

"Don't answer that," the lawyer advised Raber.

"You told us on the morning of the search warrant that you were worried about a break-in, but when we began to open the wooden boxes, you suddenly departed. Who reported a break-in? Your departure seems strange—both then and now—especially for a peace officer claiming he was concerned about a possible break-in."

Raber was sweating.

"You know," Bapcat said, "we asked Sheriff Cruse to attest to your value as his deputy, but as you can see, the sheriff isn't here, and now you must be wondering what we will think about that. It's puzzling for sure."

"Could it be that the sheriff sees no value in you?" Zakov chimed in.

"The sheriff's a busy man," the lawyer said.

"Certainly true," Zakov said. "Or this also may be Cruse's subtle way of informing Deputy Raber that he's on his own. It's well known that the sheriff is a cautious man."

"Don't listen to this garbage," the lawyer said.

"I don't know nothing about no deer-meat shipments," Raber said.

"Plural?" Zakov said immediately. "Shipments, as in more than one?"

"Slip of the tongue," the lawyer said. "A simple case of *lapsus calami*. No transcription here, no formal record; this is simply a conversation."

Echo came forward and said, "To be precise, which is expected of those of us who practice before the bar, *lapsus calami* refers solely to a 'slip of the pen,' a written slip, and what we have here is *lapsus linguae*, a verbal slip of the tongue," Echo said. "Rest assured, said *lapsus linguae* will invite extensive questioning. As it stands, it seems to provide the deputies here with motivation and reason to investigate any long-term relationship between Mr. Nesmith, Nesmith Victuals, and Deputy Raber."

"Do what you have to do," the lawyer said.

"Hey!" Raber said with a pained yelp.

"Not to worry, Deputy. These men are only fishing," the lawyer said, looking calm and bright.

Bapcat leaned toward the Houghton deputy. "Our *fishing* has taken us out to Central mine to talk to your stepfather." Bapcat saw Raber claw at the table. "He a hunter too?"

"*Do* you hunt, Deputy Raber?" Zakov asked, joining in.

"None of this is relative to anything," the lawyer said. "My client will answer no further questions."

Echo came into the conversation again. "When did Deputy Raber's status shift from a favor for friends to client?"

"We're done with this nonsense—now," the lawyer said.

"Nonsense?" Zakov said. "You see, the mine operators send someone from their mouthpiece firm as a favor, and as soon as the discussion turns to illegal deer, the man is declared a client. This, of course, makes us wonder what the mine operators have to do with illegal deer." Zakov looked at the deputy. "Do you understand what your attorney is telling us through his actions—the fact that the mines, having sent him, will take him away if things start to look bad for their reputations?"

"Ignore their yammering," the lawyer said.

Raber's eyes showed uncertainty.

"Today we just talk," Echo said. "Next time we call, there will be an arrest warrant followed by an arraignment."

The lawyer grabbed the deputy and physically steered him out of the room.

Echo looked calmly at the game wardens. "Engineers look to build foundations, prosecutors to crack them. I think today we made a fine start on a crack." To Zakov he said, "You should consider a career in the law."

Zakov beamed at his partner as they left Echo's office. "Career in the law; you heard the man."

"This was nothing but play today," Bapcat said. "No formal rules, no stakes—a skirmish, and nothing more than that."

"Did we not make our deputy friend wonder if he is all alone?"

"The question is, what does he do now, and where the hell is Davidov? Two of us aren't enough to go around, and we can't expect Cruse and his people to help us. We've got to be smart in choosing what we do while we're waiting to see what Deputy Raber and the others do."

Echo came outside and joined them. "You know that Nesmith and his attorney have already fallen on their sword for the meat and all the illegalities surrounding it, which came as a surprise to me. What does it tell you?" he asked Bapcat.

"Not sure. How about you?"

"The Rees, Robinson, and Petermann man's presence suggests that the mine operators have some stake in the outcome here, which I must confess I cannot yet ascertain."

Bapcat rolled a cigarette for the man and handed it to him, then proceeded to tell him the full and unabridged story of what was happening away from the street, where strikers and strike-breakers were butting heads.

When the game warden finished, Echo blew a smoke ring and sighed. "Gentlemen, I think we might expect with some certainty that the worst is yet to come. How is Cruse involved?"

"We don't know," Bapcat said. "So far it seems he just does what the mine operators and MacNaughton want, but who knows?"

"MacNaughton's role?"

"No idea at this point, but if we had to point a finger at the main man, it would be Cap'n Hedyn."

"What's next for you fellows?"

"A day off to think," Zakov said.

"Spoken like an attorney," Echo said. "You men stay in touch. Lucas will have a deep and abiding interest in the case, or cases, you develop, you can depend on that."

"Can you help get search warrants for the Champion depot by talking to your counterpart in Marquette?"

"I can make some calls. Anything else?"

"Food," Zakov said, and Echo laughed.

"Also high up on a lawyer's hierarchy of values."

95

Red Jacket

SUNDAY, NOVEMBER 2, 1913

Bapcat had talked to Assistant Prosecutor Echo twice the day before, and once again that morning, Echo revealing Lucas's interest. Like O'Brien, Lucas was from a miner's family that had struggled their whole lives. Bapcat wanted a sit-down with MacNaughton.

"He sent his family away and sleeps in different places every night. Moving target," Echo added. "Never without his bodyguards."

"It's hard to hide a group," Bapcat said.

Echo was quiet momentarily. "I'll talk to Lucas and get back to you."

Bapcat gave him Vairo's telephone number and made a note to tell Harju they needed a telephone installed on the hill. It seemed it was getting so you could do little without a telephone. *You come into the job expecting to be outside in the woods, and you spend more time inside four walls.* Telephones speeded things up and let you do multiple things at once, and not waste time on travel. Echo and Lucas were working the request, but Bapcat had Vairo get in touch with Bruno Geronissi and ask him to come for a meeting.

• • •

"*Dottore*," Bapcat greeted him when Geronissi came swirling in with a cape draped over his shoulders.

"*Signore* Vairo told me you wanted to see me."

"You know what goes on around here. You have your finger on the pulse." Geronissi made a dismissive hand gesture and Bapcat continued. "MacNaughton: I want to sit down with him, talk across a table, eye to eye."

"He has his own army and moves around alla time," Geronissi said.

"I've heard that."

"What's your interest in MacNaught?"

"Time he and I met."

"MacNaught, he don't like make no talk with regular people."

MacNaught—not even his full name, just the blunt front—a slight. No wonder Big Jim's ducking. "I don't want him to kiss me, just talk."

Geronissi chuckled. "And you think Bruno, he know where MacNaught go?"

"I think *Dottore* Geronissi knows how to find out."

"Another favor; you sure?"

"Yes, and there's no time to waste."

"You think some storms, they comin' close?"

"Don't you?"

Geronissi said, sniffing, "*Si,* like poison in air."

"You know the operators are poisoning streams and ponds, flooding dens, slaughtering deer, cutting timber so there's no nearby firewood?"

"Bruno knows they also cut down the fruit trees, so no fruit for people, poison some wells if somebody too tough in strike, maybe set house fires."

"I don't know, but I want to look him in the eye and hear what he has to say."

"Can't make such meeting," Geronissi said.

"Just help me find him and I'll figure out things from there."

Geronissi gave him a lingering look of appraisal. "You do all that shit for *animali?* I'm glad you game warden, not *la polizia.*"

Strange comment. Hard to have to ask for help from the likes of Bruno, but he could think of no other way. It was reduced to priorities.

"*Grazie, Dottore.*"

"*Ciao.* We talk soon," Geronissi said, got up, and swept away.

A six-foot-tall raven wobbled into the bar and stood across from Vairo. A white face emerged from under a large, black-cloth beak. "*Sambuca,* Dominick, *si non ti dispiaci.*"

"What you supposed to be today, Carlo?" Vairo asked the costumed man, who shrugged and said, "Bird of hope."

"Wearing all black?"

The man held up the drink. "This damn strike, he got everyt'ing downside up, eh?" Carlo's vulpine mouth opened, showing badly yellowed teeth as he chugged the shot in one gulp.

Bapcat looked to Vairo for an explanation of the costume. " 'Alloween, for Italians. All Souls, eh?"

96

Kearsarge

FRIDAY, NOVEMBER 7, 1913

Zakov had gone north into the woods to search for Canady yew and deer, while Bapcat unhappily remained townside, waiting for word from Echo or Geronissi.

The assistant prosecutor finally called and said he was sorry, but he couldn't figure out a way to get to MacNaughton. Geronissi sent a messenger telling Bapcat to meet a man named Marinello that morning, in Kearsarge. The building stank of creosote and old smoke. Marinello, editor of *Il Minatore Italiano* in Red Jacket, stood with a pair of men who looked like miners.

"I get word you want to meet MacNaught," the mustachioed editor said.

That shortened name again. "True. Can it be done?"

Marinello looked him over. "MacNaught, he been having secret meetings with miners, tries convince come back work, bring others."

"I'm not a miner."

"This morning he meet three men near here. He never meet them before."

"What's your role?"

"Delivery boy. In September, I write strike not so good for Italians. MacNaught, he drop by one day, tell me I seem like reasonable man, he like reasonable men, and *grazie-prego,* can I introduce him to other reasonable men, Italian miners."

"You get to pick the men?"

"*Si,* I pick, he talks, tells them to tell others quit strike and go back work."

"I'm not Italian," Bapcat said.

"What you are?"

"One hundred percent nobody knows." *Or cares.*

"*Bene,* you come."

"Why?"

"Favors—you *capisce?*"

Bapcat understood. *Marinello owes Geronissi, same as me.*

• • •

It was 10 a.m. Kids were in school, non-striking miners were underground, most other people working, and the streets seemed relatively empty as the editor led the three men to a house with a man in a black suit on the porch. The man carried a sawed-off shotgun, and wore a black fedora. He nodded to Marinello and opened the door.

Just inside were five more men in black suits—bodyguards—and MacNaughton, lean, well over six feet tall, broad-shouldered, straight hair combed neatly back, tiny rimless eyeglasses, slate-gray eyes, pink face from a fresh shave, pressed white shirt, black tie, jacket off, red braces over his shirt, holding out his hands in welcome: Jesus welcoming the multitudes.

Bapcat took the chair on MacNaughton's right, closest to him, and watched Marinello leave. The two miners who had accompanied him also sat down, a bit farther away and said nothing. Bapcat could tell they were nervous.

"Thank you for coming, gentlemen. My good friend, Mr. Marinello, tells me you are reasonable fellas, pressured to strike by socialists and the other radicals from out west. I'm not going to ask you to come back to work in the mines. But I'm going to make you an offer that will benefit all of us."

MacNaughton made no eye contact, stared off in the distance, reciting something scripted in his mind. "Interested?" the C & H boss man asked.

Bapcat's companions said nothing. He said, "We'll listen."

"For every man you talk into coming back to work, I will give you the equivalent of his first day's wages as a reward."

The two miners blinked.

MacNaughton rolled his eyes and complained. "Marinello keeps sending us deaf and dumb mutes."

"You want to pay us to recruit for you?" Bapcat asked.

MacNaughton was surprised at what was being said to him. "It's a simple proposition."

Bapcat said, "Rather than recruiting men, why don't we talk about your deer bounties instead?"

MacNaughton began to blink at a sheet of paper in front of him. "*Which* one are you?"

Bapcat turned his lapel to show his badge. "Bapcat, Deputy State Game, Fish and Forestry Warden."

MacNaughton's scowl faded to a blank. "Your name is not one put forth by Marinelli. Where is he?"

"Gone," the nearest guard said. "You want we should go fetch him?"

"No," MacNaughton said, and the bodyguards began to step toward Bapcat and the miners with their revolvers out.

Bapcat said, "These are simple questions, Mr. MacNaughton. Who is paying men to kill deer and leave them to rot? Who is poisoning the streams and ponds and wells? Who is cutting timber so there's no firewood? Who is setting fire to private homes, and who is cutting down fruit trees so there can be no harvest next spring? Who is doing these things, sir?"

Bapcat saw his two companions squirming.

"Get Marinelli," MacNaughton said to the nearest guard.

"Are you going to answer me, sir?" Bapcat asked. "Why are you asking these men to recruit their friends back to work when you're trying to starve them and their families?"

"Joshua," the mine boss said.

A bodyguard started to step toward the table, but just then, the front door flew open and the exterior guard came stumbling in backward with Zakov pushing him, holding a black Colt .45 to the man's head. "Let us now each and all exercise keen and pragmatic judgment in these delicate circumstances," the Russian exhorted.

MacNaughton rose to his feet. "I have no idea what you are talking about, sir, and I resent this intrusion. We are leaving now. Joshua."

With that, the leader of the Keweenaw's copper industry ran out of the house and got into a vehicle, which raced away.

"This is true, what you say—the mine operators, they do these bad things?" one of the men asked.

"*Somebody's* doing them," Bapcat answered.

"You got balls, talking to MacNaught that way," one of the men said.

"*Or un sacco di stupidita*," the other one whispered.

The two miners departed on shaky legs, and Zakov and Bapcat walked back to where the Russian had parked the truck.

"I don't think MacNaughton knows what I was asking about," Bapcat told his partner.

"Which suggests perhaps the impetus comes from *below* him," the Russian said.

"Maybe, but the fact that MacNaughton is still trying to use miners to recruit miners tells me the strike is hurting him and his operations more than he wants to let on." *It says there's desperation in the air, on all sides.*

"How the heck did you find me?" Bapcat asked the Russian.

"Game wardens," Zakov said. "We are adept in the black arts, the magic of detection."

"Cut the crap."

"I was driving through Kearsarge, saw you, followed and waited, just in case."

"How did you know when to come in?"

"I didn't. I got bored. Pure luck I came through the door when I did."

97

Bumbletown Hill

SATURDAY, NOVEMBER 8, 1913

The witch had roared to life two days before, on the sixth of November. Lake Superior's surface water had remained strangely warm all fall, and Bapcat knew that when sudden winds swept down from Canada, there would be a snowstorm of epic proportions. He'd been in one in 1905, and had been trapped in the woods for a month. These winds, like those of eight years before, had come up fast from the northeast, the temperature fell just as quickly, and rain began and turned to sleet, coating everything with two inches of ice before it turned to snow, turning the world white and making all men blind.

The night before, Bapcat had tried to call Harju to request a telephone for the house, but the clerk at Petermann's told him the lines were down, and he had no idea how long the outage would last. It was the same with electric power in nearby towns. Bapcat had trudged back up to the cabin through deep snow.

"Canady yew?" Bapcat asked his partner, who had been north in the woods and only returned an hour ago, yet had not even mentioned the storm.

"As reported, mostly in dark canyon bottoms, and judging by the specimens I saw, they appear to be untouched since last winter. Yard browse, I conclude, to be eaten only when it is nearly the last choice, like borscht for me."

"Deer?"

"A few, and some sign, but no rotting carcasses."

"Too far from settlements to bother with," Bapcat said. "Maybe. Did you look for bats?"

"In *this* weather?"

Bapcat grinned. "I was beginning to think you didn't notice there is a storm." Then, "I think we should try to estimate the extent of the siege activities, you up here, me south of Houghton. Or vicey versey. Your choice."

"Here suits me," Zakov said. "It will be some days before we can move. Trees are down everywhere, drifts are up to my head, and it is looking like Siberia. Where will you start?"

"I'm thinking Painesdale, which in my mind seems to be the southwest fringe. We know there is activity east toward Chassell."

Zakov said, "The strike seems more violent and vehement south and north, softer in the center. Why would this be?"

"If I were smarter, I might manage an equally smart guess," Bapcat said.

"You are plenty smart, wife."

Meant to say more schooled, not smarter.

"Impressions of MacNaughton?" Zakov asked.

"He doesn't look people in the eye, but I think I saw fear."

"Not many people are direct," the Russian said. "In some cultures direct eye contact is taken as an insult, or worse—a call for combat to the death."

"Where did you come up with the Colt?" The semiautomatic pistol had only been issued to the US military a couple of years ago.

"Harju left one for each of us, but when he saw how attached you are to your beloved Krag, he gave both to me."

The Russian went and fetched a second weapon, a box of cartridges, and two spare magazines, and set them in front of Bapcat. "It is a hand cannon," Zakov said. "A man-stopper."

"I hope it never comes to that," Bapcat said.

"Greed sometimes situates violence within whispering distance," the Russian said.

"Thanksgiving, I intend to go to Jaquelle's, spend some time with the boy and her. You want to come with me?"

"One of us should remain here," the Russian said. "How is the boy doing?"

"Adjusting," Bapcat said with a chuckle. "Grudgingly."

"You should be a good papa and explain to this boy the sheer folly of resisting the Widow Frei."

"I'm not his father," Bapcat said, jarred by the concept.

"Yet," the Russian whispered. "Wife."

"There are moments," Bapcat said, pointing the empty Colt at a wall.

"These are, of course, mutually frustrating moments," the Russian said officiously, "and here I must posit a question stimulated by our readings in

Tiffany's. That is, if I shot you, my wife, would I be compelled by law to testify against myself?"

"Let me know when you get that worked out. We should be patrolling. Deer will not be moving much, so they'll be easy targets," Bapcat said. "I'll go south, and you can take care of this area."

"To enforce what?" Zakov asked. "You unilaterally suspended the law, at least for these surrounds."

"Just make sure hunters have licenses."

Zakov said sarcastically, "Yes, of course; the state treasury must have its pound of flesh."

98

Trimountain, Houghton County

THURSDAY, NOVEMBER 13, 1913

The storm south of Houghton was much milder than to the north. Early today Bapcat had intercepted twenty hunters in the Obenhoff Lake country and checked their licenses. He wrote no citations, gave only verbal warnings.

It felt good to have been outside for nearly two days as he trudged up the trail past Trimountain Peak, toward the mining village of Trimountain down the hill to the east. Most of all he was looking forward to a fine dinner at Shewbart's Cafe in town, and a room at Vijver's Boardinghouse, which Harju had recommended in one of their conversations. Sunday and Monday he had slept in his sleeping bag and bedroll in the woods, and each morning had brushed away fluffy new snow before making his tea fire.

This morning he had found two headless deer, but he was unable to back-track the hunter or hunters because they had carefully kept to rocky areas. This was the first evidence of the siege he had come upon around here, and knowing the kill was certain and heavier east of Trimountain and Painesdale, toward Chassell, he guessed that Obenhoff was the southwestern edge of the scheme. He wondered what Zakov was discovering up north.

When he was in sight of the town's main street, four men stepped into the alley, blocking his way. All wore black coats adorned with round white buttons with CITIZENS' ALLIANCE printed in red. As he walked toward them, they formed a wall. He said, "Hungry man here, gents. Make a hole, please."

All four men wore gun belts with the small .38s issued to special mine deputies. *Buttons, not sun-star badges. Choices here: Push through, stop, retreat, or close on them, and engage.* He decided to close in order to reduce their space to maneuver, to keep their flanks tight. Harju had advised against this, warning him to keep distance in order to spot threatening actions, but Bapcat's instincts pushed him to get closer and use his presence to dictate circumstances. In a four-on-one-situation, most would assume the group would have the advantage, but he intended to crumple their leader immediately and remove whatever sass he had. As he drew closer, he reached back, slid his bayonet out of the scabbard on his pack, and snapped the blade on the barrel of the rifle. He did this while maintaining eye contact with the man to his far right.

Affixing the bayonet happened with such speed that the men didn't react until he had turned the rifle slightly. The blade gleamed and all four of them took a half stumble backward.

"Who're *you?*" the big man on the right challenged.

"Bapcat, Deputy State Game, Fish and Forestry Warden. Who're you?"

"Fed-up citizens," the erstwhile leader barked.

"At least you're fed," Bapcat quipped.

"Had our fill of troublemakers and damn radical socialists," another of the men grumbled.

Bapcat moved the rifle slightly and the men pulled back again. "You don't want trouble, boys—not tonight, not with me, not here. He rolled his lapel to show his badge, asked, "Where're your badges?"

"You see our authority, sir," the leader said pretentiously. "We are committed Alliance men."

"That has no legal standing," Bapcat said. "Alliance . . . does that mean you're union men?"

This garnered a group snort of derision. "We represent citizens fed up with damn unions and their radical socialist leaders."

"So you fellas aren't socialists?"

This time they didn't step back, and he said, "Men, I'm not real sure what a radical socialist is, so step out of my path, or you and your attitudes are going to get sliced to ribbons." He wiggled the bayonet. The men flinched. "One more warnin,' boys. Step aside."

Their postures told him they were fixated on the bayonet and his upper body. He moved his head, and his eyes, slightly left, pausing long enough for the men to react, and then came straight up with the rifle butt under the leader's chin, crumpling him in place, pivoted, and racked a shell into the chamber. "Lead or steel, boys. Your choice. Me, I like both."

The group's belligerence was replaced by visible fear.

"All right, hands up and on top of your heads."

The three men complied, and he took each of their weapons and put them on the ground. The leader suddenly grabbed at his leg and Bapcat snapped a heavy punch to the man's temple and he went back down face-first and sighed. He then took the leader's sidearm.

"Take the big boy and go," Bapcat ordered the Alliance men. "I see you again, you'll be jailed for obstructing a state officer in pursuit of his duty. That's a felony, men."

He thought he'd read this in *Tiffany's*, but wasn't sure where. The men didn't argue, just scooped up the big man and headed for a side street.

One of the men yelled back, "You ain't real law—just a damn game warden."

Bapcat made the bayonet flick again. "Game warden with a fang," he called back. He dumped the loose cartridges into his pack and put the pistols on top.

• • •

Othar "Old Bill" Shewbart was longtime beaver trapper, a bear-size man with a large square snout, gentle mannerisms, and a soft voice. His wife put up meals that were better than the fanciest places in Houghton or Red Jacket, and at half the price.

The owner was at the counter, but there were few customers. "Look what done crawled up out of the cedar swamps," the bearded man greeted him.

Bapcat looked around. "Business slow, or do you just need a bath?"

"That's a worn-out joke. It's been this way since the strike came in and people hit the road. The strikers got no money to spend on good food."

"You know anything about a so-called Alliance, Billy?"

"It's just starting up; why?"

"You belong?"

"They came and asked, but I told 'em I ain't the joinin'-up type. Truth is, Lute, lots of people in these parts have had enough of this whole mess."

"Who asked you to join?"

"Some of the other businessmen."

"They say who's behind it?"

"Everybody, they claim."

"That's where they got money to print buttons—from everybody?"

"What're you sayin', Lute?"

"Mine operators, not businessmen, that's my guess." Bapcat told his friend what had happened, and Shewbart scowled. "What's their problem with you, Lute?"

The game warden showed his badge, and Shewbart scowled even deeper. "You got to be crazy to take a job like that in normal times, never mind during a strike. What's wrong with you?"

"No beaver," Bapcat said. "A man has to earn a living."

Shewbart still trapped as a sideline. "You know how many beaver licenses been sold in Houghton and Keweenaw counties for this trapping season?"

Bapcat didn't know.

"Two up your way, and only thirty down here," Shewbart said. "Beavers is disappearing, just like the copper will one day be gone, and then what?"

"Why the attitude about game wardens, Billy?"

"What's out in the woods is ours. This ain't your damn Europe with kings and potentates. You game wardens all want to take away what's rightfully ours."

"No, Billy, we're trying to make sure everybody plays fair, and that it will still be there for your kids and grandkids." Oates and Jones had presented it this way at the Sault meeting, and Bapcat had liked the words, the logic, and the sentiment.

Bapcat knew his friend's feelings were far from rare, here or out west, and such views had to get changed if game wardens were going to make a difference.

"Give me the benefit of the doubt, Billy, and ask the wife to whip up a chicken dinner for your old pal."

"You miss trapping, Lute?"

"Sometimes, Bill. Sometimes." *But less and less.* More and more he found himself thinking and wondering about, and missing, Jaquelle Frei and the boy. The feelings seemed foreign and he had no idea how to sort them out, only that he felt them, and powerfully.

"You read any papers or been out to the woods?" Shewbart asked.

"Woods."

"Papers say this storm, she sink two ships in Superior, eight in Huron, maybe two hundred and fifty hands lost. Dozens of ships run aground, probably more lost in Lake Michigan, but I ain't heard on that yet. Had a ship founder out by Gull Rock. The lifesaving boys from the Portage and Copper Harbor stations banged their way north in boats and got all hands to safety. I guess it was tough business, but you live up here, you learn weather can kill you," Shewbart said, snapping his fingers. "Like that. You'd think sailors would learn to read the weather better."

It occurred to Bapcat that up in Copper Harbor, Jaquelle and Jordy had probably been clobbered worse than anywhere. He found his heart racing, wondering how they were.

99

Bumbletown Hill

THURSDAY, NOVEMBER 20, 1913

Bapcat needed uninterrupted sleep—a lot of it. He had been resting poorly when he did, and slept little in the cold and sleeting onditions. Deer hunters were out, but most had had the required licenses. He had seen only two headless deer carcasses anywhere west of Trimountain and Painesdale, despite covering a lot of ground on foot, several miles a day along streams and in what looked to be good deer country.

Storm gone, the daytime temperatures were hovering in the low twenties, and he guessed this sustained cold had put the deer into the annual rut, which made male deer stupid. With it happening now instead of earlier, hunters should be doing quite well. Even so, Bapcat had heard almost no shots, and seen few deer on poles at hunting camps. Next year the law was likely to be for bucks only, and for a lot shorter season, and in Harju's opinion, "It'll be real messy the first time around."

Trekking up the hill he saw the truck and another automobile and arrived to find Zakov in conversation with a lanky man with a prominent Adam's apple and a thin nose.

"Here he is," Zakov said, "entering stage left on cue, fresh from policing Coxey's bloody army."

What the hell was the Russian talking about: Coxey's Army? Before Cuba, he sort of remembered talk about a bunch of unemployed workers who had marched on Washington to demand that the government create jobs, but this was all he could recall.

Zakov, always in love with the sound of his own voice, continued. "This fine individual is one August Beck of Calumet and Hecla."

"Responsible for company security," the man said. "Mr. MacNaughton asked me to look into certain allegations you made after illegally intruding upon a private assembly you were unauthorized to attend."

"Whole lot of words for what amounts to bear crap," Bapcat said. "What gets you fellas most, me at your meeting? Or what you people are doing to make life impossible for strikers and their families? Or me calling you out on it?"

The direct questions seemed to take the man off guard. *Clearly the type who likes to deal from power.*

"Mr. MacNaughton is unaware of any alleged illegal and immoral activities."

"Not anymore he ain't, because I told him. And we'll be glad to walk him out to any of his properties and show him the evidence. Tell him to open his damn eyes and take a look around. Even a child can see what's going on."

"There's no call for that tone," Beck countered.

"The world looks different from my boots," Bapcat said. "What the hell do you want here, Beck?"

"Civil discourse."

Zakov said, "I have volunteered to give the gentleman a tour. There are ample things to see close to here."

Bapcat set down his rifle, opened his pack, and took out the confiscated revolvers.

"I prefer my Colt," Zakov said.

Bapcat looked at Beck. "I encountered something called the Citizens' Alliance, over in Trimountain. You know anything about these vigilantes?"

Beck wouldn't look at him. "Sorry."

"For a security man, you seem a far piece out of the picture, Beck, both big and small."

"Professionals work rationally, on facts, not conjecture."

"What people like you prefer is to bully from behind a thin shield of law."

"We are a nation of laws."

"We're a nation of people who make and change the laws," Bapcat countered. "We *make* the laws, not the other way around. Hell, you've already got too damn many special deputies all over the place, and they're all armed. Now, about this so-called Citizens' Alliance: Who runs the outfit?"

"As previously stated, I have never heard of this group."

"I took those four revolvers off deputies who appeared to have replaced their badges with Alliance buttons, and tried to act like this so-called Alliance has the force of law."

"These men threatened you?"

Bapcat smiled. "They tried. Is that your intention, too?"

"I am employed solely to gather facts and report back."

"Good; tell your boss that most people around here are sure nobody can take a shit unless C and H says so, and C and H means MacNaughton. We all know this because we see it every day."

"There is no point to continuing this conversation," Beck said.

"Let us dispense with meaningless banter" Zakov said.

"Can't continue what isn't," Bapcat said. "Go out to the damn mines and see for yourself, if you really don't know."

"Mr. MacNaughton wishes me to inform you that he is a law-abiding citizen of the highest moral character, and he abhors all questionable actions."

"That's a pretty good joke," Bapcat said. "Really—all questionable actions, even if they make a profit for the men back in Boston, or crush a union forever, along with its families?"

"I have never worked for a finer man," Beck said.

Zakov stepped in. "How banal. That only attests to your limited experience or to pathetic values, Mr. Beck, not to MacNaughton's quality."

Beck didn't linger, and hurried away.

"I guess he doesn't want the tour," Zakov said.

"MacNaughton sent him to cover himself and the company politically. Beck not taking the tour suggests he already knows what's going on."

"Which means MacNaughton knows," Zakov said.

"Not necessarily. You ever have a boss you couldn't tell bad news to?"

"I walked one such man out to meet the Japanese."

"How was your patrol?"

"Very few deer, even fewer hunters. Word seems to be widespread that there are no deer up here."

"The mine owners are succeeding," Bapcat said.

The Russian looked deep in thought. "Mother Nature has a role, I believe. In our discussions in Sault Ste. Marie, it was suggested that hunting practices have significant effect, and deer up here have been overhunted since before the strikes."

"We are our own worst enemies?"

"An inescapable conclusion."

"And I made it worse."

"*We* did," the Russian said.

"Russians know Mother Nature?"

"*Rodina*, we say, and this serious word means *motherland,* but Mother Nature, Mother Russia, motherland—it is all the same, *da*."

Bapcat didn't understand the point, but nodded to be polite. His mistake in judgment had hurt the situation. *How does a man atone for ignorance and poor judgment?*

100

Copper Harbor

THURSDAY, NOVEMBER 27, 1913

Zakov agreed to join Bapcat on his Thanksgiving trip, and they drove up to Copper Harbor, cursing the road the whole way, which was little better than a widened wagon trail, and so rocky it relentlessly pounded the vehicle, causing a flat tire as light snow fell. The ground, where it wasn't rock, was frozen from two weeks of below-freezing nights.

"It will be a considerable challenge to drive this road in spring when the mud comes," the Russian said, adding, "it was mud that stopped Napoleon."

"I thought it was your army."

"Only after the *rasputitsa* mired his army and allowed us to slaughter them like animals in a pen."

• • •

Widow Frei was waiting for them. She wore a long black skirt, a diaphanous white blouse with a frilly collar, and a long string of raw agates. She had cut her hair since Bapcat had last seen her, and it took him by surprise. The boy looked uncomfortable in an obviously new white shirt, tie, and jacket, with black knickers and the ends of his spindly legs tucked into polished boots.

"Do those hurt your feet, boy?" Zakov asked, pointing at Jordy Kluboshar's new boots.

"Only when I walk in them," the boy said.

"A lame and likely excuse to help him escape chores," Frei said. She gave Bapcat a peck on the cheek.

"How'd you like the storm?" Zakov asked the boy.

"I guess I seen my share of snow blowing around before this one," the boy retorted.

"You heard about Moriarty?" the widow asked.

"No," Bapcat said.

"He hanged himself behind his establishment."

"Suicide?"

"Moriarty wasn't the kind of man to be strung up by others. They were far too fearful. Damn few would have had that kind of nerve," she said. "Much less ability."

"When?"

"Ten days ago, or so," she said.

"Who found him?"

"I don't know."

"Did the county medical examiner come up?"

"I run my own business, and mind it, too."

Bapcat laughed. "You also know every damn thing that goes on up here."

"Wyoming is hardly Copper Harbor," she said.

"Jaquelle."

"Yes, he and the sheriff came up and took care of the remains."

Bapcat tried to remember the last time he'd talked to Hepting, but couldn't.

After dinner they sat on the apartment's side porch. The sun was out, temperature in the forties.

"Indian summer," Frei said. "My knees say we're in for more snow soon."

Bapcat set his slouch hat on the floor, rolled a cigarette, smoked slowly, and dozed off. When had he seen the colonel—May? It felt like years ago. His mind drifted back to Marquette. At their first meeting, Oates and Jones had asked about Cruse and Hepting and Captain Hedyn, but not about MacNaughton. And now, six months had passed.

Bapcat suddenly sat up.

"What is it?" Jaquelle Frei asked.

They had laid out his target in the first five minutes, and somehow he had missed the signal. He felt like a fool. Apparently, they were seeing Hedyn as a market hunter, but they were obviously operating on incomplete information, because nobody had ever seen what was actually happening in Copper County.

Did they expect me to go right at Hedyn from the beginning, and if so, why didn't they say anything? Good God!

Bapcat pulled the Russian aside. "Stay tonight. We'll take the boy hunting and stay the night."

"What's changed?"

"My memory," Bapcat said.

He used Frei's telephone to place calls to both Oates and Jones. Neither man answered.

The men and boy hunted in the afternoon, and Jordy Kluboshar shot a large buck with almost black fur, and Bapcat and the Russian shot smaller animals. There was wolf sign in the area, and they got home long after dark, having to drag three carcasses out of the woods and along steep ridges to where the truck was parked.

Bapcat fell asleep with Jaquelle's head on his shoulder. "I won't ask when you're coming back," she whispered. "I can see in your eyes you are on a crusade."

"You don't know me well enough to say that," he protested.

"Honey, you don't have to *see* a fire to know it's burning."

101

Wyoming (Helltown)

FRIDAY, NOVEMBER 28, 1913

The next morning, they drove up the hills to Mandan, where the train line from Houghton terminated, and used the railroad phone to call Oates and Jones. Their secretaries said both men were in meetings. Bapcat said he would call Jones around 3 p.m., from Sheriff Hepting's office in Eagle River.

Bapcat had never been in Helltown in daylight, but he had often smelled it from concealment in the forest. Today he sensed a new air, one with less edge and easier breathing—if you ignored the floozy on the sidewalk coughing blood into the snow. Where Moriarty's place once stood was a squat black cairn.

The owner of the Coppertown Tavern told them Moriarty's body had been taken by Hepting and the coroner to Eagle River. There seemed to be no sorrow or remorse over the Irishman's demise.

"There was a man named Fisher around town," Bapcat said.

"Never heard of him," the barman said.

"I saw him come into your place one night," Bapcat countered.

"That don't make him special. I can't remember everyone."

"Especially someone you'd rather forget?"

"Your words, not mine," the man said.

"How about Pinnochi?"

"Why would I know him?"

Odd response. "Most people would say they don't know him."

"Well, I don't know nobody," the man said.

"Not even your good customers?"

"If they got cash in hand, I know 'em. If not, I don't."

"This Fisher you never heard of—maybe he couldn't be heard of after Moriarty killed himself."

"Could be like that," the man said. "I wouldn't know."

"Who takes over Moriarty's place now that he's gone?"

"Nobody. Help yourself to what's left. It burned to the ground that very night."

"Act of God?" the Russian asked.

"Everybody seems to have an opinion."

"What's yours?" Zakov asked.

"Act of God's as good as any."

"Makes one embrace fate," Zakov said.

"Especially in this hole in the woods," the man said.

"Anyone knows anything that relates, we call that material in the law," Zakov said. "Expect a visit from Sheriff Hepting."

"People in this town got a lot worse things to worry about than Johnny Hepting," the man said.

"Name one," Zakov said.

"Winter."

"I suggest you add *us* to your short list," Bapcat told the man, and turned away.

102

Eagle River

FRIDAY, NOVEMBER 28, 1913

Jones answered his own phone immediately, and Bapcat launched directly at him.

"When you talked to me about the job in May, you asked me about a certain captain, and about my hands. I think you knew about the fight. You've got someone inside."

"I can't go into that," Bapcat's boss said. "Neither confirm, nor deny."

"What the hell does *that* mean?"

"It means telephones have many ears."

Bapcat went silent. "How do we talk?"

"Not like this," Jones said.

To hell with it. "There's no market-hunting here. It's something different—a lot different."

"Not on the telephone, Deputy."

"I intend to put the heat on the man we talked about. A lot of heat."

Long pause. "Keep us apprised of your progress and needs, and be careful."

"While we're talking, you might want to find out what you can about an Ascher deputy named Fisher."

"No names, Lute."

"Just check on him, sir," Bapcat said, and hung up. "Maybe we *don't* need a damn telephone," he told the Russian.

"I don't understand," Zakov said.

"Party lines," Hepting said from the side of the room. "Each line serves many, and all can listen to each other."

God, Bapcat thought. "We came through Helltown. They say you picked up Moriarty after the suicide."

"Well, it's true enough he was hanged, but it's hard to string yourself up with half your head gone and no pistol on the ground where you're hanging," Hepting said.

"Murder?"

"No point in making it public. Better to keep it quiet, let rumor and gossip reign, see what speculations percolate."

"This is an established investigative procedure?" Zakov asked.

"More my take on such things," the sheriff admitted. "If we tried to chase every wrong, we'd have no time to take care of important things."

"They burned his building," Bapcat said.

"It was still standing the day we retrieved the body."

"Not anymore. You hear the name Fisher while you were up there?"

"Should I have?"

"Just wondering."

Hepting cracked his knuckles. "The thing about being a small county sheriff is, you're damn limited in everything you do, or can do."

"He goes by the name of Frank Fisher, but his real name is Frankus Fish. He was a Rough Rider, a sergeant with a foul temper and a taste for torturing his own men."

"And you think he's here why?"

"I *know* he's here, not why. He came in as an Ascher detective, but that may be only a story. I don't know. I saw him once coming out of Moriarty's at night."

"You were at Moriarty's?"

"Not exactly there, but we talked."

"Where?"

"In his privy."

Hepting grinned. "Talk about taking away a man's dignity."

"I talked to Moriarty early last month, not long after Fisher is supposed to have shown up asking questions about Pinnochi."

"Why?"

"I don't know that. Could be he's looking for me."

"Why you?"

"Bad blood."

"Man with a grudge?"

"Could be."

"Why?"

"I stopped him from doing what he liked to do."

"What happened to 'forgive and forget'?"

"Some men never forget anything. Zakov and I are going to put the heat on Cap'n Hedyn."

Hepting cringed visibly. "Not a good idea to bite the bulldog."

"Depends on how hard you bite," Bapcat said. "Alone, he's less than inspiring. I already met with MacNaughton."

"How?" Hepting looked surprised.

"My take on the book."

"What book do we refer to?" Zakov asked.

John Hepting said, "The one everyone quotes and few read. You want my help, Lute?"

"Your hands are full with the strike. Just keep an ear out for Fisher."

En route to the hill, Zakov said, "You are an exceedingly complex man."

"Is that good or bad?"

"Much of both, I think."

"The days ahead could get intense and messy."

"There is no revelation in these words you choose. When you killed the Spaniards in Cuba, how did you feel when it was done?"

"Unhappy; happy; sad, maybe; glad; a little sick to my stomach."

"When I dispatched my general, I felt nothing but elation," Zakov said. "Then and now."

"You mean, for walking him toward the enemy troops?"

"I don't like leaving critical things to chance, wife. It was coincidence only to those back in our lines. The shell exploded a split second after I put a bullet in the back of the monster's head."

"You left your escape to chance."

"My personal survival was never the point," Zakov said, "only his death."

"Why are you telling me this?"

The Russian took his hands off the steering wheel and the truck began to slide wildly around before he took control again. "I like staring into the unknown and unpredictable," he said. "This is no doubt a serious character flaw."

103

Redridge, Houghton County

FRIDAY, DECEMBER 5, 1913

Rollie Echo called John Hepting, who called Petermann's store in Allouez. Petermann sent a messenger up to the hill, telling Bapcat to call Echo as soon as he could. They called from Petermann's and immediately raced to Houghton to meet the assistant prosecuting attorney.

"Solid but unverified information," Echo told them in his office in the county courthouse. "Your Davidov is allegedly holed up in Redridge. I have detailed directions."

"You're coming with us?"

"It behooves one to occasionally leave the confines of his office and mingle."

No idea why the back-office man suddenly wanted outside, but so be it. "Where in Redridge?"

"There's a backwater off the dam pond, a cranberry bog off the backwater on the northeast side, an abandoned cabin on the property, and a barn."

"Who owns the property?"

"Champion Mining sold it to Philamon Hedyn."

This stopped Bapcat in his tracks. "The captain's brother?"

"So it appears. The purchase was completed this past summer, in June."

"Is there a connection between Davidov and Hedyn?"

"Unknown," the assistant prosecutor said.

It was midafternoon when Zakov bounced the truck through a stump field along a rutted wagon track off the main road from Houghton. The stump field connected to the cranberry marsh, and the house and barn sat atop a slight rise above the bog, which was covered with a layer of thin black ice over black muck, making the footing look secure, which it wasn't.

The log house was two floors with a cedar-shingle roof and a chimney. A ladder had been affixed to the roof to allow for snow removal.

"Apparently we're about a quarter-mile due east of the village," Echo announced.

"You've been out here before?" Zakov asked.

The prosecutor said, "My point is that this place is not nearly as isolated and remote as it appears from this vantage. How will you gentlemen go about this?"

Bapcat looked at Zakov. "House first, then the barn. I'll take the front, you take the back. Mr. Echo, place yourself down that way so that you can see the barn, but stay close to the truck. Are you armed?"

"Some people rely on prayer," Echo said. "My personal preference is to run when danger looms." There was almost a smile.

Zakov and Echo nodded at Bapcat's plan, and the game wardens headed for the unpainted building. Vigorous knocking brought no response from inside the house. Bapcat tested the front door, pushed it inward, and peeked inside. *Dark, little light.* He walked through to the kitchen to the back stoop and waved for Zakov to join him in searching the house. Bapcat saw that Echo was positioned to watch the barn.

The game wardens searched methodically.

"Someone's been here," the Russian said. "Tobacco on the kitchen floor, bread crusts in the snow off the back stoop. Some kind soul likes to feed small carnivores."

They heard Echo yelling, and ran outside to see him gesturing north.

"A man came running out of the barn," Echo shouted excitedly.

"Shall we lose the packs?" Zakov asked, smiling.

"Your leg up to this?"

"It seems strong enough most of the time. We shall see."

Snow was dusting the frozen ground, and they ran parallel to the fleeing man's prints, which showed his gait getting longer, suggesting he was taking longer strides and tiring. *Afraid, confused, not used to running, looking for a hide*, Bapcat told himself, and signaled for the Russian to stop and kneel.

"Let us hope he finds no second wind," Zakov said, his chest heaving.

"You all right?"

"At the moment, but the future is at issue. My style is more plodding than fire-eating pursuit."

They sat quietly, scanning the area ahead of them, a broad field and a tree line. They could smell smoke from the town's mill and feel the dull thud of mill presses crushing tons of rock hauled in from the Baltic Mine.

Rumbling ground was such a common thing in mining towns that it was rarely acknowledged, but this time something about the vibration nipped at Bapcat's subconscious. *Sound beneath the stamp-mill vibrations, softer, more rhythmic, thut-thut-thut.*

Train?

Before he could say anything, the Russian was running forward, yelling, "Train—hear it?"

He did.

"Trainman on the run," the Russian said over his shoulder. "He doesn't have the patience to sit. The train means distance, safety." The Russian pointed at the rail bed ahead and the running figure. "He's making for the train."

They pursued across a swale and through a maple tree line into an expanse of barren fields with several small wooden houses. They could see the elevated track bed and a train chuffing westward, a black locomotive, coal tender, four cars, and a caboose.

Bapcat stopped, looked left, and saw a stick figure running hard, two hundred yards in the lead, on an intercept course for the train at a place where the tracks seemed to dip, which would make it easier for a man to board, especially a tired man.

Bapcat tore past Zakov. "Get back to Echo and the truck. Get into Redridge, fast!"

The Russian immediately peeled off and headed back toward the house while Bapcat fixed his mind on the run and nothing else. Lungs burning, he tried to empty his mind and keep pounding forward. Impossible to gauge how long he had been running when he realized the runner would catch the front part of the train before him, and rifle in hand, he put his head down and tried to run without thinking, to glide until he began to approach the train. Only then did he turn his attention to the challenge.

The last car had platforms front and back. He thought he had a chance at the front platform of the last car, and if he missed, there was an outside chance he could recover sufficiently to grab the back of the caboose as it passed by. He knew if he put all his effort at the tail end, a miss would mean he'd lost the man, which was all he could think about.

Closing on the train, he picked a place on the front step and platform of the last coach car, ran up the incline, and leapt, banging his shoulder on a rail and going down hard on his knee on a metal step. He was immediately up and moving to the third car, where he shouldered open the door and entered in a low crouch, rifle up and ready.

What he saw were rows of small pink faces looking back at him, mouths agape, eyes wide. *Children.* He flashed his badge, said "Game warden," and all the children's arms and hands pointed forward in unison.

"What is this train, girl?" he asked a child as he advanced.

"School train, sir, Atlantic Mine, Redridge, Beacon Hill."

Easing his way into the next car, he held up his badge and all the children again pointed. He ran forward and found Davidov facedown on the platform of the second coach, his left arm bent in an unnatural position, his head covered with blood.

Bapcat pulled the man inside the coach, propped him in a seat. The children stampeded when the man shrieked in pain, and Bapcat told him, "Shut up. These children have more courage than you."

The game warden said to a little girl nearby, "Scarf."

She immediately handed him a yellow bandanna. The game warden used the cloth to fashion a sling to immobilize Davidov's injured arm, and told the man to stop whining.

The girl came over to him. "Mister, did you hurt him 'cause he was naughty?"

"He hurt himself."

"Why?"

"I don't know, kid."

When the train jerked and chugged to a stop at the Redridge station, Zakov came hurtling aboard and helped him get the injured man down to the ground.

"Who are all the brats?" the Russian asked.

"School train. They helped me."

Zakov stopped and dramatically held out his hands. "Thank you, our dear friends. You are now all hereby appointed honorary Michigan Forest Scouts, the first in county history."

The children had spilled out of all the cars to watch what was happening, and when Zakov spoke, they all began to cheer and clap, and wave their hats.

"I am a regular Pied Pipersky," the Russian proclaimed.

"I had no choice; they gave me no choice," Davidov cried.

Assistant Prosecuting Attorney Echo studied the man and said, "You will have choices from us, sir, but you may not find them to your liking."

"My arm hurts *bad*," Davidov said, and Zakov immediately slapped the arm hard, making the man scream and wince with pain.

"Was that necessary?" Bapcat asked his partner.

"For him, no. For me, yes, of course."

A schoolboy approached. "Is that the man who cuts off deer's heads?"

Bapcat looked at the boy. "What did you just say?"

"Is that the man who cuts off deer's heads?"

"Does that happen around here?"

"Yes, sir."

"Where?"

"Behind our school."

"Where might that be?"

The boy pointed east. "Painesdale."

"What's your name?"

"Johnny Haluska."

"You live near here?"

"Yeah."

"Do you know how to use a telephone, John?"

"They got one at Redridge Co-op."

Bapcat gave him Vairo's and Petermann's phone numbers. "You see people with deer, call either of those numbers and tell whoever answers what you saw, who, and when."

The game warden led the boy outside. "Show me your house."

The kid pointed. "Third one on left, over there."

"Let's quick go see your ma."

"My ma don't speak good English. Am I a good Forest Scout now?"

"Our top scout, John."

"Do I get a badge?"

"You bet, but not today."

Bapcat told Echo, "We need to make a stop before we go back."

"I want to lodge him and charge him as soon as possible. Get him in a cell, see if it helps his memory."

"We've got to get him medical attention first," Bapcat reminded the assistant prosecutor.

"Is it always this exciting?"

"This is quite uneventful, actually. He didn't even want to fight," Zakov said.

• • •

The clapboard Redridge dispensary sat along the road between the steel dam on the Salmon Trout River impoundment and Lake Superior, both of which could be seen in the distance, great hulking gray presences. There was a greeting station just inside the front entrance, next to a waiting room for ambulatory patients, and a hallway with treatment rooms reaching off to the left.

Having Rollie Echo along helped get Davidov seen to quickly by a wizened doctor named Venelaste, who set the arm break, splinted it, sewed twelve stitches in the man's head cut, and bandaged him.

"What about pain?" Davidov asked through clenched teeth.

"Endure it the way our savior endured it on the cross," the enigmatic doctor said.

Bapcat could smell alcohol on the doctor. *A lot of alcohol.* "All right to talk to the patient?" he asked the doctor, who belched, shrugged, and shambled away.

"I had no choice," Davidov said immediately.

"No choice in what?" Bapcat countered.

Davidov looked up at him. "The boxes."

"What boxes?"

The man looked befuddled, and Bapcat could see him laboring to sort pain from his thoughts, his answer a heavy sigh. "Why am I here?"

"Trespass," Bapcat said.

"But you and your partner were on the train from Marquette," Davidov said, obviously still trying to clarify earlier exchanges.

"Yes, we were. Why were you hiding in the barn?"

"*Barn?*"

"I saw you come out and run," Rollie Echo said. "Why were you in the barn, and why did you run?"

"I didn't run," Davidov insisted.

"I was right behind you," Bapcat said.

"I was late for my train."

"The *school* train?"

"I ride it to Beacon Hill and take it back to Painesdale."

"Why would you go to Beacon Hill when you could wait right here for the train to return?"

"This is just how I like to do it," the man said vaguely, his eyes darting.

"You do this regularly, do you?"

"I've done it."

"Prevarication provokes," the assistant prosecutor said menacingly.

"It's the truth, I've caught this train before."

"By jumping aboard as it passed."

"I'm a railroad man; we develop certain skills."

"You broke your arm and cut your damn head. *Those* skills?"

"You don't understand," Davidov said.

"Have you caught the train after previous episodes of trespass?" Echo asked.

"I did not trespass."

"You have permission to be on that property?"

"Of course. I'm a law-abiding citizen."

"Written permission?" Bapcat asked.

"Verbal."

"From the owner?" Echo asked.

"Yes, from the owner," the trainman insisted.

"Gerlach?" Bapcat asked.

"Who is Gerlach?"

"The owner. You said you had permission."

"I do. Reverend Philamon Hedyn's the owner, not someone called Gerlach."

Bapcat watched the man's expression and saw it change to one of deep concern as he replayed the exchanges and suddenly seemed to suspect he had given up something he shouldn't have.

Bapcat said, "You said you had no choice, and they gave you no choice. Do you remember those words from the train?"

"I was in pain," the man said.

"No choice but trespass, or something more serious?"

"I'm not saying any more," the man said, lifting his chin defiantly. "I want my lawyer."

"Why do you need a lawyer if you're innocent?"

"It's my right."

"Is it? Why pay a lawyer when all you have to do is be honest with us. You claim someone named Hedyn is the property owner, not Gerlach?"

"Yes. I'm in pain, and I think you're trying to trick me."

"Trick you into what?"

"I'm not sure," the man admitted. "I feel confused."

"We know who owns the property, and when it was purchased," Echo said.

Bapcat said quietly, "Nesmith of Houghton claims he killed all the deer, and he took total responsibility for the boxes."

"So I can go?" the man asked, hope in his voice.

"Of course not," Echo said. "You're under arrest for trespass."

"That's not fair. I have permission. Ask the Hedyns."

"The Hedyn of Copper Harbor?"

"Central Mine," the man insisted, "not Copper Harbor."

He said Hedyns, plural. "Thank you," Bapcat said. "Was that so hard?"

"Was what so hard?"

"Telling us what we wanted to know," Echo said, touching the man's shoulder. "You're under arrest."

"For a trespass that wasn't a trespass?"

"For trying to elude game wardens and an officer of the court."

"How was I to know who you were? Times are dangerous, you know."

"We met on the train recently," Zakov reminded him. "Talked about wooden boxes and their ore contents."

"I don't remember you," the man insisted.

"Don't say any more," Echo said. "Save what you have to say for your lawyer."

"I'm telling you I have verbal permission. Why would I lie?"

"Permission given when?"

"I don't remember the exact date."

"You're still going to jail," Echo said. "You fled."

"Nobody told me stop."

"You looked right at me and fled."

"I didn't know who you were."

Bapcat said, "You're a railroad man. Do you run away from every passenger you don't know?"

The man hung his head. "It's not the same thing," Davidov protested.

Echo said, "A judge and jury will decide what is and isn't."

Zakov helped the prisoner into the truck and Echo pulled Bapcat to the side. "Why did you go after trespass?"

"I wanted to get him talking. We had Nesmith's confession, but this guy fled town, and today he fled us. He's scared. I wanted to get him off balance, then go back to the boxes."

"What do you think you have?"

"An opening back to Reverend Hedyn." *Maybe to both brothers.*

"He'll deny giving permission."

Bapcat grinned. "I don't give a damn. This will give me a chance to squeeze him."

"To get his brother?"

"I'm guessing it will at least get his attention."

"Your interview style would shame most senior law students. Maybe you should consider a career in the law."

"I don't want to steal my wife's dream," Bapcat said.

Echo asked, "You're married?"

Bapcat pointed at Zakov. "My fine wife."

Echo exhaled loudly. "I don't want to know any more. Do you still need to stop in Painesdale?"

"Yes."

"I'll put the prisoner on the Copper Range from there."

"No need. We'll take you into Houghton so you can book the man. We can come back afterward."

104

Painesdale, Houghton County

SUNDAY, DECEMBER 7, 1913

The prisoner was lodged into custody late Friday, and the game wardens spent the night at a hotel in Houghton. Saturday morning they drove south to Painesdale, where they spent all day in the woods behind the school, along the Little Otter River, eventually discovering eight headless carcasses. Obviously the operators were not abandoning their plan.

It was approaching one in the morning as Zakov drove the truck through the north end of Painesdale. Suddenly they heard volleys of shots from the west. Both men pointed in the same direction, and the Russian turned sharply down the nearest road, which turned out to be Baltic Street. As they drove, they heard another fusillade. "Rifle," Zakov said, "heavy caliber."

Bapcat heard at least twenty shots and guessed there had been more. "Sounds like someone is killing a herd," he said as they heard a final shot and jerked to a stop at the dead end, a heavy wooded area on a low hill directly in front of them. Both men grabbed their weapons and moved to the thick cover, where they separated slightly and moved in slowly, listening for sounds that didn't belong. In the distance they heard crows, human shrieks and screams. Bapcat was tempted to go back, but the shots had come from the woods, and they needed to search there first.

The game wardens emerged from the woods two hours later to find the area swarming with Houghton county deputies, all of them armed and edgy.

They identified themselves to a deputy and told him they had gone to investigate shots, thinking there were poachers at work.

"They were poachers, all right, but they were hunting men. All the shots seemed to go into the two end houses on the south side," the deputy said. "Got two dead, a third who probably won't make it, and a little girl who got hit twice, but she'll probably live. You find anything out there?"

"Nothing," Bapcat said, and looked up to see Dr. Robair Labisoniere, the Barber, come out of the first house, rolling a cigarette.

"Goddamn ambuscade," he greeted them when they joined him. "You boys sure do get around. Where the hell did *you* come from?"

"Sergeant over there said people are dead," Bapcat said.

"Inside the house it looks like an abattoir."

"Victims?"

"Two dead, side by side, and near as I can tell the same damn bullet killed the both of them. Went all the way through the first house into the third floor of the second and blew their heads apart. What're the chances? We've got two wounded, one mortally.

"The man of the house ran down to Siler's Hotel to use a phone, call for medical help from a mine doctor, and I got called after the doctor got here and found the bodies. The doctor drove his buggy like a madman, which seems somehow fitting. This whole Painesdale lot is mad. How many murders will it take?" The Barber didn't finish. Instead he sucked deeply on his cigarette.

"We heard shots from the woods," Bapcat said. "We were less than a minute behind the shooter."

"More than one," the doctor said. "One neighbor claims thirty rounds."

"I counted twenty at one point," Bapcat said. The doctor was no doubt right about multiple shooters.

"You fellas find anything out there?"

"Nothing," Bapcat said.

"This is the death knell for the strike," the doctor said. "Most mines are already digging rock again. Both the dead men are scabs, brothers, supposed to start work Monday morning. You can bet WFM men are involved in this, and now they've given the lunatic Citizens' Alliance a cause. Retribution will be in the air. MacNaughton hates Finns, and everybody knows this. Expect them to catch the brunt."

"You think these people were murdered?" Bapcat asked.

"If I had to guess, I would think the shots were fired to intimidate and deliver a message, but bad luck turned it into murder."

Big Jim Cruse came out of the house closest to the woods and waddled over to them. "I hear you State boys are trying to make some trouble for Deputy Raber, one of my best men."

"Made trouble for himself," Zakov retorted. "Perhaps you should focus on the case at hand."

Cruse said, "Go on and git before you foul up my investigation."

Bapcat looked at all the deputies and soldiers and neighbors milling around and said, "We wouldn't want that."

"Sass me," the sheriff said, "I'll run you in for interfering with a police investigation."

"Almost be worth the trouble, just to see if you *can* run," Bapcat said, and steered his partner away before both their mouths got them into trouble.

"You make me weary," Zakov said as they got the truck started.

105

Central Location

TUESDAY, DECEMBER 9, 1913

It had snowed all night. They drove the Ford down into Allouez, but reports said the roads ahead were badly iced and the going slow. They grabbed their packs and weapons, took the electric out to Mohawk, and transferred to the Keweenaw Central to Central Depot, Central Location's rail station.

Philamon Hedyn was splitting wood behind his church. Although he was a small man, he swung the long-handle double-bit ax with ease and power.

"Reverend," Bapcat greeted him.

Hedyn ignored them, drove the ax into another piece of wood, and sent two halves hopping into the air.

Bapcat rolled a cigarette for Zakov and himself, lit them, and blew smoke into the icy winter air.

Eventually the minister buried the blade into a large stump and glared at them. "We don't abide evil weed," Hedyn said.

"We, meaning you and the Lord?" Bapcat countered. "I don't remember anything about evil weeds in the Good Book."

"Blasphemer," Hedyn said, spitting.

"Is that any way to talk to people who are trying to help you?" Bapcat asked.

The man continued to glare.

"We asked around about your stepson's involvement in an illegal deer case. Now we find out you gave hunting permission to one of your son's confederates and fellow suspect, a railroad man named Davidov."

No reaction from the reverend. Keep pushing, Bapcat told himself. *Get a reaction of some kind, anything.* "The Houghton County prosecutor saw Mr. Davidov on *your* Redridge property."

Hedyn smiled. " 'Ave yer fun, ladies, 'ave your fun whilst you can."

"Davidov has given a written statement that you gave him permission, and as you well know, illegal activity on your property also implicates *you*."

"Don't waste your smoke, lads. This will all come to naught."

Said Bapcat, "Well, you might be right, Reverend, but next time we come back, we'll be with Sheriff Hepting, and we'll have statements from multiple witnesses. We'll be coming for *you*."

Hedyn snatched up the ax. "Be gone, Satan."

"We'll be bringing search warrants."

The minister turned his back on them and went back to splitting wood.

"Our intent here?" Zakov asked as they boarded a southbound train.

"Fuel."

"For?"

"Remains to be seen."

"He's more irritated than intimidated."

"Those two things are cousins," Bapcat said, and the Russian smiled and nodded.

106

Red Jacket

FRIDAY, DECEMBER 12, 1913

Bruno Geronissi sat at a small table against the back wall in Vairo's saloon with Lute Bapcat. Two days ago, all the mine operators had given their employees an unexpected paid day off to enable them to attend Citizens' Alliance rallies. The *Gazette* reported that ten thousand had turned out in the streets of Houghton, and an astounding forty thousand in Red Jacket, which seemed ludicrous until Geronissi pointed out that the operators had rented trains to carry miners north to Red Jacket from the other mine areas. A recent *Gazette* headline had proclaimed FOREIGN AGITATORS MUST BE DRIVEN FROM THE DISTRICT AT ONCE.

"That thing down Painesdale," Geronissi said, "those Alliance guys, they say it's mainly Finns make and keep the strike. They say all Finns are poisonous slime."

"You believe it's mainly Finns?"

"No. There are plenty of *Italianos* right in middle of the whole thing."

Since the killings in Painesdale, there had been four days of mass beatings, street assaults, and random shootings, but so far, no more fatalities. Bapcat and just about everyone could feel a surge of energy in the vigilante efforts, and it seemed sure to worsen. Bapcat knew in his gut that the union strikers would not back off. Couldn't the operators understand their stubbornness?

Harju had come over from Marquette for a night and brought the new badge for Zakov. Bapcat had asked him to have one made, identical to his own. The partners pinned their badges on under their coat lapels. Trading the one badge back and forth had become a burden and now they could both present a badge when it was needed. Bapcat chided himself for not taking care of this detail earlier, and took it as more evidence of his need to smarten up.

Harju explained that when he had gotten warrants and gone to serve them to the railroad people in Champion, with the help of county deputies, the four suspects were gone, allegedly to Detroit, where more—and better-paid—work awaited. The warrants were no good that far away from the county where they had been issued, unless a capital crime was involved, which meant the four men were safely away from Upper Peninsula, Houghton, and Marquette County courts.

Raber had been charged with complicity in an illegal deer-killing scheme by prosecutor Lucas, and the deputy had been arrested, but the judge had released him on his own recognizance and Sheriff Cruse had put him right back on the payroll, history repeating itself.

Nesmith continued to insist through his lawyer that he had killed all the deer in the boxes. He was out on bail and his building physically released after the evidence had been transferred to the county, but the evidence had quickly disappeared and charges against Nesmith dropped by order of the judge. Rollie Echo sent a messenger with a note: *Lute—Nesmith attends Hedyn's church. Raber too, but not regularly. Keep in touch. Rollie.*

Hepting refused to help Bapcat squeeze Hedyn's brother, and the two of them had gotten into a heated argument, with Bapcat challenging the sheriff's lack of grit, and the sheriff accusing Bapcat of trying to "soldier through the case without evidence of any kind." Hepting added: "You ain't up on that Cuban high ground this time, Lute. You got to use your brain instead of that bloody Krag you drag around all the time."

"What good's a brain without resolve?" Bapcat threw back at his friend.

They had not spoken since.

Back at Vairo's, Bapcat said, "Bruno, another favor. You got a man who can follow people pretty good?"

"Perhaps I know such a man."

"I need such a man."

Geronissi smiled and touched his wineglass to Bapcat's. "*Si,* for you."

But when Bapcat got down to specifics, Geronissi balked and started acting nervous. "Favor or not?" Bapcat pressed.

"Listen, my friend. Hedyn's preacher brother, he's no problem, eh? But this captain, he got the long arm and a longer memory, *tui capisce?*"

"You afraid?"

"Is only prudent. You know this word, *prudent?*" Geronissi said.

"Yeah, it means coward," Bapcat said.

"No, you wrong! Good hunter, he better have the caution, patience."

"I just want their movements tracked, nothing else. Information only."

Geronissi mulled it over, said, "I get back to you," downed his wine, got up, and strode out of the tavern.

Dominick Vairo brought over two bottles of beer. "On me. *Salute.*"

"*Salute*. You feel what's in the air?"

"All the damn time, and violence, it make me sick, but Christmas, she come soon, everybody takes break, step back, take care of *bambinos,* go to church, pray."

The two men clicked bottles. "Peace," Bapcat said.

Fig Verbankick came in wearing a black bowler and a black overcoat that stretched almost to his ankles. He sported a bushy drooping mustache.

"BEER!" the little man shouted.

Bapcat said, "Hey Fig, how's Herman?"

The strange little man looked confused. "ASK HERMAN!" he yelled, then, "BEER!" Verbankick put a handful of money on the bar and Frank Rousseau asked, "Beer for just you, or the whole damn house, Fig?"

"EVERYBODY BEER!" Fig shouted enthusiastically. "FIG BUYS BEER!"

Bapcat remarked, "That's real generous, Fig; where'd you get all that money?"

Verbankick's hooded eyes narrowed and a sneer formed. "ASK HERMAN!"

"Who looks after Fig?" Bapcat asked Vairo.

"Nobody. He seems to do just fine himself. He's just a little slow, not stupid, but put him out in the bush and he's the equal or better of any other man."

"He come in here often?"

"No, he just started showing up recently. Why?"

"No reason."

Geronissi popped through the side door from the stairwell up to the Italian Hall and motioned for Bapcat, who went over to him.

"Talk outside," Geronissi said, and they went into the wide hallway and pushed open the doors. "Okay, I got this guy, Judah Capicelli, but *you* tell him what you want. I don't want no details, okay?"

"Agreed. Send him up to the hill tonight."

• • •

Capicelli appeared at the house on the hill just before midnight. "Our mutual friend sent me," he announced.

"You know Captain Madog Hedyn?"

"Everybody knows him."

"He's got a brother, a minister up at Central Location. I want both of them followed everywhere—who they meet, where, how long, everything—every day, every detail."

"That ain't no one-man job," Capicelli said. "I'm just one man, *Dottore*."

"You know others you can rely on?"

"I got four brothers."

"Use them."

"Start when?"

"Tomorrow."

"Until?"

"We'll have to see."

"What about the cops?"

"They won't bother you. Their hands are full with the strike. Just don't be obvious."

"When you want reports?"

"Nine, Friday mornings, down in the woods behind the cabin at the bottom of the hill. But if the captain or his brother take off into the woods, I want to know that right away." Bapcat pointed, told him where.

"You want we should follow these men into the bush?"

"Nope, that's our specialty."

107

Bumbletown Hill

FRIDAY, DECEMBER 19, 1913

On Wednesday, Zakov had caught a man with a headless deer near Hill Creek west of Ahmeek, but after a long talk, he had decided the man had only been hungry and wanted the meat—that, finding it headless, he had decided to capitalize on his luck. The Russian was elated when he came back to the hill and reported his experience to Bapcat. "The bonus-givers did not think through their strategy. Winter is preserving the meat. The hungry don't care about heads."

"So?"

"If there is a hole in their logic in one place, there will be more. This is an axiom of military intelligence."

Bapcat smiled. *Finally, a small break for miners and their families; more to the point, maybe one for us.*

This morning Judah Capicelli reported on the movement of Reverend Philamon and brother Madog Hedyn. "Both men go to their work and come straight home when they're done," Capicelli said. "Both have some visitors at their houses in the night, but never late."

"What sorts of visitors?"

The man shrugged. "Without someone inside, no way to know. And in winter everyone dress pretty much the same."

"Ask your brothers to jot down descriptions as best they can, especially if they notice anything different."

"What does this mean, different?"

"Tell me about what you saw this week. You said lots of visitors at night."

"Yes, every night."

"Groups, or single visitors?"

Capicelli took off his chook and rubbed his matted hair. "Usually two or more; only one time, just one man alone."

"That's what I mean by different. Tell me about the man who came alone."

"He carried a rifle."

"What kind?"

The man squinted. "Like yours."

"You're sure?"

"No mistake. Not so many rifles like that."

Frankus Fish. "Good job. How long was he there?"

"Minutes."

"He left alone?"

"With a box."

"What kind of box?"

"Hedyn stepped onto the porch with him and gave him the box."

"You saw this?"

"Yes, but it doesn't mean he did not arrive with it."

Nor that he did. "See you next week."

"You got tracks down here in the woods," Capicelli said.

"Yours?"

"Not mine. Two men, one heavy, with big feet, and one small one."

"Show me."

Capicelli took him to the tracks. "They come in from the road above Allouez."

"You followed them?"

"I stayed back in the woods, kept them in sight."

"Why such caution?"

"Why not?"

Bapcat examined the tracks. "Last night."

Capicelli nodded.

"We're being watched," Bapcat told Zakov as soon as he got back to the house.

"By whom?"

"One tall man, big feet, one small person. Tracks in the woods at the bottom of the hill lead out to the road."

"There is no tactical advantage down there other than concealment. We hold the high ground. If they are below, they are observers only."

"Your professional opinion?"

"*Da*, of course."

"What if they're amateurs, or stone-stupid? I'd like to know who, and why."

"Let us endeavor to answer this most intriguing interrogatory."

• • •

At nine o'clock under a clear, starry sky with a partial moon, Bapcat watched two men slog through the woods toward him. He could see their breath clouds smudging the pristine night air. Zakov was posted low, toward the village, and his instructions were to trail any intruders heading toward his partner.

Moonlight on snow afforded remarkable visibility. Both men carried long guns, slung over their shoulders.

The pair settled beside some large popples. One took out a spyglass and extended it to look up at the house before passing it to his partner. They did not speak.

A match flared momentarily and went out. Bapcat was close enough to hear the sound. *Checking the time? Both men seem edgy. The cold maybe? Got to be hovering near zero tonight.*

Shots erupted from the two men, tongues of flame leaping out of barrels toward the house on the hill, two rounds from each man, and just as quickly, not more than a second's delay after that, three shots from below the men. Bapcat heard the bullets hit and the men go down hard on their faces into the snow. *Zakov?*

The last shot came from where he thought Zakov had placed himself.

A few minutes later, the Russian came over, breathing hard. "One man. He ran after I shot. I don't think I hit him, but I think I helped quicken his pace. What the hell is going on?"

Bapcat didn't answer, just beckoned for Zakov to follow him over to where the two men lay on the ground.

Bapcat felt the pulse of the smaller man, and announced, "Dead."

The bigger man was in agony, rolling around, scissoring his legs, hands opening and closing like claws.

"Get down to Petermann's, call for medical help, and call Hepting," Bapcat said. Zakov took off immediately.

The injured man looked up at Bapcat in the moonlight. “You the bastard game warden?”

“Probably.”

“Didn’t come to kill, just to scare you,” the man said with a pained grin. “Why you shoot us?”

“Somebody shot you, but not us.”

“Cap’n,” the man mumbled.

“What’s your name?” Bapcat asked.

“Mangione,” the man said, blood bubbles cascading from his mouth.

“Cornelio?”

“*Si*.” The alleged assassin.

“Who sent you, Cornelio?”

“Cap’n.”

“Captain who?”

“I go to *il inferno*. I see you there,” the man said, coughing. He let loose a long exhalation, shuddered, went silent, and lay still. Bapcat checked for a pulse. None. He looked through the man’s pockets, found two fifty-dollar gold pieces, a paper with Bapcat’s name and address, but nothing to confirm the man’s identity as Cornelio Mangione, *assassino professionista*.

The pair had each thrown two rounds at the house. The angle from down here was poor at best. Would they have shot more if they had not been attacked? *Somebody cut them down, two kills in three shots, good shooting. How does one part relate to the other?*

An out-of-breath Zakov came back with the doctor. “John and the medical examiner are coming.”

“The tall one is Mangione,” Bapcat told his colleague. “Check the little man for papers.”

Zakov went through his clothes. “Nothing.”

The game wardens followed the lone shooter’s tracks out to the road above the village. There were fresh vehicle tracks in the snow. “Dropped off,” the Russian proclaimed.

“Mangione said he and his partner were just trying to scare us.”

“Someone else, it would appear, had a different agenda.”

“When Mangione and the other man got up to the trees, they checked for the time, I think. Why would they do that?”

“To coordinate with another party?”

"Presumably not the party who shot them."

"Who knows."

"Could it be they expected other shots from above? But no . . . Mangione said they just wanted to scare us, so it was probably just them alone down here."

"Why check the time?" Zakov asked. "Odd."

Bapcat closed his eyes. "They were expecting more shots from above. The car dropped them at the base of the hill and went up. Maybe it was supposed to drive up top and throw some rounds at the house."

"Purely speculative."

"Tell me the story doesn't hold together."

"It is a fine story, I think, as much fiction as fact."

"Fiction and fact don't vary that much. If the story is accurate, the dead men were double-crossed. They expected help from above, not an attack from below. Bapcat said. "They were out to get us when the other attacker got into position, only he came after them instead of us."

108

Red Jacket

WEDNESDAY, DECEMBER 24, 1913

Bapcat argued with Jaquelle Frei about Christmas. She wanted him in Copper Harbor, and he told her he couldn't get away because of the cases they were working on—that she should bring Jordy south to the hill, where they could celebrate Christmas together. After a lot of swearing, cajoling, and huffing, she compromised; she would bring the boy today, but they would get a "civilized" room in the Calumet Hotel on Fifth Street in Red Jacket, and spend Christmas there. She refused to stay in the "damn barn on the hill."

She had tried to convince him that Hancock would be even better, but he had stood his ground, his mind made up: Red Jacket. She talked about driving south, but he convinced her to drive her car to Mandan, park it there, and take the train south. He told her he would meet the boy and her at the Red Jacket depot at six that night.

Late morning they drove to Vairo's saloon to see Dominick and Geronissi. Capicelli was due to report again Friday morning, and Bapcat wondered what the Hedyn brothers had been up to. In fact, he found himself thinking about little else, and decided such narrowness was yet more proof of his shortcomings.

It was noon, and Dominick had a huge jar of fresh pickled eggs on the bar, along with plates and bowls of antipasto and a crock of pickles. The tavern was wall to wall with drinkers, men in dark suits, white shirts, a few with ties, always black, black bowler hats, occasionally a fedora.

"You'd think everyone would be in church or at home getting ready for the big day," Bapcat grumbled at the crowded tavern.

"Church is for women," Vairo said. "We heard you fellas had some trouble up your way, that you shot Cornelio Mangione."

"We didn't shoot anyone."

"Too bad," Vairo said.

Bapcat saw Fig Verbankick in a black overcoat sitting at the end of the bar with a glass of whiskey, his face flushed, eyes glazed. He started to say something to Fig, but the little man was staring straight ahead, ignoring everything and everyone around him.

Eventually the crowd was fewer than twenty patrons. Vairo and Rousseau were behind the bar, holding court, Rousseau manipulating a deck of cards.

Bruno Geronissi came in and sat at a small table. Bapcat joined him.

"Where's your pet Russian?" the Italian asked.

Bapcat nodded toward the men gathered at the bar. "Games of chance, *Dottore*."

"How things go?"

"Capicelli's good. Got his brothers working, too."

"All good men," Geronissi said.

"You hear about Mangione?"

Geronissi flicked a hand, like he was swatting away an invisible fly. "Hear this, hear that."

"Dead," Bapcat said. "He and another man fired shots at our place and a third man shot them both dead."

Geronissi barely moved his eyes to look at the game warden. "You seen this with your own eyes?"

"Capicelli saw their tracks from the previous night and showed me. The Russian and I went down there to see what might happen, and that's when the shooting took place."

"The shooter?"

"Skedaddled. Zakov shot at him."

"Hit?"

"No blood trail."

"Unh," Geronissi said.

"We think Mangione and his partner just wanted to scare us."

"Unh," Geronissi said ambivalently. "You *sure* that Mangione, he is *morto?*"

"The two bodies are in Eagle River. The sheriff's keeping them there until his investigation's complete."

"When this happen?"

"Friday last."

"Long time keep bodies."

"John Hepting does things *his* way."

"I hear this. What you do for Christmas?"

"Got people coming, *Dottore*."

"Good; a man should not be alone at Christmas."

Geronissi had one drink, excused himself, and swept out of the tavern.

All sorts of noise was coming from the stairwell that led up to the Italian Hall on the floor above. It was packed with women and children. Some looked into the bar as they passed by the door, and Rousseau went over and closed the door.

"What's all the commotion?" Bapcat asked.

"The union's throwing a party for the strikers' families. They got candy, little gifts for the kiddies," Vairo said.

"Good," Bapcat said, thinking that he had no positive images or memories of Christmas as a kid, no memories at all. Christmas had been just another day.

Anna Clemenc came into the bar and waved at Vairo and Rousseau, who held up a card. "Hey, Annie, quick game? Maybe you win a little bail money for the new year."

The towering woman belly-laughed. "I got enough to handle upstairs."

"How many you got?"

"We've lost count," she said happily. "Five hundred at least, not more than a thousand—take your pick in between. Kids—so loud!" she added.

"They just excited," Vairo told her. "*Natale!*"

Clemenc went into the stairwell and closed the door to the saloon. *Handsome woman,* Bapcat noted. *Intense eyes.*

Vairo pushed a mug of beer toward Bapcat, who watched Verbankick drink down a jigger of whiskey.

"Fig's hitting it pretty hard," Vairo pointed out.

Rousseau said, "One of his moods; won't hardly talk to nobody. Usually we can't shut him up. You got plans tomorrow?"

"Yep."

"What about the Russian?"

"Don't know. Ask him."

Vairo said, "He ain't got no place to go, me and Maria bring him to dinner at our place here. What you do today?"

"Sit right here, smoke, relax, think."

"Drinks on me," Vairo said. "Okay?"

"I'm not much of a drinker."

"We got food—olives, eggs, pickles, meat, cheese, good stuff. *Mangia, mangia.*"

"I will."

Zakov came over. "What time do the widow and boy arrive?"

"I meet them at the station at six. What're you doing tomorrow?"

"I have an appointment with a lady," the Russian said.

"She have a name?"

"Yes—Four o'Clock, at Nelly Gold's House of Sport."

The men laughed. Zakov asked, "What *is* that damned cacophony in the stairwell?"

"Christmas party for the strikers' kids. You have Christmas in Russia?"

"Only in odd-number years," the Russian said, deadpan.

Bapcat tried to process the words.

"Joke," Zakov said. "I keep thinking about last week."

"Me, too. Everything we saw tells me the dead men were set up."

"Do you think we'll ever get this Gordian knot undone?"

"Gordian knot?"

"Gordius, King of Phrygia, tied this fastidiously complex knot and declared that he who could undo it would become the next ruler of Asia."

"Phrygia?"

"It was an ancient kingdom somewhere inside what is now Turkey, and was in those days the gateway to Asia."

"Like China and Japan?"

"All of Asia. Alexander the Great, upon hearing this, withdrew his sword and chopped the knot and it fell apart."

"Did this Alexander then become King of Asia?"

"Alas, no. He got close, but nobody can become king of Asia."

I am ignorant. "Did you learn all this in school?"

"Yes, and much, much more."

"But the story doesn't make sense," Bapcat said. "The king said he who could undo the knot would become king. Alexander didn't undo it, he *cut* it. That's cheating."

Zakov stared at the other game warden. "I am loath to admit this, but not once have I ever considered this unique logic you present. To me, *undo* meant getting the knot apart in any way possible, but if technically it had to be untied in order to qualify, you're no doubt right. Alexander cheated, which if one buys into the legend, would explain why he perished short of achieving his objective. Were we dons in academe, we might author a paper or a scholarly screed, make a career of the knot that undid Alexander."

Sometimes I understand nothing this man says. "So we don't have an *actual* knot here?" Bapcat asked.

"Metaphorically it's a knot."

"Then we should cut it, metaphorically."

"And how might one organize *that?*" the Russian queried.

"Don't ask me," Bapcat confessed with a nervous laugh. "I don't even know what a metaphor *is*." The Russian laughed with him, and Bapcat felt lighthearted. It felt good. He was looking forward to seeing Jaquelle.

It was getting late, darkening outside, spitting snow. The din above the bar was beyond description: shrill voices, stomping feet making the floor above resound like drums. Bapcat looked up at the ceiling and Rousseau said, "They have a play or something for the children. They stomp the floor with their feet to applaud."

Bapcat took a sip of wine and chewed an olive, spitting the pit onto a plate on the bar. The noise above suddenly grabbed his attention. Dominick Vairo raised an eyebrow at the same moment, and just then, the stairwell was suddenly inundated with sound—pounding and crashes. Vairo ran to the door and pulled it open only to reveal a mass of intertwined bodies, writhing, screaming, clawing at each other, many of them babbling incoherently about a fire. Vairo began grabbing at people and trying to pull them free of the pile, but they were wedged too tight, and a continuous wail filled the bar and crushed all other sounds. Bapcat and Zakov were there with him, trying to help, but it was futile.

Vairo said, "Ladder to fire escape is outside."

My God, it was the Chicago theater all over again. But where was the smoke? Chicago had smoke. You could smell it before you saw it.

The game wardens ran outside and quickly scrambled up the side of the building to a door that opened onto the landing by the meeting hall's ticket office. Inside they found adults and children screaming, some of them running around and waving their arms, while others were at the top of the stairs above the jam, trying to pull people upward and away from the writhing pile.

The two men worked their way down, accepting injured and dead from below and passing them back until they were at the front line of bodies, working frantically but as gently as possible to extract people. All the while, the elongated, shrill scream continued.

Zakov worked a boy loose and looked at Bapcat and shook his head, and handed the dead child up to hands behind them, saying *Gentle* to those above.

"Where's the actual fire?" Bapcat asked. "I don't smell smoke."

"What fire?" someone behind him said.

Bapcat peeled a woman away from the mass. She had a broken arm and bloody mouth. He got her to her feet and helped her move back next to those behind them. He looked down and saw a child on her back, eyes open and staring up, unmoving.

"*Pinkhus, help me!*" Bapcat got a hand under the girl and Zakov a hand under her other side, and they pulled her up to them. When helping hands reached for her, Bapcat said no, and he and the Russian climbed up the stairs and carried her into the auditorium where bodies were being laid out in rows. They lay her down with them.

"You're weeping," Zakov said.

"We know her."

He heard the air go out of Zakov, followed by a choking sound. "Draganu Skander," he said, stifling a sob. "Beloved quiet one," he said.

Bapcat pulled his friend back to the stairs. "We can't help her, *gospodin*. The others need us now."

Eventually the wall of twisted, crushed, broken, bleeding suffocated corpses and wounded began to clear as rescuers from below began to make headway toward those trapped at the bottom of the stairs. Someone passed a ladle of water to Bapcat, who drank and held it for Zakov, who handed it to Dominick Vairo, who looked hot and shaky. Tears and sweat everywhere, vomit, blood, shit . . . it was like a battlefield.

"Keep working," Bapcat said.

It was well after dark, light snow still falling, breath clouds shrouding the street where hundreds of people had gathered in silence, staring at the scene as bodies were carried out: relatives, neighbors, the curious, police, firemen, deputies, a conglomerate of sorrow. And agony.

Bapcat and Zakov went down the outside fire escape and back into the bar. Vairo looked disconsolate, pointing at his empty cash register drawer and empty shelves where bottles had been only hours before. "Cleaned out," he said.

"What is the time?" Zakov asked.

Vairo looked at his watch. "Seven."

"Widow Frei," the Russian said to Bapcat.

Photographer Nara poked his head into the saloon from the hallway and waggled a finger at Bapcat "We're going to shoot in here, make a record. We didn't expect to see you here."

Bapcat wiped at his eyes with the heel of his hand, and as they went into the street and started to move through the crowd, he saw Jaquelle and Jordy at the edge of the jam. There was no talking, no sound other than muffled coughs. Bapcat, Zakov, Frei, and the boy all embraced, and Jaquelle said to the Russian, "You are going to get a room and eat with us tonight."

"I can still help," Zakov said.

"You can't," Bapcat said. "Let others take it from here."

It was a two-block walk to the Calumet Hotel, and the whole way they were moving against crowds of curious and panicked people surging toward the Italian Hall.

"How?" Jaquelle asked as they walked through the fresh snow.

"It just happened," Bapcat said.

"So many children," she said. "Innocents."

That word stuck in Bapcat's mind, and no matter how hard he tried to banish it, the word remained, blinking like a candle the wind was trying to extinguish.

109

Red Jacket

THURSDAY, DECEMBER 25, 1913

They ate a meager breakfast in the hotel dining room before first light. The place was crowded, the other patrons quiet, the town reeling under the tragic events of yesterday's disaster.

Someone at a nearby table said quietly, "I heard seventy, and I heard eighty; I don't think they even know how many yet. The whole thing was chaos."

Bapcat had given Jordy his gift before they went to breakfast. It was a Krag-Jørgensen.

"It came from Denver. I had to mail-order it."

"Just like yours?" the boy asked.

"Just like mine."

"We'll have *our* Christmas later," Jaquelle whispered to him.

"We have to get back," he told her.

"I know. We'll be here."

Vairo and Rousseau were in the tavern. The Barber was with them, and they each had a glass of amber liquid in front of them.

The smell of death hung in the air. "You're here," Bapcat said.

Labisoniere said, "The world gone mad."

"How many dead?"

"Seventy-three. There were seventy-four, but a girl in one of the morgues acted as Lazarus and came back to life. She'll live. Or she won't," he added. "Once again I find myself asking, What are you two doing here?"

"Fate" Zakov said. "We were here when it happened."

"You heard someone call *Fire?*"

Bapcat said, "We heard stamping feet and a scream that never ended. There was no yell of *Fire* down here, and we didn't hear it mentioned until later, when we were pulling people out, and even that was just panic."

"Well, witnesses are saying it got yelled upstairs. That's what caused the stampede. There was never any fire."

"Why would someone do such a thing?" Vairo asked.

The doctor said. "Think of all that has transpired these past five months—the killings, beatings, all of it."

"Intentional?" Bapcat asked.

The Barber shrugged. "A prank gone wrong, a bored child? Who knows. But we will spend all day today making out death certificates. Paper brings us into the world and paper takes us out. There are bodies spread among several different temporary morgues, but they all have the same look inside: rows of dead innocents struck down without reason."

"What can we do to help?" Bapcat asked.

"Keep Cruse away from me. He's telling newspapers the union did this to its own people in order to create sympathy."

An outraged Zakov said, "Slanderous, libelous, scandalous nonsense!"

"Yet that is what our dear sheriff is saying, unchallenged. I asked him if a reward would be offered as it was after Seeberville, and he glared at me like I am a cretin, and he said, 'It was an accident.' I told him I heard him tell reporters the union had engineered the event, and therefore he had linked cause with effect, which removed it from the realm of accident. He ordered me to mind my own business."

"Is there a victim list?" Bapcat asked.

"Not yet. We're working diligently on assembling one. Every morgue is in pandemonium as adults search for their children and children search for their parents and relatives search for loved ones, and the nosy come just to satisfy their morbid sense of curiosity. It is sad . . . so damn sad. Eventually we'll get the dead identified and a list made."

"There's a girl, Draganu Skander," said Bapcat. "I will help when it is time to bury her."

The Barber took out a small notebook and pencil and made a note.

"*We* will help," Zakov said.

"Anything more on the robbery?" Bapcat asked.

"Not one of our regular customers," Rousseau answered. "We are like a family here. This was an outsider taking advantage. Family does not steal from family."

"It was beyond chaos—it was pure Dante," Zakov declared.

“There are opportunists everywhere,” Rousseau said. “You should see *Italia*.”

“Can I use your telephone?” Bapcat asked Vairo.

“Line was cut yesterday. Go next door to A and P Tea and tell Frankie Meyers I sent you. Show him your badge. He was up there last night with you boys, pulling out bodies.”

“No party line?”

“No, we each got our own.”

“And only yours got cut?”

Vairo shrugged.

Photographer Nara went up the stairs with a camera on his shoulder, his brother and another camera behind him.

Next door, Meyers looked exhausted, his back bent. He barely looked at the badge and just pointed at the phone. Bapcat got the number he needed from his own notebook and placed the call to Rollie Echo’s home number.

“Echo.”

“Bapcat.”

“Where are you?”

“Red Jacket.”

“You heard the news.”

“Zakov and I were there.”

“You were inside the Italian Hall?”

“Downstairs in the bar. We helped pull out bodies.”

Echo took a long time to respond. “We should talk, soon.”

“Cruse is telling reporters the union did this to its own people as a way to stimulate sympathy.”

“We saw that in today’s paper. You got a theory?”

“Not yet. You?”

“Not for phone talk. The Fat Man is acting like chief engineer on the whitewash express.”

“On whose orders?”

“Guess.”

MacNaughton. “Where’s your boss?”

“Somewhere up there with you, wringing his hands. The Fat Man and the Citizens’ Alliance want an inquest to empanel jurors, to be impartially selected by the Fat Man himself, not by the medical examiner.”

"Can he do that—legally?"

"Lucas talked to Judge O'Brien, and he acquiesced; he's fed up with everyone and everything."

"They told Cruse yes?"

"More like they didn't tell him no."

"And you?"

"Disappointed in my friend. Deeply so."

"Where exactly *is* your boss?"

"The unanswerable question. Supposedly he is up there with you, taking statements and talking to witnesses. He calls me every hour or so, says there's too many, too much, a biblical flood of information to be sorted through. I want to talk to sane, calm men, like you and Zakov."

"All right, we'll call back."

"What're you doing now?"

"Going to find a father to tell him his daughter is dead."

"Done this sort of thing before?"

"No."

"Make up words to say and put them in your head and think only about those words, not what they mean, and not what you've seen. Be prepared for any kind of reaction. It's always different."

"You've done this?"

"Too many times to count."

They found Jerko Skander in his shack, on his back, blood everywhere, a large knife by his side, his eyes open, same as his daughter. Bapcat said, "We'll tell the Barber, and let him decide what has to be done here. Do you think he is with his daughter now?"

Zakov said, "He made vertical cuts down his arms. He intended to die, not simply to make a plea for help. It would seem we are late with the news of the child. As to your question, Heaven is a pathetic fable, a narcotic for the masses. What great, loving God would randomly extinguish the lives of so fucking many innocents on the eve of his big-shot son's alleged birthday?"

110

Bumbletown Hill

FRIDAY, DECEMBER 26, 1913

Capicelli was on time.

"Did you know anyone in the Italian Hall?" Bapcat asked, guessing that from now on, the disaster would serve as some sort of marker in the lives of everyone who lived in the area.

"Everybody knows someone. Word is youse was there, helping rescue people."

"Not much rescue with so many dead," Bapcat said. "What do you have for us?"

"Tuesday night this peculiar fella came up to the Rev'rend's house. They talked at the door, and then the fella, he went over to the church and went inside. He not come out till after he was inside almost one hour, so I stand and wait, and suddenly I see my brother Paulie, who's following the captain. We look at each other, like, what is this? And Paulie he tells me, 'My man inna church too—got there before your man.'

"So then the peculiar fella comes outta the church, starts walking toward the depot, and he's yelling to beat all get-out, only there's a pretty stiff wind, and we ain't quite close enough to make out what it is he's yellin' about. Then my man comes out of the church and goes home, and the captain comes out and Paulie follows him."

"What was so peculiar about the one fella?"

"I dunno. Maybe how short he was, how funny he looked in an overcoat that almost dragged on the ground, big black hat pulled down over his eyes, big, bushy black mustache, you know—peculiar."

"What time was this?"

"Around nine. You want us to keep on?"

"Please."

"You know what's going on?" the man asked.

"Not quite."

"You want we meet again next week, Friday?"

"Yes," Bapcat said, guessing it would be sooner.

Trudging up the hill to meet Zakov at the truck, the word innocent continued to roil his mind, but more than that, he wondered if cameras like the one Nara used might someday be smaller and be of some value to police and game wardens. Maybe if there were cameras that also acted like telescopes, they would be good tools for the sort of work Capicelli was doing.

The mental meanderings of an uneducated man, he chided himself. *Stay here in the now, not in the make-believe world of what might be. Accept the world as it is, not what it might become in some imaginary future.*

111

Red Jacket

SUNDAY, DECEMBER 28, 1913

The massive St. John the Baptist Croatian Catholic Church on Seventh Street was overrun with mourners and the curious, inside and out. Bapcat and Zakov sat at the ends of two pews, across from each other, a small white coffin bearing the body of Draganu Skander between them in the aisle. The congregants were a single mass of black clothing.

There were four men assigned to each body. Bapcat's partner, a stranger, sat beside him, Zakov's partner beside him. Ten caskets were lined up in the church on unpainted sawhorses. Fresh flowers were on the coffins, and Bapcat wondered where in the world they had gotten them in December, in the Keweenaw. Other churches in town had caskets, as well, no one house of worship carrying all the burden.

The overpowering smell of tallow, incense, human perspiration, and wet leather hung in the air as Father Niklas Polyek droned on in a language Bapcat couldn't understand. Croatian and Latin were both strange in cadence, in tone. The massive priest with his square-cut black beard stood in a pulpit shaped like a ship's bow and cast his thundering voice out over the crowd, echoes ricocheting in the cavernous church like runaway bullets, crossing each other, magnifying each other, canceling each other.

Polyek suddenly switched to English and his big hands were balled into hairy fists as he said without prologue, "I know we got Alliance spies out here in God's house. To you I say, you watch us today. You watch how we bury our dead without tears. This strike our people make is moral and makes God happy. These murders are criminal, mortal sins. You Alliance men must understand Croatians are people of iron will. We will die before we surrender, and these little children's broken bodies are to us the bodies of soldiers fallen in war. You are warned here today by me—and by God Himself. Amen."

The priest concluded by crossing himself and making his way back to the altar and the bevy of altar boys and priests in colorful garb assisting him.

Bapcat heard music he had never heard before, coming from an organ in the loft above, slow, heavy music filled with inexpressible sadness. Yet people did not sob or let their emotions loose. They brooded in steely silence, their faces dark masks of anger.

When Polyek finished the mass, he signaled the pallbearers to stand by their coffins, and when the music changed they hefted their loads and marched slowly into the street where thousands were gathered, waiting quietly, too many to count. The church's bells began to peal and blend into a chorus of bells across the city. The procession moved north on Seventh toward Pine. There they merged onto the road where horse-drawn hearses waited for them to load the coffins. Out front were automobiles also carrying bodies, and the main sounds were the engines of motorcars, the whinny of horses, and boots sliding through the snowy mush. It had been salting snow all day, but on the way to the staging area on Pine, the snow picked up and the wind gave it some added muscle.

A brass band struck up a heart-rending dirge ahead of them, and Bapcat couldn't tell where in the procession they were. Once they had Draganu Skander safely in her hearse, Bapcat, Zakov, and the other two bearers fell in behind it to walk to Lake View Cemetery, carefully avoiding steaming horse apples as they marched.

Bapcat saw Jaquelle Frei and Jordy walking to his right, their eyes straight ahead.

By the time the front echelons of the long procession reached the graveyard gate, the tail of the procession, two miles back, was just moving out of Red Jacket. Bapcat would later hear that more than five thousand people had marched two miles in the snow and mud, and an estimated forty thousand more had formed a gauntlet through which the dead and marchers passed.

Bapcat and Zakov and their partners removed the casket from the hearse and walked it into the Roman Catholic section of the cemetery, where last night a single large trench had been dug as a mass grave. Boards had been fixed around the trench to allow for foot traffic, to get the bodies into the hole, and Bapcat and Zakov helped to lower Draganu into her final resting place. They stepped back into the crowd to await whatever ceremonies would come next as snow continued to fall and wind gusted from the northwest.

There were twenty-five dead Catholics and twenty-eight dead Protestants, each denomination consigned to their separate part of the cemetery, which struck Bapcat as strange and wrong. They had lived and died together; why could they not pass into eternity together?

A different priest appeared and conducted a ceremony in the same strange language Bapcat had heard in the church. People were packed into the graveyard, including dozens who had climbed trees and hung on branches like fat black birds. With all the thousands in attendance, the fresh snow had been mashed into brown sludge, and it was six o'clock and dark before the final interments were completed. All the mourners left as they had arrived, en masse, as silent as death.

Jaquelle and Jordy walked with the game wardens. "How can this happen?" the Widow Frei asked.

The men had no answers for her, remained silent.

John Hepting materialized from the crowd. "You seen MacNaughton?" the Keweenaw County sheriff asked.

Bapcat shook his head.

"Sonuvabitch isn't here. None of the operators are here, not a goddamn one. Did you hear what happened to Moyer?"

"The union's president?"

"The same. Alliance men grabbed him in his hotel in Hancock, beat the shit out of him, shot him, dragged him across the canal, and put him on a train to Chicago with two of Cruse's men as guards. Some say MacNaughton was there, but I don't know about that. Sonuvabitch has been afraid to show himself much since all this began. He likes to work through other people, not directly."

"Why Moyer?" Bapcat asked.

"On Friday, Moyer accused the Alliance of creating the Italian Hall panic."

"After Cruse accused the union on the day it happened."

"There it is."

"MacNaughton's idea to give Moyer the heave-ho?"

"What do you think?" the sheriff said noncommittally.

"The governor should have kept all of the soldiers here, John, not just a few men from the local armory. As soon as they withdrew the violence got bad, fast."

"Our prissy and inept Governor Ferris did not want the State to take sides."

"When there is an oppressor and the State takes no sides, it is in fact siding with the oppressor," Zakov declared. "This state has no position on mass murder?"

"Apparently not," Hepting said. "In Ferris's view, this is a private matter, not a public issue."

"You could say that about every murder," Bapcat said.

"Look around," Jaquelle Frei said. "There are tens of thousands of people here. How private is *that?*"

"You finished with Skander?" Bapcat asked his friend.

"He's already in the ground."

"What about Cornelio Mangione?"

"The body has been released to his family."

"And the man with him?"

"Nobody knows who he is. We buried him in a pauper's grave. What the hell went on that night, Lute?"

"We gave our statements," Bapcat said.

"Between us, off the record."

"We think Mangione and his friend got set up. They were sent to rattle us so that someone could take them out while their focus was on us."

"Any notions who?"

Bapcat shook his head.

"Coroner's inquest tomorrow," Hepting said. "Lucas is overwhelmed, said the people should judge for themselves. At least two-thirds of the jury will be Alliance men. You two were in the hall Christmas Eve. I talked to Dominick."

"We were there."

"Any thoughts?"

They stopped walking. "What are you driving at, John?"

"There are multiple reports and descriptions of a man wearing an Alliance button who yelled *Fire* and was seen to run away."

"I'm sure Cruse will be on it," Bapcat said sarcastically.

"The Fat Man couldn't care less. Moyer is gone, out of the picture. Now the operators just want all the bodies in the ground and all this shit done and gone. Cruse made his accusation while the dust was still in the air and the bodies still being brought down, and you can bet he didn't take that shot without permission or direction. Good tactics, to attack first."

Zakov said, "The best strategy for overwhelming your enemy is to follow success with excessive force. You do not defeat an enemy face-to-face; you make him break and run, and destroy him from behind."

"What if you don't overwhelm him?" Bapcat asked.

"Counterattacks can be overwhelming and reverse the momentum."

"You think the union will retaliate, John?" Bapcat asked.

Hepting said, "I think this is the end, Lute It may drag on, but it's over. Christmas Eve drove the price too high."

"Justice thwarted," Jaquelle Fred said indignantly.

"There's been neither justice nor fair play since day one here," Hepting said. "Why should that change?"

Bapcat faced his friend. "If you had the guilty man here now, what would you do to him?"

"The one who yelled *Fire*, or the one who put him up to it?"

"Both."

"I ain't much on theoreticals," Hepting said.

"You must have some thoughts."

The sheriff chewed his bottom lip. "Time will tell," he said, starting to walk away from them, but wheeling back suddenly. "A surface captain from C and H came forward and gave a description entirely different from any others provided. He claimed he was in the street out front, passing by, and he saw a man run out the front door minutes before the disaster."

"How different?" Bapcat asked.

"Called the man a ginger-head."

"And?"

"Questionable; an outlier."

"Maybe he's right and the others wrong."

"Said captain works for Madog Hedyn."

"Track-covering?"

"I can't say that; not yet. What I do know is that everyone hooked to the operators is pointing a finger, and all their fingers point at the same place—at the union."

"Conspiracy," Zakov said.

Widow Frei asked, "John, do you honestly think the union would kill its own women and children to gain sympathy for the larger cause?"

Hepting looked at Bapcat. "The sheriff in me would arrest the two and seek justice within the system. The other part of me—the part I think of as a man—well, he wouldn't bother troubling the system. And hell no, Jaquelle, I don't."

"The blackest of talk from a peace officer," Zakov said.

"There can come a time when you have to lay aside your badge and oath and pay homage to a higher authority."

As Hepting walked away Bapcat leaned over to Zakov. "He knows who did this."

"Which part?"

"Both . . . all."

"Why doesn't he tell us?"

"He thinks we know, too, and he wants space for himself."

"*Do* we know?"

Bapcat nodded solemnly. "Probably."

"When will you share with your partner?"

112

Central Location

WEDNESDAY, DECEMBER 31, 1913

Zakov parked the Ford between a boulder and a poor-rock cascade, backing it into place, and Bapcat helped him cut several cedar boughs to cover the vehicle's front.

They each carried a pack and a rifle, .45s in closed holsters. Snowshoes were lashed to their pack frames. Each took a white sheet and covered his regular clothes, the packs and rifle, so that they wouldn't stand out at any distance.

The two men moved quickly down to the river. The temperature back in town was hovering near zero, snow steadily piling up. The temperature was lower here in the middle of the peninsula's spine. The drive up had been hard, but by pushing and taking chances, they had gotten through.

Word had come this morning from Capicelli to meet him as quickly as they could get here. Jaquelle and Jordy were back at the hill, waiting.

The game wardens got close to the river and Capicelli stepped out of the tree line. "You fellas look like coupla damn ghosts."

"What's going on?" Bapcat asked, getting right to business.

"Cap'n Hedyn come to his brother's house with that peculiar little fella and a big man carrying the same weapon you got. Four of 'em took off with packs and rifles to the north. Paulie's bird-dogging them. I take you to find them, then you two are on your own. Me and Paulie, we're done with this, okay?"

Bapcat slid off his pack, his mackinaw and wool sweater, rolled both, and wrapped them with twine, lashing them to the top of the pack frame. Zakov did the same without being told. In winter, sweat was your enemy. If you had to move fast and far, you stripped and added layers only when you stopped for any time.

"Prob'ly won't need *les raquettes*," Capicelli said.

"Better to have and not need then to need and not have," Bapcat said tersely. He had lived in the bush for years, knew what he was doing. Winter here could kill fast.

"Suit yourselves," the man said, taking off in front of them.

Capicelli took them up into steep, rocky country west of the village, aiming on a diagonal for the top of the spine. They took a knee at the top to wait for the man to range and find sign, which he did in less than five minutes, coming back so they could see him, waving for them to follow to the northeast.

The ground up here was surprisingly flat, but mostly devoid of trees. *Been logged*, Bapcat told himself, which meant there was probably a mine shaft nearby. Central's miners had worked the Northwest Mine, south of town. What was up this way?

Their guide veered into a narrow defile between two hard rock spines that stuck up like black incisors. The sign led them eventually to a flat area, where the hard climb finally ended. Capicelli immediately knelt and used his hand to tell them to do the same. He immediately moved right, working his way through the edge of the trees, with a relatively open field to his left and in front of Bapcat and Zakov. The sign showed the trail going into the field straight ahead.

"We're close," Bapcat said. "Let's add layers, drop packs here."

Off in the distance Bapcat thought he saw another man moving toward Capicelli and held his breath until the two turned and started back.

"Paul," the brother said. "Four men, three hundred yards ahead. They found a deer in a snow cone and killed it. They're butchering it now, got a fire going, and they're passing around a bottle."

Zakov's eyes widened.

"Hedyn brothers?" Bapcat asked.

"And two more," their scout reported.

"One with a Krag?" he tapped his own rifle to show the man.

"Same."

"Why are they stopped up here?"

The man grimaced. "Don't know; just are. Don't think they were looking for deer, but they saw breath coming up from snow piled against small white pine and shot into it. Deer got in there to keep warm."

"What's up here?" Zakov asked.

Capicelli said, "This whole mountain under us is a beehive of levels, stopes, tunnels, adits. This was the old Copper Falls mine from the way back. We're leaving," Capicelli added. "Don't know what this is about, and don't want to."

"Thanks," Bapcat said, and watched the men slide back the way they had come.

Bapcat whispered, "Wish we knew what brought them up here."

Zakov replied, "Von Clausewitz reminds us that our intellect always hopes for clarity and certainty, but our natures often find uncertainty fascinating."

"Van who?"

"*Von* Clausewitz, the great Prussian general and military strategist."

"Prussian, like a Polish-Russian?"

"Prussians are Germans."

"Why don't they call themselves Germans, then?"

"Too complicated to explain," Zakov said, showing his frustration.

He knows how little I know. Why is he with me? "Let's move forward," Bapcat said.

They rearranged some of their clothing so that they were almost entirely white, and went right through the woods where the Capicelli brothers had been. The wind was blowing steadily but lightly, the gusts done for now, steadying to a biting wind from the north-northeast. *We're in for it,* Bapcat told himself. He didn't understand why, but up here you could go from a clear day to a complete and total whiteout in minutes, and the whiteout could last for days once it descended.

Even with the wind, he could smell smoke, could tell it was a small fire, an experienced woodsman's fire.

The field to their left was on a slight rise, and as they worked back to the north they saw the men, not thirty yards away, tucked inside a tree line. Just as the brothers had reported, he saw the Hedyns, Sergeant Frankus Fish, and, as he had suspected, Fig Verbankick. He now understood why the word innocent kept tugging at his mind.

"Did you know?" Zakov asked.

"Suspected, I think, but didn't know for sure until now."

A small deer carcass hung from a tree branch by its hind legs, the cape hanging down the front legs, dragging on the ground, bones showing where they had carved meat off the skeleton. It was last spring's fawn and would taste good; thus, the smell of meat cooking in a pan on the open fire.

Why are they here? Bapcat wondered.

Frankus Fish stayed apart from the others, on guard, his rifle in one hand, his eyes roving continuously.

"Who is he?" Zakov asked.

"Rough Rider."

"With you?"

"We were never chums."

"Why is he here?"

"Ascher Agency."

"How can you know this?"

"Remember our stop in Seney?"

Zakov nodded.

"Rudyard Riordan told me about him, and later I saw Fish in Helltown. I don't know what his game is. He might be hunting me."

"You have bad blood?"

"I crossed him once, made him lose face."

"In Cuba?"

"Yes, before we went up the hill."

"A long memory is a curse," the Russian said.

Fish motioned north and said something to the Hedyns that Bapcat couldn't make out. The brothers looked up, nodded, and prodded Verbankick. The three of them left camp.

"Stay with Fish," Bapcat said, "no matter where he goes," and crawled to his right as quickly as he could slide along, looking for cover to carry him in the direction of the three men.

He saw that they stopped no more than fifty feet from the camp. Fig Verbankick was carrying a rifle. *Strange.* Bapcat crept along wooded cover to a place in some rocks beyond where the three men stood, and there he saw what they were looking at: a hole, perhaps twenty feet across, gaping and black. Bapcat crawled closer so that he could hear.

"DARK!" Fig said loudly and shakily as Philamon Hedyn attached a rope to Verbankick's miner's harness, the sort they used to make vertical ascents and descents along steeply angled stopes in deep mines.

"The bats shine in the dark," Hedyn said.

"BATS SLEEP ALL WINTER," Fig shouted. "DARK!"

"You'll be able to see just fine when your eyes get accustomed to the dark. Fire your rifle now and let's make sure it hasn't frozen.

"BEER!" Fig screamed, and the shout and the unexpected rifle report made Bapcat flinch.

"Not long, okay?" Fig said, whimpering like a child.

"Just shoot a few; it's your reward. You like to shoot, right?"

"*LIKE* SHOOT! Herman's okay?"

"Herman's fine," Hedyn said. "Get down on your belly and we'll let you down."

Verbankick pivoted and tried to run, but Cap'n Hedyn swatted him in the head and drove a fist into this belly, and the little man went facedown in the snow, moaning, "I DON'T WANT TO BE HERE!"

"Herman will think you're a baby," the captain said.

Fig glowered, pushed backward on his belly, holding onto the rope, which the two men gripped, slowly lowering the man into the hole.

"DARK, DARK, DARK!" Verbankick squealed.

The brothers grunted under the effort.

"BEER!" Fig screamed from inside the hole. "DARK!"

"He's sure got the lungs," Philamon told his brother, and the two of them started laughing.

"DON'T SEE NO BATS!" came a shout from the hole.

Philamon eased toward the lip. "Feel around with your feet."

"OKAY!"

"See the bats yet?"

"NO!"

"You feel ground yet with your feet?"

"YEAH, DARK—GET ME OUT, DON'T LIKE THIS!"

"Good Lord, son. It's dark out here, too. Remember, this is your reward, and wait until Herman hears. Relax, all right?"

"DON'T WANT TO RELAX!"

The captain said, "Let's go, Phil, this storm's stiffening."

Hedyn let go of the rope and it snaked across the white snow and dropped into the darkness.

"UH . . . OH!" came a shout from the hole.

The Hedyns walked side by side toward the fire, and Bapcat got to his feet and into step behind them in the darkness. They needed to get Fig out, but couldn't do that until the Hedyns and Fish were accounted for. He hoped Zakov was close by.

The meat on the fire was pungent, and as Bapcat sniffed there was a shot near the fire and Philamon Hedyn collapsed to the ground.

"My brother," Madog Hedyn said unemotionally.

"No witnesses," Fish said. "Those are our orders."

"*I* give the orders," Madog Hedyn retorted with a snarl.

A shot cut him down beside his brother, and Fish said, "No witnesses, little man."

It was all silent, but as his heart slowed, Bapcat heard the wind through the trees, some limbs beginning to bend and chatter and crack in the wind, the meat popping and the small cooking fire hissing. When another shot rang out, he instinctively ducked behind a tree and fought to catch his breath, his heart pounding, breathing too fast.

He eased forward, and reached over to check Philamon for a pulse. Finding none, he crawled over to Madog, who had a small pistol in his hand, and no pulse.

Zakov said, "I'll check the other one, then . . . Nothing. He's gone. Where is number four?"

"Underground," Bapcat said.

"Fish is hit in the head. In this dark, pure luck for the shooter."

Bapcat's hands shook as he tried to roll cigarettes. "What just happened?"

A distant voice echoed behind them. Bapcat said, "Fig!"

They went to the hole. "FIG!"

"GET ME OUT!"

"We're going to get you out."

"DARK! I . . . DON'T . . . WANT . . . TO . . . BE . . . HERE . . ."

"Fig, it's Bapcat and Zakov, the game wardens. Remember us?"

"HELP!"

"Get a rope," Bapcat said, and Zakov took off to fetch their packs while Bapcat tried to keep the man below as calm as he could.

Zakov came back, panting. "Snow's getting heavier."

They each carried hundred-foot-long loops of half-inch hemp in their packs. Bapcat sat down and quickly spliced them together.

"No lights," Zakov said. "How will he feel the rope?"

Bapcat thought for a moment, grabbed a snowshoe, and tied the end of the rope to the toe brace.

"This is crazy," Zakov said. "Is the wood strong enough?"

"It's ash, cut in August, which is as strong as it gets. I want him to sit on the shoe and hang on. As we pull him up, the shoe will act like a small platform. It's narrow enough that he may be able to hook his feet underneath."

"You've done this before?"

"It seems to work in my mind."

"I find no reassurance in hypotheticals."

"Fig, stand where you are! We're lowering a snowshoe on a rope. When you get hold of it, put it on the ground. Put the toe forward, the skinny part, and get a good hold on the rope. It'll be like riding a broom horse, You ever do that, Fig, ride a broom horse?"

"YEAH!"

"When we begin to pull you up, wrap your legs around the snowshoe and cross your ankles. You've got to hang on tight. Are you hearing me? Don't let go of the rope, no matter what."

"DARK!"

"Fig!"

"OKAY!"

"You understand what we're going to do? You have to help us to help you."

"OKAY!"

The game wardens launched the shoe over the lip into the black void.

"How the hell will he see it?" Zakov asked.

"Fig, are your hands out?"

"OKAY!"

They played the rope out slowly and deliberately until it began to oscillate.

"Fig, tell us if you can hear anything."

"HEAR YOUSE!"

"Fig!"

"OKAY!"

"About halfway," Zakov reported. "A hundred feet, give or take. We've got to be close."

"I HEAR!" Verbankick screamed. "I HEAR!"

"Is it close, Fig?"

"DON'T KNOW."

"Keep your arms out, and yell if you feel anything."

The rope stopped abruptly and there was slack.

"Fig!"

"GOT ROPE, GOT ROPE, GOT ROPE!"

"Feel the snowshoe?"

"YEAH!"

"Put it on the ground, toe pointed forward—away from your bum."

"OKAY!"

Bapcat tested and felt tension on the rope. "We have weight," he told the Russian. "Loop the other end around your waist."

Zakov did as instructed. "I hope we don't all end up down in that hole."

"Fig, you holding tight?"

"YEAH, TIGHT!"

"Here we go, Fig. Be brave!"

"BRAVE!"

The two men started reefing and pulling, establishing a slow and steady retrieve and lift, backing away from the hole.

"Fig?" Bapcat yelled.

"YEAH!"

"He's getting close," Bapcat told Zakov.

When Verbankick slid over the lip into the snow, he began screaming, and he kept screaming as they dragged him away from the pit until he was clear. They dropped the rope, ran forward, grabbed him under the armpits, and hauled him to his feet. The man wept, covered his face and mumbled, "Ghosts!"

Bapcat said, "Open your eyes, Fig. It's us. We're not ghosts."

Fig looked at them tentatively, and back at the hole. "Do that . . . AGAIN?"

They hoisted the bodies of the dead men into trees and lashed them in place to keep the wolves off them. The venison was overdone, but they gave Fig some on a stick and he devoured it. They put out the fire, gathered their packs and the dead men's weapons, and started hiking.

"You okay, Fig?"

"Ask Herman," an exhausted Verbankick whispered hoarsely.

113

Eagle River

THURSDAY, JANUARY 1, 1914

John Hepting came to the door of his house with sleep in his eyes.

"Make us some coffee, John," Bapcat said. "A lot of coffee. And get some dry clothes and blankets for Mr. Verbankick."

The sheriff did as he was asked, and when cups of hot, fresh coffee were poured and Fig was in dry clothes, Bapcat said, "Don't say anything until we're finished. The Hedyns and another man are dead."

"You kill them?"

"No. Be quiet, listen, and don't interrupt us."

Bapcat turned to the little man. "Fig, you okay? Warm enough?"

"ASK HERMAN."

"Drink your coffee, Fig. Why did they put you in that hole?"

"ASK HERMAN!"

"Herman's not here, Fig. You have to tell us."

Verbankick sobbed and teared up. "THEY KILL HERMAN!"

"No, Fig. Herman's fine. He's okay. He's just not here right now. We need you to tell us what happened, all right?"

"Okay."

"They put you in the hole. I saw them."

"Reward!"

"I don't understand. What reward?"

"BIG JOKE, HA-HA-HA!"

"You made a big joke?"

"YEAH, YEAH, YEAH! HA-HA-HA!"

"At Vairo's?"

"YEAH!"

"You yelled something—that was the joke, right?"

"BEER!" Verbankick said, giggling.

"You were upstairs?"

"With lots of monkeys."

"No monkeys up there, Fig. Just children, kids."

"MONKEYS!"

"Listen to me, Fig. They were kids, lots of kids. It was a party."

"Finns not people," Verbankick said shakily. "Just monkeys."

Bapcat drew a deep breath and tried to steady himself. Neither Zakov nor Hepting moved, much less drank their coffee. "You yelled *Beer,* not *Fire?*"

"No, Fire bad, Beer is joke."

He yelled Beer and it was heard as Fire, and now seventy-three people were dead. *Good God.*

"The Hedyns wanted you to play a joke on the monkeys?"

"YEAH!" Verbankick said, nodding animatedly.

"Fig, you used to do everything with your friend Herman, but not recently. Why's that?"

"Reverend."

"I don't understand."

"Tell Fig to stay away from Herman or they kill him."

"Who?"

"I don't KNOW!"

"Did you want to play the joke on the monkeys?"

The man shook his head vigorously.

"But you did."

"I don't, they kill Herman."

"Who would kill Herman, Fig?"

"Monkeys," Verbankick said.

"You want something to eat, Fig?"

"ASK HERMAN!" he shouted. "Am I in trouble?" he asked sheepishly.

Bapcat looked over at Sheriff John Hepting.

"He's not in trouble with me," Hepting said.

"Bad storm outside tonight, John. Can we bunk here?"

"Sure, and we've got a bedroom for Fig."

With Fig put to bed, they made more coffee and smoked. The wind howled outside, buffeting the sides of the house, making windows rattle.

Bapcat explained, "They used a rope to lower him into a mine opening and threw the rope in behind him. I think they wanted it to look like some sort of an accident."

"Tell me about the shootings," Hepting said.

"A man called Fisher, an Ascher detective, shot both Hedyns, but Madog didn't die right off, and shot Fisher dead."

"You witnessed this?"

"Both of us saw it," Zakov said.

Hepting pulled on a cigarette, took a sip of coffee, and leaned into the table toward Bapcat. "All right, what the hell is all of this?"

"We'll probably never know," Bapcat said. "Madog was running the whole thing to deny food, fuel, and so forth to the strikers. His brother was helping. Fisher was there to oversee everything and clean it all up."

"Who brought this Fisher in?"

"We'll never know, but we can guess."

"You think he's that ruthless?"

Bapcat spread his hands apart, imploring. "Fig's not responsible, John."

"What do you propose?"

"Take him somewhere safe, set him up to live out his life."

"Herman?"

"We tell him what's going on. I think he'll help."

"You think this can work?"

"I don't like the alternatives, and John, I'm figuring a whole lot of people already know, or will figure this out pretty fast. Fig was drinking at Vairo's that day—overcoat, hat, mustache, Alliance button. Just the way some witnesses described. And then he was gone, and the panic began. I don't think he yelled Fire. I think he yelled Beer."

There was a long silence.

"Maybe the courts should handle this, make it official. There are places, asylums."

"Fig's not insane, John. Everybody knows him and how he is. He would never do anything like this on his own."

"Seventy-three dead, fifty-three of them children," Hepting said disgustedly. "For what?"

"To crush the union," Bapcat said, "no matter the cost."

"MacNaughton wins," Hepting said.

EPILOGUE

Red Jacket

TUESDAY, JANUARY 6, 1914

"We got the trouble," Dominick Vairo said with a pained sigh. "Ghosts upstairs. Nobody wanna drink with all those dead kiddies . . . nobody wants drink with ghosts."

Zakov said, "There are no ghosts, but for some reason, too many humans prefer feelings to facts."

"This fact clear," Dominick said. "Me and Rousseau losin' our shirts."

Hepting sipped his glass of Bosch and seemed preoccupied.

"John?" Bapcat said.

"Newspapers are saying Henry Ford down there in Detroit will pay five dollars a day just to put together his automobiles. That's more than a sheriff gets paid."

"Or game wardens," Zakov added.

"Five dollars a day—that's the nail in the coffin for the mines. They can't match that, or won't. Making cars would be a helluva lot less riskier for workers. Ironic. MacNaughton kills the union, and Ford kills the mine operations by taking Copper's labor."

"You're guessing," Vairo said. "Ground here still got lots copper."

Hepting rolled his eyes and Vairo walked away.

"Where's Fig?" the sheriff asked.

Bapcat said, "He has a younger sister. He's living there now. We won't see him again. But that hole we pulled Fig out of, there'll probably be a lot of answers down there when the thaw comes."

John Hepting drained his beer glass and stood up. "I've arranged to have that hole covered when spring comes, Lute. Someday, someone may find it and figure it out, but until then, I say, sleeping dogs and all that. There are some answers the world can live without."

ABOUT THE AUTHOR

Joseph Heywood is the author of *The Snowfly* (Lyons Press), *Covered Waters* (Lyons Press), *The Berkut, Taxi Dancer, The Domino Conspiracy,* and all the novels comprising the Woods Cop Mystery Series. Featuring Grady Service, a detective in the Upper Peninsula for Michigan's Department of Natural Resources, this series has earned its author cult status among lovers of the outdoors, law enforcement officials, and mystery devotees. Heywood lives in Portage, Michigan, and in the Upper Peninsula.

For more on Joseph Heywood, visit the author's website at www.josephheywood.com.